A CARTOON NETWORK ORIGINAL

The AMAZING WORLD OF GUMBALL™

SCRIMMAGE SCRAMBLE

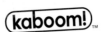

THE AMAZING WORLD OF GUMBALL: SCRIMMAGE
SCRAMBLE, March 2018. Published by KaBOOM!, a
division of Boom Entertainment, Inc. THE AMAZING
WORLD OF GUMBALL, CARTOON NETWORK, the
logos, and all related characters and elements
are trademarks of and © Cartoon Network. (S18)
All rights reserved. KaBOOM!™ and the KaBOOM!
logo are trademarks of Boom Entertainment, Inc.,
registered in various countries and categories. All
characters, events, and institutions depicted herein
are fictional. Any similarity between any of the names,
characters, persons, events, and/or institutions in this
publication to actual names, characters, and persons,
whether living or dead, events, and/or institutions is
unintended and purely coincidental. KaBOOM! does
not read or accept unsolicited submissions of ideas,
stories, or artwork.

For information regarding the CPSIA on this printed
material, call (203) 595-3636 and provide reference
#RICH - 771145.

BOOM! Studios, 5670 Wilshire Boulevard, Suite 400, Los
Angeles, CA 90036-5679. Printed in USA. First Printing.

ISBN: 978-1-68415-217-9, eISBN: 978-1-64144-031-8

A CARTOON NETWORK ORIGINAL

The AMAZING WORLD OF GUMBALL™

SCRIMMAGE SCRAMBLE

created by **BEN BOCQUELET**

written by **MEGAN BRENNAN**

illustrated by **KATE SHERRON**

with **CHRISTINE LARSEN & JENNA AYOUB**

colors by **VLADIMIR POPOV**

with **KATE SHERRON & LAURA LANGSTON**

letters by **MIKE FIORENTINO**

cover by **JENNA AYOUB**

designers **JILLIAN CRAB & GRACE PARK**

assistant editor **MICHAEL MOCCIO**

editor **WHITNEY LEOPARD**

with special thanks to **MARISA MARIONAKIS, JANET NO, CURTIS LELASH, CONRAD MONTGOMERY,** and the wonderful folks at **CARTOON NETWORK.**

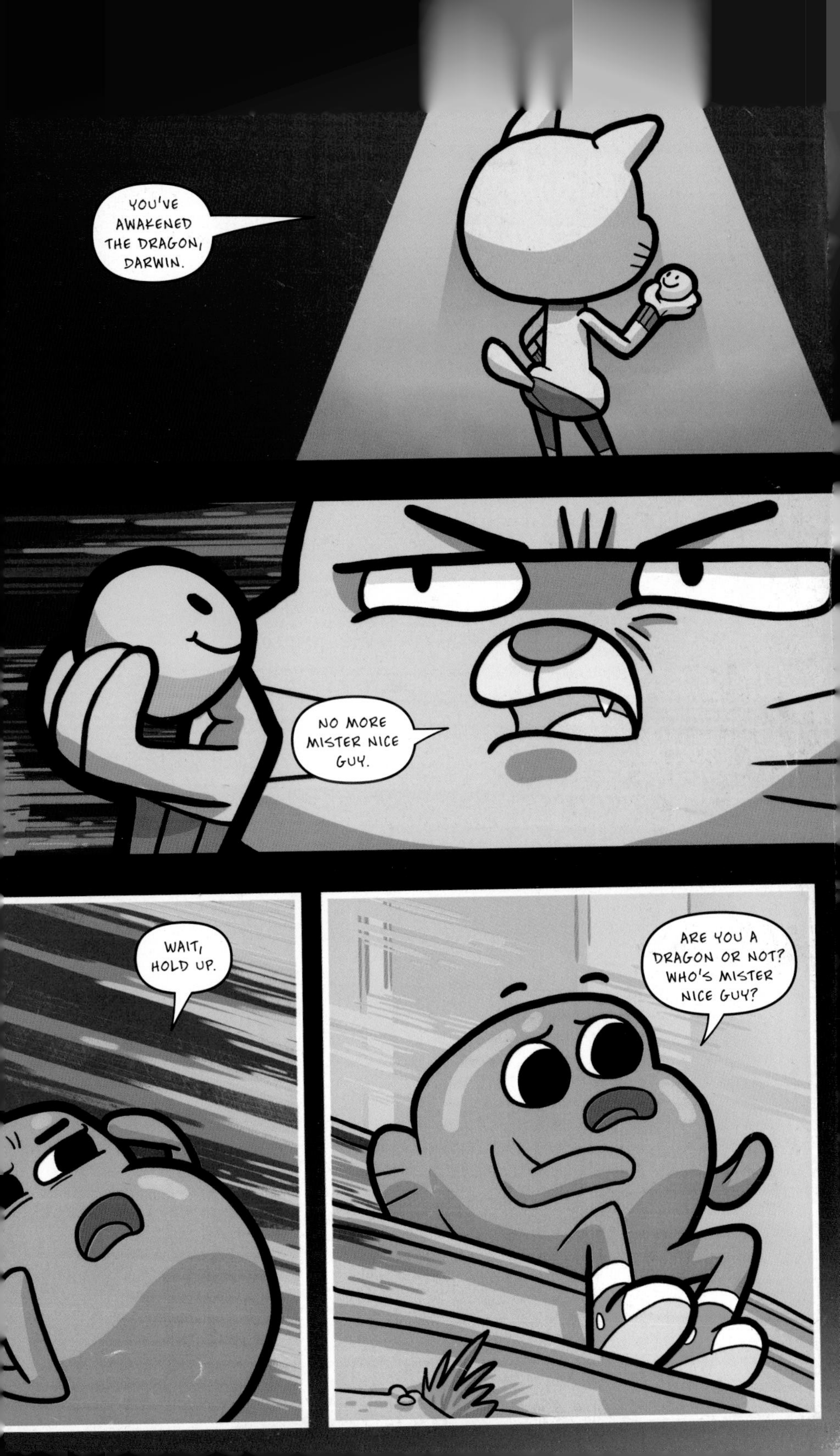
YOU'VE AWAKENED THE DRAGON, DARWIN.
NO MORE MISTER NICE GUY.
WAIT, HOLD UP.
ARE YOU A DRAGON OR NOT? WHO'S MISTER NICE GUY?

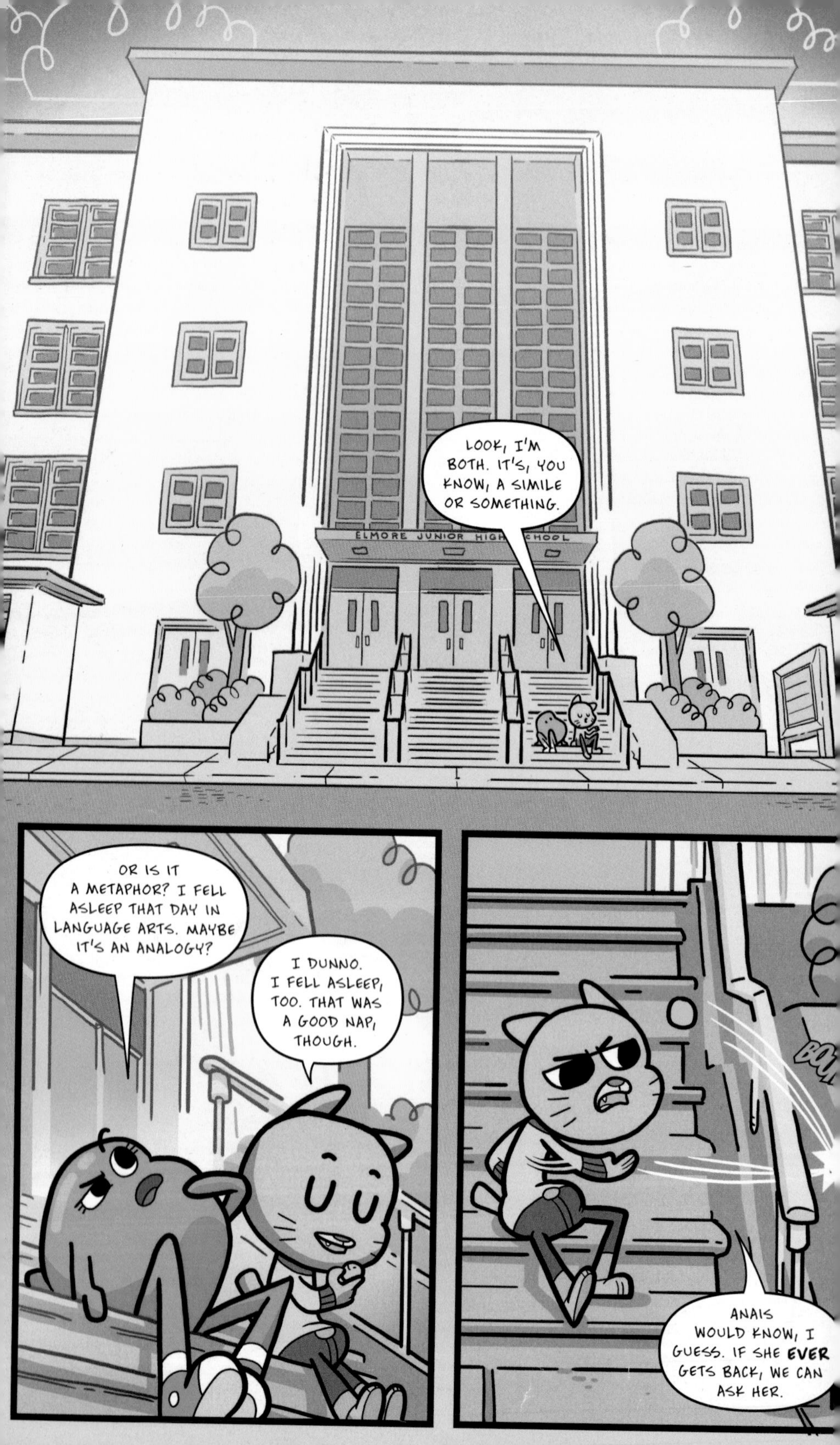
ELMORE JUNIOR HIGH SCHOOL
LOOK, I'M BOTH. IT'S, YOU KNOW, A SIMILE OR SOMETHING.
OR IS IT A METAPHOR? I FELL ASLEEP THAT DAY IN LANGUAGE ARTS. MAYBE IT'S AN ANALOGY?
I DUNNO. I FELL ASLEEP, TOO. THAT WAS A GOOD NAP, THOUGH.
ANAIS WOULD KNOW, I GUESS. IF SHE **EVER** GETS BACK, WE CAN ASK HER.

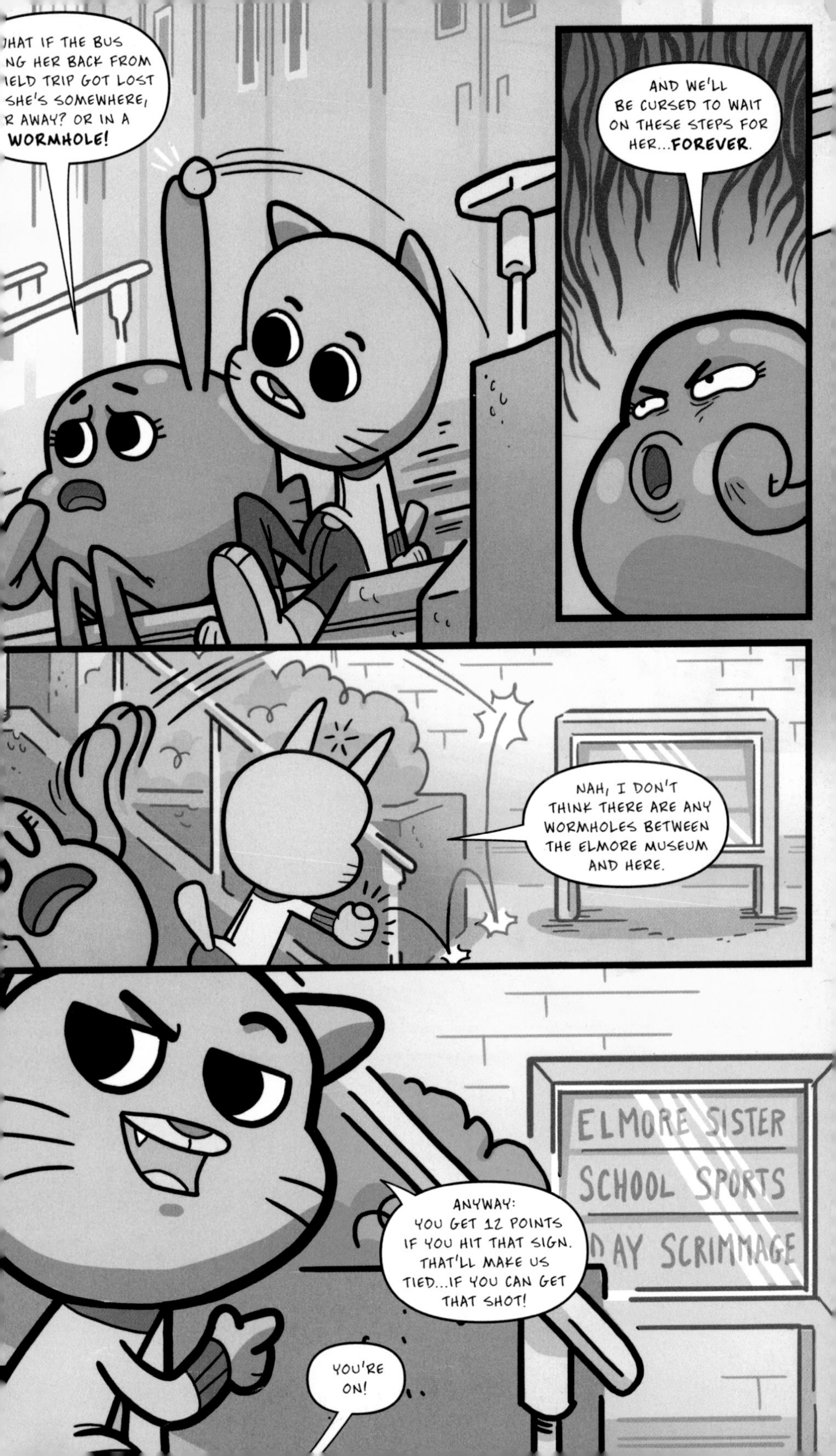
WHAT IF THE BUS
NG HER BACK FROM
IELD TRIP GOT LOST
SHE'S SOMEWHERE,
R AWAY? OR IN A
WORMHOLE!
AND WE'LL BE CURSED TO WAIT ON THESE STEPS FOR HER...FOREVER.
NAH, I DON'T THINK THERE ARE ANY WORMHOLES BETWEEN THE ELMORE MUSEUM AND HERE.
ANYWAY: YOU GET 12 POINTS IF YOU HIT THAT SIGN. THAT'LL MAKE US TIED...IF YOU CAN GET THAT SHOT!
ELMORE SISTER SCHOOL SPORTS DAY SCRIMMAGE
YOU'RE ON!

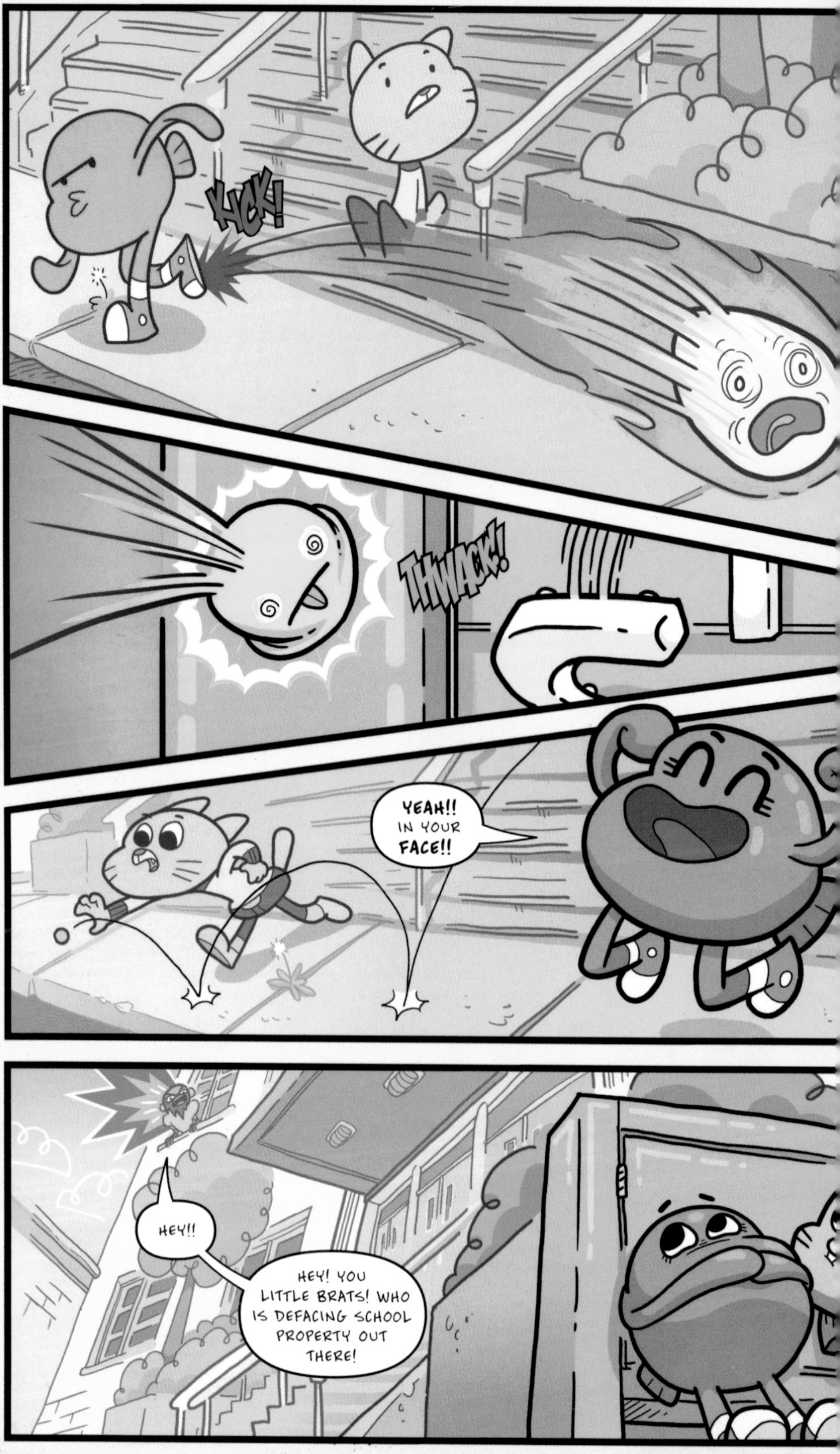
KICK!
THWACK!
YEAH!! IN YOUR FACE!!
HEY!!
HEY! YOU LITTLE BRATS! WHO IS DEFACING SCHOOL PROPERTY OUT THERE!

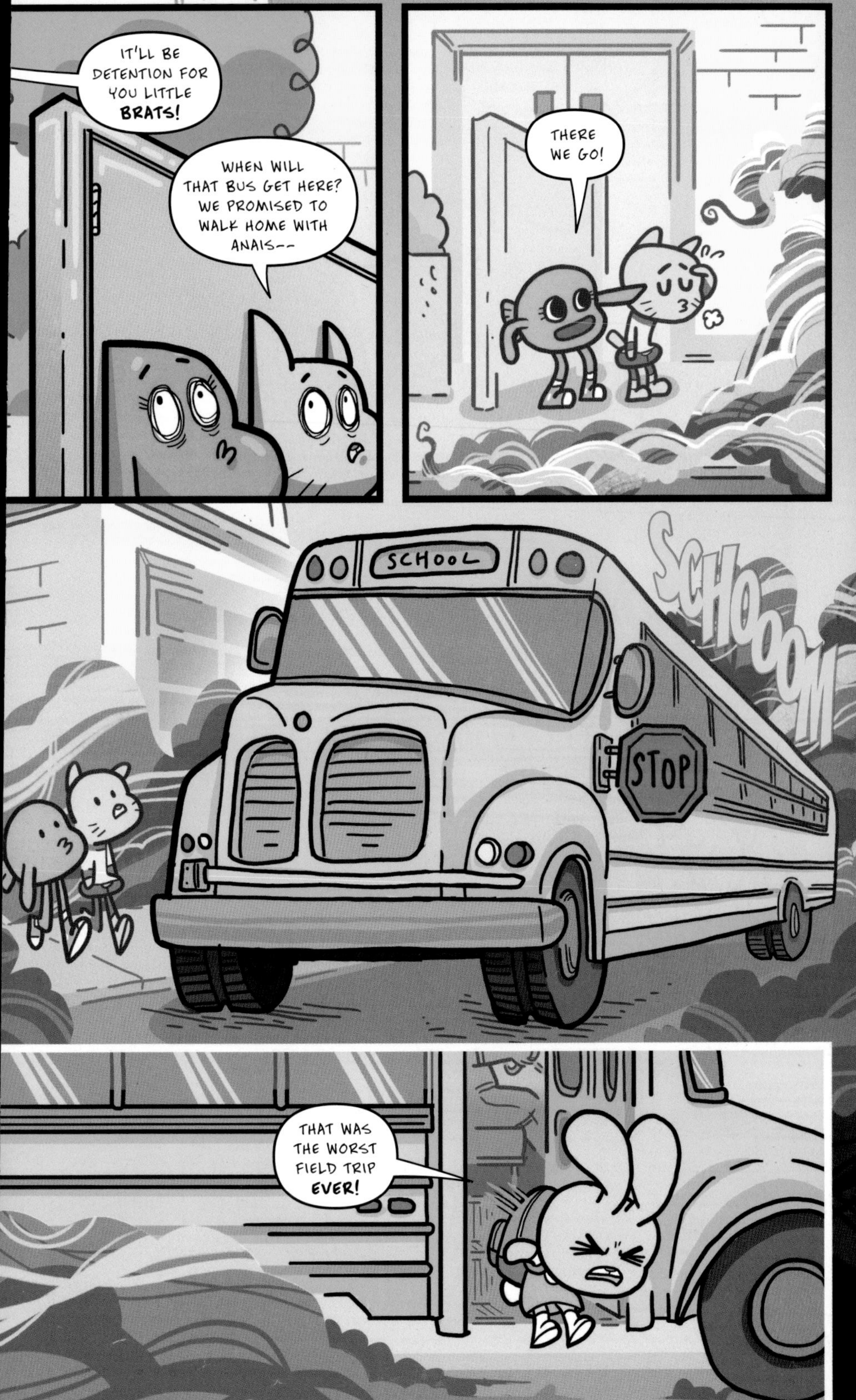

IT'LL BE DETENTION FOR YOU LITTLE BRATS!
WHEN WILL THAT BUS GET HERE? WE PROMISED TO WALK HOME WITH ANAIS--
THERE WE GO!
SCHOOL
STOP
SCHOOOOM
THAT WAS THE WORST FIELD TRIP EVER!

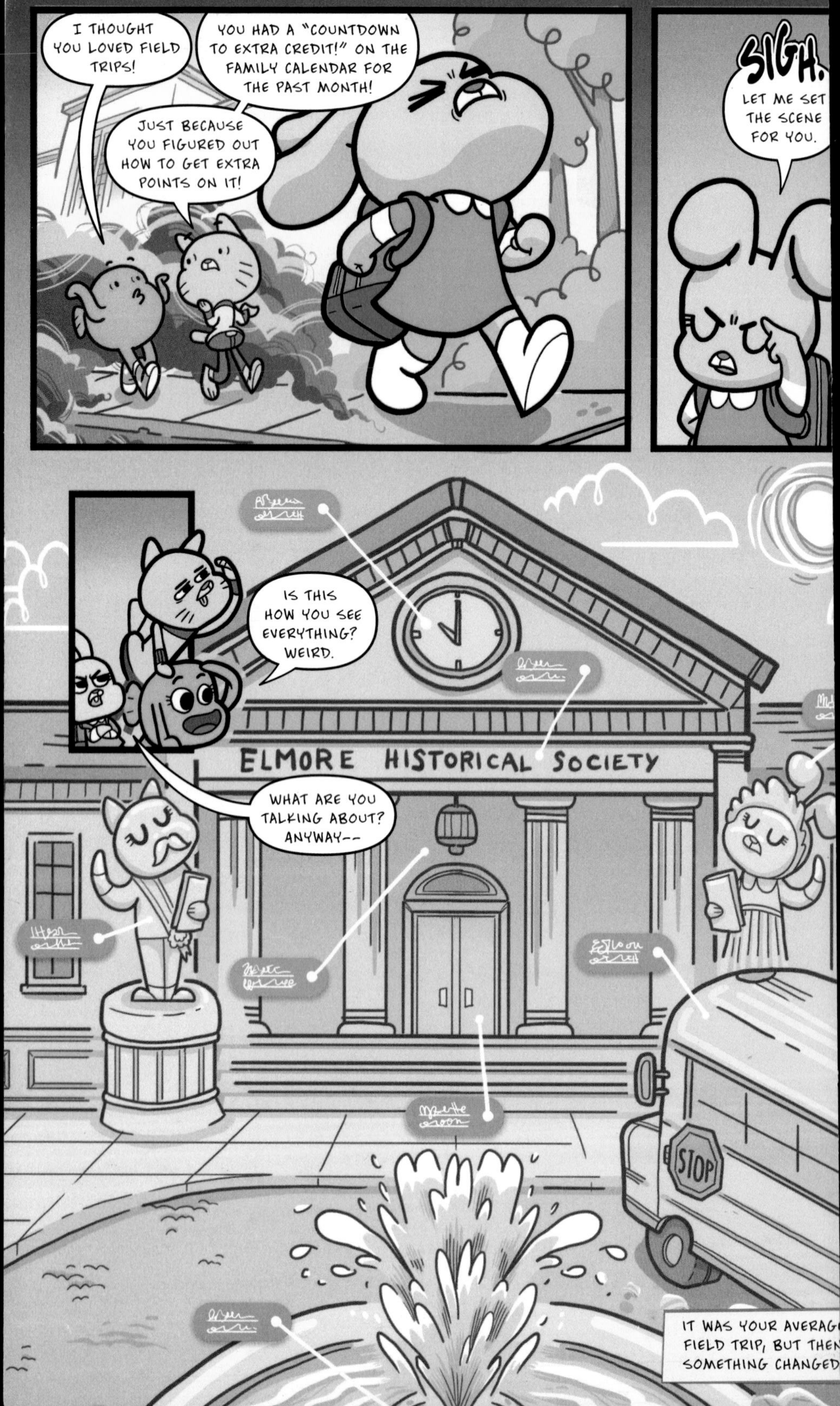
I THOUGHT YOU LOVED FIELD TRIPS!
YOU HAD A "COUNTDOWN TO EXTRA CREDIT!" ON THE FAMILY CALENDAR FOR THE PAST MONTH!
JUST BECAUSE YOU FIGURED OUT HOW TO GET EXTRA POINTS ON IT!
SIGH.
LET ME SET THE SCENE FOR YOU.
IS THIS HOW YOU SEE EVERYTHING? WEIRD.
ELMORE HISTORICAL SOCIETY
WHAT ARE YOU TALKING ABOUT? ANYWAY--
STOP
IT WAS YOUR AVERAGE FIELD TRIP, BUT THEN SOMETHING CHANGED

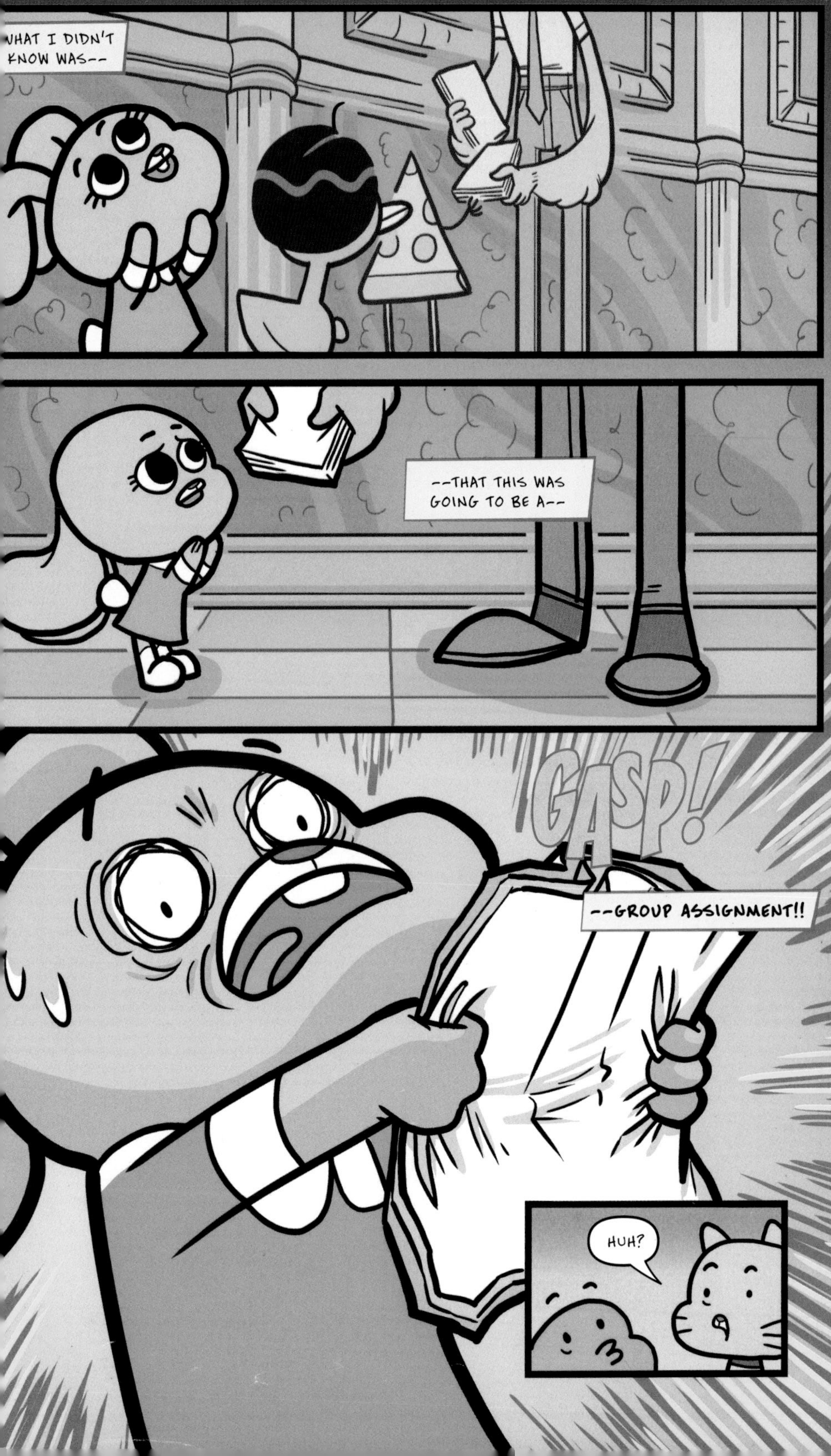
WHAT I DIDN'T KNOW WAS--
--THAT THIS WAS GOING TO BE A--
GASP!
--GROUP ASSIGNMENT!!
HUH?

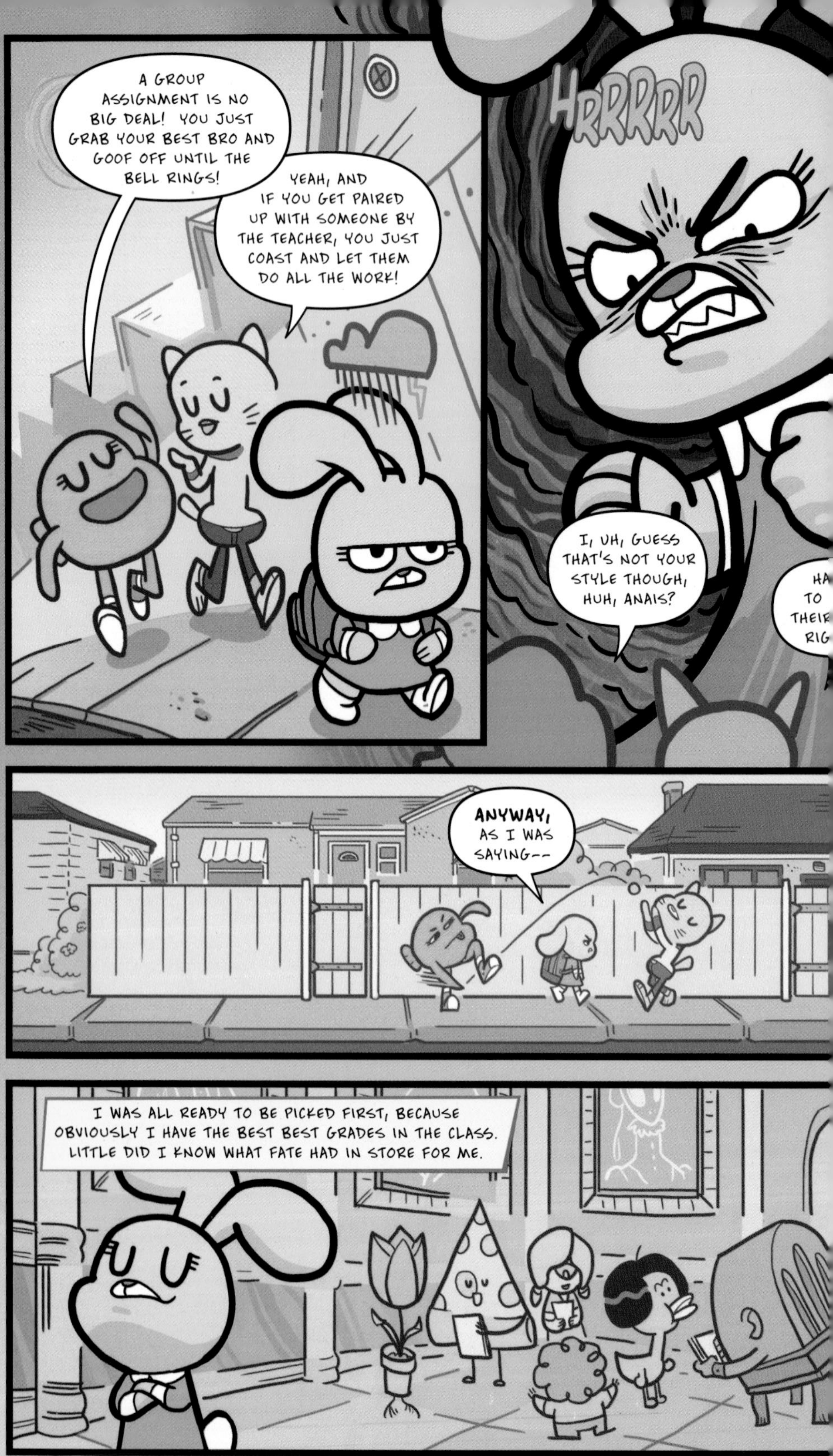
A GROUP ASSIGNMENT IS NO BIG DEAL! YOU JUST GRAB YOUR BEST BRO AND GOOF OFF UNTIL THE BELL RINGS!
YEAH, AND IF YOU GET PAIRED UP WITH SOMEONE BY THE TEACHER, YOU JUST COAST AND LET THEM DO ALL THE WORK!
HRRRRR
I, UH, GUESS THAT'S NOT YOUR STYLE THOUGH, HUH, ANAIS?
ANYWAY, AS I WAS SAYING--
I WAS ALL READY TO BE PICKED FIRST, BECAUSE OBVIOUSLY I HAVE THE BEST BEST GRADES IN THE CLASS. LITTLE DID I KNOW WHAT FATE HAD IN STORE FOR ME.

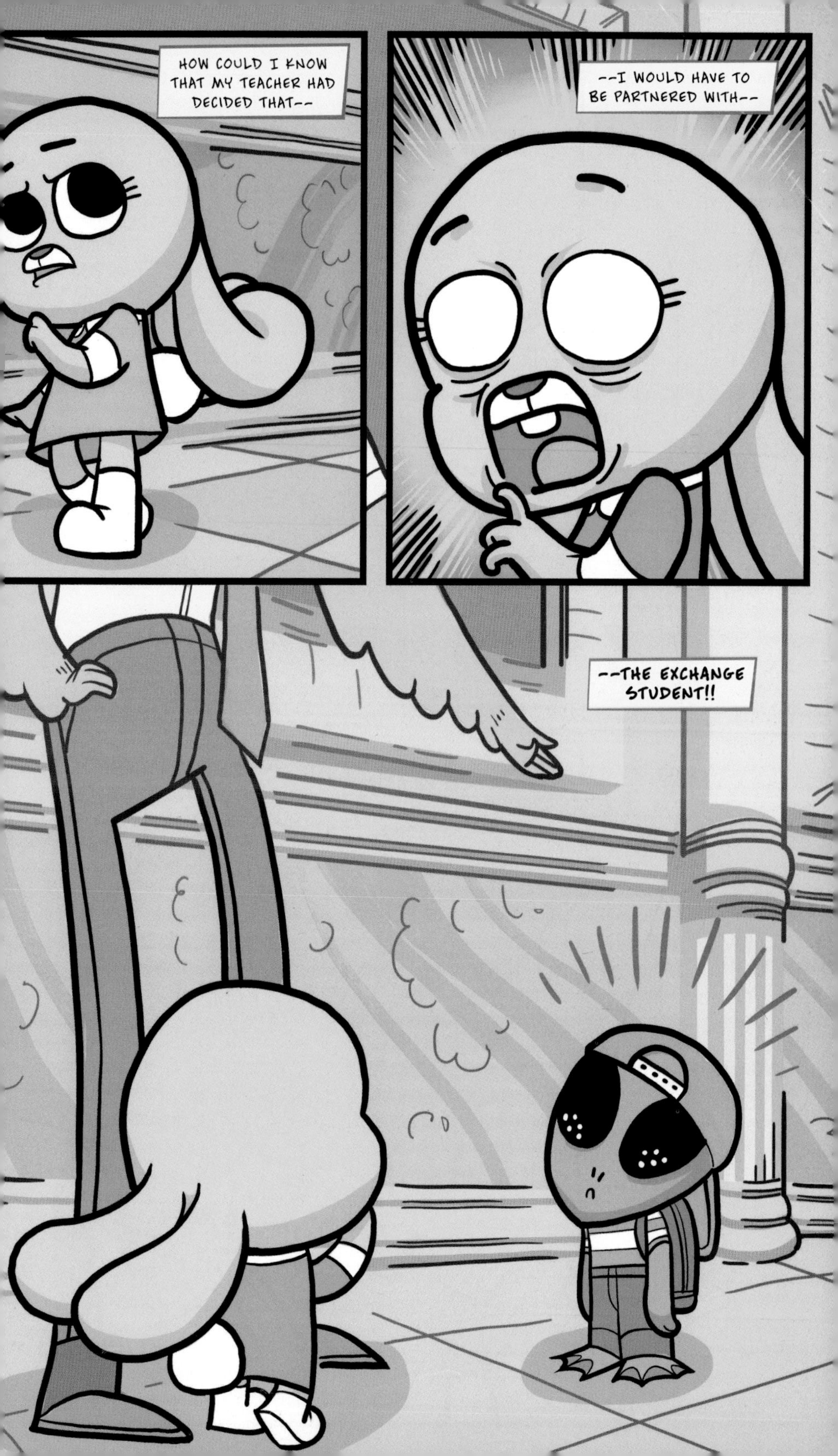
HOW COULD I KNOW THAT MY TEACHER HAD DECIDED THAT--
--I WOULD HAVE TO BE PARTNERED WITH--
--THE EXCHANGE STUDENT!!

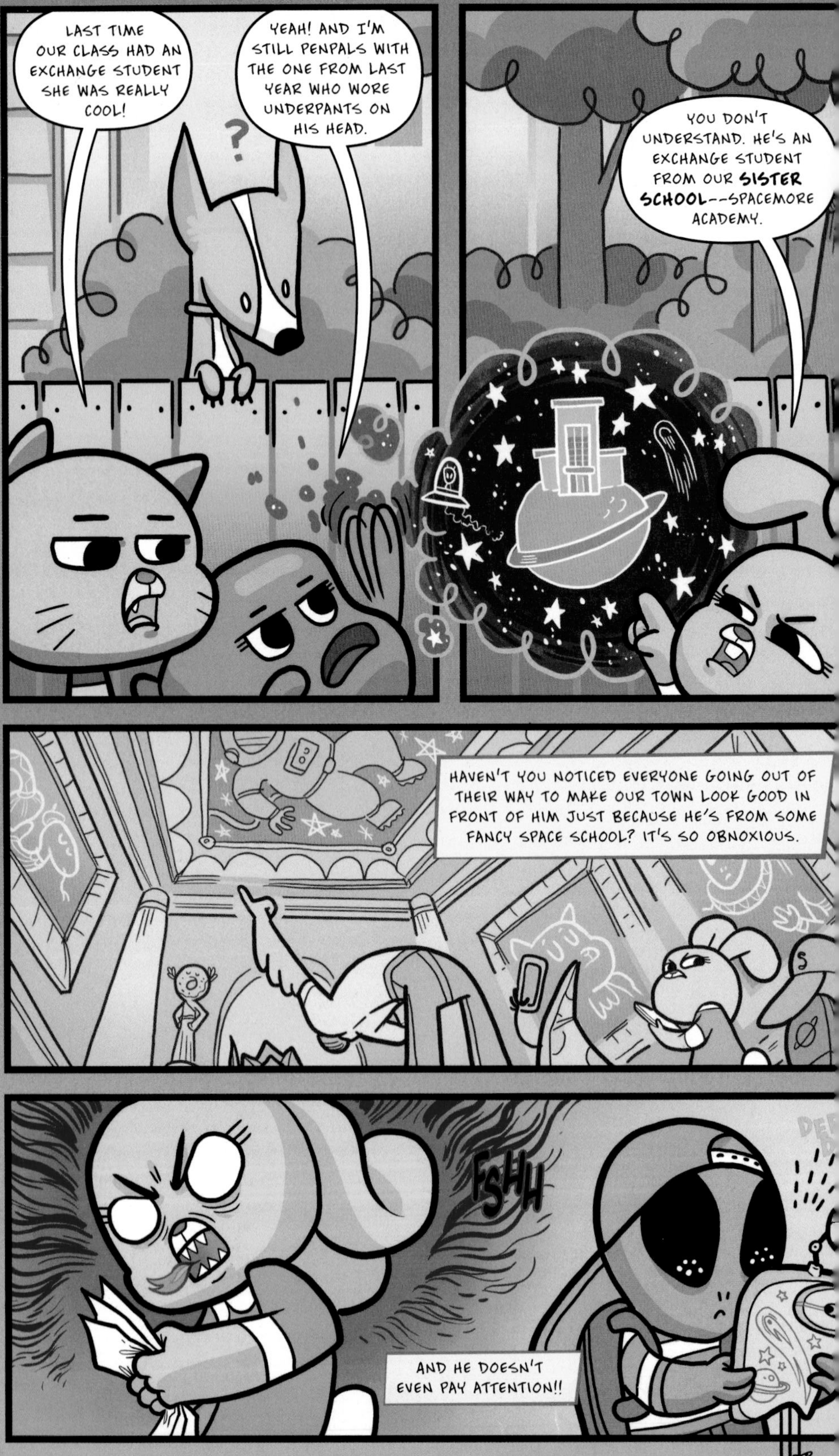
LAST TIME OUR CLASS HAD AN EXCHANGE STUDENT SHE WAS REALLY COOL!
YEAH! AND I'M STILL PENPALS WITH THE ONE FROM LAST YEAR WHO WORE UNDERPANTS ON HIS HEAD.
?
YOU DON'T UNDERSTAND. HE'S AN EXCHANGE STUDENT FROM OUR **SISTER SCHOOL**--SPACEMORE ACADEMY.
HAVEN'T YOU NOTICED EVERYONE GOING OUT OF THEIR WAY TO MAKE OUR TOWN LOOK GOOD IN FRONT OF HIM JUST BECAUSE HE'S FROM SOME FANCY SPACE SCHOOL? IT'S SO OBNOXIOUS.
FSHH
AND HE DOESN'T EVEN PAY ATTENTION!!

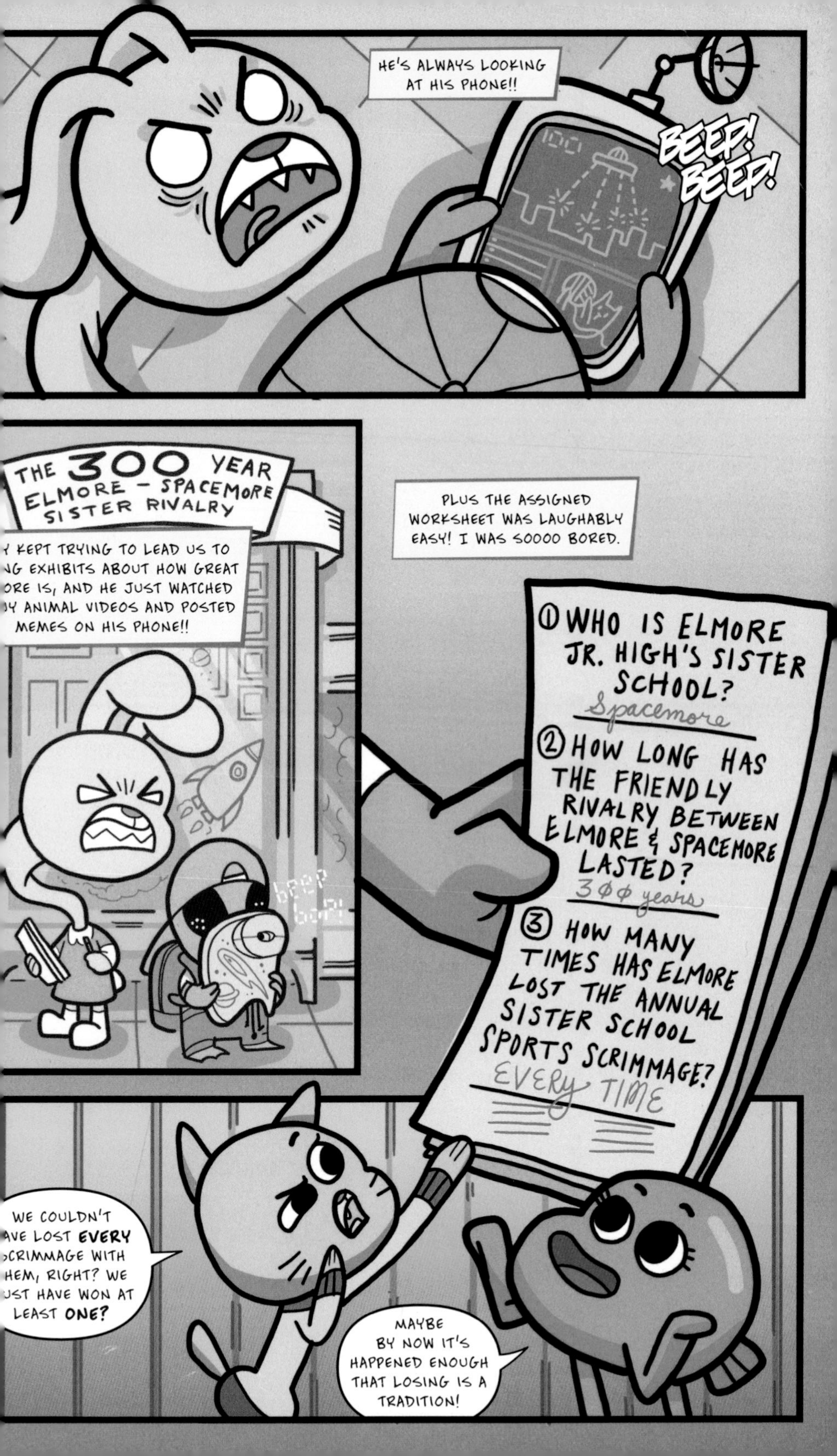

HE'S ALWAYS LOOKING AT HIS PHONE!!
BEEP! BEEP!
THE 300 YEAR ELMORE – SPACEMORE SISTER RIVALRY
Y KEPT TRYING TO LEAD US TO NG EXHIBITS ABOUT HOW GREAT ORE IS, AND HE JUST WATCHED Y ANIMAL VIDEOS AND POSTED MEMES ON HIS PHONE!!
PLUS THE ASSIGNED WORKSHEET WAS LAUGHABLY EASY! I WAS SOOOO BORED.
① WHO IS ELMORE JR. HIGH'S SISTER SCHOOL?
Spacemore
② HOW LONG HAS THE FRIENDLY RIVALRY BETWEEN ELMORE & SPACEMORE LASTED?
300 years
③ HOW MANY TIMES HAS ELMORE LOST THE ANNUAL SISTER SCHOOL SPORTS SCRIMMAGE?
EVERY TIME
WE COULDN'T AVE LOST EVERY SCRIMMAGE WITH HEM, RIGHT? WE UST HAVE WON AT LEAST ONE?
MAYBE BY NOW IT'S HAPPENED ENOUGH THAT LOSING IS A TRADITION!

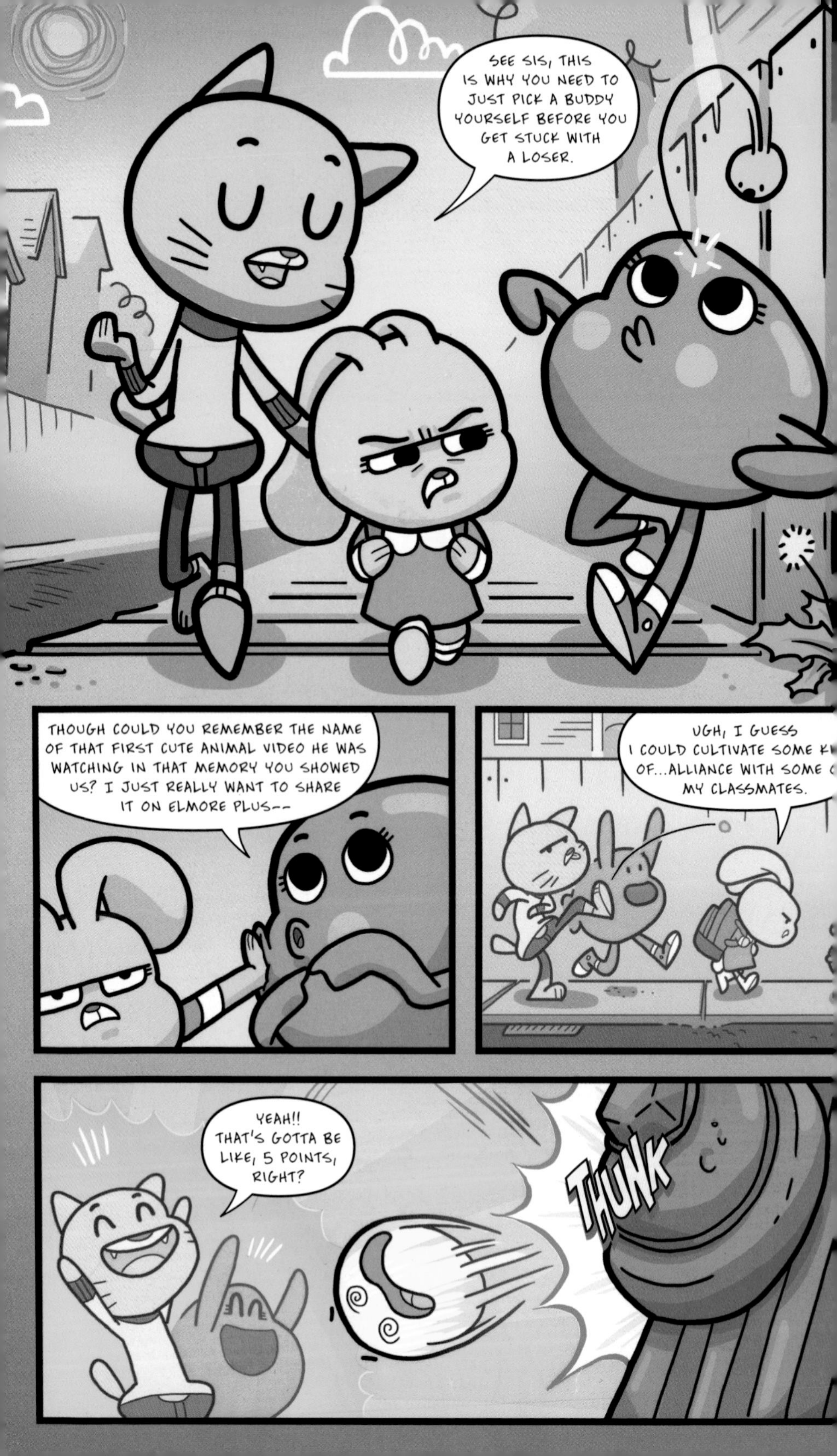
SEE SIS, THIS IS WHY YOU NEED TO JUST PICK A BUDDY YOURSELF BEFORE YOU GET STUCK WITH A LOSER.
THOUGH COULD YOU REMEMBER THE NAME OF THAT FIRST CUTE ANIMAL VIDEO HE WAS WATCHING IN THAT MEMORY YOU SHOWED US? I JUST REALLY WANT TO SHARE IT ON ELMORE PLUS--
UGH, I GUESS I COULD CULTIVATE SOME K OF...ALLIANCE WITH SOME MY CLASSMATES.
YEAH!! THAT'S GOTTA BE LIKE, 5 POINTS, RIGHT?
THUNK

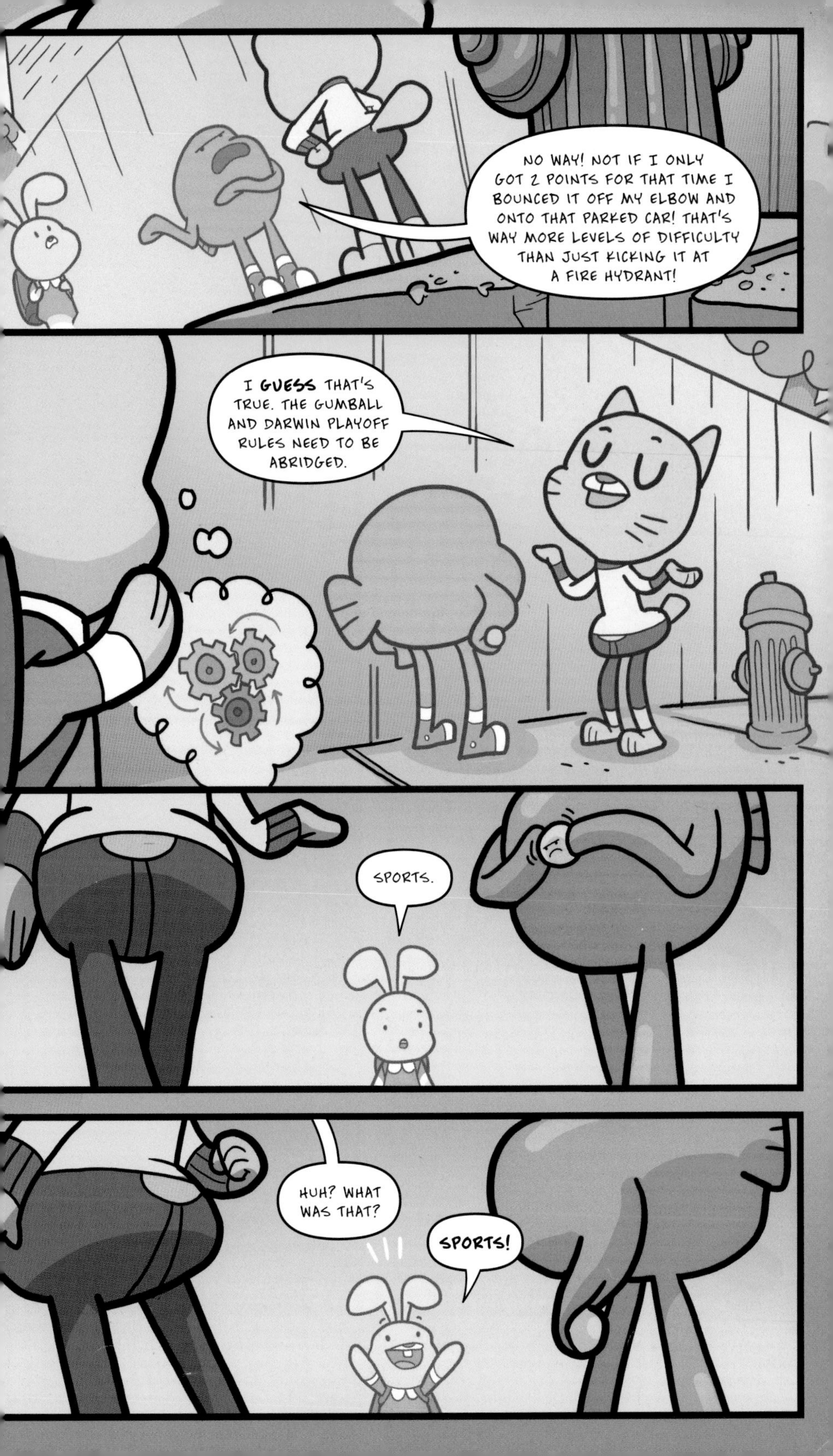

NO WAY! NOT IF I ONLY GOT 2 POINTS FOR THAT TIME I BOUNCED IT OFF MY ELBOW AND ONTO THAT PARKED CAR! THAT'S WAY MORE LEVELS OF DIFFICULTY THAN JUST KICKING IT AT A FIRE HYDRANT!
I GUESS THAT'S TRUE. THE GUMBALL AND DARWIN PLAYOFF RULES NEED TO BE ABRIDGED.
SPORTS.
HUH? WHAT WAS THAT?
SPORTS!

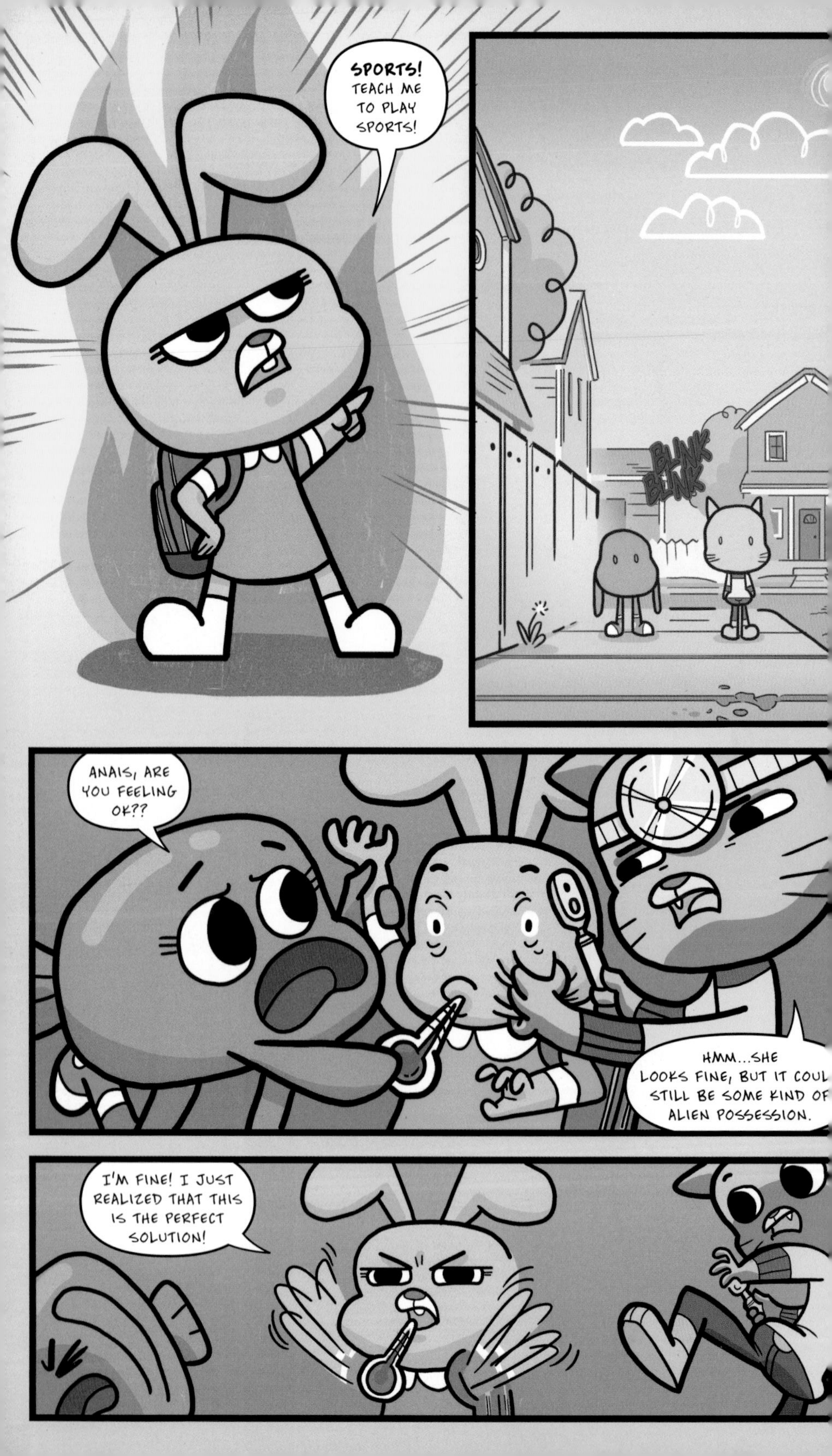
SPORTS! TEACH ME TO PLAY SPORTS!
BLINK BLINK
ANAIS, ARE YOU FEELING OK??
HMM...SHE LOOKS FINE, BUT IT COUL STILL BE SOME KIND OF ALIEN POSSESSION.
I'M FINE! I JUST REALIZED THAT THIS IS THE PERFECT SOLUTION!

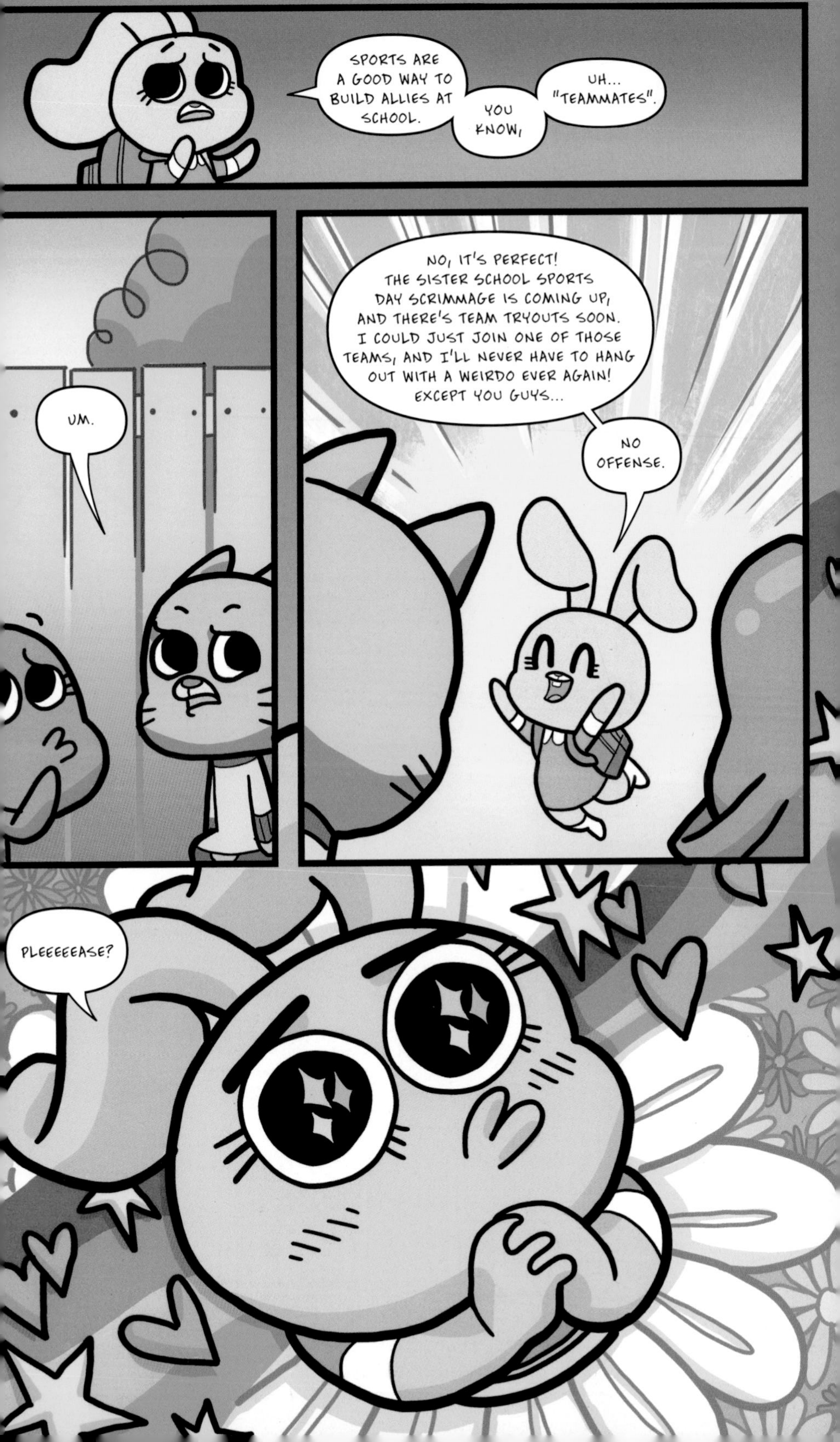

SPORTS ARE A GOOD WAY TO BUILD ALLIES AT SCHOOL.
YOU KNOW,
UH... "TEAMMATES".
UM.
NO, IT'S PERFECT! THE SISTER SCHOOL SPORTS DAY SCRIMMAGE IS COMING UP, AND THERE'S TEAM TRYOUTS SOON. I COULD JUST JOIN ONE OF THOSE TEAMS, AND I'LL NEVER HAVE TO HANG OUT WITH A WEIRDO EVER AGAIN! EXCEPT YOU GUYS...
NO OFFENSE.
PLEEEEEASE?

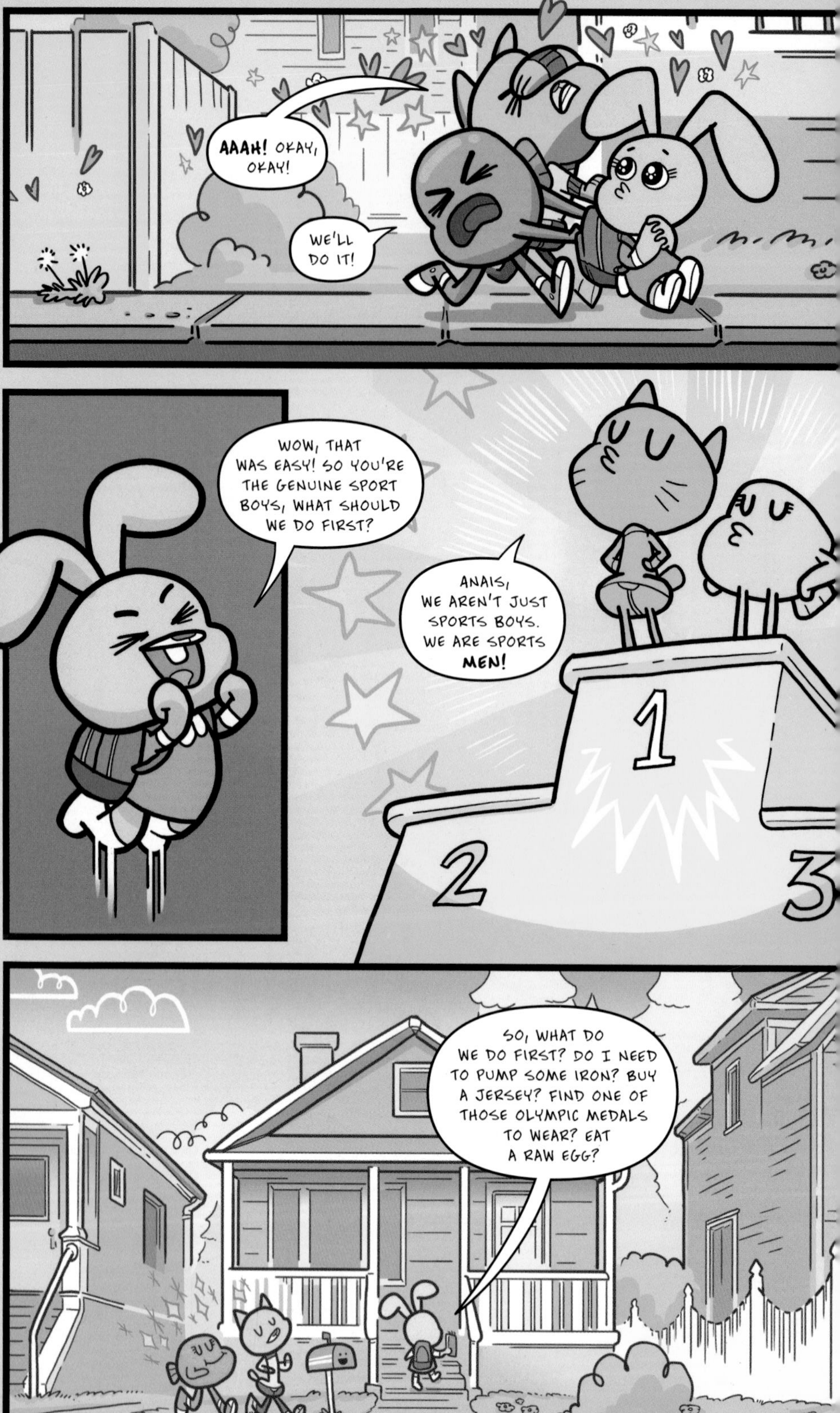
AAAH! OKAY, OKAY!
WE'LL DO IT!
WOW, THAT WAS EASY! SO YOU'RE THE GENUINE SPORT BOYS, WHAT SHOULD WE DO FIRST?
ANAIS, WE AREN'T JUST SPORTS BOYS. WE ARE SPORTS MEN!
1
2
3
SO, WHAT DO WE DO FIRST? DO I NEED TO PUMP SOME IRON? BUY A JERSEY? FIND ONE OF THOSE OLYMPIC MEDALS TO WEAR? EAT A RAW EGG?

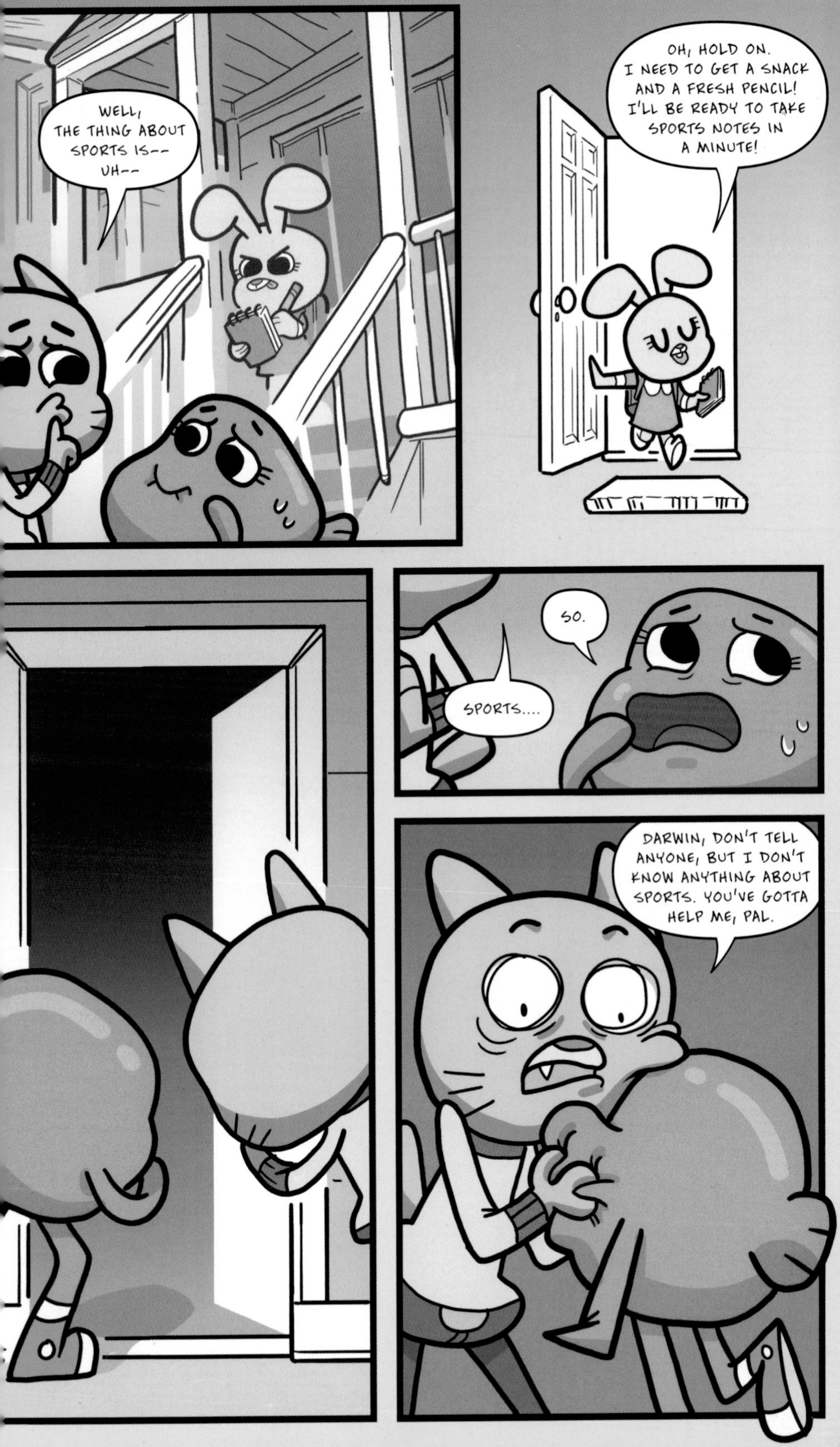
WELL, THE THING ABOUT SPORTS IS-- UH--
OH, HOLD ON. I NEED TO GET A SNACK AND A FRESH PENCIL! I'LL BE READY TO TAKE SPORTS NOTES IN A MINUTE!
SO.
SPORTS....
DARWIN, DON'T TELL ANYONE, BUT I DON'T KNOW ANYTHING ABOUT SPORTS. YOU'VE GOTTA HELP ME, PAL.

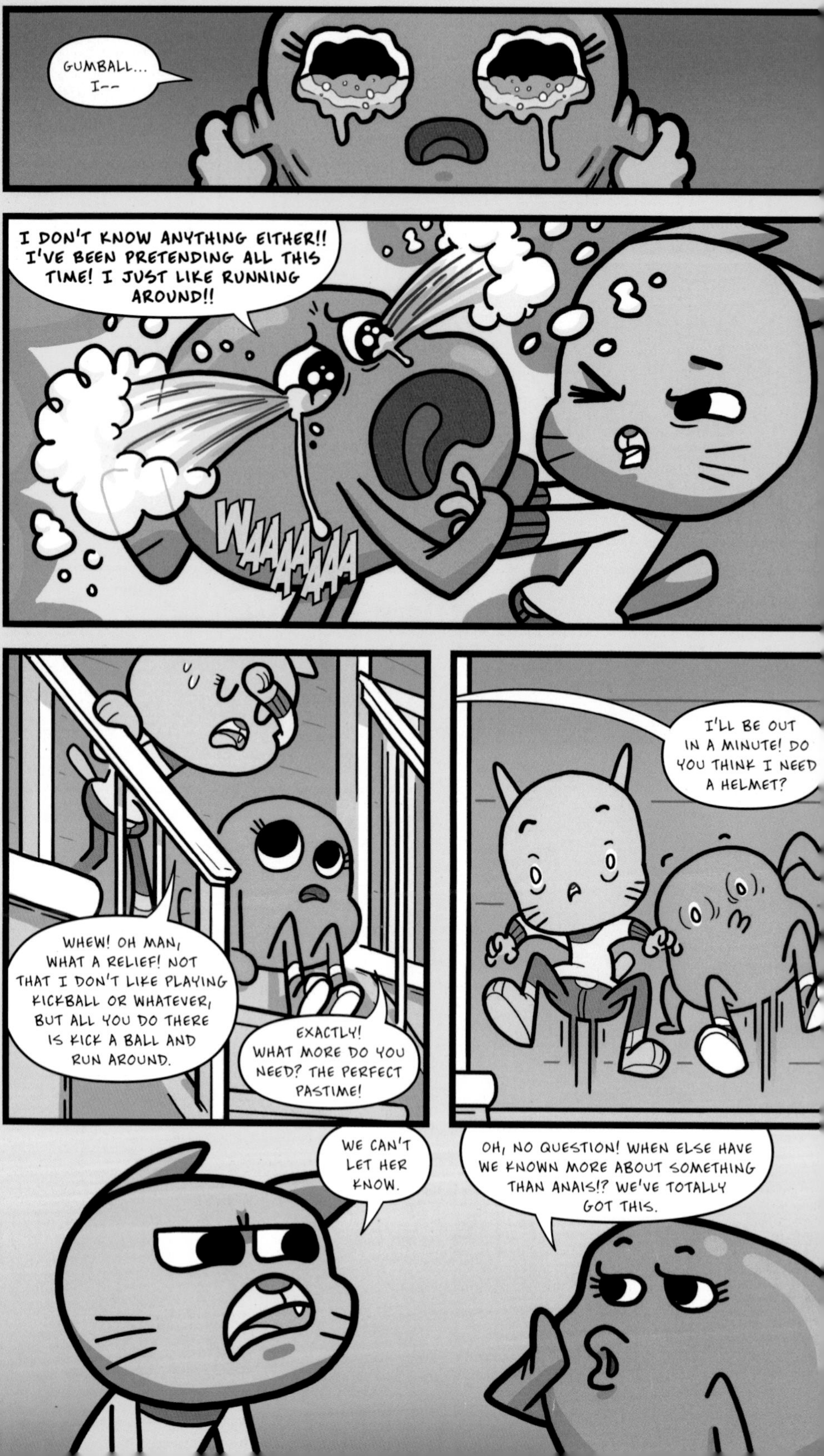
GUMBALL... I--
I DON'T KNOW ANYTHING EITHER!! I'VE BEEN PRETENDING ALL THIS TIME! I JUST LIKE RUNNING AROUND!!
WAAAAAAAAAA
WHEW! OH MAN, WHAT A RELIEF! NOT THAT I DON'T LIKE PLAYING KICKBALL OR WHATEVER, BUT ALL YOU DO THERE IS KICK A BALL AND RUN AROUND.
EXACTLY! WHAT MORE DO YOU NEED? THE PERFECT PASTIME!
I'LL BE OUT IN A MINUTE! DO YOU THINK I NEED A HELMET?
WE CAN'T LET HER KNOW.
OH, NO QUESTION! WHEN ELSE HAVE WE KNOWN MORE ABOUT SOMETHING THAN ANAIS!? WE'VE TOTALLY GOT THIS.

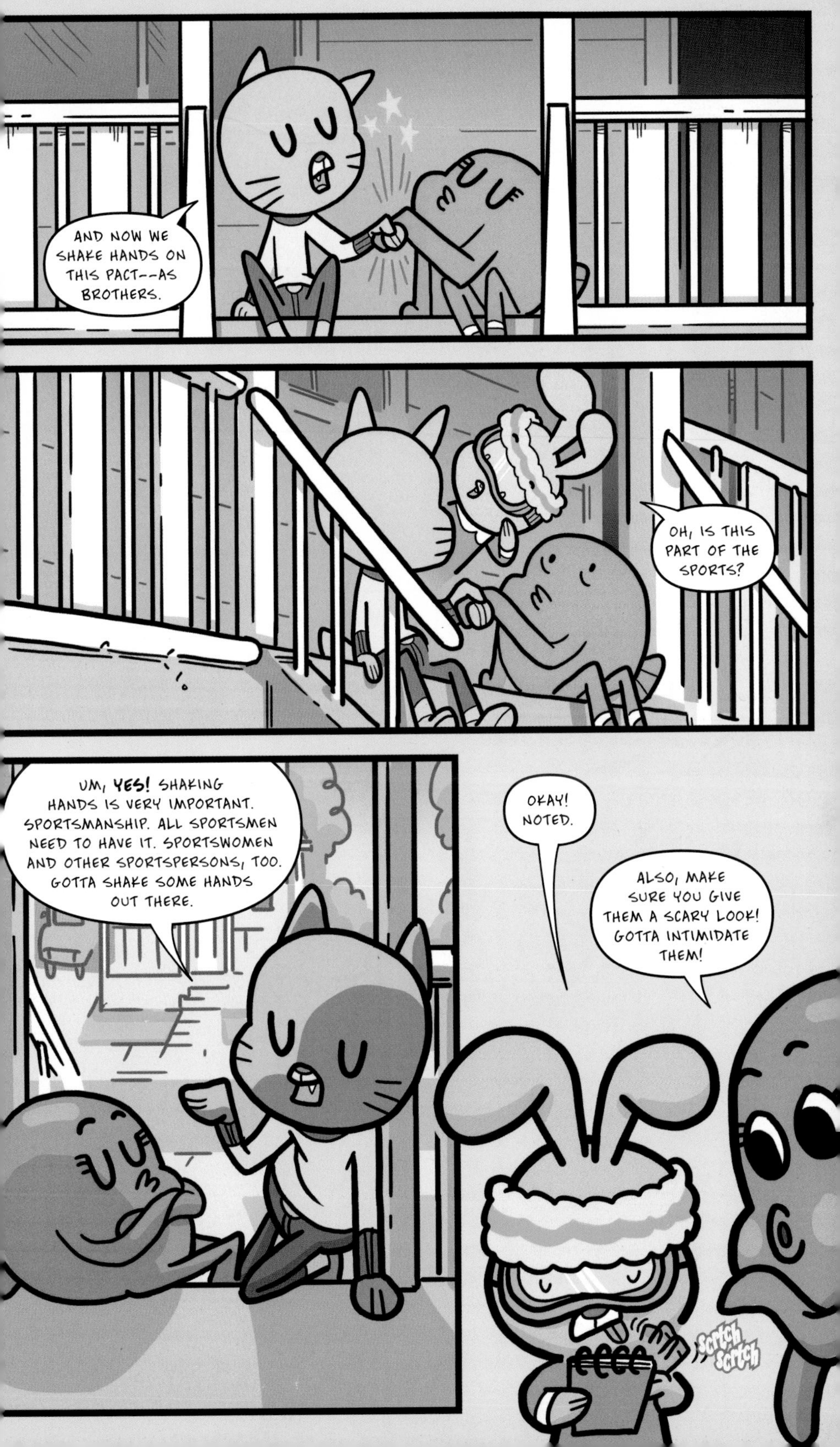
AND NOW WE SHAKE HANDS ON THIS PACT--AS BROTHERS.
OH, IS THIS PART OF THE SPORTS?
UM, YES! SHAKING HANDS IS VERY IMPORTANT. SPORTSMANSHIP. ALL SPORTSMEN NEED TO HAVE IT. SPORTSWOMEN AND OTHER SPORTSPERSONS, TOO. GOTTA SHAKE SOME HANDS OUT THERE.
OKAY! NOTED.
ALSO, MAKE SURE YOU GIVE THEM A SCARY LOOK! GOTTA INTIMIDATE THEM!
SCRTCH SCRTCH

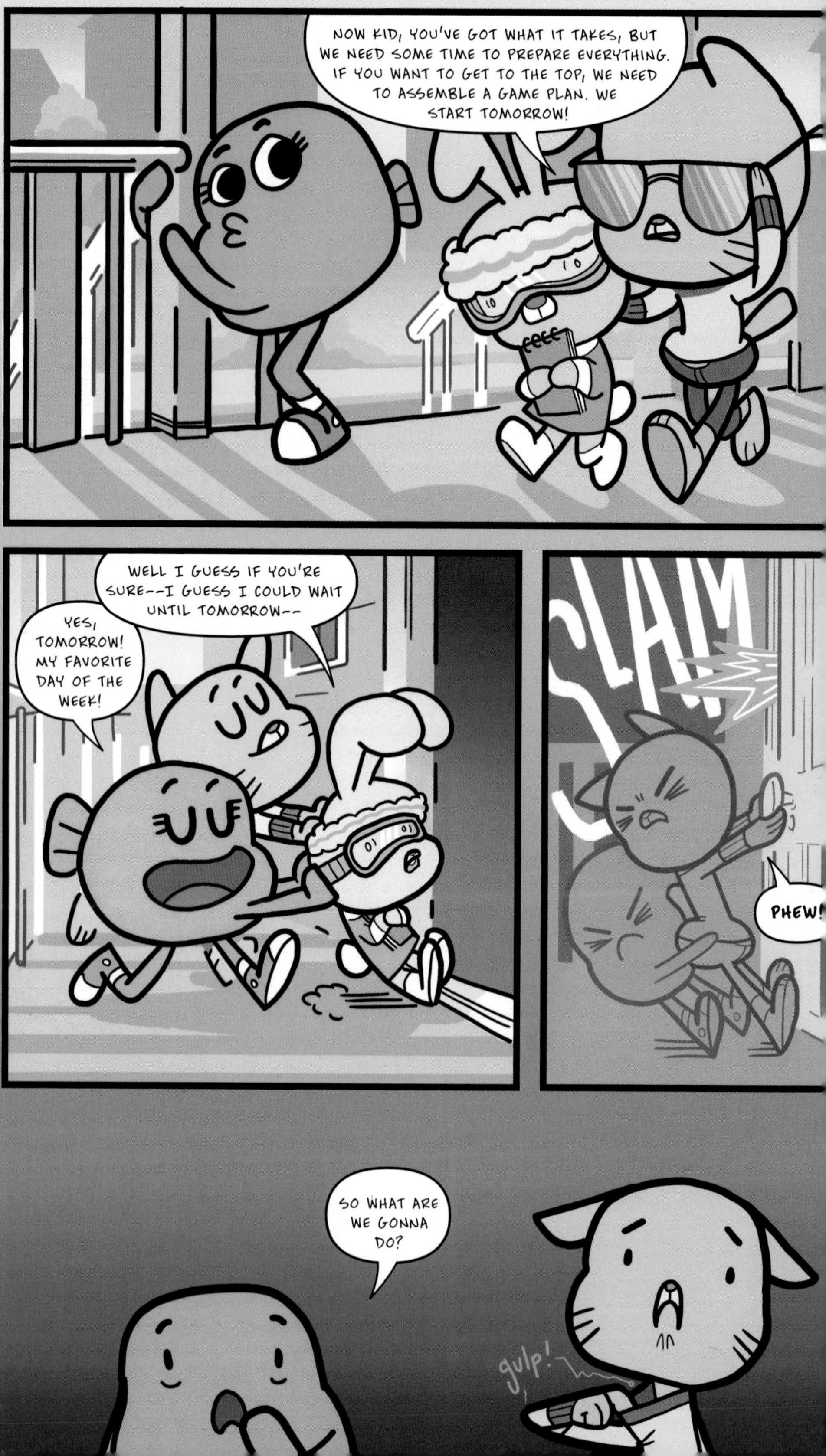
NOW KID, YOU'VE GOT WHAT IT TAKES, BUT WE NEED SOME TIME TO PREPARE EVERYTHING. IF YOU WANT TO GET TO THE TOP, WE NEED TO ASSEMBLE A GAME PLAN. WE START TOMORROW!
WELL I GUESS IF YOU'RE SURE--I GUESS I COULD WAIT UNTIL TOMORROW--
YES, TOMORROW! MY FAVORITE DAY OF THE WEEK!
SLAM
PHEW!
SO WHAT ARE WE GONNA DO?
gulp!

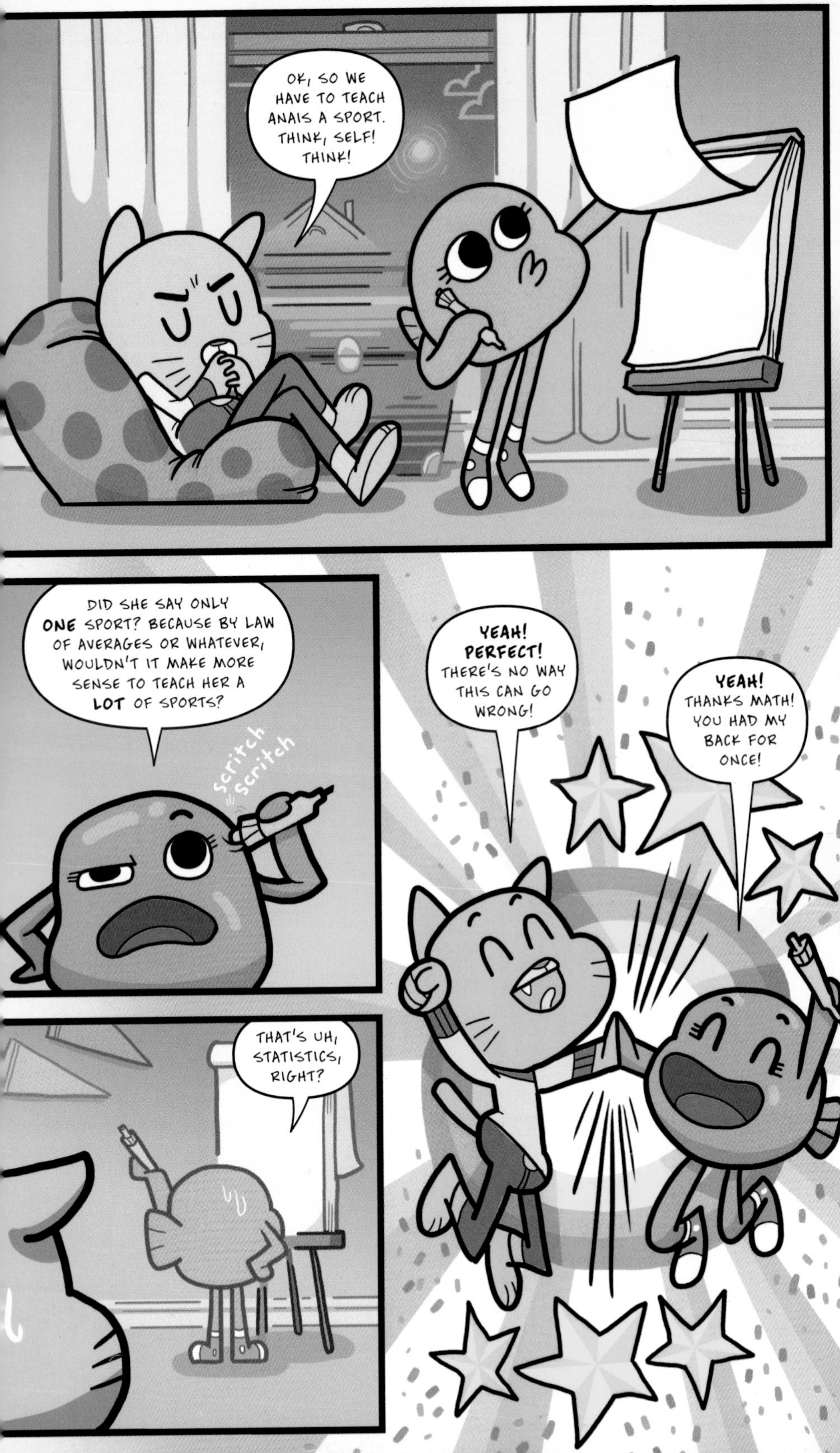
OK, SO WE HAVE TO TEACH ANAIS A SPORT. THINK, SELF! THINK!
DID SHE SAY ONLY ONE SPORT? BECAUSE BY LAW OF AVERAGES OR WHATEVER, WOULDN'T IT MAKE MORE SENSE TO TEACH HER A LOT OF SPORTS?
scritch scritch
THAT'S UH, STATISTICS, RIGHT?
YEAH! PERFECT! THERE'S NO WAY THIS CAN GO WRONG!
YEAH! THANKS MATH! YOU HAD MY BACK FOR ONCE!

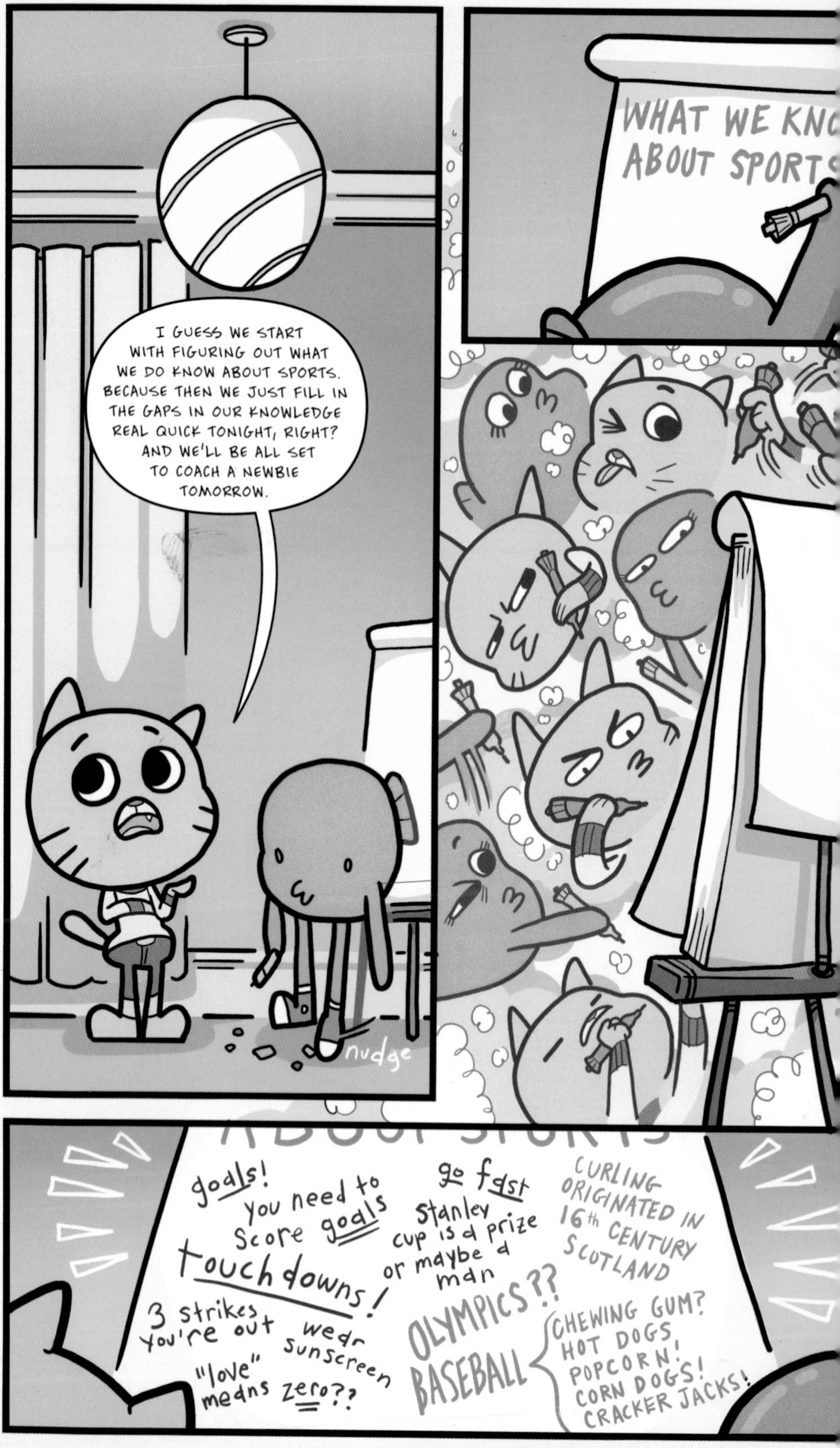
I GUESS WE START WITH FIGURING OUT WHAT WE DO KNOW ABOUT SPORTS. BECAUSE THEN WE JUST FILL IN THE GAPS IN OUR KNOWLEDGE REAL QUICK TONIGHT, RIGHT? AND WE'LL BE ALL SET TO COACH A NEWBIE TOMORROW.
nudge
WHAT WE KNO
ABOUT SPORTS
goals! you need to score goals
touchdowns!
3 strikes you're out
wear sunscreen
"love" means zero??
go fast
Stanley cup is a prize or maybe a man
OLYMPICS??
BASEBALL
CURLING ORIGINATED IN 16th CENTURY SCOTLAND
CHEWING GUM? HOT DOGS POPCORN! CORN DOGS! CRACKER JACKS!

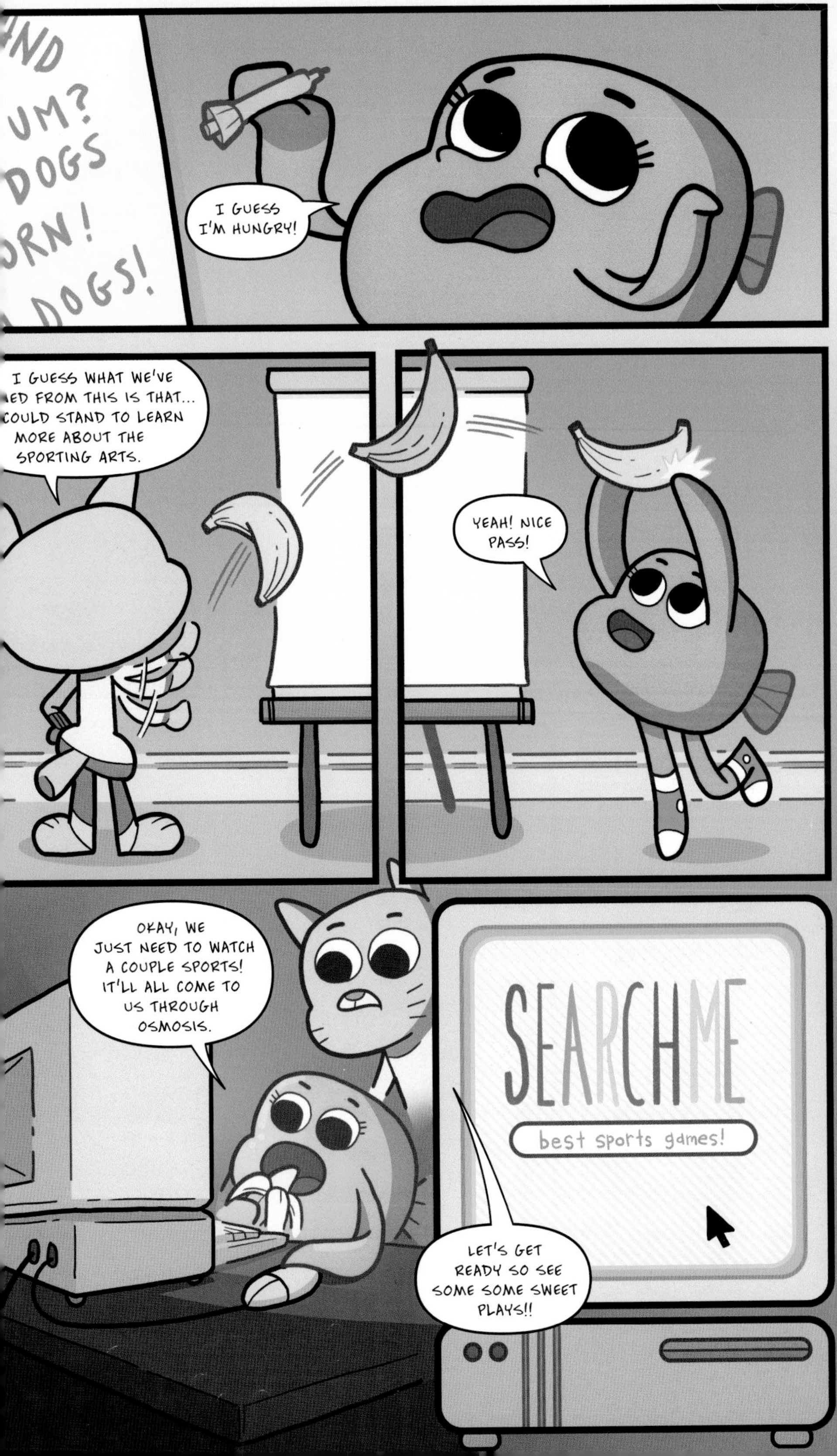
UM?
DOGS
I GUESS I'M HUNGRY!
I GUESS WHAT WE'VE
COULD STAND TO LEARN MORE ABOUT THE SPORTING ARTS.
YEAH! NICE PASS!
OKAY, WE JUST NEED TO WATCH A COUPLE SPORTS! IT'LL ALL COME TO US THROUGH OSMOSIS.
SEARCHME
best sports games!
LET'S GET READY SO SEE SOME SOME SWEET PLAYS!!

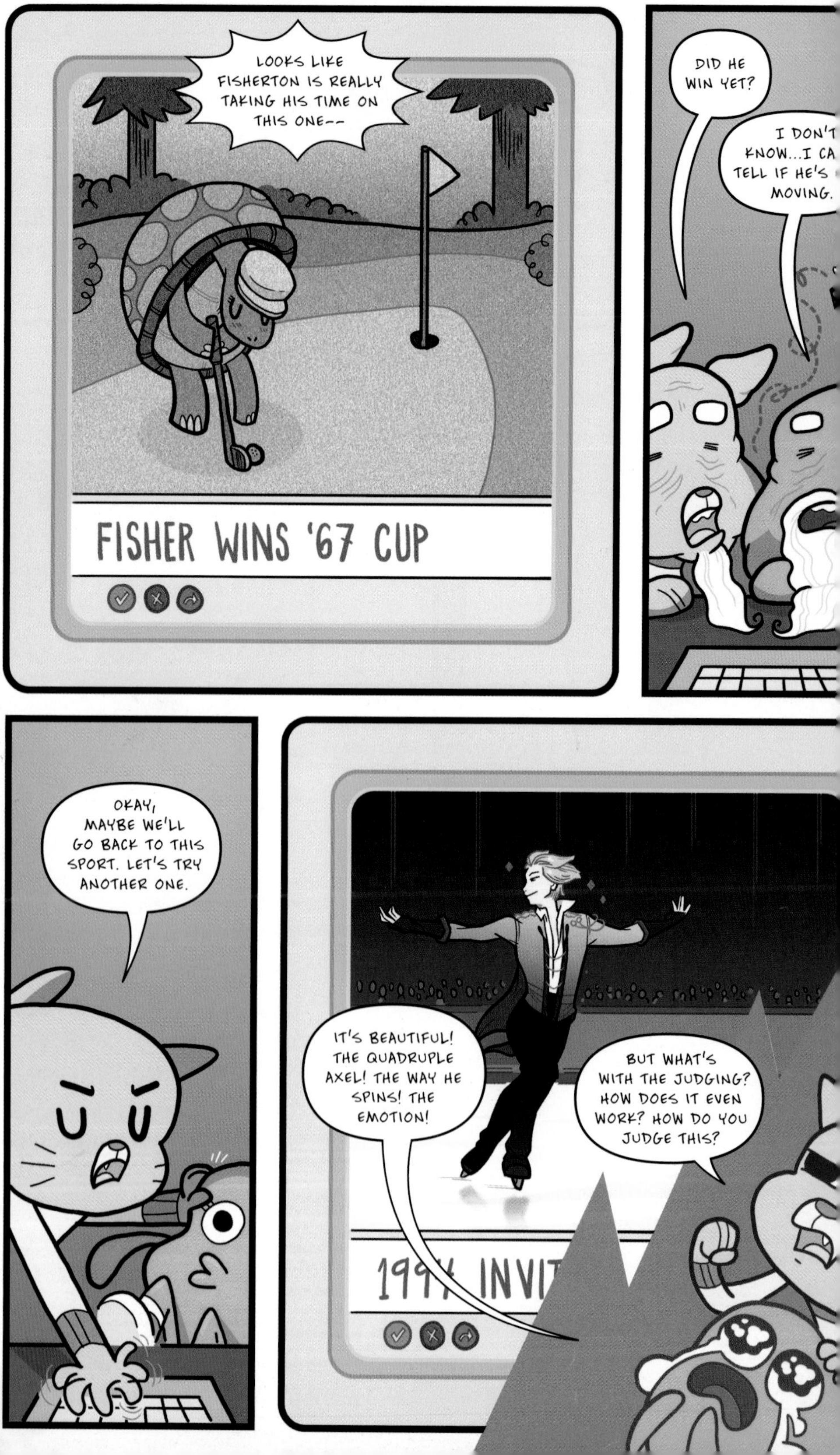
LOOKS LIKE FISHERTON IS REALLY TAKING HIS TIME ON THIS ONE--
FISHER WINS '67 CUP
DID HE WIN YET?
I DON'T KNOW...I CA TELL IF HE'S MOVING.
OKAY, MAYBE WE'LL GO BACK TO THIS SPORT. LET'S TRY ANOTHER ONE.
IT'S BEAUTIFUL! THE QUADRUPLE AXEL! THE WAY HE SPINS! THE EMOTION!
BUT WHAT'S WITH THE JUDGING? HOW DOES IT EVEN WORK? HOW DO YOU JUDGE THIS?

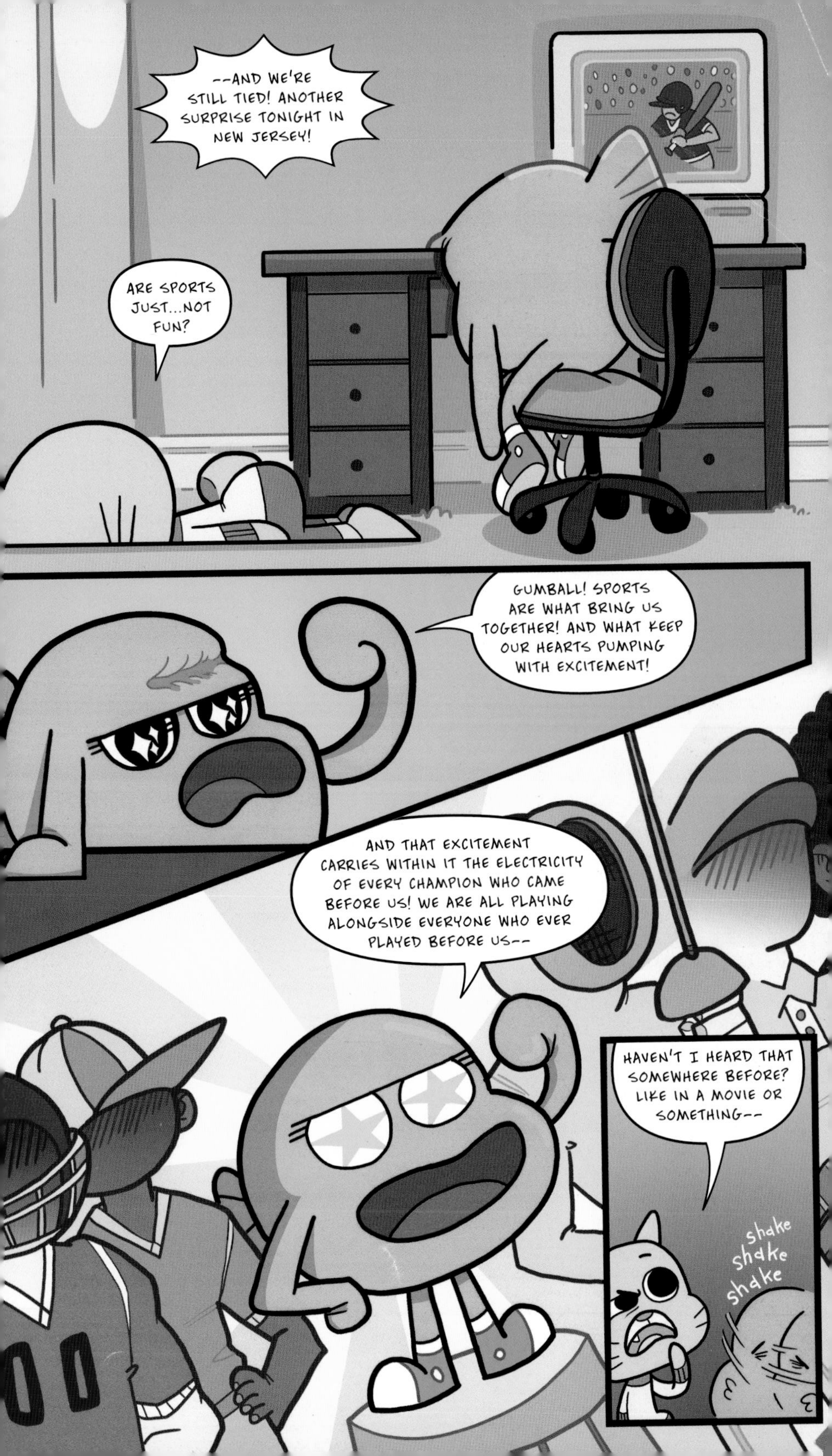
--AND WE'RE STILL TIED! ANOTHER SURPRISE TONIGHT IN NEW JERSEY!
ARE SPORTS JUST...NOT FUN?
GUMBALL! SPORTS ARE WHAT BRING US TOGETHER! AND WHAT KEEP OUR HEARTS PUMPING WITH EXCITEMENT!
AND THAT EXCITEMENT CARRIES WITHIN IT THE ELECTRICITY OF EVERY CHAMPION WHO CAME BEFORE US! WE ARE ALL PLAYING ALONGSIDE EVERYONE WHO EVER PLAYED BEFORE US--
HAVEN'T I HEARD THAT SOMEWHERE BEFORE? LIKE IN A MOVIE OR SOMETHING--
shake shake shake

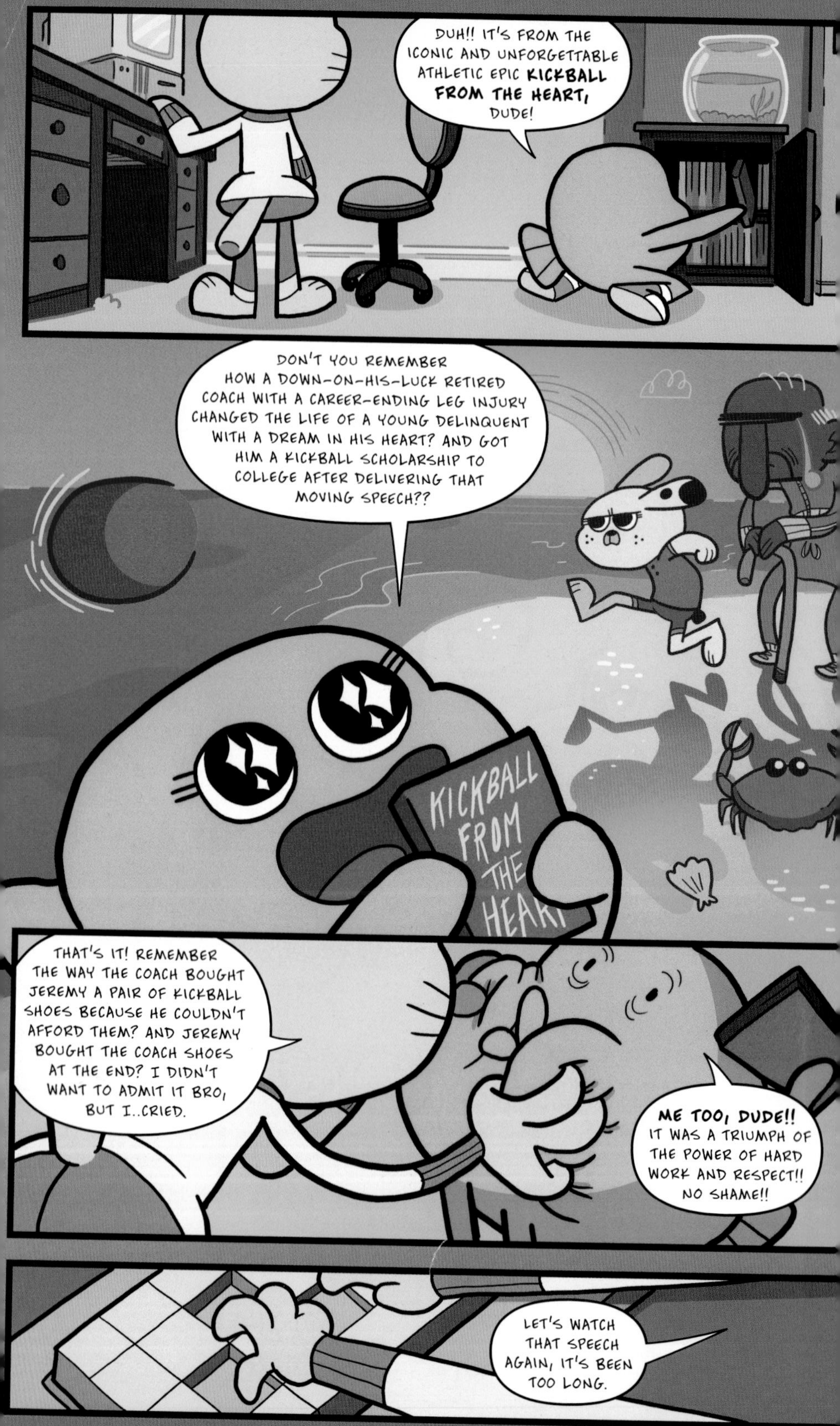
DUH!! IT'S FROM THE ICONIC AND UNFORGETTABLE ATHLETIC EPIC **KICKBALL FROM THE HEART,** DUDE!
DON'T YOU REMEMBER HOW A DOWN-ON-HIS-LUCK RETIRED COACH WITH A CAREER-ENDING LEG INJURY CHANGED THE LIFE OF A YOUNG DELINQUENT WITH A DREAM IN HIS HEART? AND GOT HIM A KICKBALL SCHOLARSHIP TO COLLEGE AFTER DELIVERING THAT MOVING SPEECH??
KICKBALL FROM THE HEART
THAT'S IT! REMEMBER THE WAY THE COACH BOUGHT JEREMY A PAIR OF KICKBALL SHOES BECAUSE HE COULDN'T AFFORD THEM? AND JEREMY BOUGHT THE COACH SHOES AT THE END? I DIDN'T WANT TO ADMIT IT BRO, BUT I..CRIED.
ME TOO, DUDE!! IT WAS A TRIUMPH OF THE POWER OF HARD WORK AND RESPECT!! NO SHAME!!
LET'S WATCH THAT SPEECH AGAIN, IT'S BEEN TOO LONG.

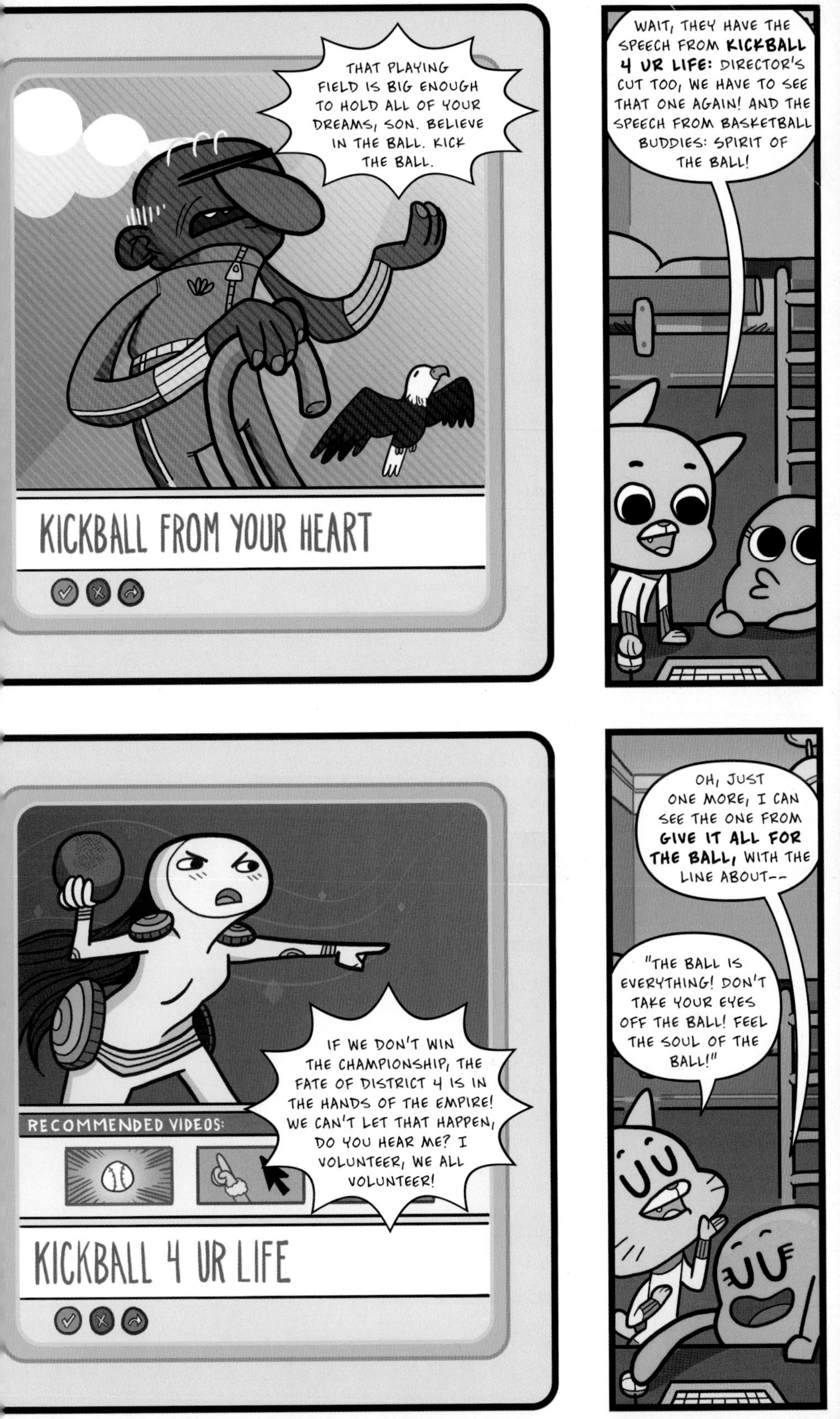
THAT PLAYING FIELD IS BIG ENOUGH TO HOLD ALL OF YOUR DREAMS, SON. BELIEVE IN THE BALL. KICK THE BALL.
KICKBALL FROM YOUR HEART
WAIT, THEY HAVE THE SPEECH FROM **KICKBALL 4 UR LIFE:** DIRECTOR'S CUT TOO, WE HAVE TO SEE THAT ONE AGAIN! AND THE SPEECH FROM BASKETBALL BUDDIES: SPIRIT OF THE BALL!
IF WE DON'T WIN THE CHAMPIONSHIP, THE FATE OF DISTRICT 4 IS IN THE HANDS OF THE EMPIRE! WE CAN'T LET THAT HAPPEN, DO YOU HEAR ME? I VOLUNTEER, WE ALL VOLUNTEER!
RECOMMENDED VIDEOS:
KICKBALL 4 UR LIFE
OH, JUST ONE MORE, I CAN SEE THE ONE FROM **GIVE IT ALL FOR THE BALL,** WITH THE LINE ABOUT--
"THE BALL IS EVERYTHING! DON'T TAKE YOUR EYES OFF THE BALL! FEEL THE SOUL OF THE BALL!"

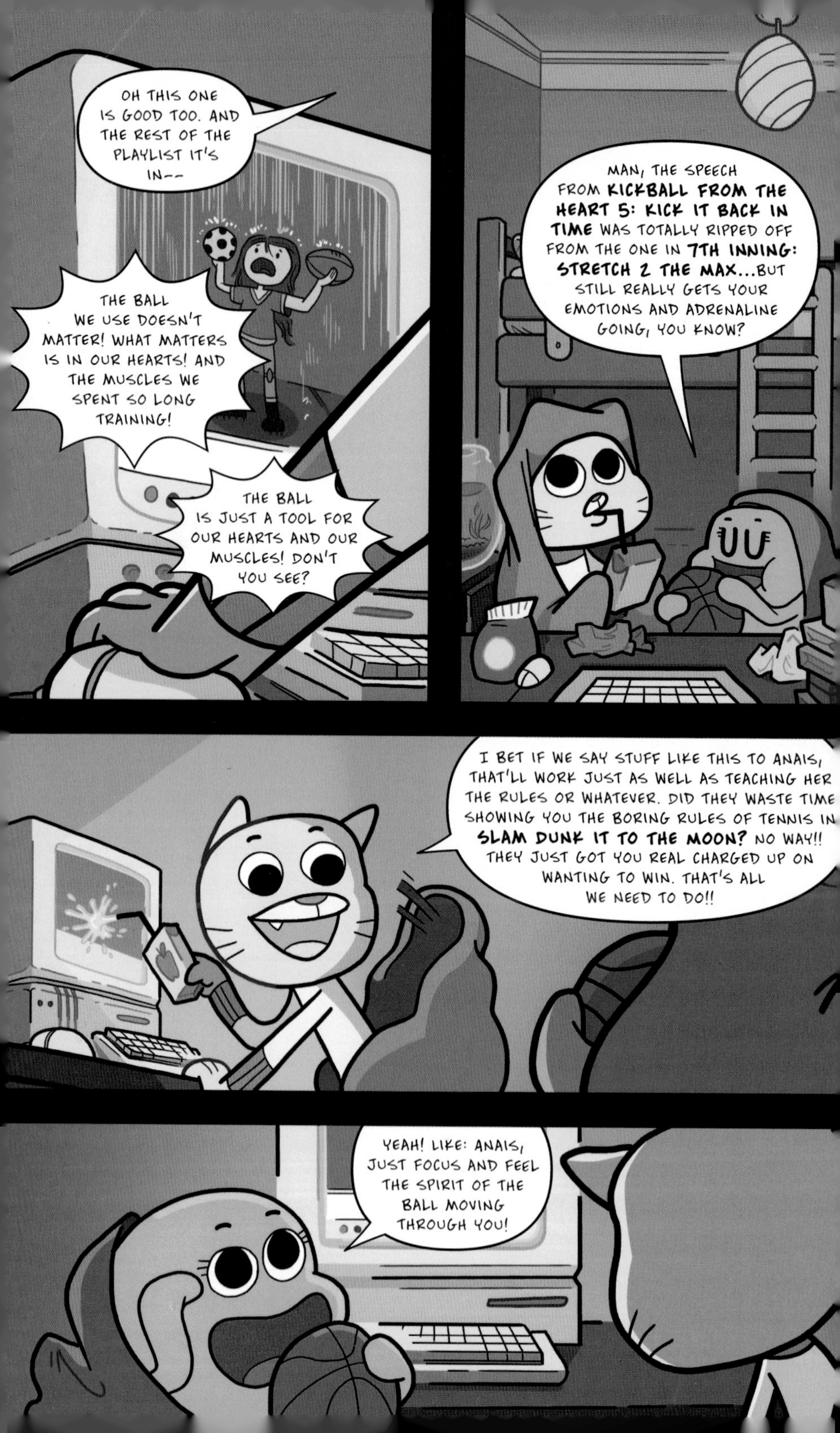
OH THIS ONE IS GOOD TOO. AND THE REST OF THE PLAYLIST IT'S IN--
THE BALL WE USE DOESN'T MATTER! WHAT MATTERS IS IN OUR HEARTS! AND THE MUSCLES WE SPENT SO LONG TRAINING!
THE BALL IS JUST A TOOL FOR OUR HEARTS AND OUR MUSCLES! DON'T YOU SEE?
MAN, THE SPEECH FROM **KICKBALL FROM THE HEART 5: KICK IT BACK IN TIME** WAS TOTALLY RIPPED OFF FROM THE ONE IN **7TH INNING: STRETCH 2 THE MAX**...BUT STILL REALLY GETS YOUR EMOTIONS AND ADRENALINE GOING, YOU KNOW?
I BET IF WE SAY STUFF LIKE THIS TO ANAIS, THAT'LL WORK JUST AS WELL AS TEACHING HER THE RULES OR WHATEVER. DID THEY WASTE TIME SHOWING YOU THE BORING RULES OF TENNIS IN **SLAM DUNK IT TO THE MOON?** NO WAY!! THEY JUST GOT YOU REAL CHARGED UP ON WANTING TO WIN. THAT'S ALL WE NEED TO DO!!
YEAH! LIKE: ANAIS, JUST FOCUS AND FEEL THE SPIRIT OF THE BALL MOVING THROUGH YOU!

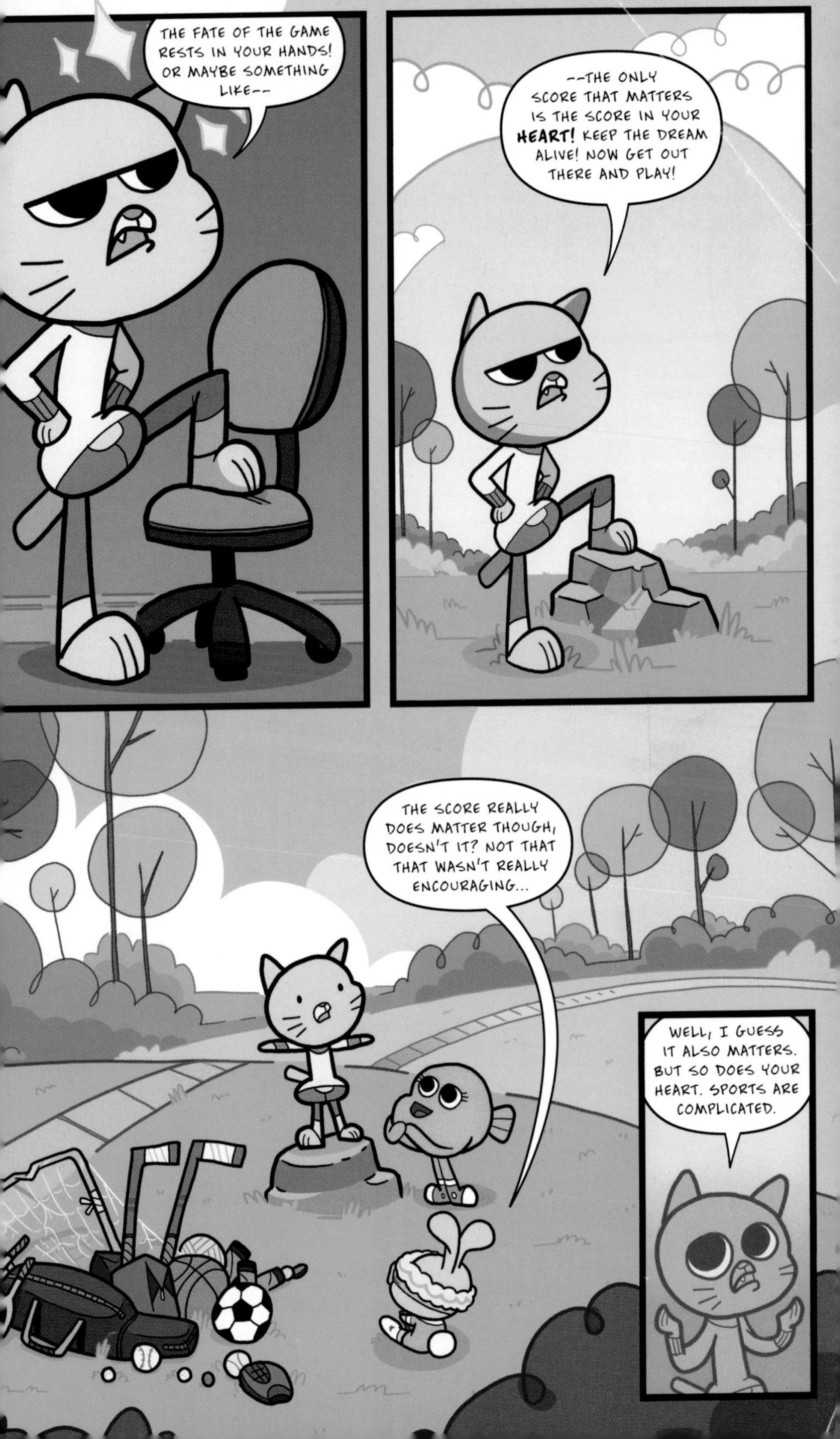
THE FATE OF THE GAME RESTS IN YOUR HANDS! OR MAYBE SOMETHING LIKE--
--THE ONLY SCORE THAT MATTERS IS THE SCORE IN YOUR **HEART!** KEEP THE DREAM ALIVE! NOW GET OUT THERE AND PLAY!
THE SCORE REALLY DOES MATTER THOUGH, DOESN'T IT? NOT THAT THAT WASN'T REALLY ENCOURAGING...
WELL, I GUESS IT ALSO MATTERS. BUT SO DOES YOUR HEART. SPORTS ARE COMPLICATED.

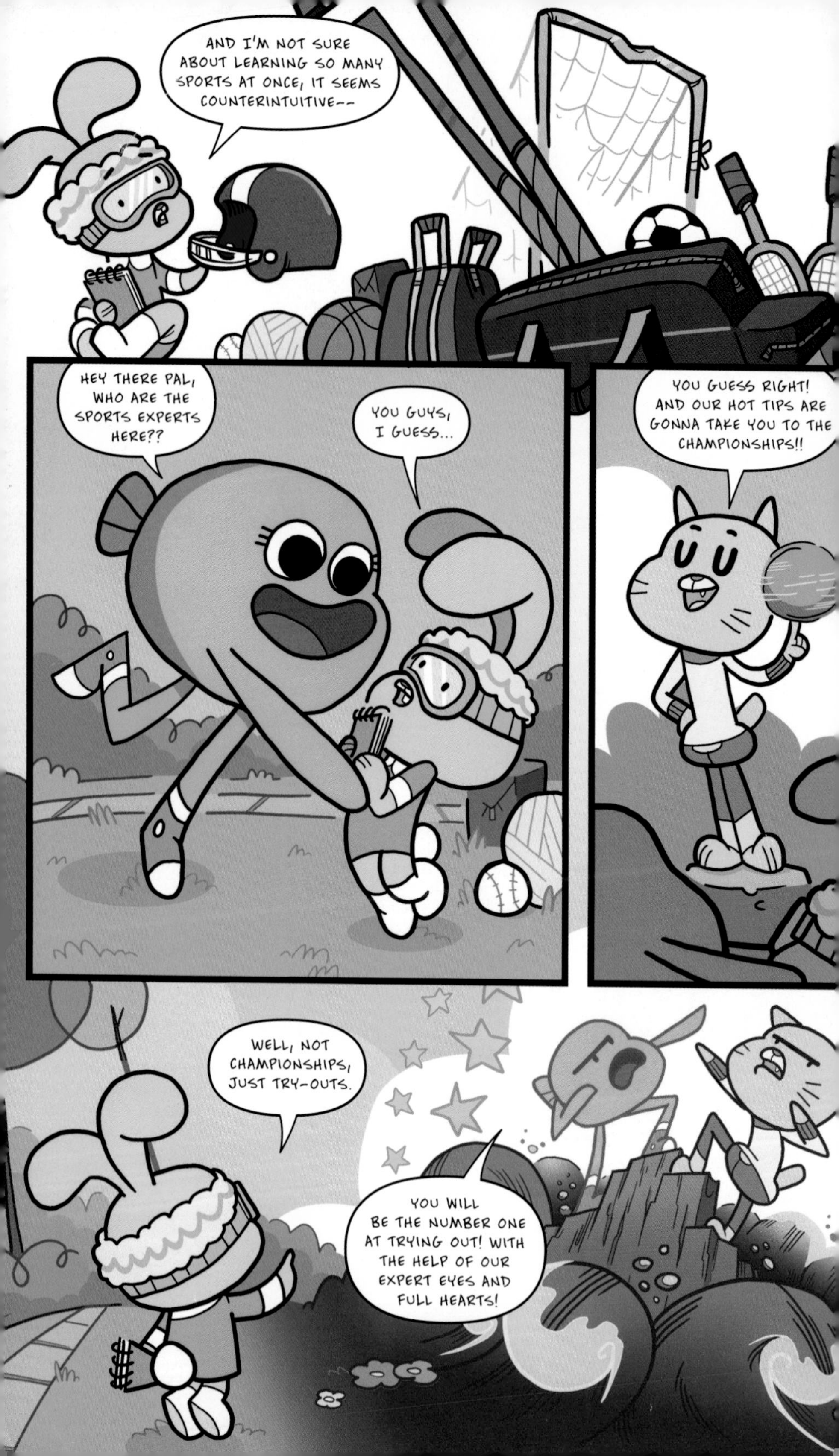

AND I'M NOT SURE ABOUT LEARNING SO MANY SPORTS AT ONCE, IT SEEMS COUNTERINTUITIVE--
HEY THERE PAL, WHO ARE THE SPORTS EXPERTS HERE??
YOU GUYS, I GUESS...
YOU GUESS RIGHT! AND OUR HOT TIPS ARE GONNA TAKE YOU TO THE CHAMPIONSHIPS!!
WELL, NOT CHAMPIONSHIPS, JUST TRY-OUTS.
YOU WILL BE THE NUMBER ONE AT TRYING OUT! WITH THE HELP OF OUR EXPERT EYES AND FULL HEARTS!

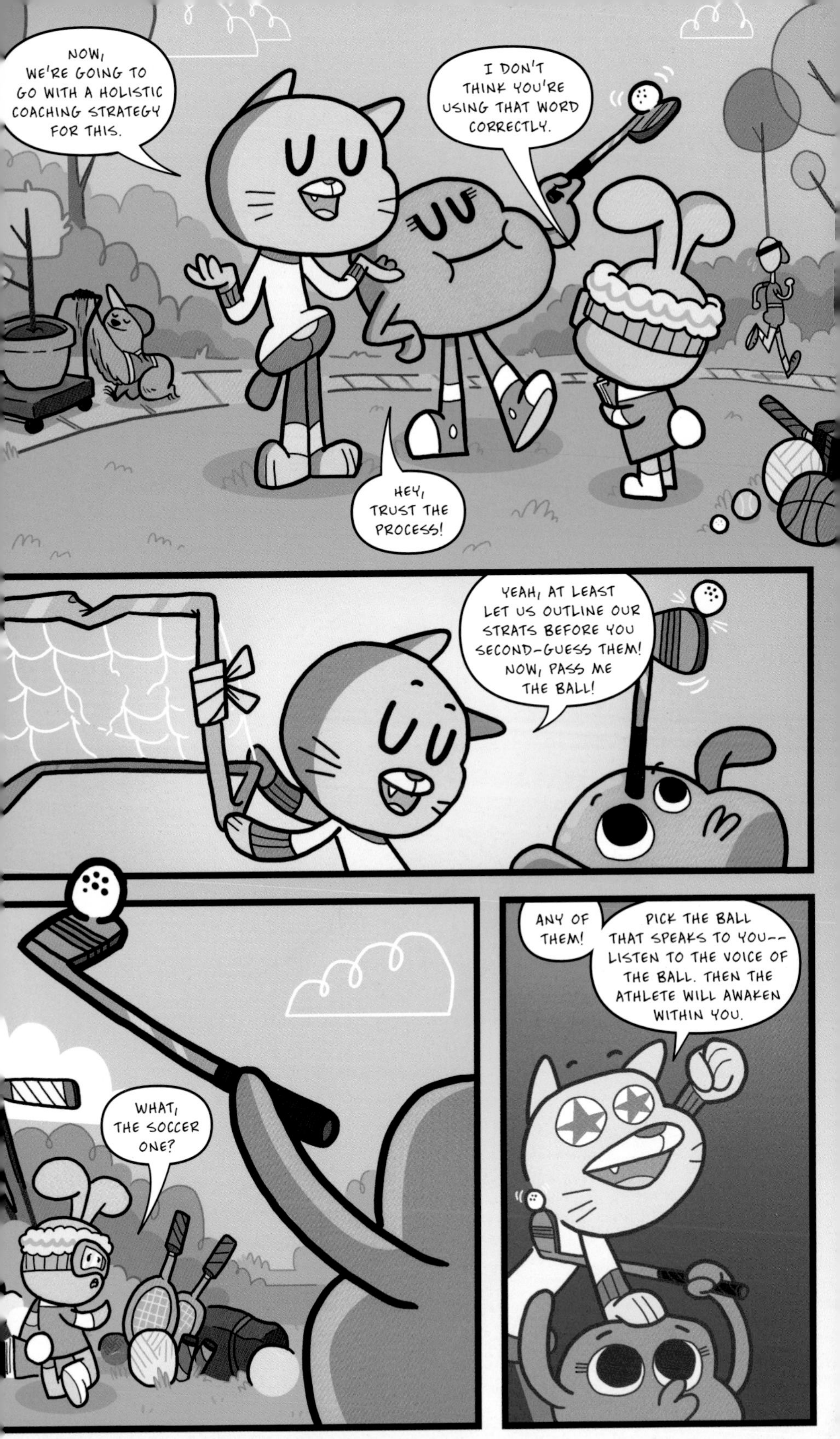
NOW, WE'RE GOING TO GO WITH A HOLISTIC COACHING STRATEGY FOR THIS.
I DON'T THINK YOU'RE USING THAT WORD CORRECTLY.
HEY, TRUST THE PROCESS!
YEAH, AT LEAST LET US OUTLINE OUR STRATS BEFORE YOU SECOND-GUESS THEM! NOW, PASS ME THE BALL!
WHAT, THE SOCCER ONE?
ANY OF THEM!
PICK THE BALL THAT SPEAKS TO YOU-- LISTEN TO THE VOICE OF THE BALL. THEN THE ATHLETE WILL AWAKEN WITHIN YOU.

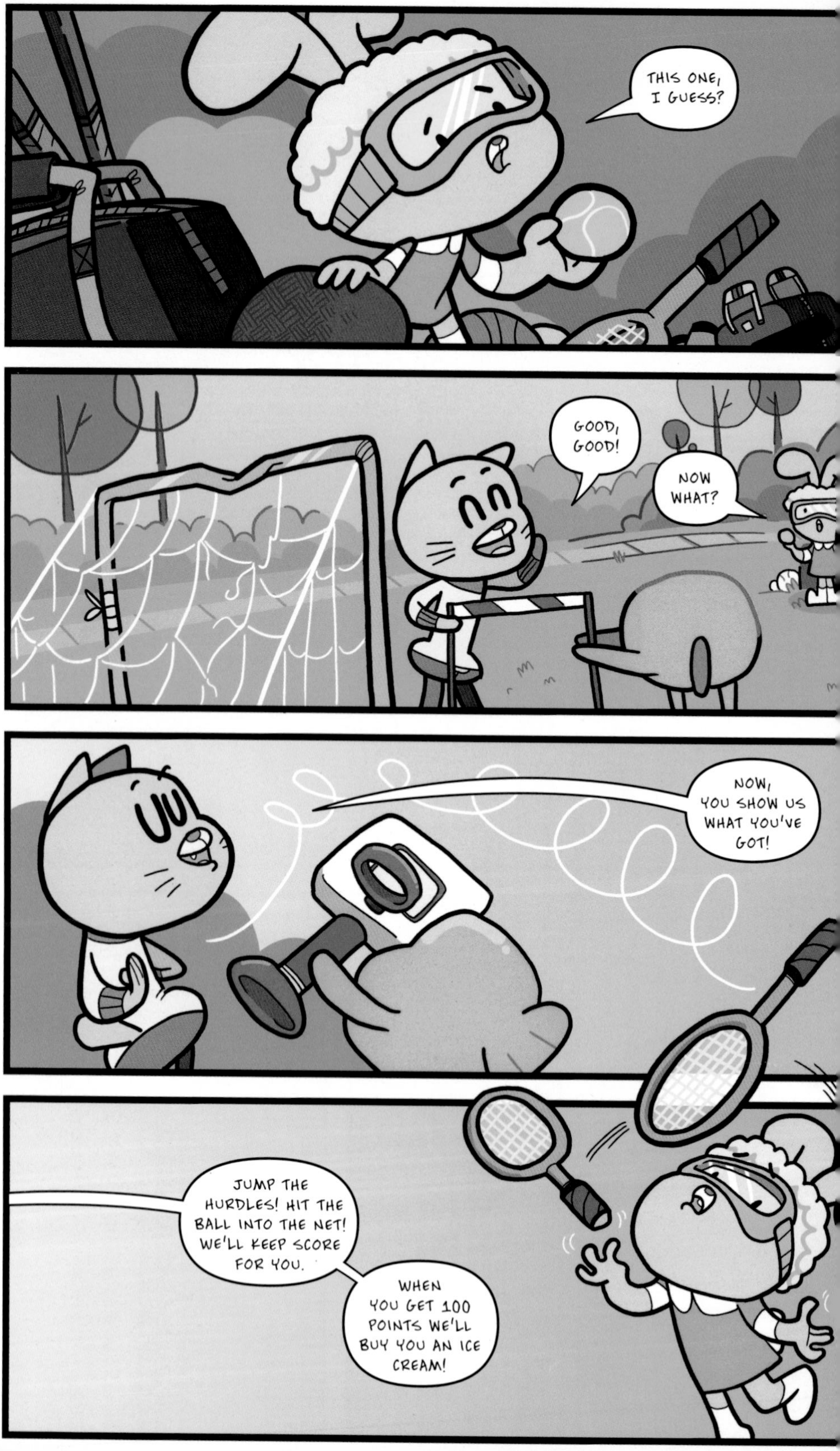
THIS ONE, I GUESS?
GOOD, GOOD!
NOW WHAT?
NOW, YOU SHOW US WHAT YOU'VE GOT!
JUMP THE HURDLES! HIT THE BALL INTO THE NET! WE'LL KEEP SCORE FOR YOU.
WHEN YOU GET 100 POINTS WE'LL BUY YOU AN ICE CREAM!

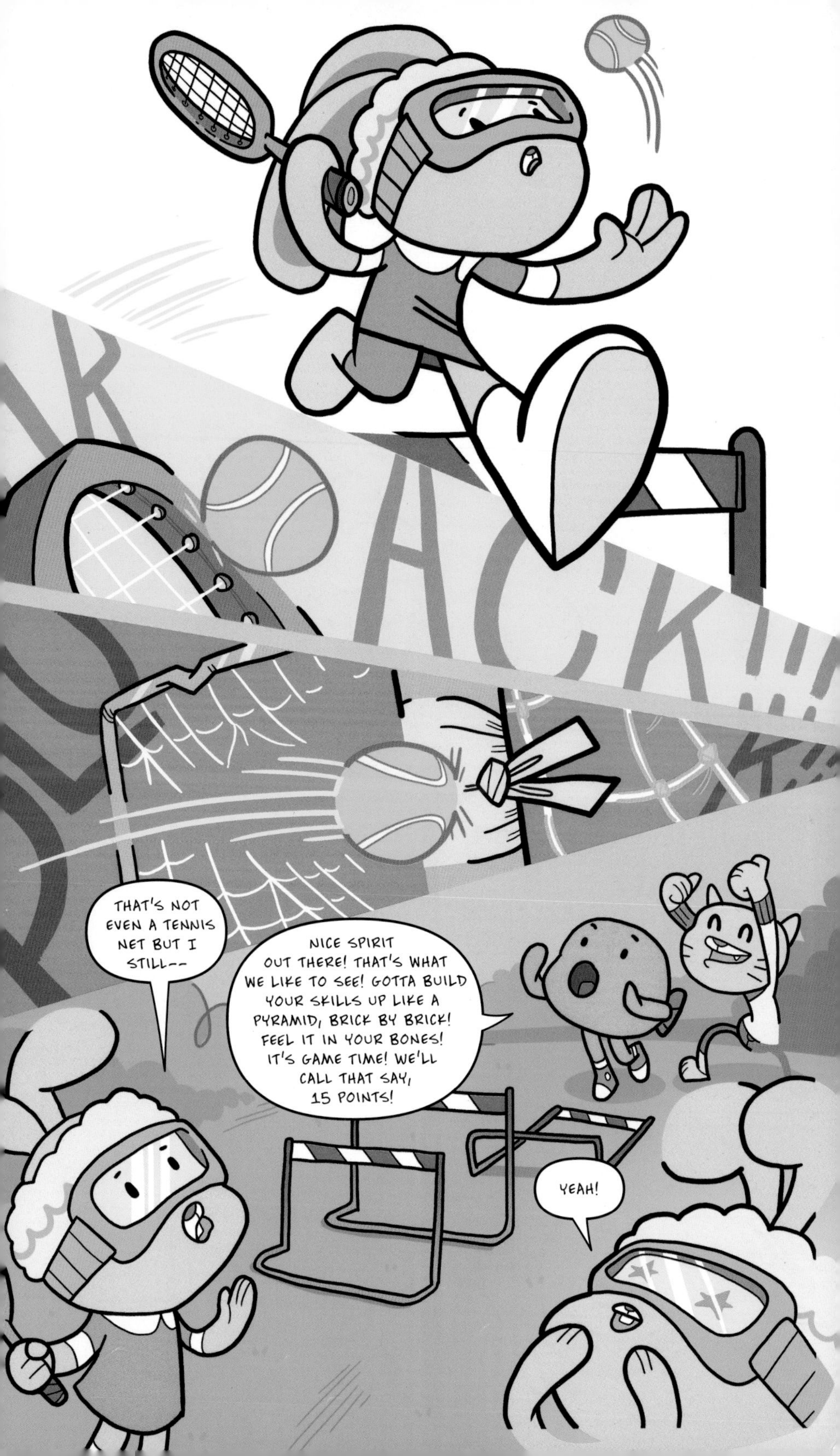

THAT'S NOT EVEN A TENNIS NET BUT I STILL--
NICE SPIRIT OUT THERE! THAT'S WHAT WE LIKE TO SEE! GOTTA BUILD YOUR SKILLS UP LIKE A PYRAMID, BRICK BY BRICK! FEEL IT IN YOUR BONES! IT'S GAME TIME! WE'LL CALL THAT SAY, 15 POINTS!
YEAH!

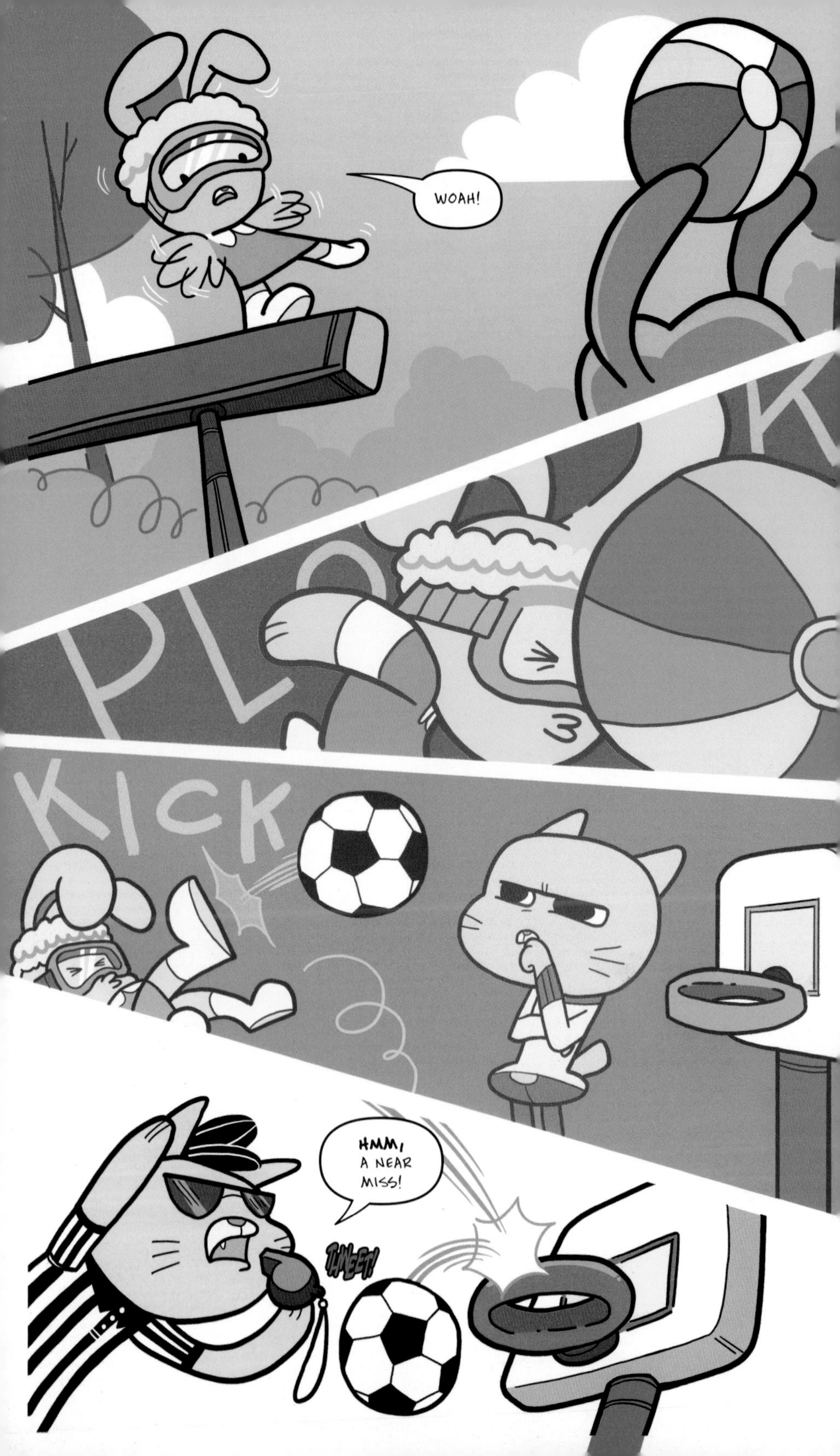
WOAH!
KICK
HMM, A NEAR MISS!
THWEET!

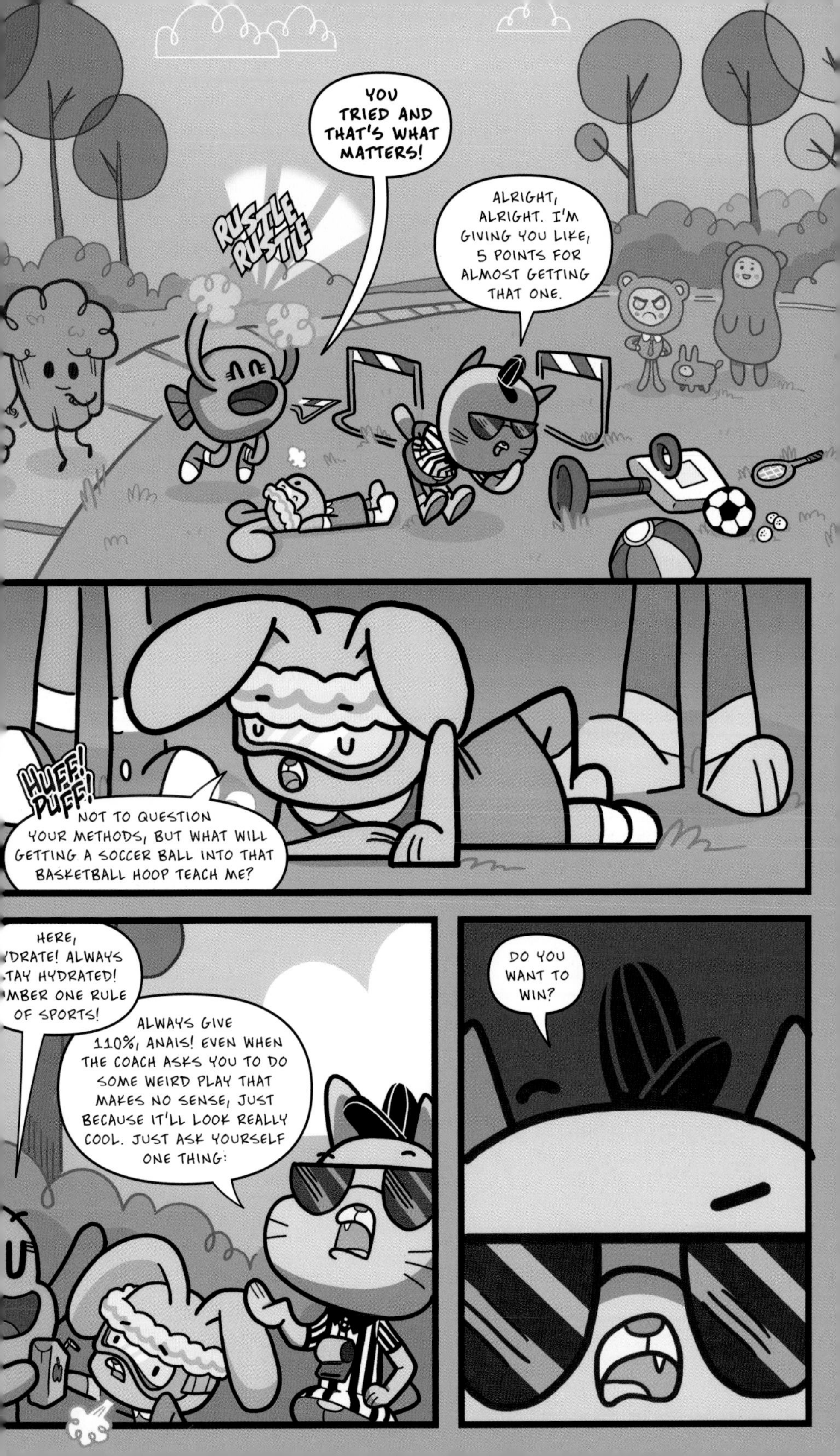
YOU TRIED AND THAT'S WHAT MATTERS!
RUSTLE RUSTLE
ALRIGHT, ALRIGHT. I'M GIVING YOU LIKE, 5 POINTS FOR ALMOST GETTING THAT ONE.
HUFF! PUFF!
NOT TO QUESTION YOUR METHODS, BUT WHAT WILL GETTING A SOCCER BALL INTO THAT BASKETBALL HOOP TEACH ME?
HERE, YDRATE! ALWAYS TAY HYDRATED! MBER ONE RULE OF SPORTS!
ALWAYS GIVE 110%, ANAIS! EVEN WHEN THE COACH ASKS YOU TO DO SOME WEIRD PLAY THAT MAKES NO SENSE, JUST BECAUSE IT'LL LOOK REALLY COOL. JUST ASK YOURSELF ONE THING:
DO YOU WANT TO WIN?

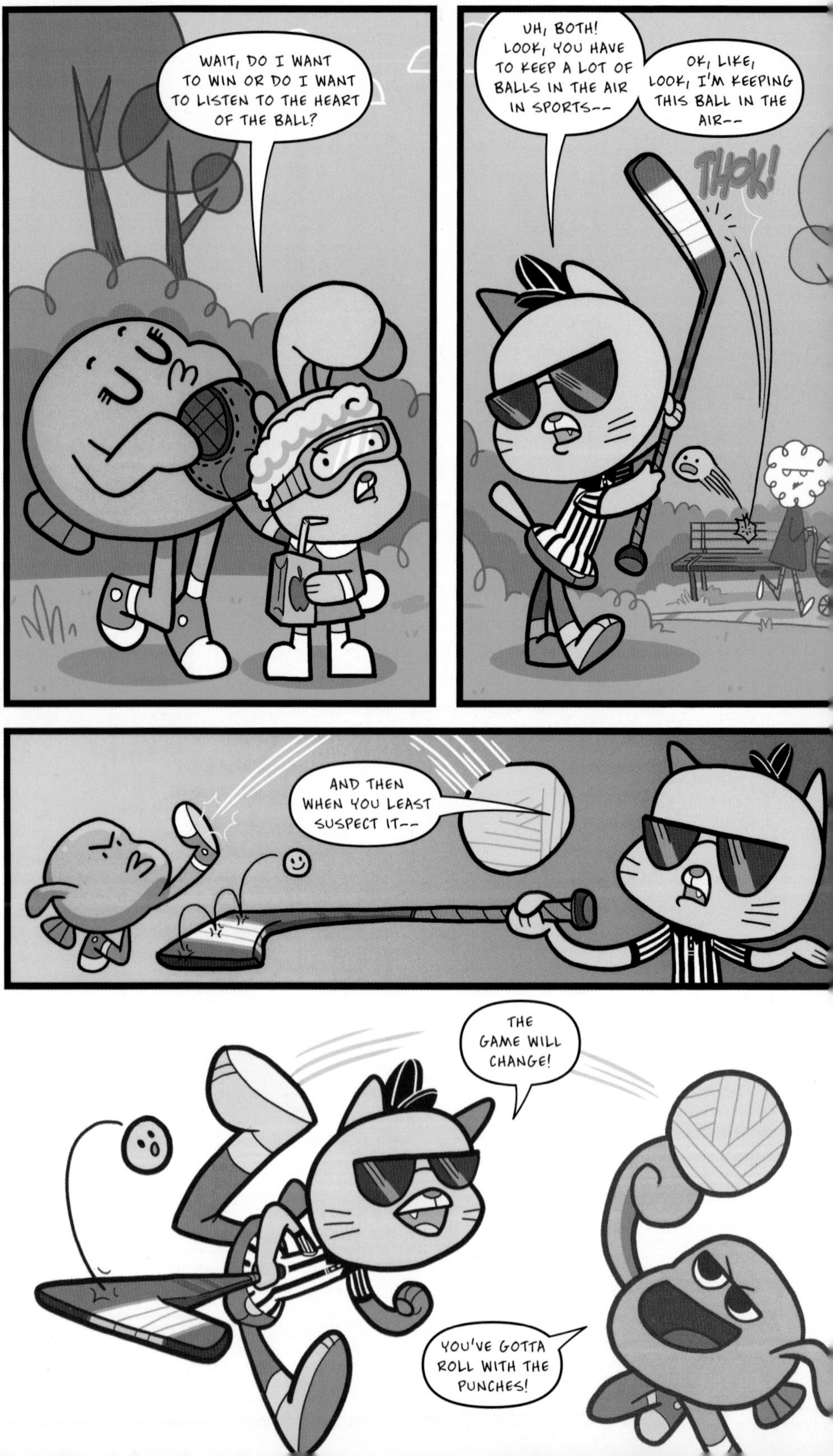
WAIT, DO I WANT TO WIN OR DO I WANT TO LISTEN TO THE HEART OF THE BALL?
UH, BOTH! LOOK, YOU HAVE TO KEEP A LOT OF BALLS IN THE AIR IN SPORTS--
OK, LIKE, LOOK, I'M KEEPING THIS BALL IN THE AIR--
THOK!
AND THEN WHEN YOU LEAST SUSPECT IT--
THE GAME WILL CHANGE!
YOU'VE GOTTA ROLL WITH THE PUNCHES!

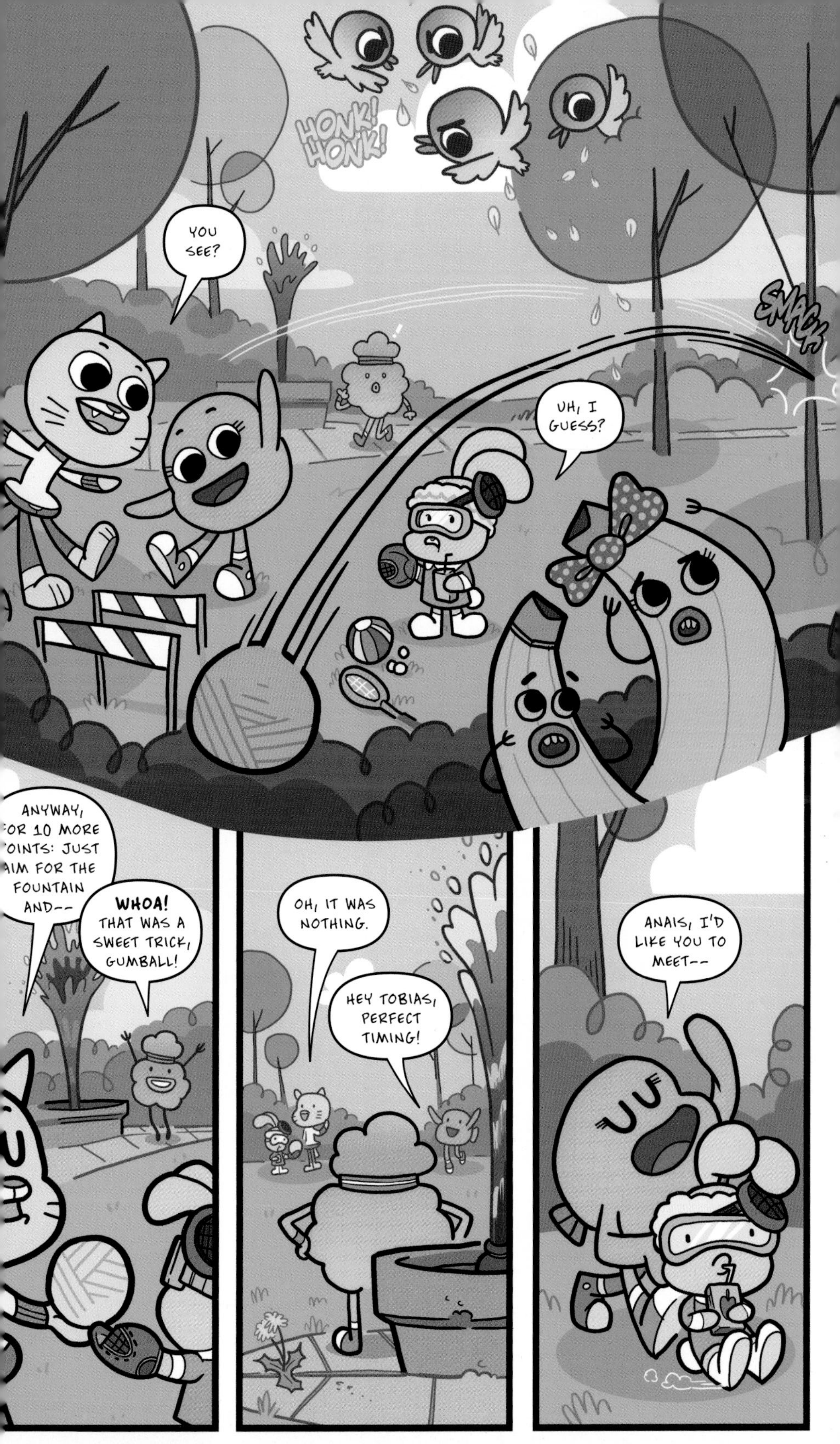

HONK! HONK!
YOU SEE?
SMACK
UH, I GUESS?
ANYWAY, FOR 10 MORE POINTS: JUST AIM FOR THE FOUNTAIN AND--
WHOA! THAT WAS A SWEET TRICK, GUMBALL!
OH, IT WAS NOTHING.
HEY TOBIAS, PERFECT TIMING!
ANAIS, I'D LIKE YOU TO MEET--

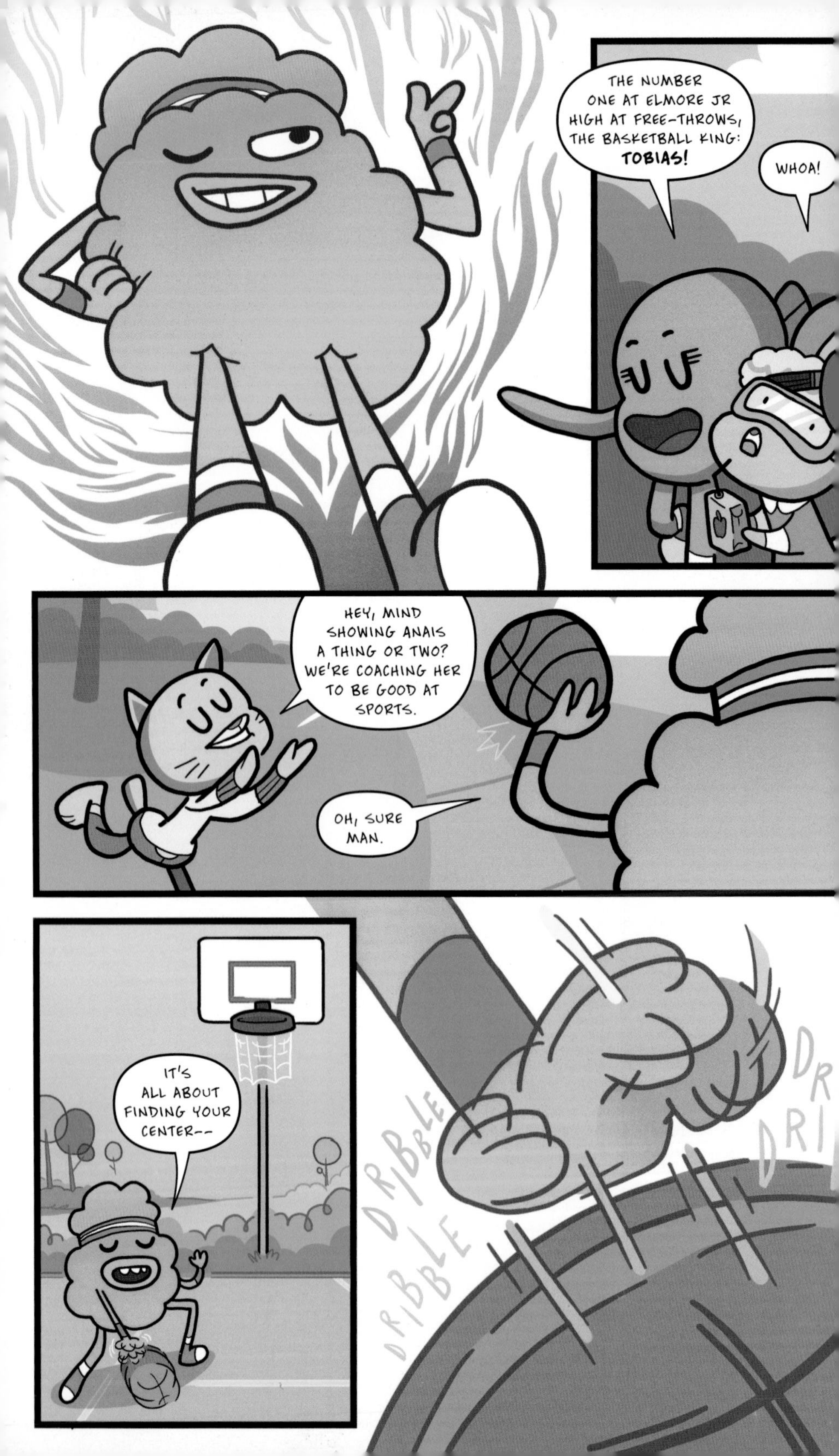

THE NUMBER ONE AT ELMORE JR HIGH AT FREE-THROWS, THE BASKETBALL KING: **TOBIAS!**
WHOA!
HEY, MIND SHOWING ANAIS A THING OR TWO? WE'RE COACHING HER TO BE GOOD AT SPORTS.
OH, SURE MAN.
IT'S ALL ABOUT FINDING YOUR CENTER--
DRIBBLE
DRIBBLE
DR
DRI

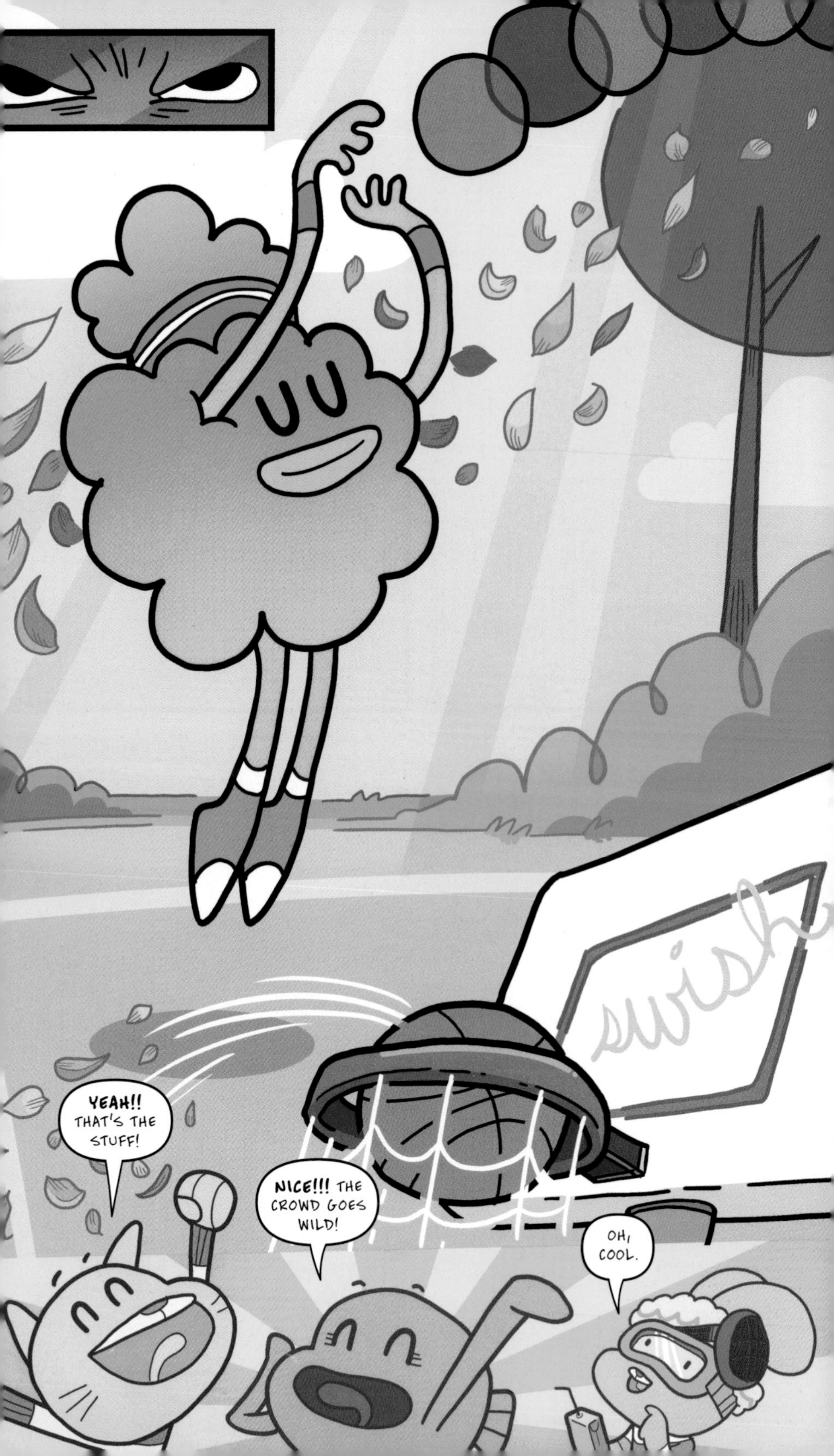
swish
YEAH!! THAT'S THE STUFF!
NICE!!! THE CROWD GOES WILD!
OH, COOL.

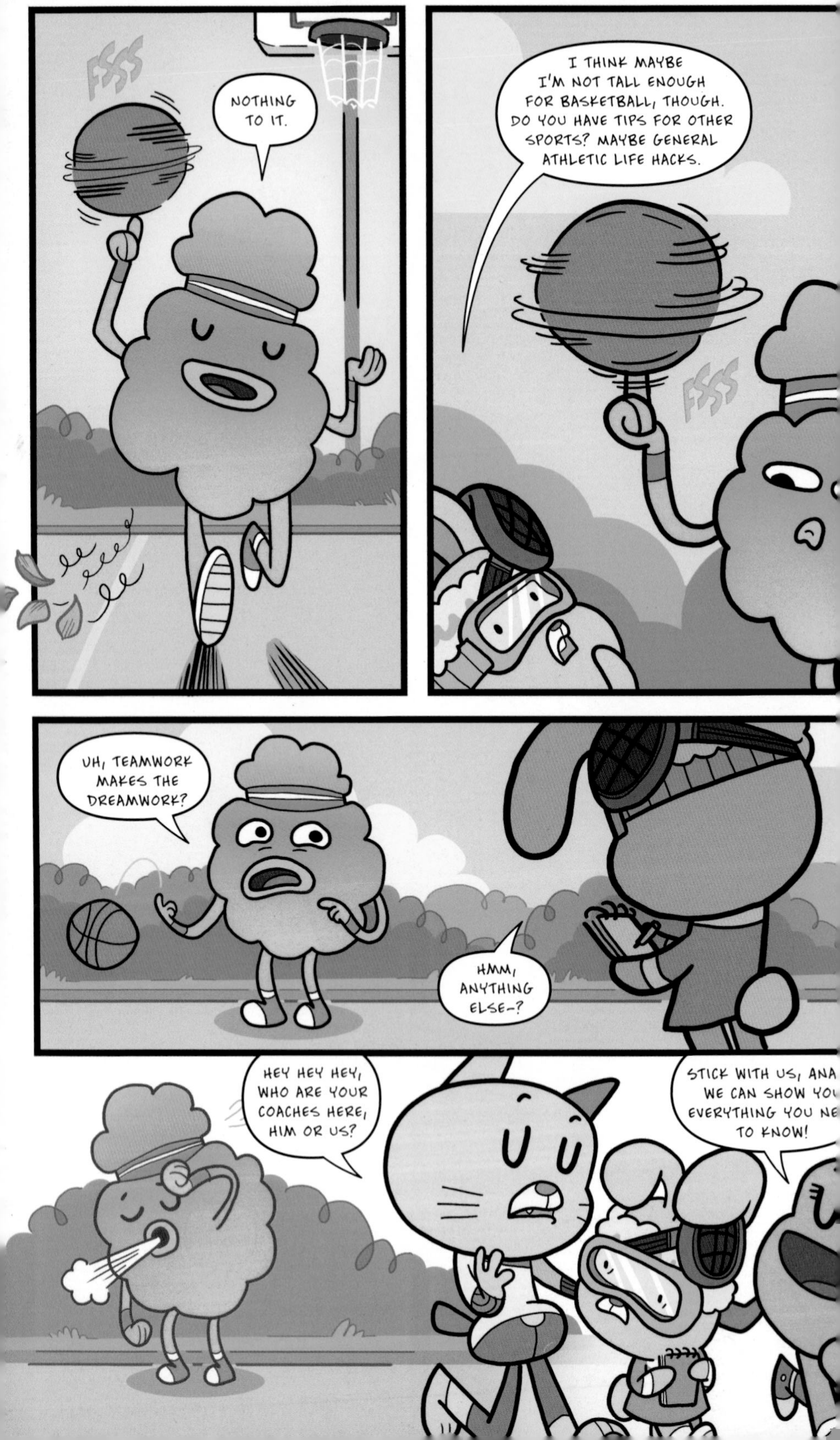
FSSS
NOTHING TO IT.
I THINK MAYBE I'M NOT TALL ENOUGH FOR BASKETBALL, THOUGH. DO YOU HAVE TIPS FOR OTHER SPORTS? MAYBE GENERAL ATHLETIC LIFE HACKS.
FSSS
UH, TEAMWORK MAKES THE DREAMWORK?
HMM, ANYTHING ELSE-?
HEY HEY HEY, WHO ARE YOUR COACHES HERE, HIM OR US?
STICK WITH US, ANA
WE CAN SHOW YOU
EVERYTHING YOU NE
TO KNOW!

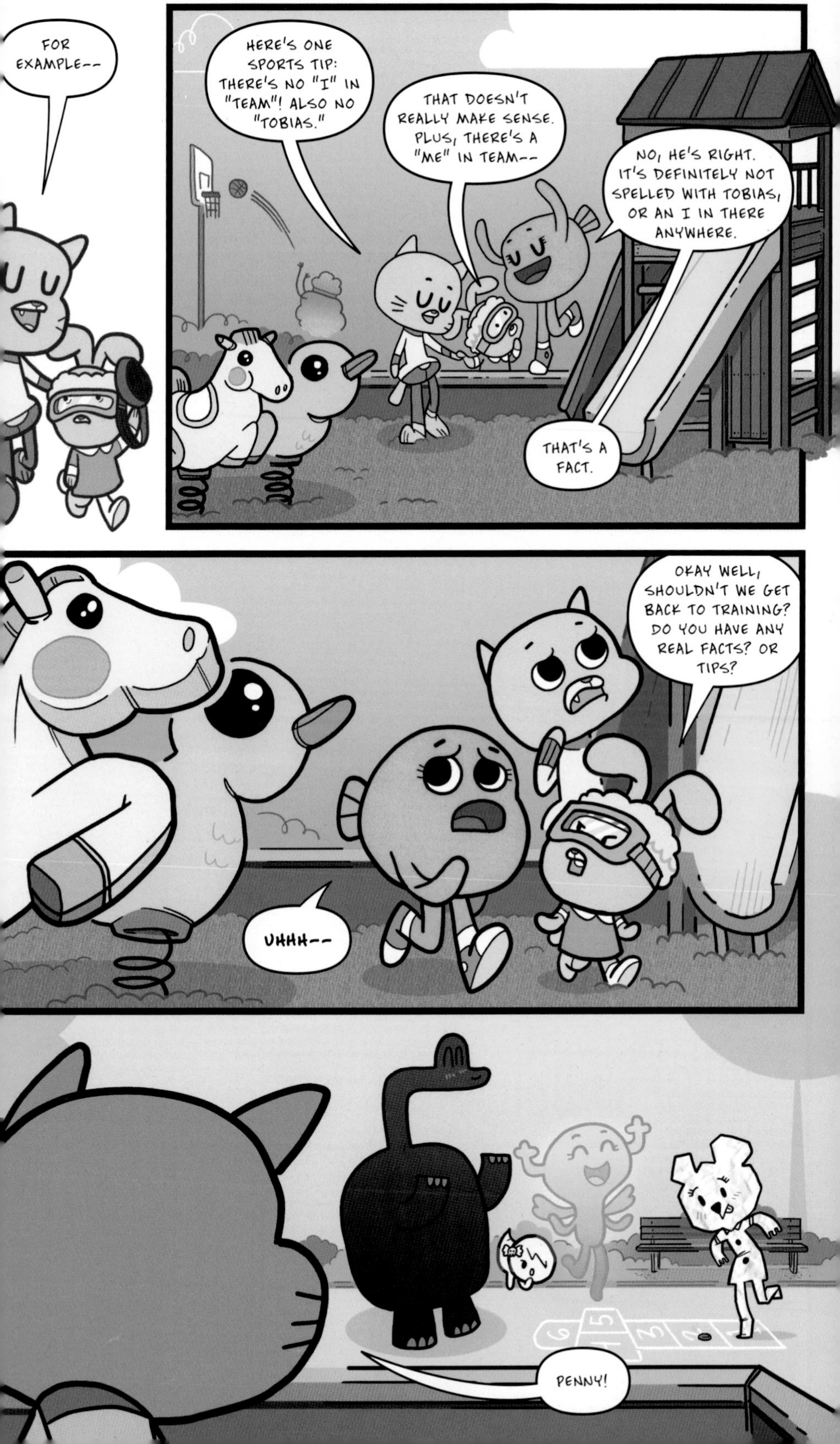
FOR EXAMPLE--
HERE'S ONE SPORTS TIP: THERE'S NO "I" IN "TEAM"! ALSO NO "TOBIAS."
THAT DOESN'T REALLY MAKE SENSE. PLUS, THERE'S A "ME" IN TEAM--
NO, HE'S RIGHT. IT'S DEFINITELY NOT SPELLED WITH TOBIAS, OR AN I IN THERE ANYWHERE.
THAT'S A FACT.
OKAY WELL, SHOULDN'T WE GET BACK TO TRAINING? DO YOU HAVE ANY REAL FACTS? OR TIPS?
UHHH--
PENNY!

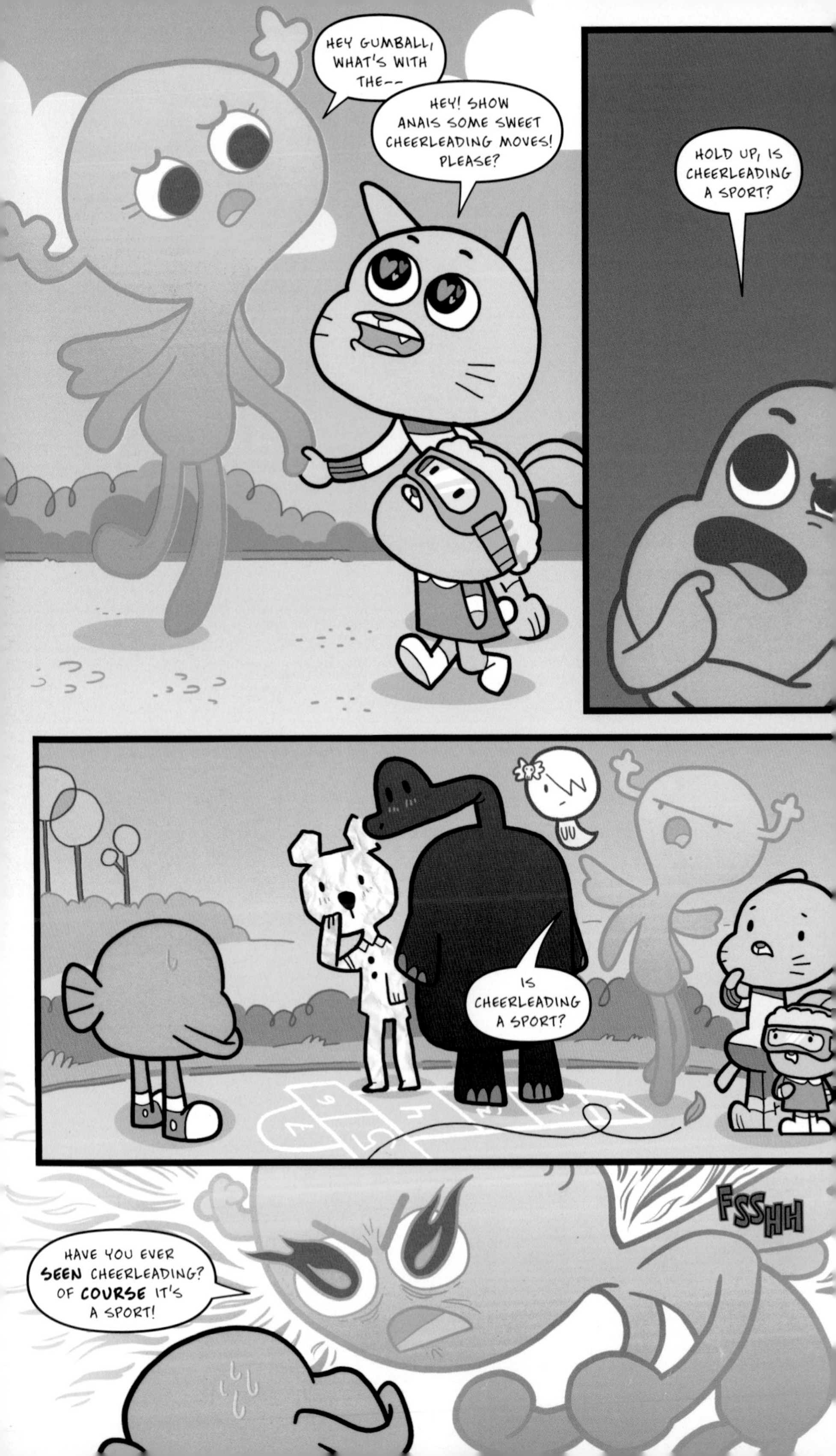
HEY GUMBALL, WHAT'S WITH THE--
HEY! SHOW ANAIS SOME SWEET CHEERLEADING MOVES! PLEASE?
HOLD UP, IS CHEERLEADING A SPORT?
IS CHEERLEADING A SPORT?
FSSHH
HAVE YOU EVER **SEEN** CHEERLEADING? OF **COURSE** IT'S A SPORT!

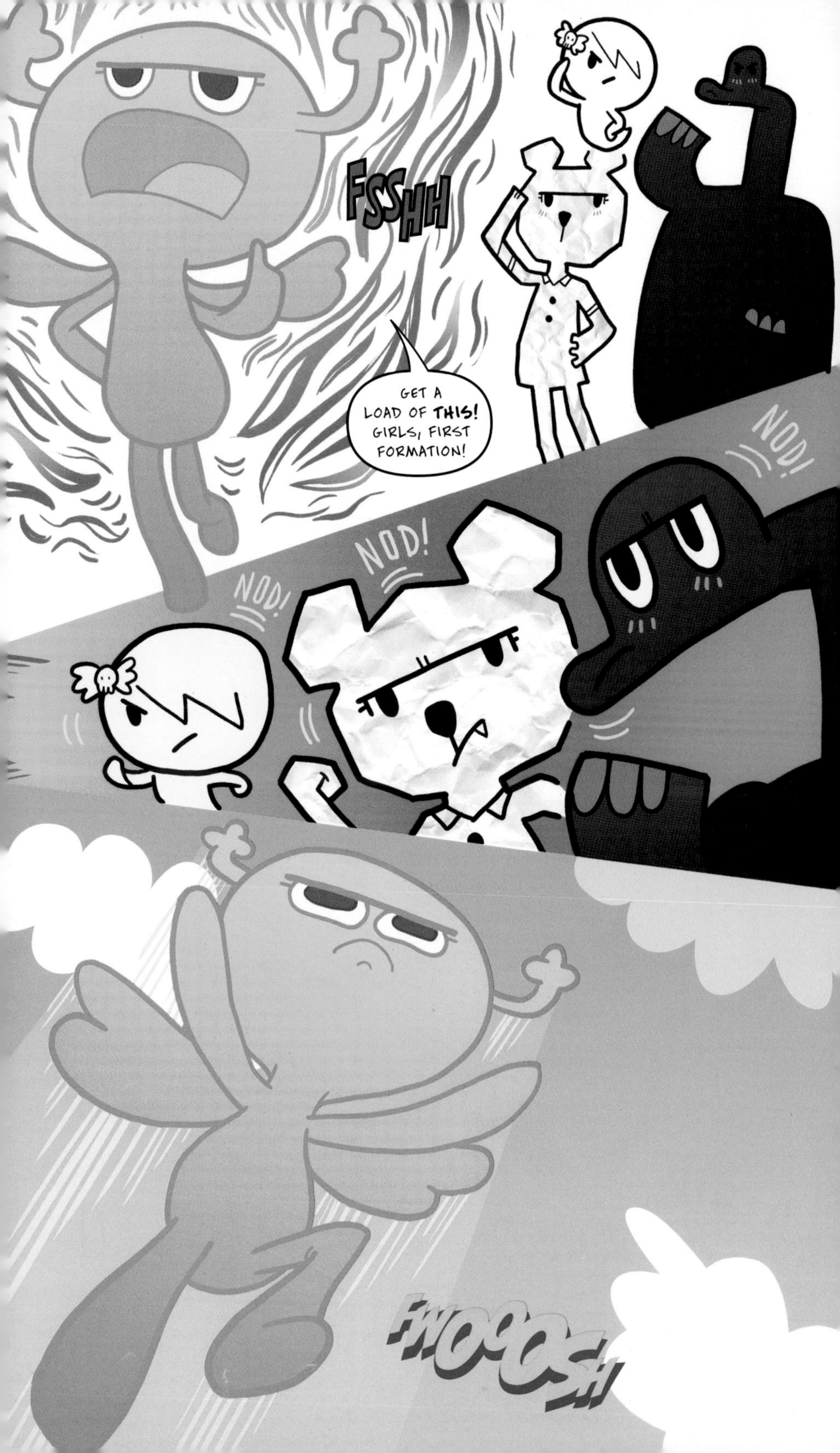
FSSHH
GET A LOAD OF **THIS**! GIRLS, FIRST FORMATION!
NOD!
NOD!
NOD!
FWOOOSH

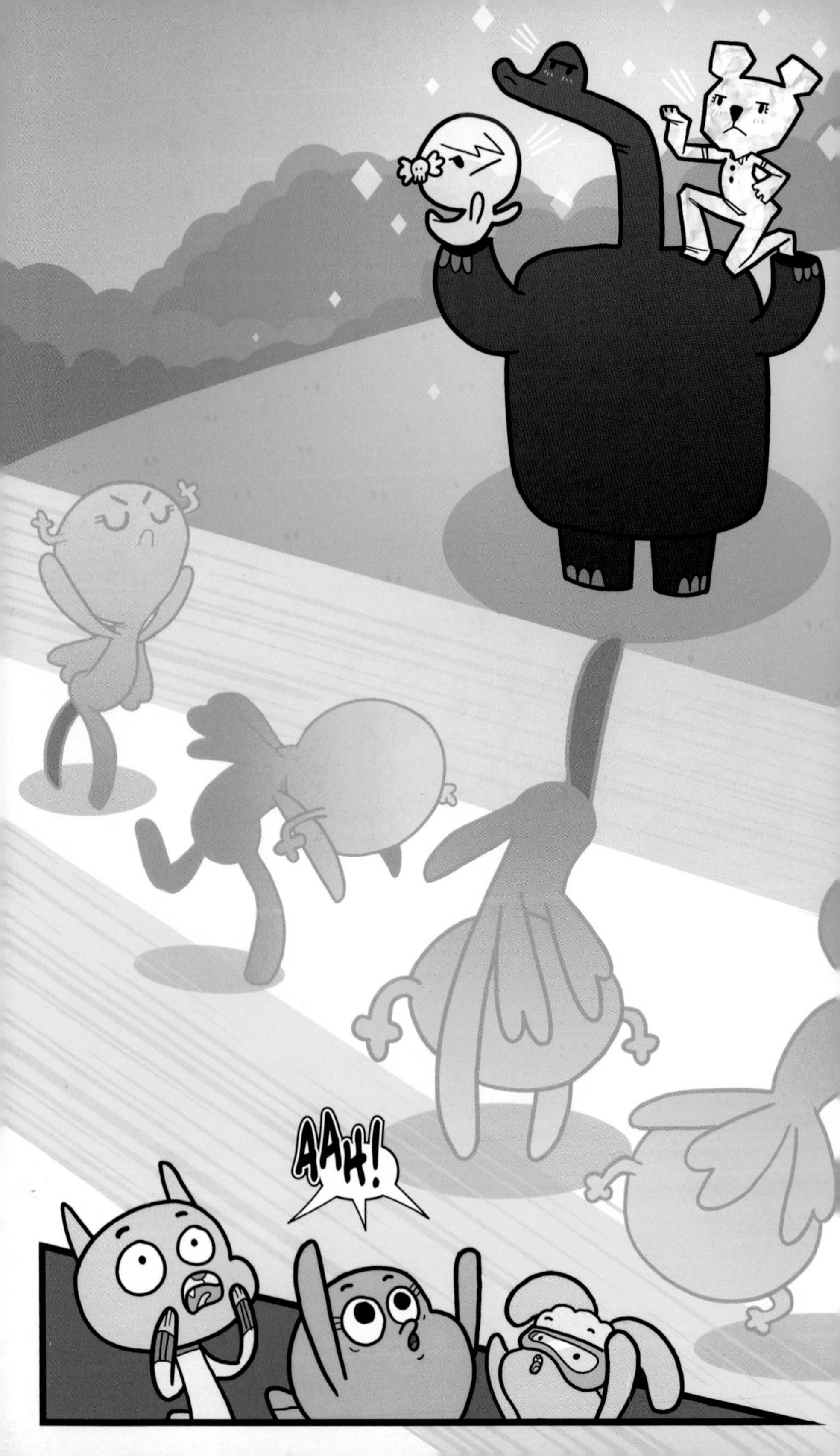
AAH!

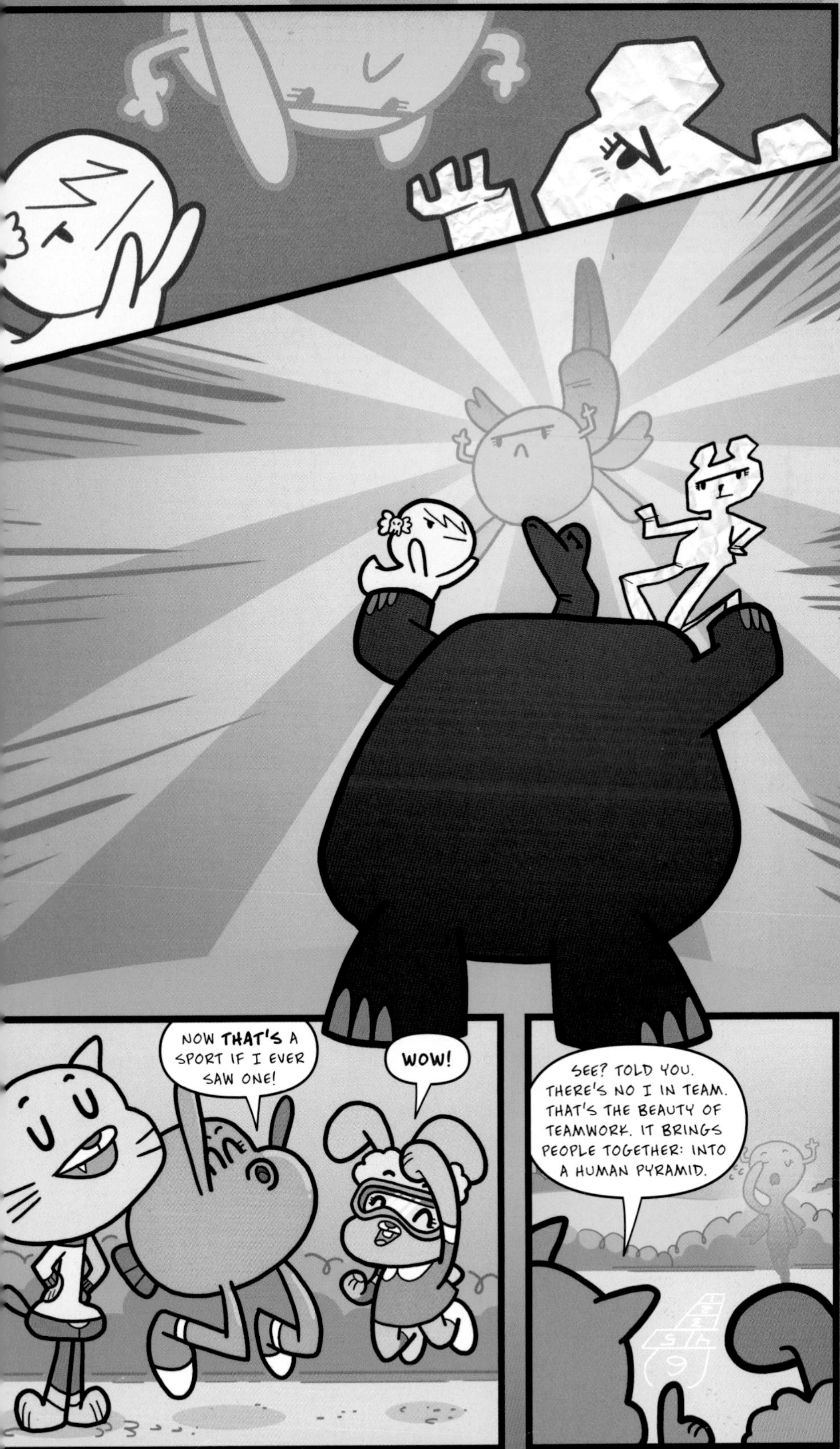
NOW THAT'S A SPORT IF I EVER SAW ONE!
WOW!
SEE? TOLD YOU. THERE'S NO I IN TEAM. THAT'S THE BEAUTY OF TEAMWORK. IT BRINGS PEOPLE TOGETHER: INTO A HUMAN PYRAMID.

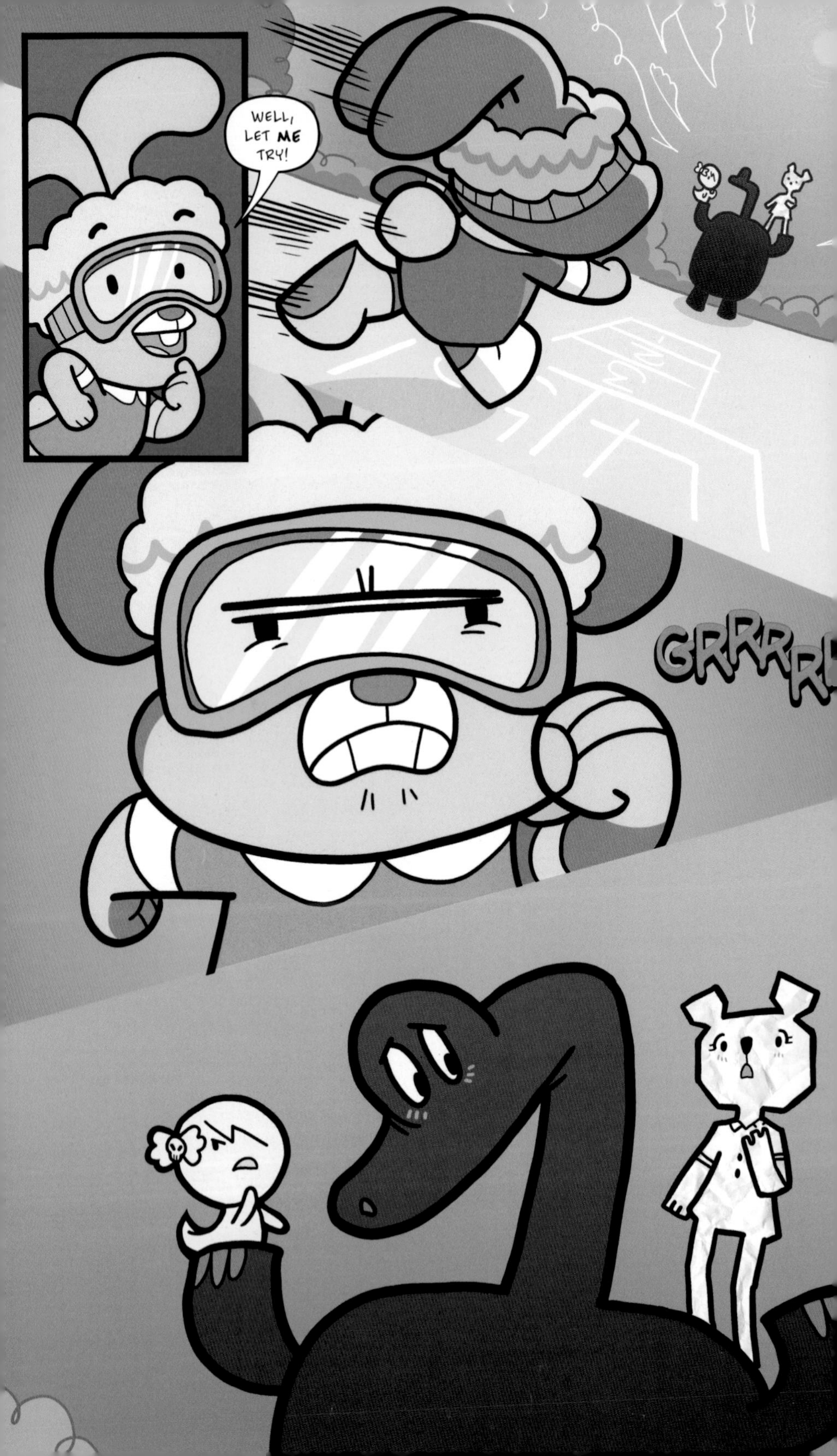
WELL, LET ME TRY!
GRRRR

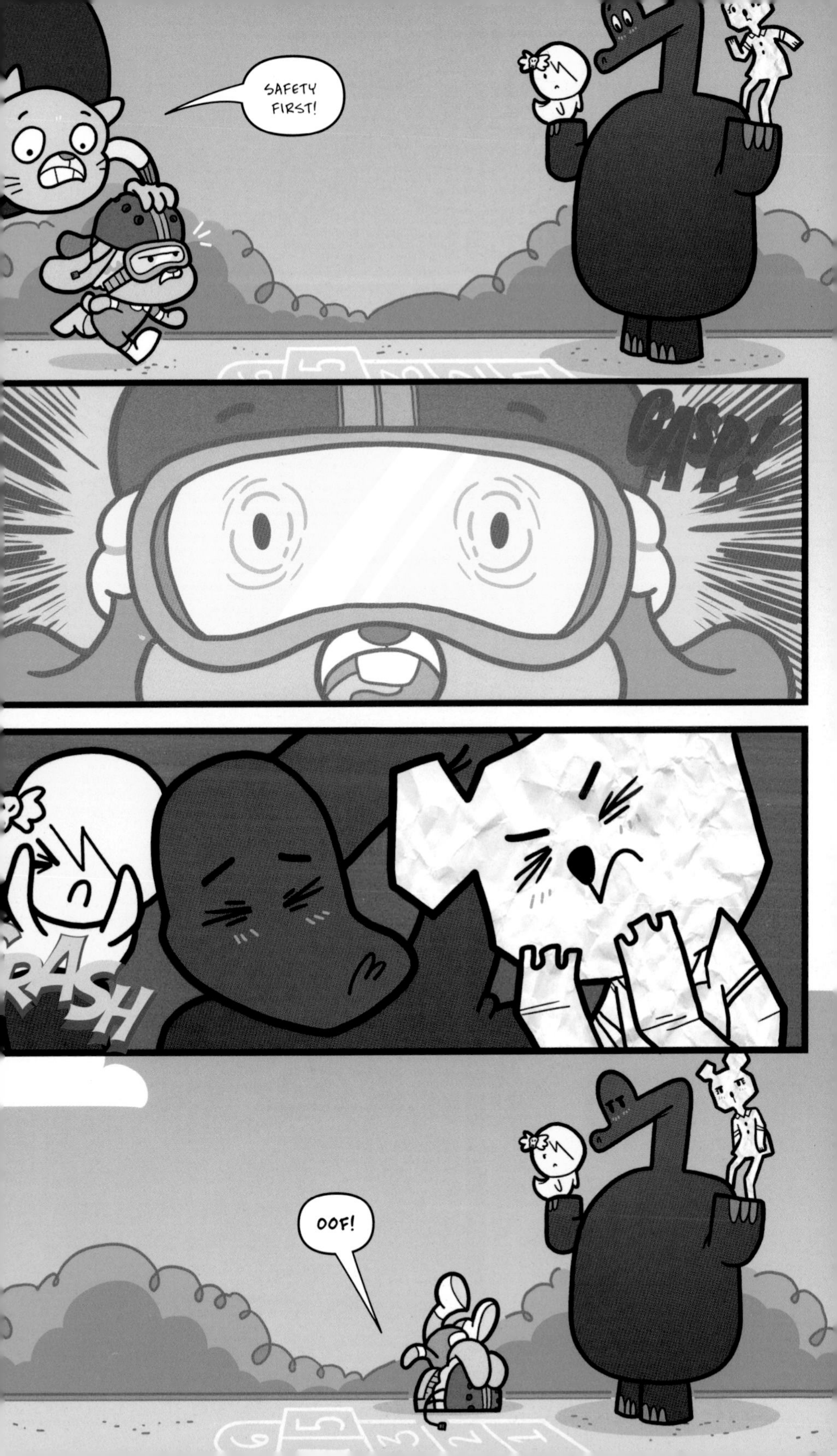
SAFETY FIRST!
GASP!
RASH
OOF!

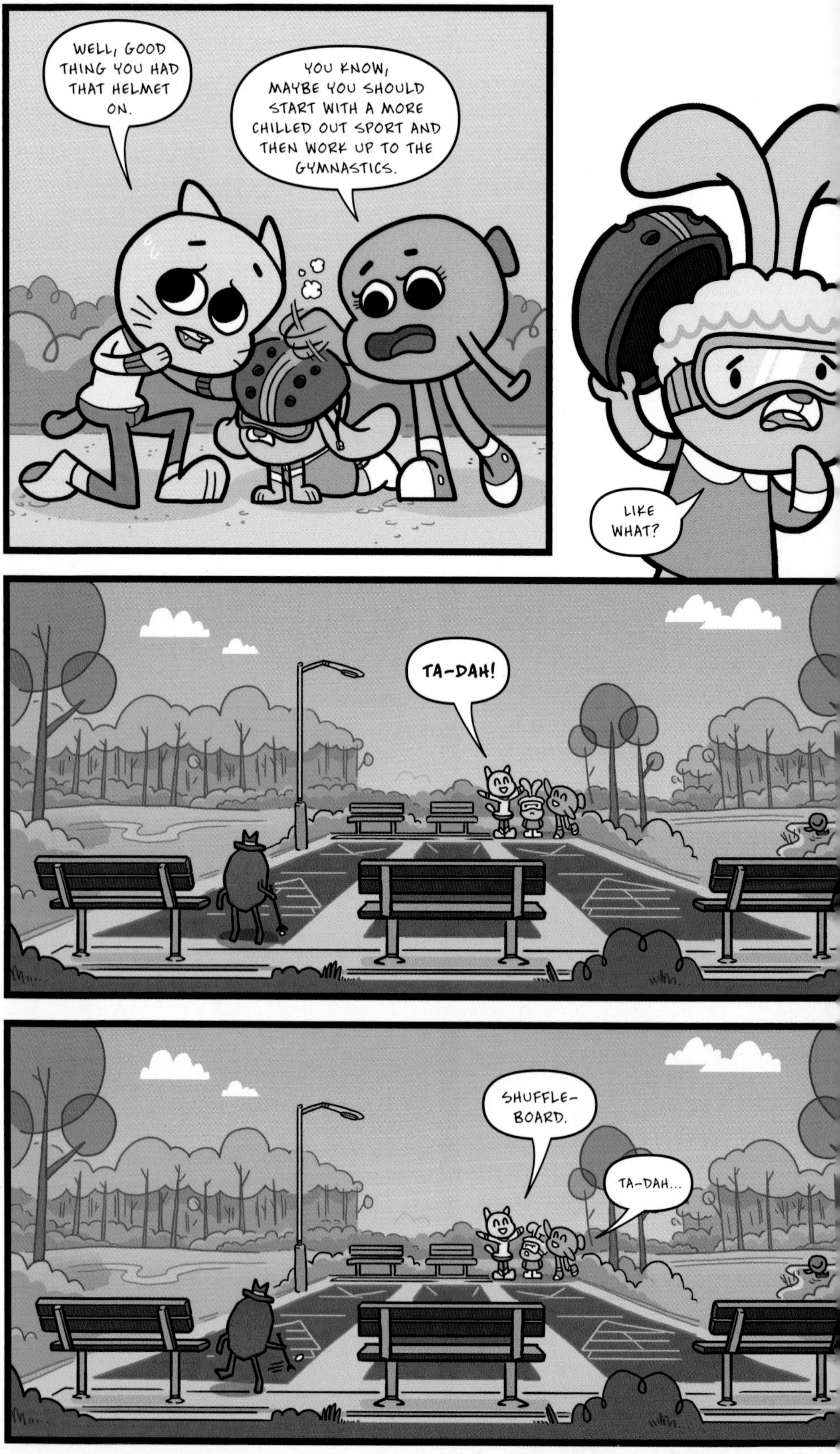
WELL, GOOD THING YOU HAD THAT HELMET ON.
YOU KNOW, MAYBE YOU SHOULD START WITH A MORE CHILLED OUT SPORT AND THEN WORK UP TO THE GYMNASTICS.
LIKE WHAT?
TA-DAH!
SHUFFLE-BOARD.
TA-DAH...

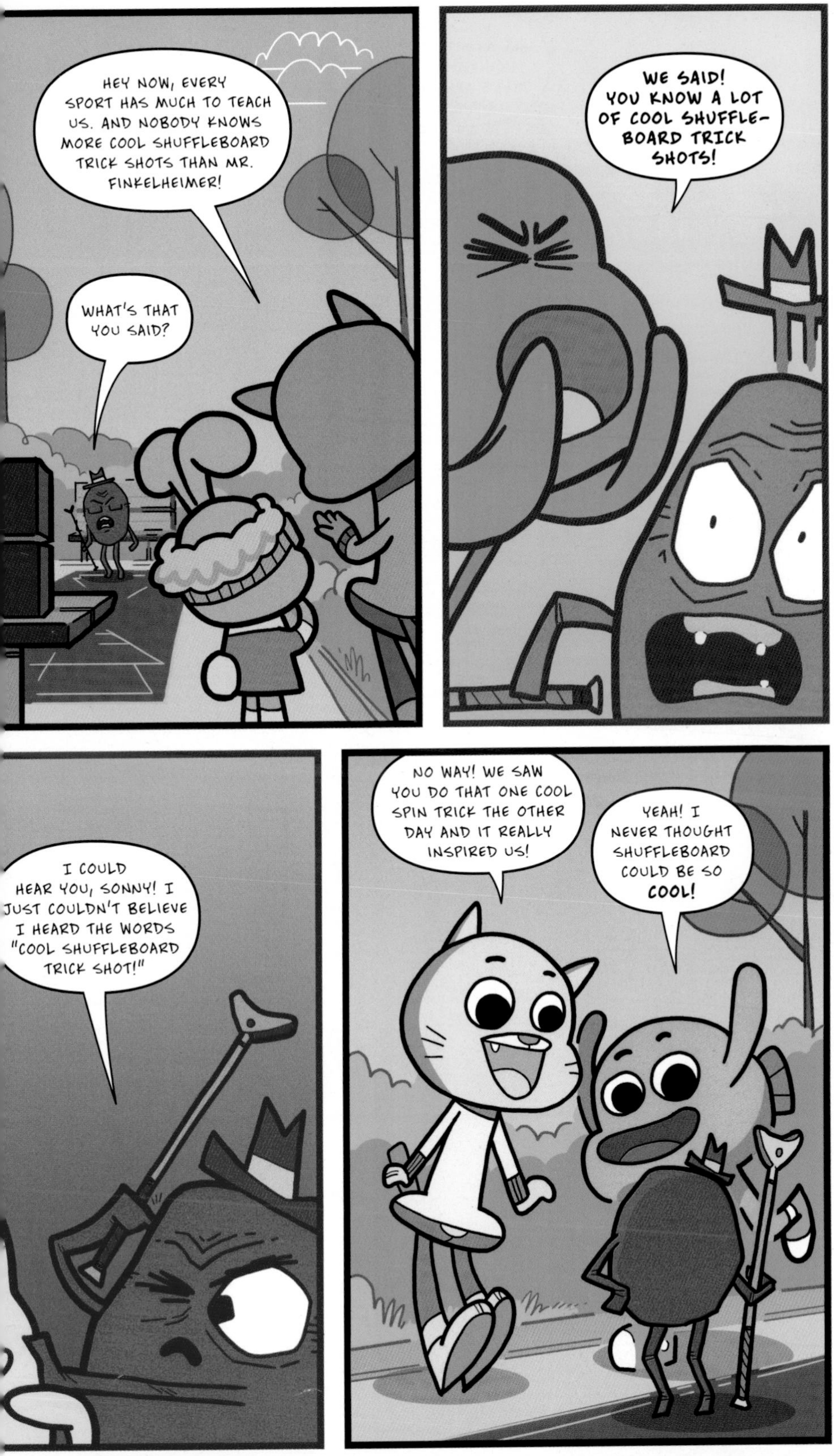
HEY NOW, EVERY SPORT HAS MUCH TO TEACH US. AND NOBODY KNOWS MORE COOL SHUFFLEBOARD TRICK SHOTS THAN MR. FINKELHEIMER!
WHAT'S THAT YOU SAID?
WE SAID! YOU KNOW A LOT OF COOL SHUFFLE-BOARD TRICK SHOTS!
I COULD HEAR YOU, SONNY! I JUST COULDN'T BELIEVE I HEARD THE WORDS "COOL SHUFFLEBOARD TRICK SHOT!"
NO WAY! WE SAW YOU DO THAT ONE COOL SPIN TRICK THE OTHER DAY AND IT REALLY INSPIRED US!
YEAH! I NEVER THOUGHT SHUFFLEBOARD COULD BE SO **COOL!**

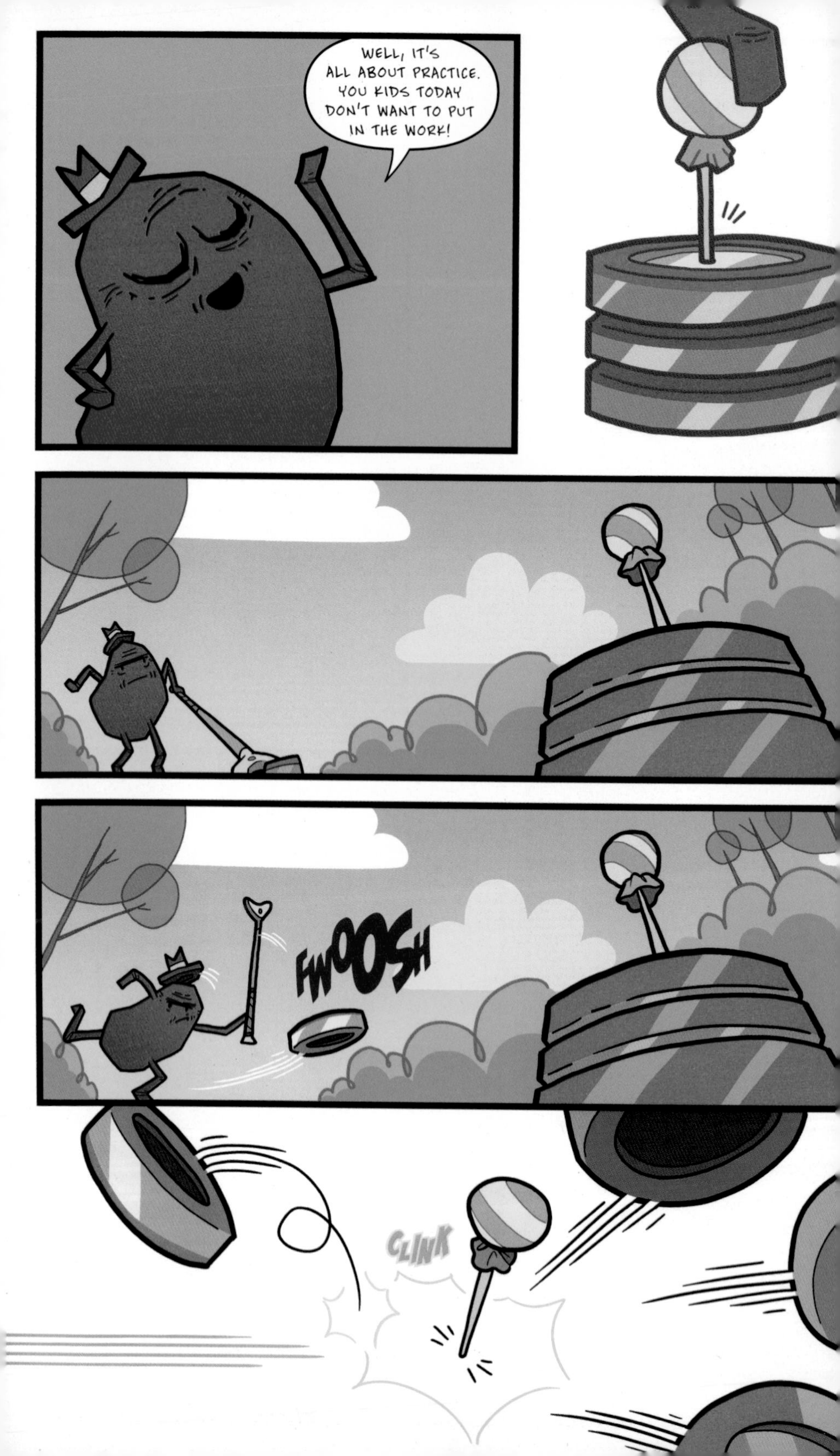
WELL, IT'S ALL ABOUT PRACTICE. YOU KIDS TODAY DON'T WANT TO PUT IN THE WORK!
FWOOSH
CLINK

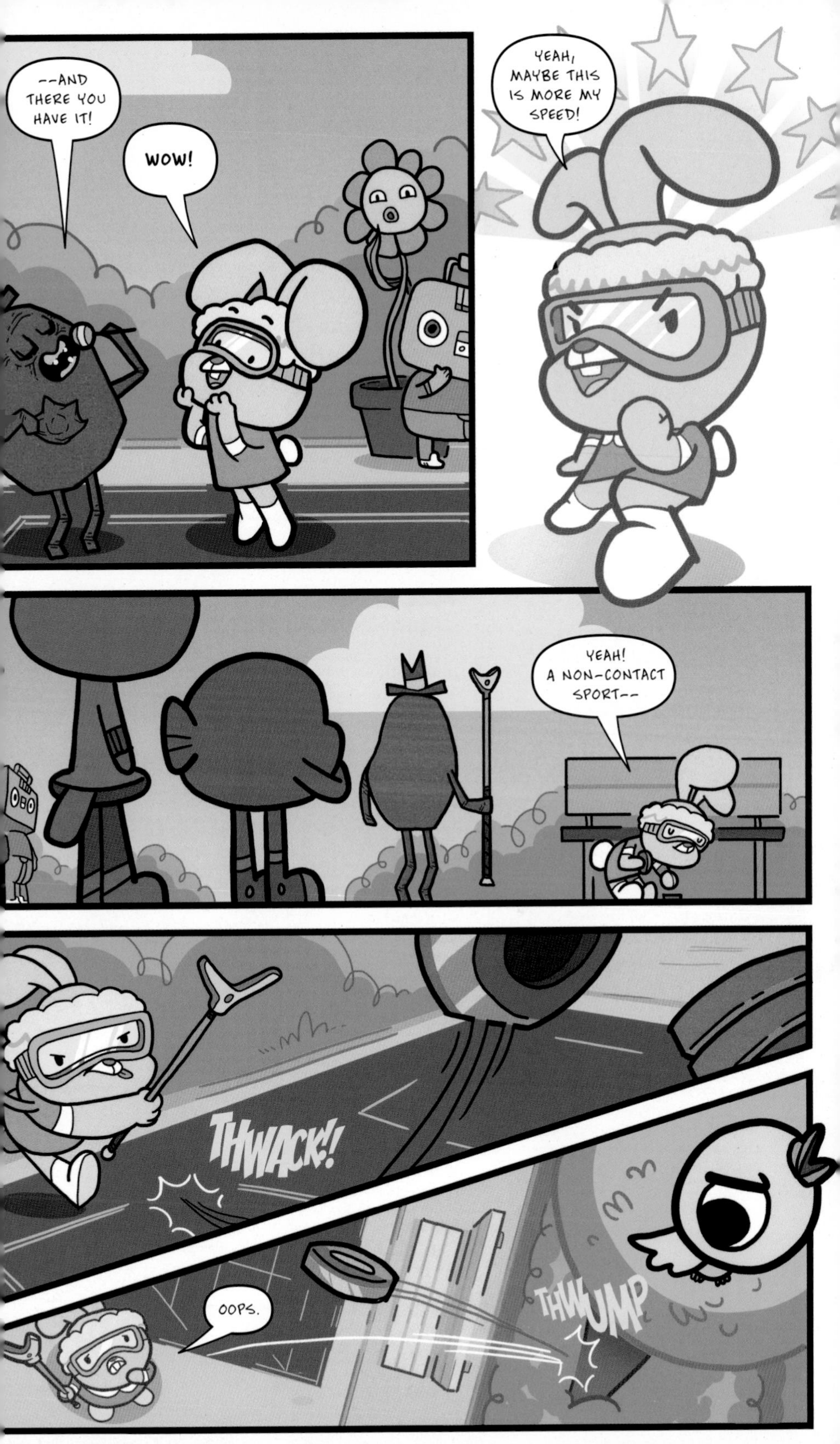
--AND THERE YOU HAVE IT!
WOW!
YEAH, MAYBE THIS IS MORE MY SPEED!
YEAH! A NON-CONTACT SPORT--
THWACK!!
OOPS.
THWUMP

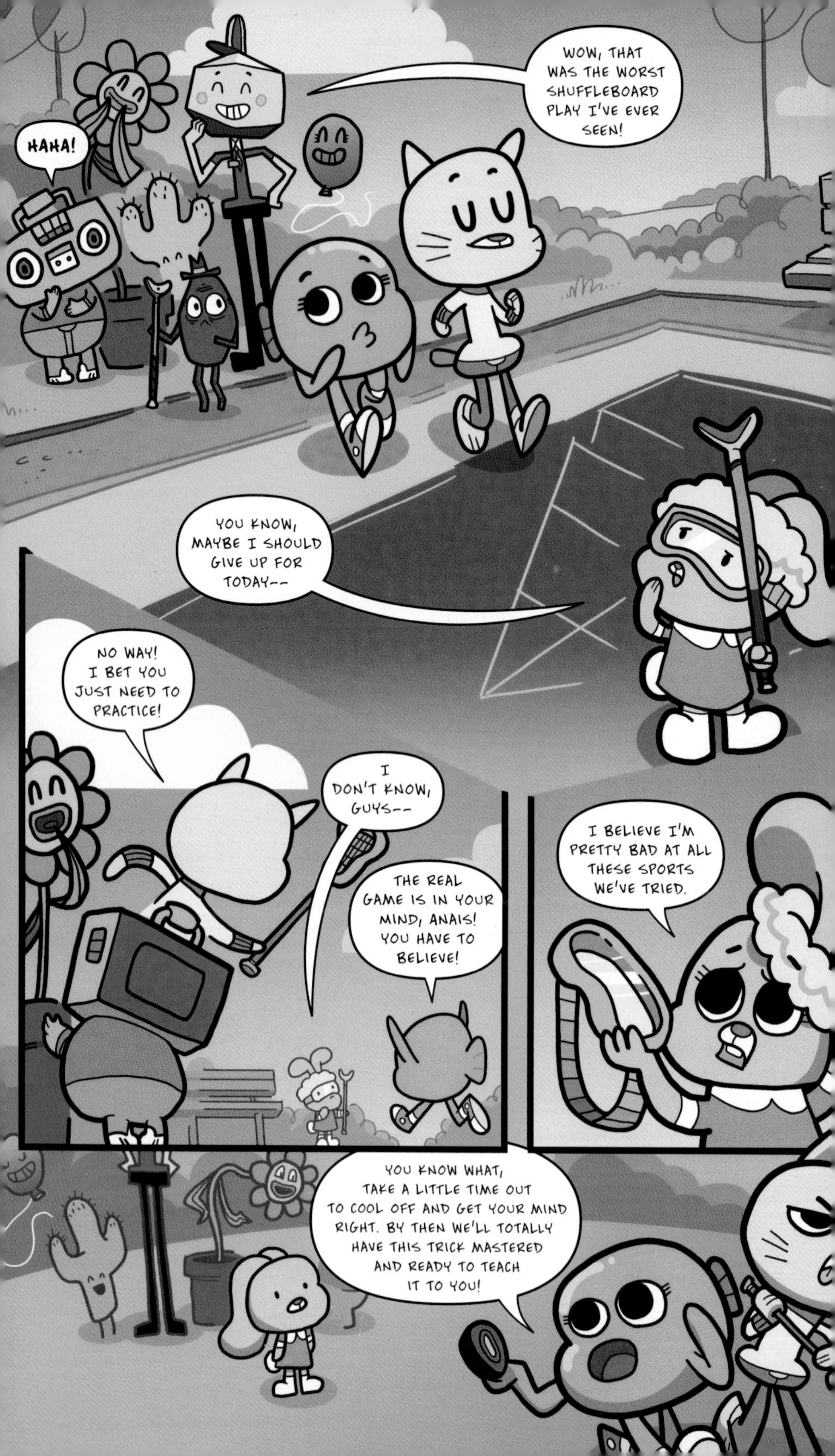
HAHA!
WOW, THAT WAS THE WORST SHUFFLEBOARD PLAY I'VE EVER SEEN!
YOU KNOW, MAYBE I SHOULD GIVE UP FOR TODAY--
NO WAY! I BET YOU JUST NEED TO PRACTICE!
I DON'T KNOW, GUYS--
THE REAL GAME IS IN YOUR MIND, ANAIS! YOU HAVE TO BELIEVE!
I BELIEVE I'M PRETTY BAD AT ALL THESE SPORTS WE'VE TRIED.
YOU KNOW WHAT, TAKE A LITTLE TIME OUT TO COOL OFF AND GET YOUR MIND RIGHT. BY THEN WE'LL TOTALLY HAVE THIS TRICK MASTERED AND READY TO TEACH IT TO YOU!

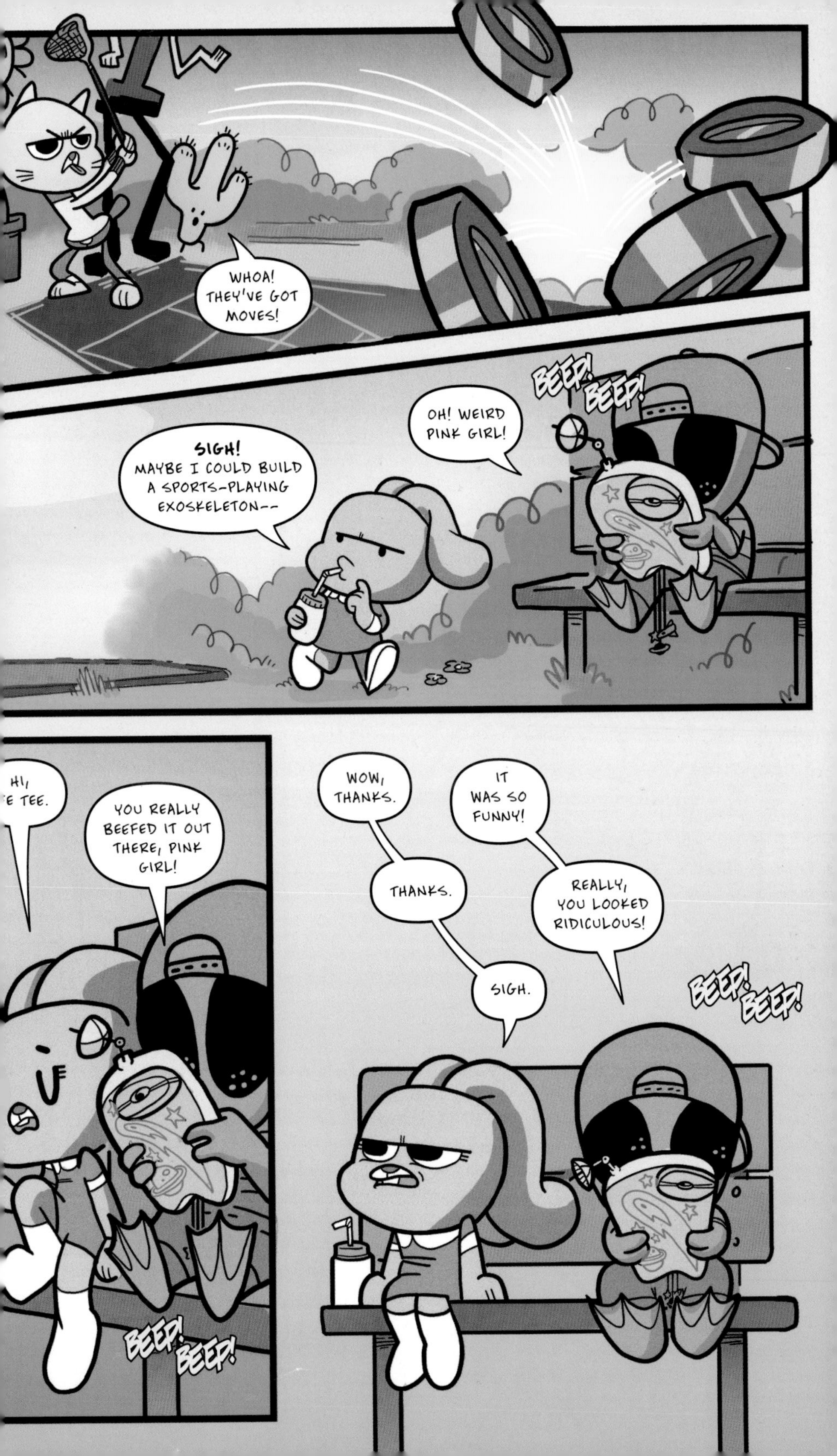
WHOA! THEY'VE GOT MOVES!
SIGH! MAYBE I COULD BUILD A SPORTS-PLAYING EXOSKELETON--
OH! WEIRD PINK GIRL!
BEEP! BEEP!
HI, E TEE.
YOU REALLY BEEFED IT OUT THERE, PINK GIRL!
BEEP! BEEP!
WOW, THANKS.
IT WAS SO FUNNY!
THANKS.
REALLY, YOU LOOKED RIDICULOUS!
SIGH.
BEEP! BEEP!

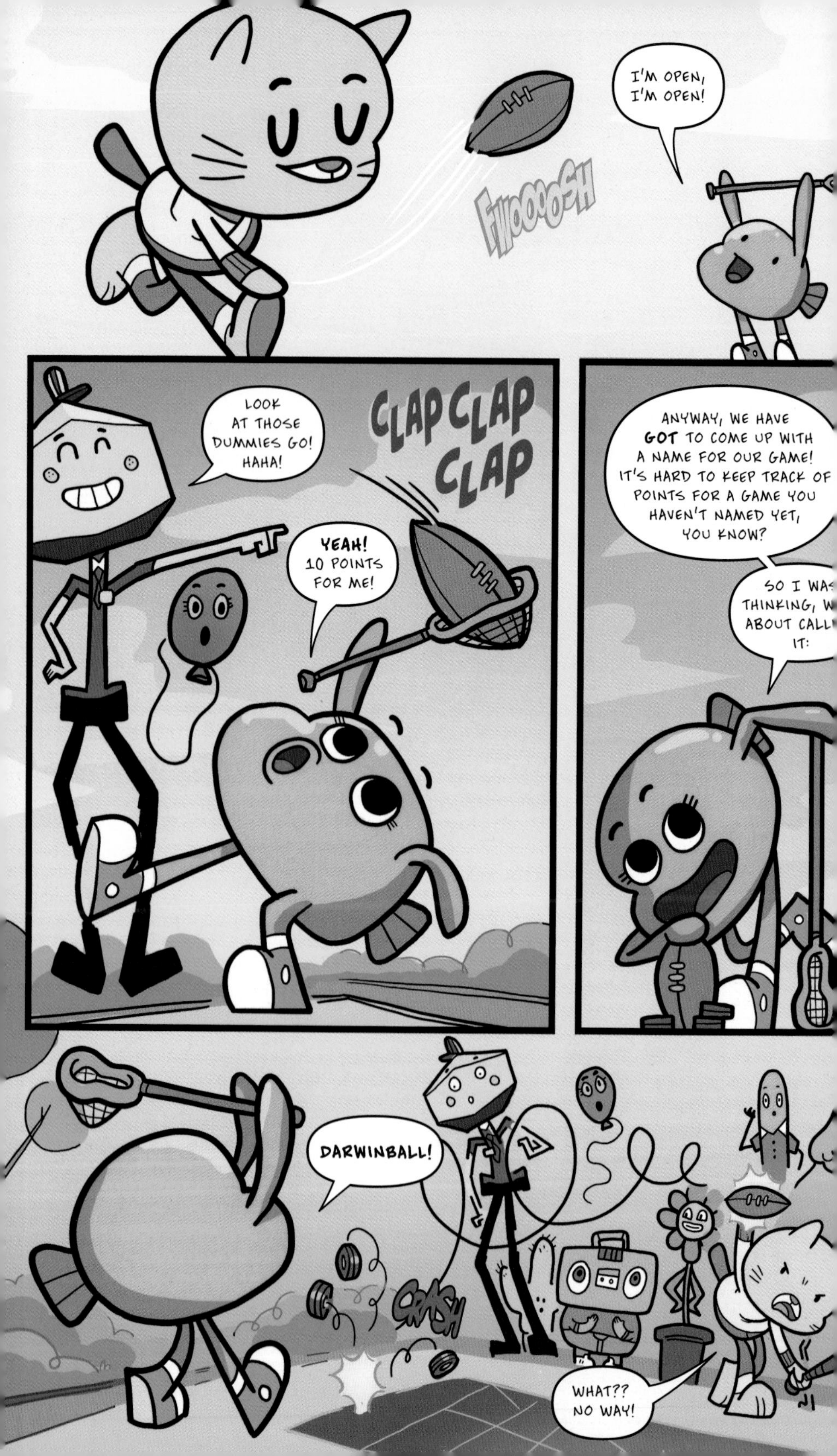
FWOOOOSH
I'M OPEN, I'M OPEN!
LOOK AT THOSE DUMMIES GO! HAHA!
CLAP CLAP CLAP
YEAH! 10 POINTS FOR ME!
ANYWAY, WE HAVE GOT TO COME UP WITH A NAME FOR OUR GAME! IT'S HARD TO KEEP TRACK OF POINTS FOR A GAME YOU HAVEN'T NAMED YET, YOU KNOW?
DARWINBALL!
CRASH
WHAT?? NO WAY!

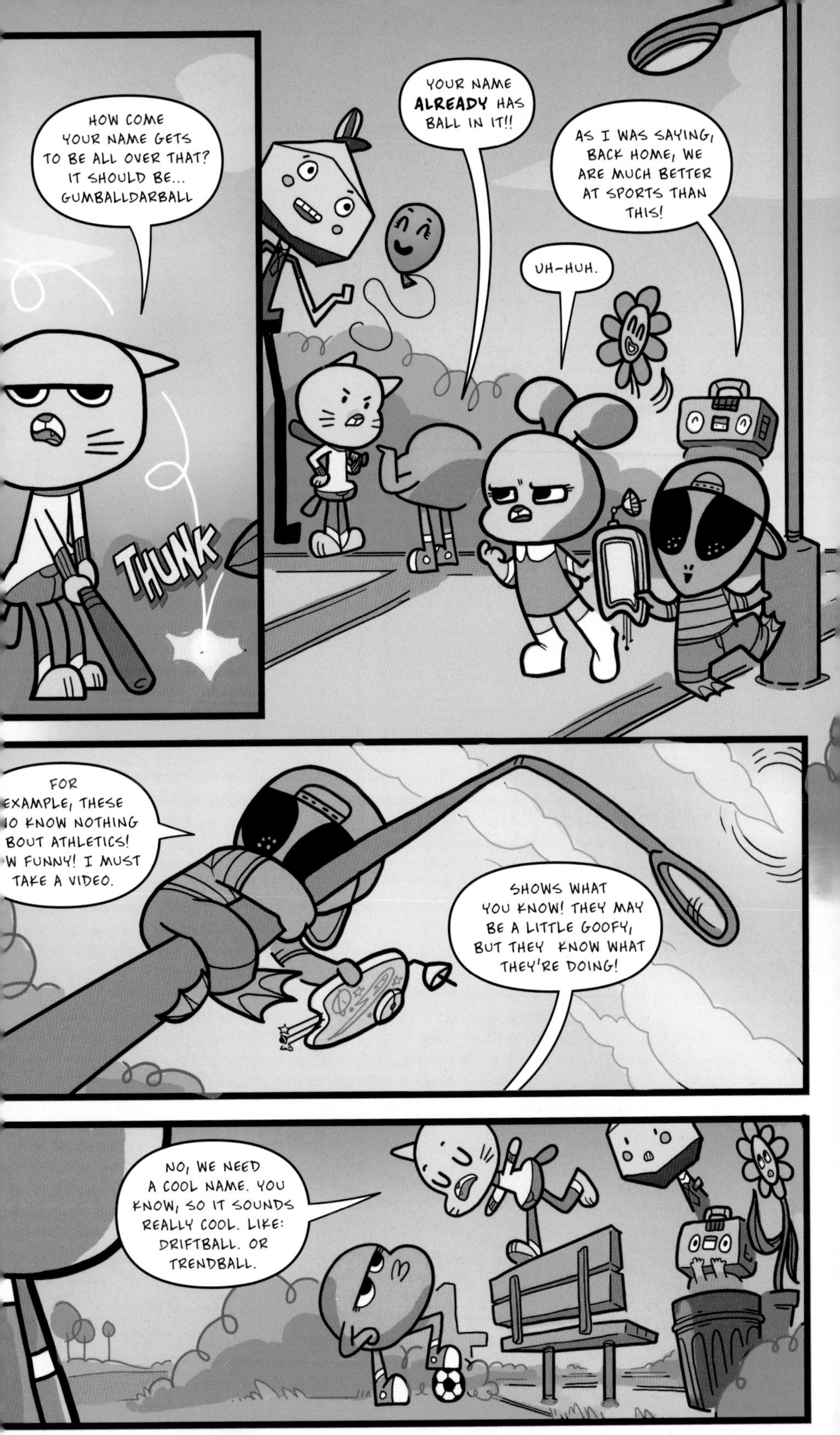
HOW COME YOUR NAME GETS TO BE ALL OVER THAT? IT SHOULD BE... GUMBALLDARBALL
THUNK
YOUR NAME **ALREADY** HAS BALL IN IT!!
AS I WAS SAYING, BACK HOME, WE ARE MUCH BETTER AT SPORTS THAN THIS!
UH-HUH.
FOR EXAMPLE, THESE
O KNOW NOTHING
BOUT ATHLETICS!
W FUNNY! I MUST TAKE A VIDEO.
SHOWS WHAT YOU KNOW! THEY MAY BE A LITTLE GOOFY, BUT THEY KNOW WHAT THEY'RE DOING!
NO, WE NEED A COOL NAME. YOU KNOW, SO IT SOUNDS REALLY COOL. LIKE: DRIFTBALL. OR TRENDBALL.

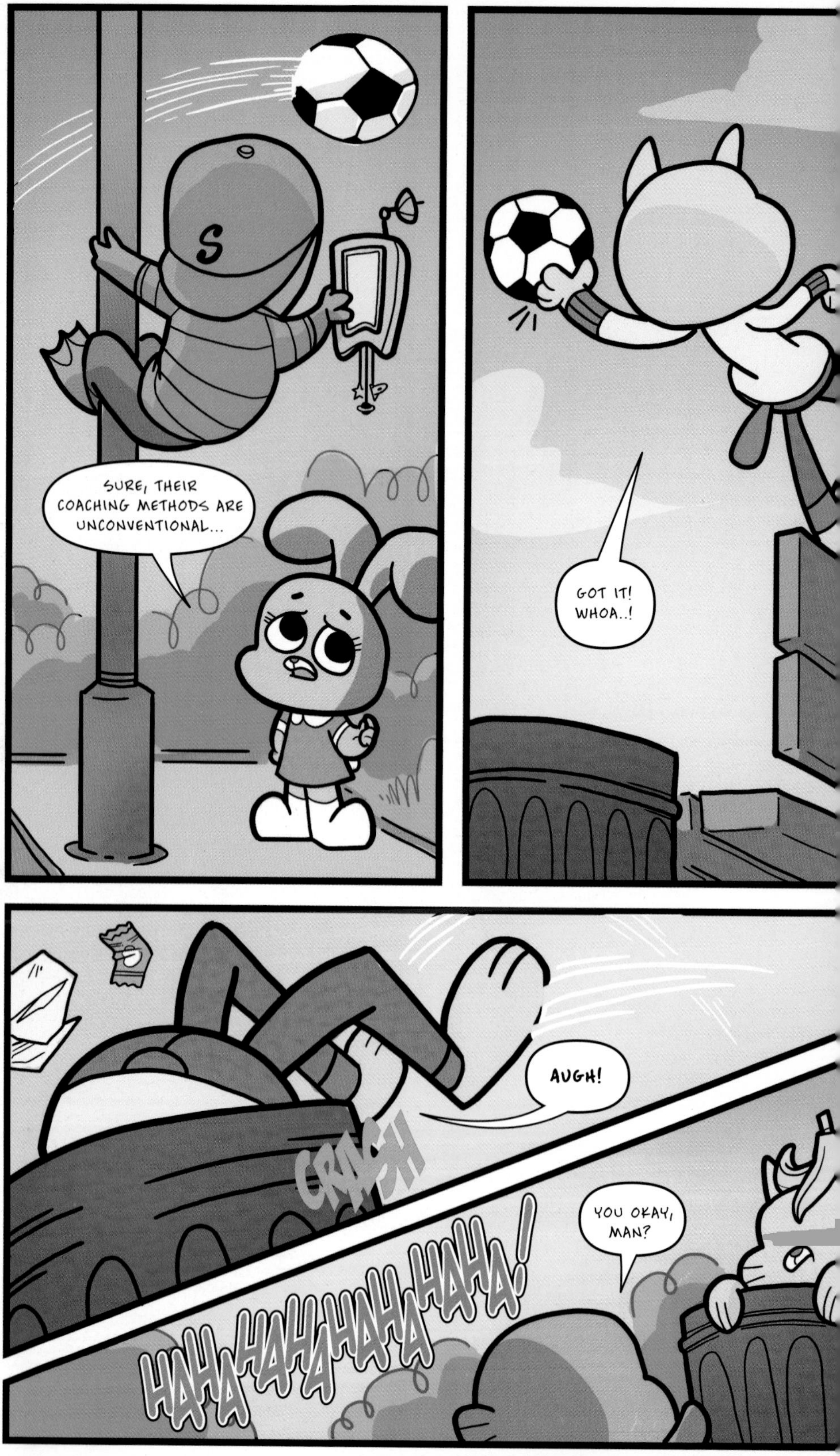
SURE, THEIR COACHING METHODS ARE UNCONVENTIONAL...
GOT IT! WHOA..!
AUGH!
CRASH
YOU OKAY, MAN?
HAHAHAHAHAHAHAHA!

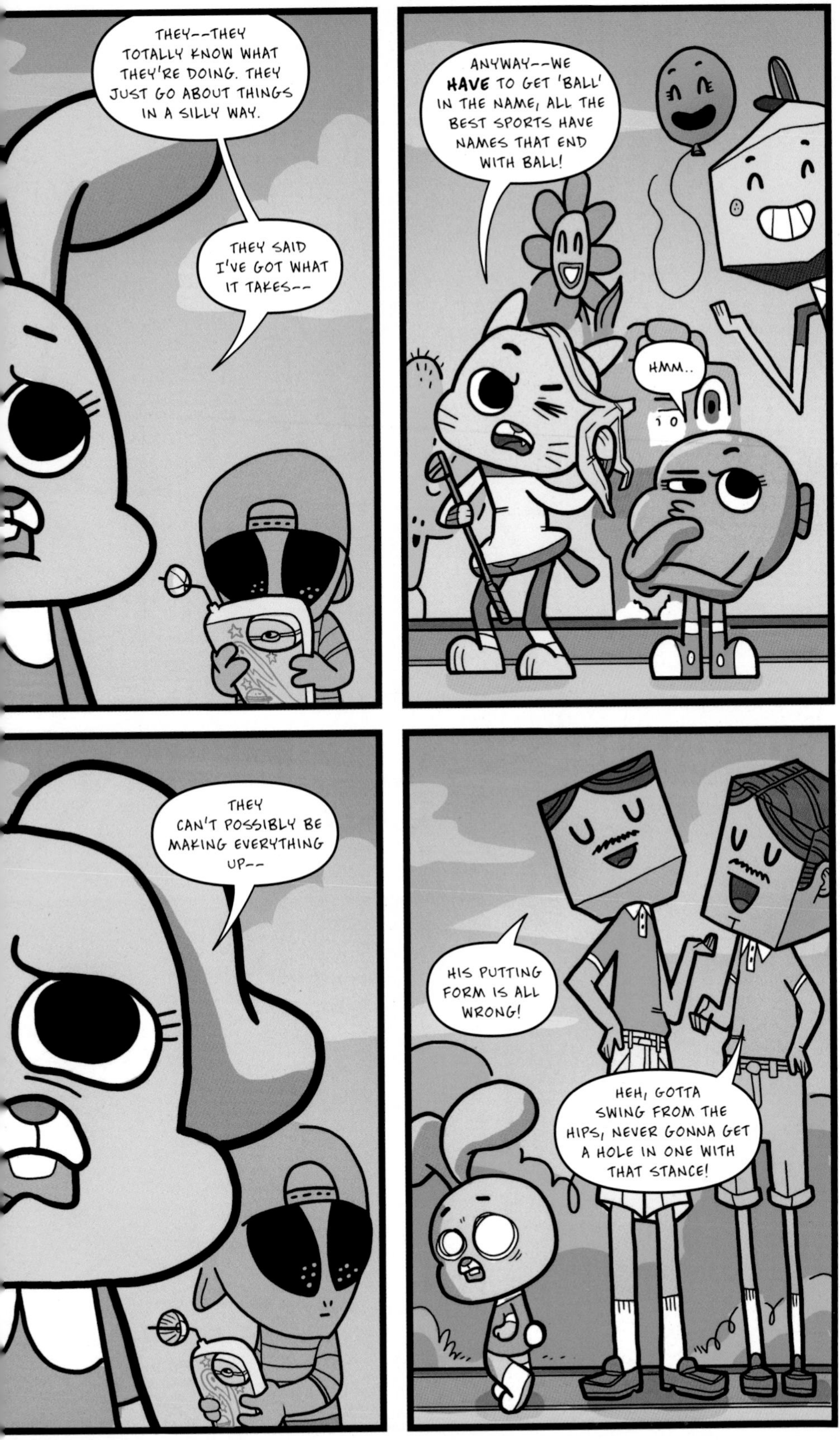
THEY--THEY TOTALLY KNOW WHAT THEY'RE DOING. THEY JUST GO ABOUT THINGS IN A SILLY WAY.
THEY SAID I'VE GOT WHAT IT TAKES--
ANYWAY--WE **HAVE** TO GET 'BALL' IN THE NAME, ALL THE BEST SPORTS HAVE NAMES THAT END WITH BALL!
HMM..
THEY CAN'T POSSIBLY BE MAKING EVERYTHING UP--
HIS PUTTING FORM IS ALL WRONG!
HEH, GOTTA SWING FROM THE HIPS, NEVER GONNA GET A HOLE IN ONE WITH THAT STANCE!

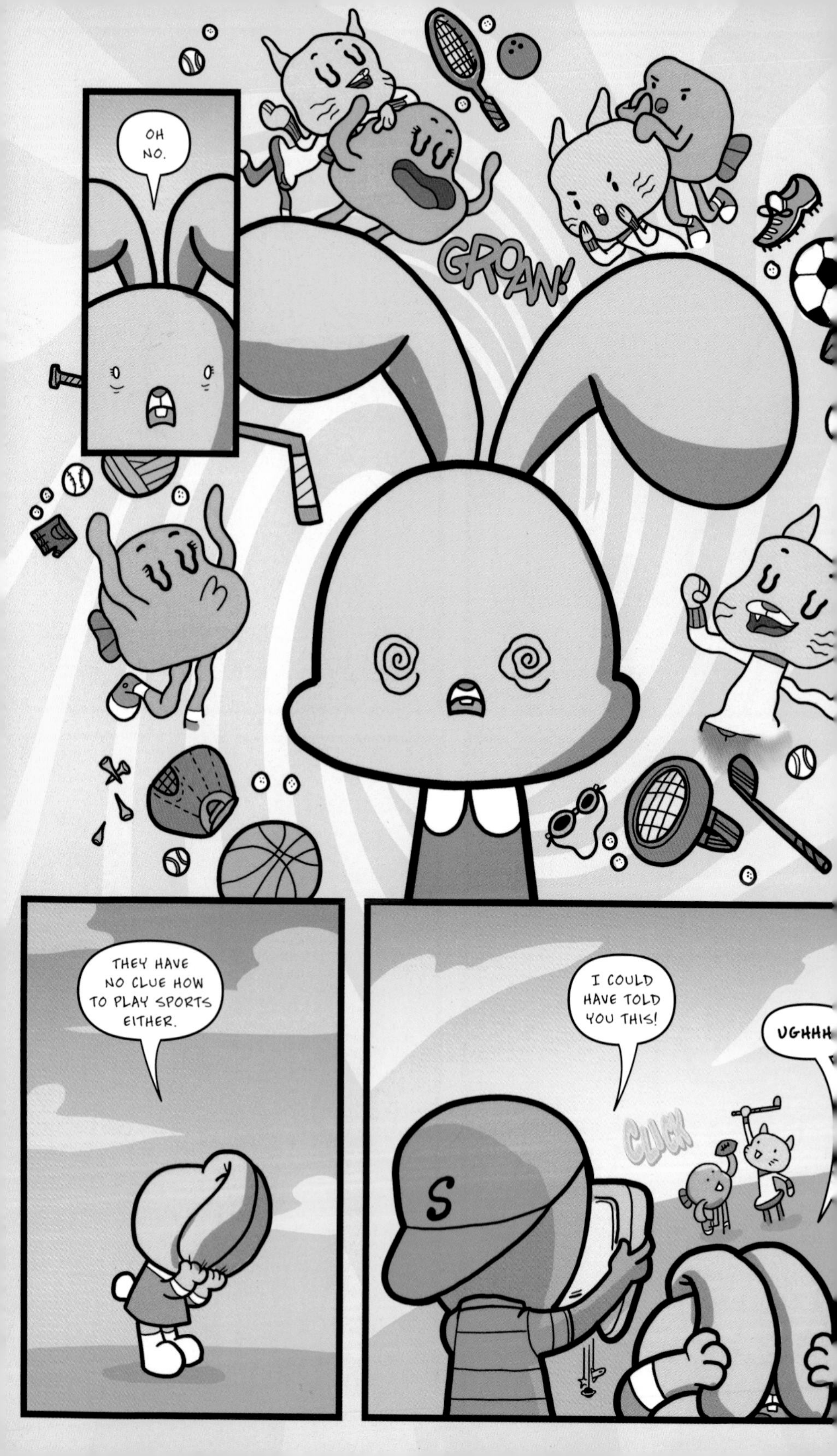
OH NO.
GROAN!
THEY HAVE NO CLUE HOW TO PLAY SPORTS EITHER.
I COULD HAVE TOLD YOU THIS!
CLICK
UGHHH

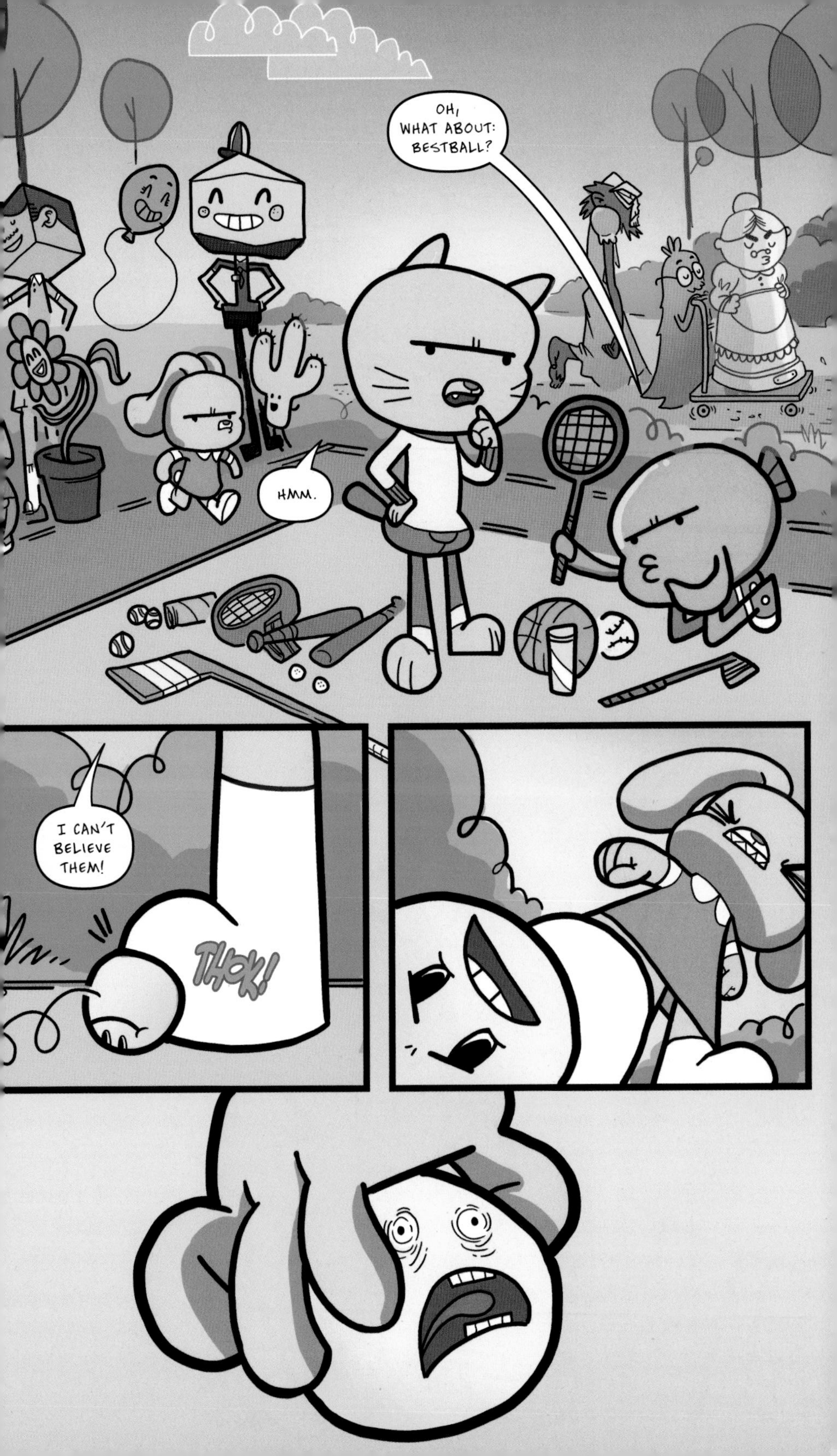
OH, WHAT ABOUT: BESTBALL?
HMM.
I CAN'T BELIEVE THEM!
THOK!

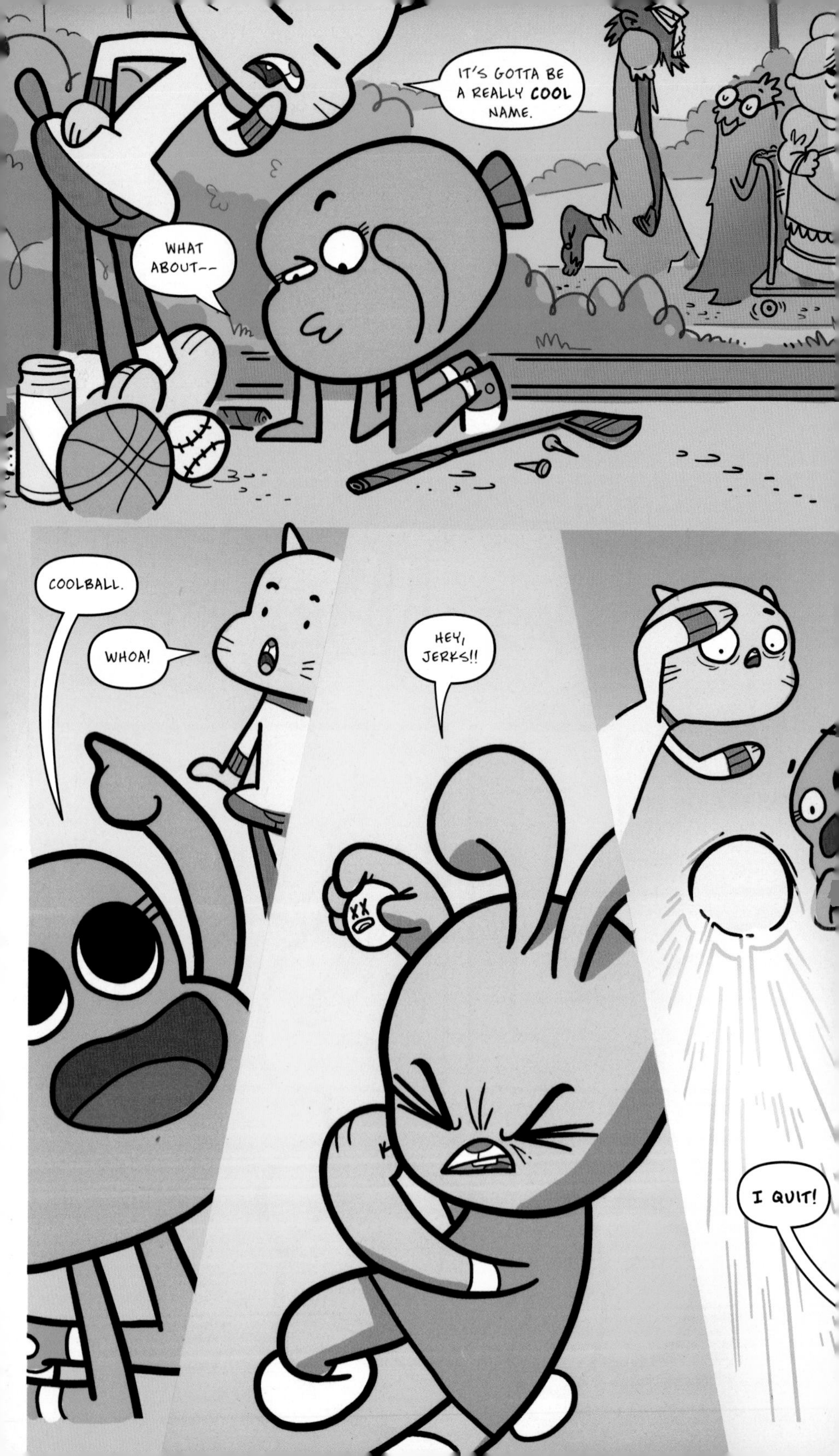

IT'S GOTTA BE A REALLY COOL NAME.
WHAT ABOUT--
COOLBALL.
WHOA!
HEY, JERKS!!
I QUIT!

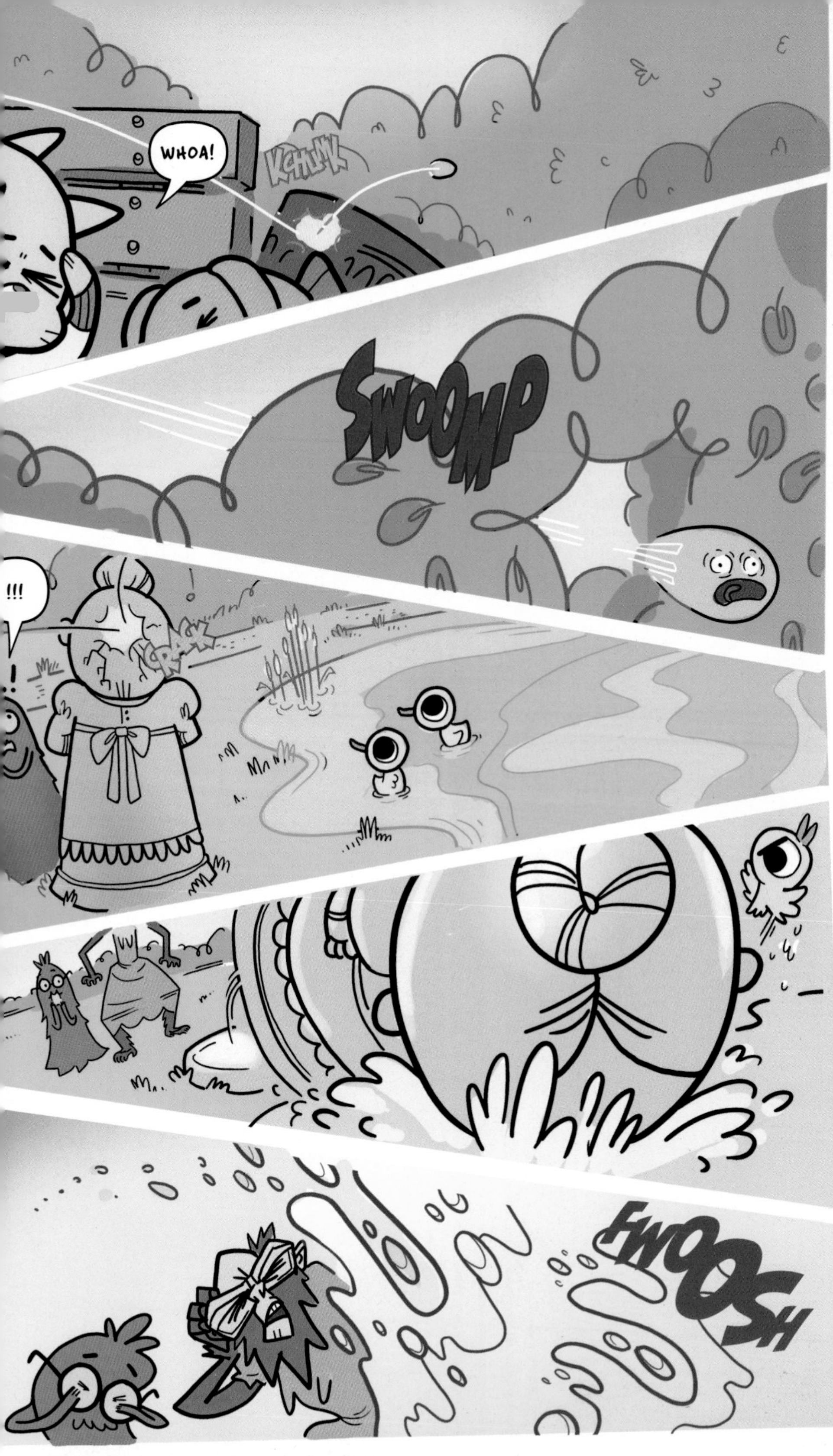

WHOA!
KCHUNK
SWOOMP
!!!
CRACK
FWOOSH

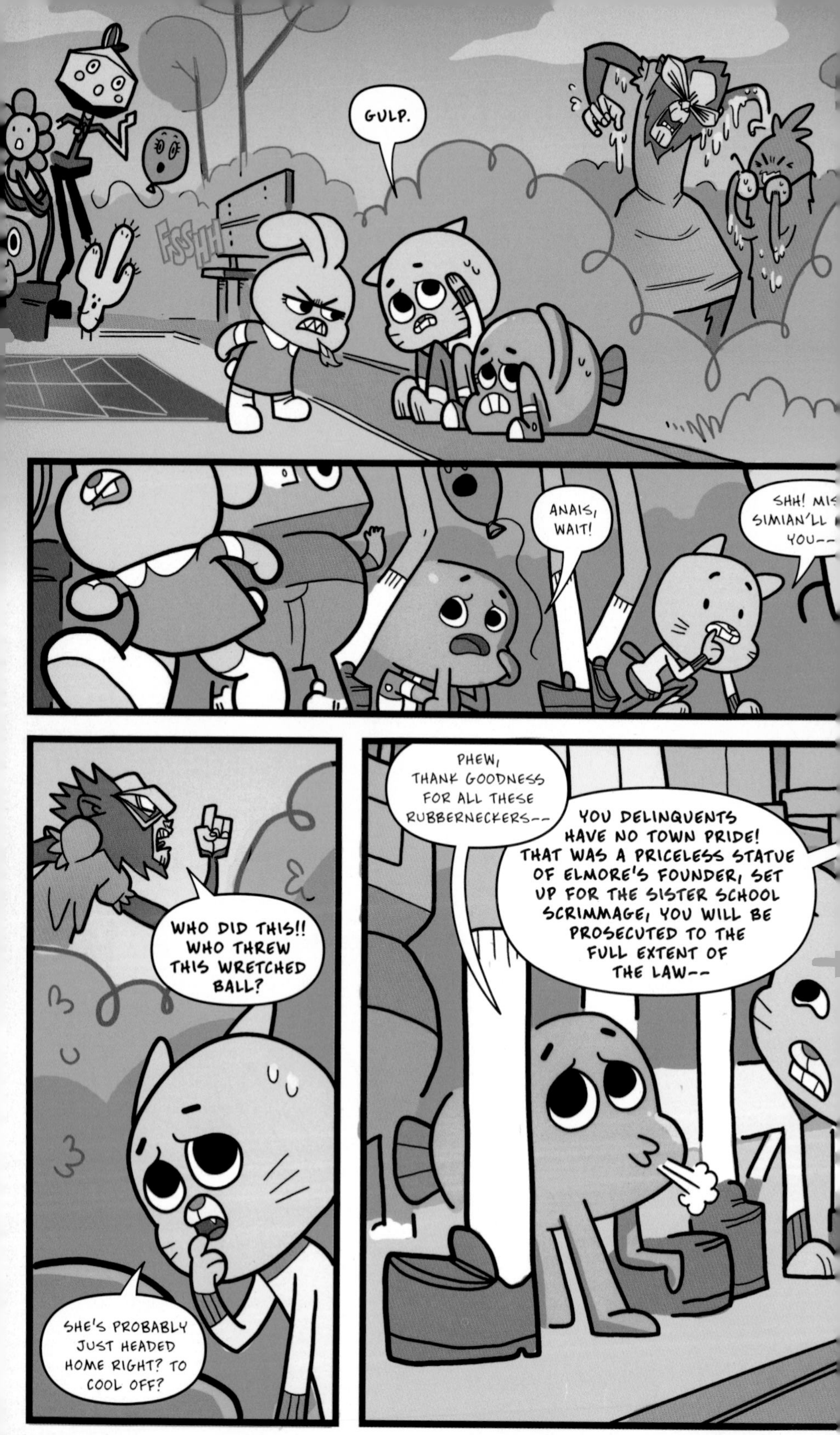
GULP.
FSSHH
ANAIS, WAIT!
SHH! MIS SIMIAN'LL YOU--
WHO DID THIS!! WHO THREW THIS WRETCHED BALL?
SHE'S PROBABLY JUST HEADED HOME RIGHT? TO COOL OFF?
PHEW, THANK GOODNESS FOR ALL THESE RUBBERNECKERS--
YOU DELINQUENTS HAVE NO TOWN PRIDE! THAT WAS A PRICELESS STATUE OF ELMORE'S FOUNDER, SET UP FOR THE SISTER SCHOOL SCRIMMAGE, YOU WILL BE PROSECUTED TO THE FULL EXTENT OF THE LAW--

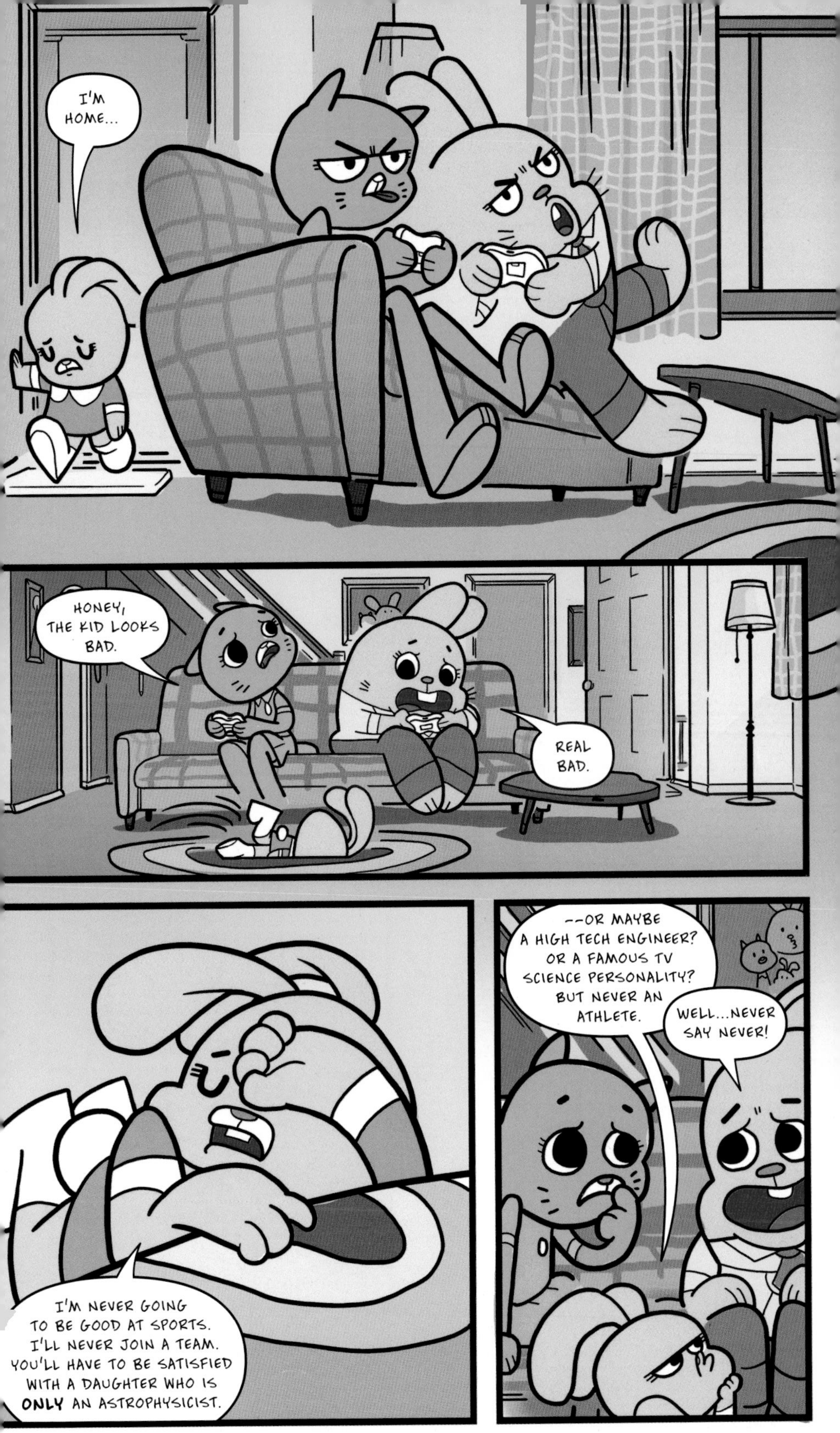
I'M HOME...
HONEY, THE KID LOOKS BAD.
REAL BAD.
I'M NEVER GOING TO BE GOOD AT SPORTS. I'LL NEVER JOIN A TEAM. YOU'LL HAVE TO BE SATISFIED WITH A DAUGHTER WHO IS **ONLY** AN ASTROPHYSICIST.
--OR MAYBE A HIGH TECH ENGINEER? OR A FAMOUS TV SCIENCE PERSONALITY? BUT NEVER AN ATHLETE.
WELL...NEVER SAY NEVER!

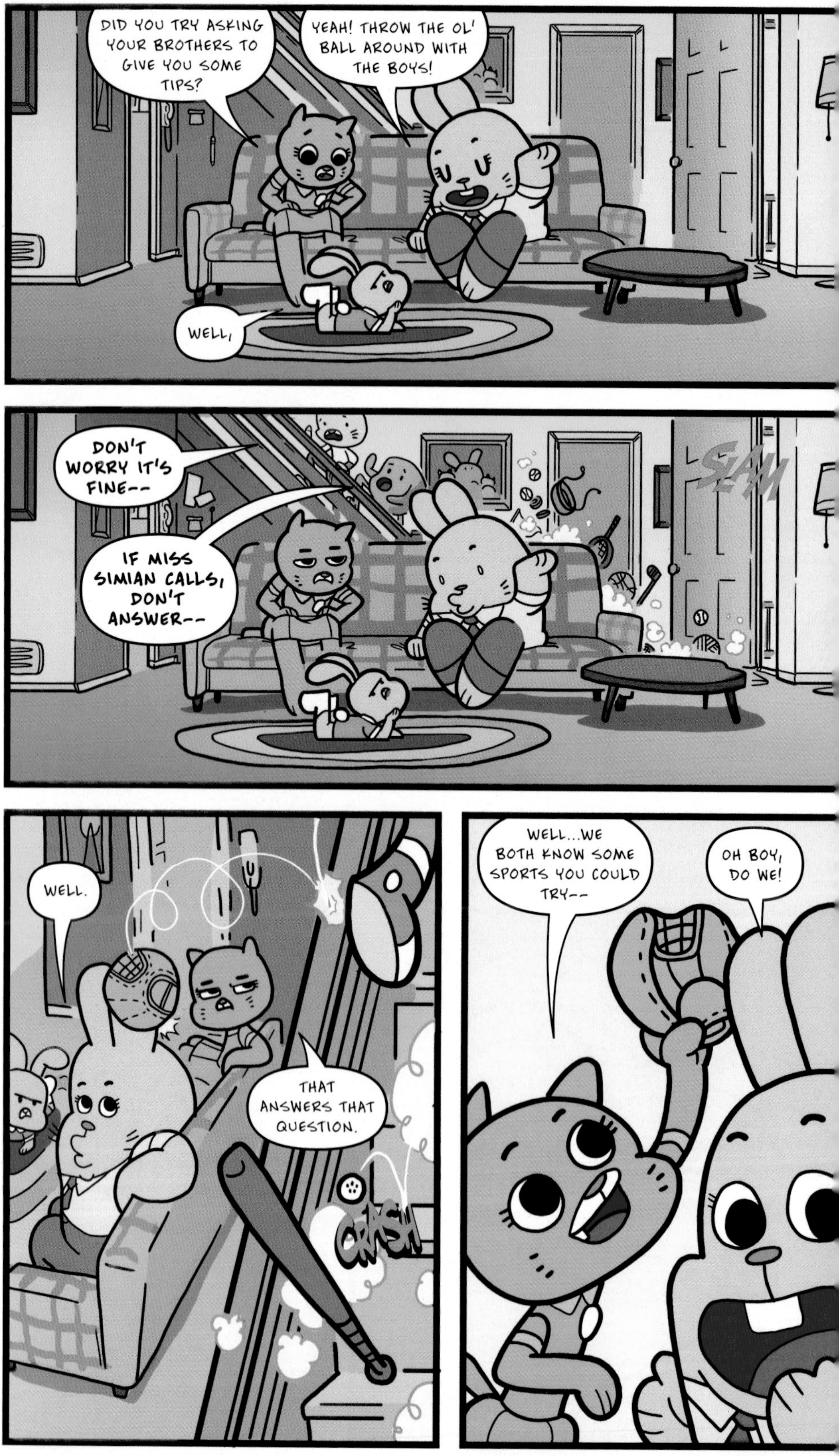
DID YOU TRY ASKING YOUR BROTHERS TO GIVE YOU SOME TIPS?
YEAH! THROW THE OL' BALL AROUND WITH THE BOYS!
WELL,
DON'T WORRY IT'S FINE--
IF MISS SIMIAN CALLS, DON'T ANSWER--
SLAM
WELL.
THAT ANSWERS THAT QUESTION.
CRASH
WELL...WE BOTH KNOW SOME SPORTS YOU COULD TRY--
OH BOY, DO WE!

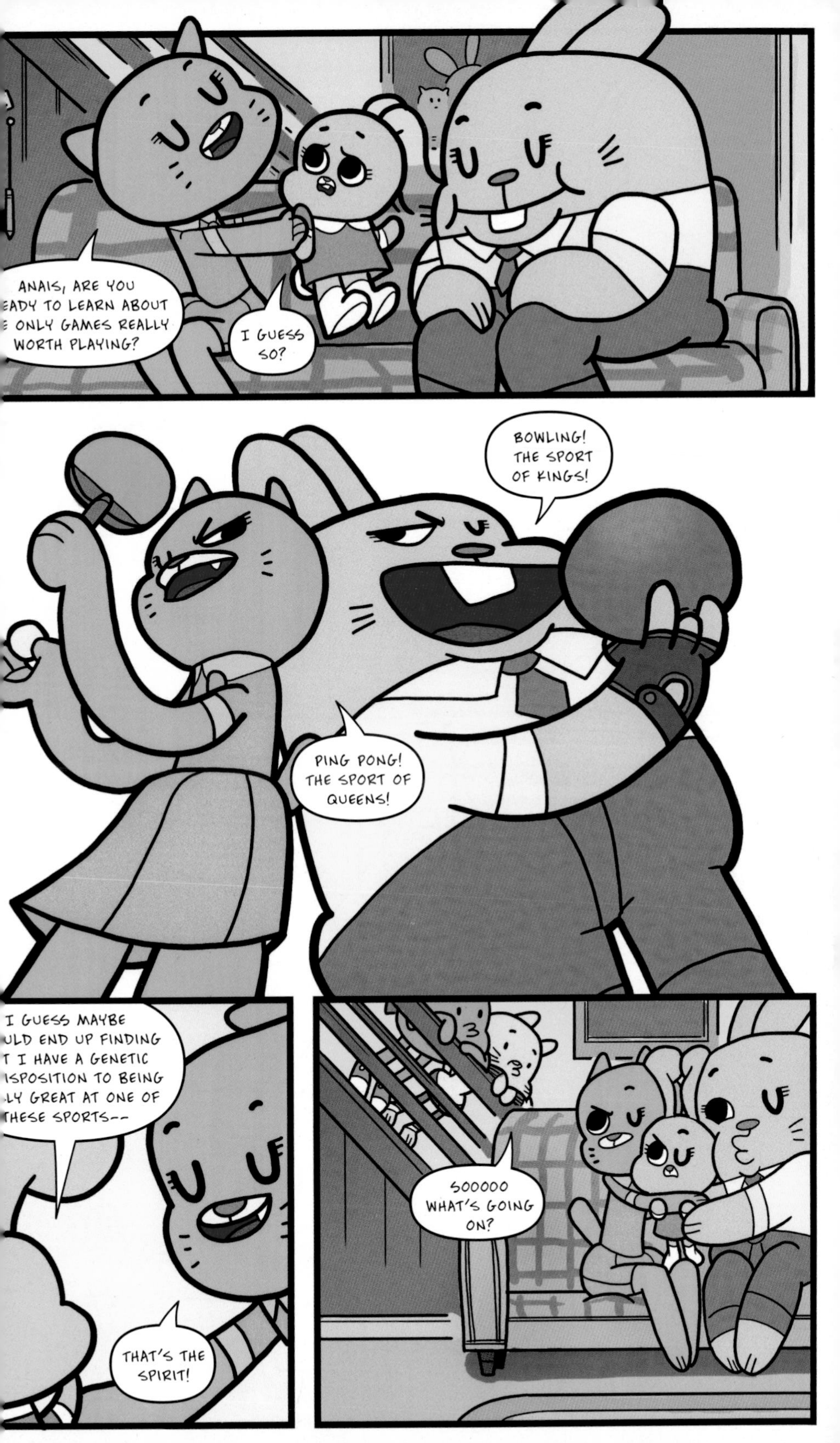

ANAIS, ARE YOU
EADY TO LEARN ABOUT
E ONLY GAMES REALLY
WORTH PLAYING?
I GUESS SO?
BOWLING! THE SPORT OF KINGS!
PING PONG! THE SPORT OF QUEENS!
I GUESS MAYBE
ULD END UP FINDING
T I HAVE A GENETIC
ISPOSITION TO BEING
LY GREAT AT ONE OF
THESE SPORTS--
THAT'S THE SPIRIT!
SOOOOO WHAT'S GOING ON?

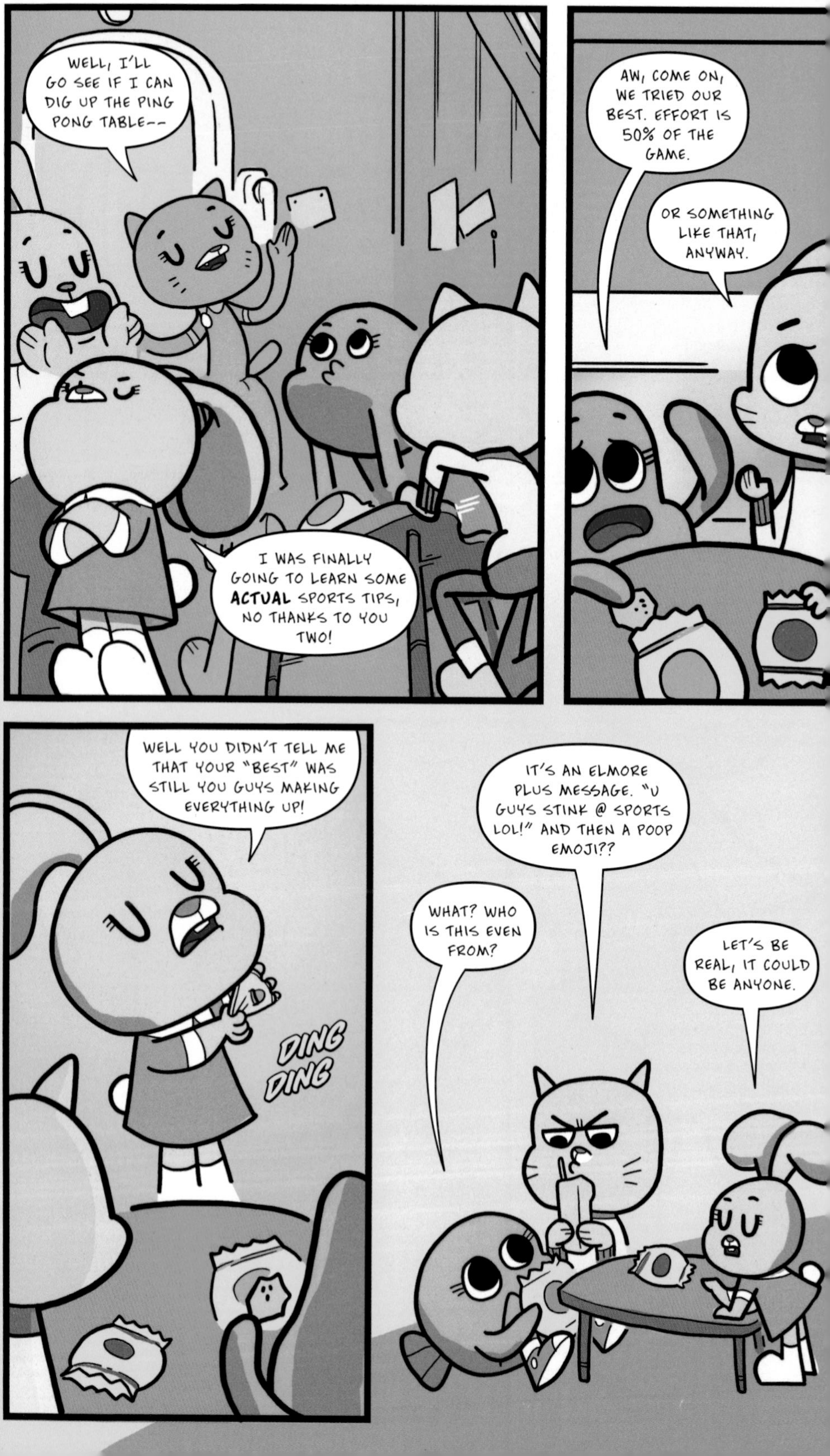
WELL, I'LL GO SEE IF I CAN DIG UP THE PING PONG TABLE--
I WAS FINALLY GOING TO LEARN SOME **ACTUAL** SPORTS TIPS, NO THANKS TO YOU TWO!
AW, COME ON, WE TRIED OUR BEST. EFFORT IS 50% OF THE GAME.
OR SOMETHING LIKE THAT, ANYWAY.
WELL YOU DIDN'T TELL ME THAT YOUR "BEST" WAS STILL YOU GUYS MAKING EVERYTHING UP!
DING DING
IT'S AN ELMORE PLUS MESSAGE. "U GUYS STINK @ SPORTS LOL!" AND THEN A POOP EMOJI??
WHAT? WHO IS THIS EVEN FROM?
LET'S BE REAL, IT COULD BE ANYONE.

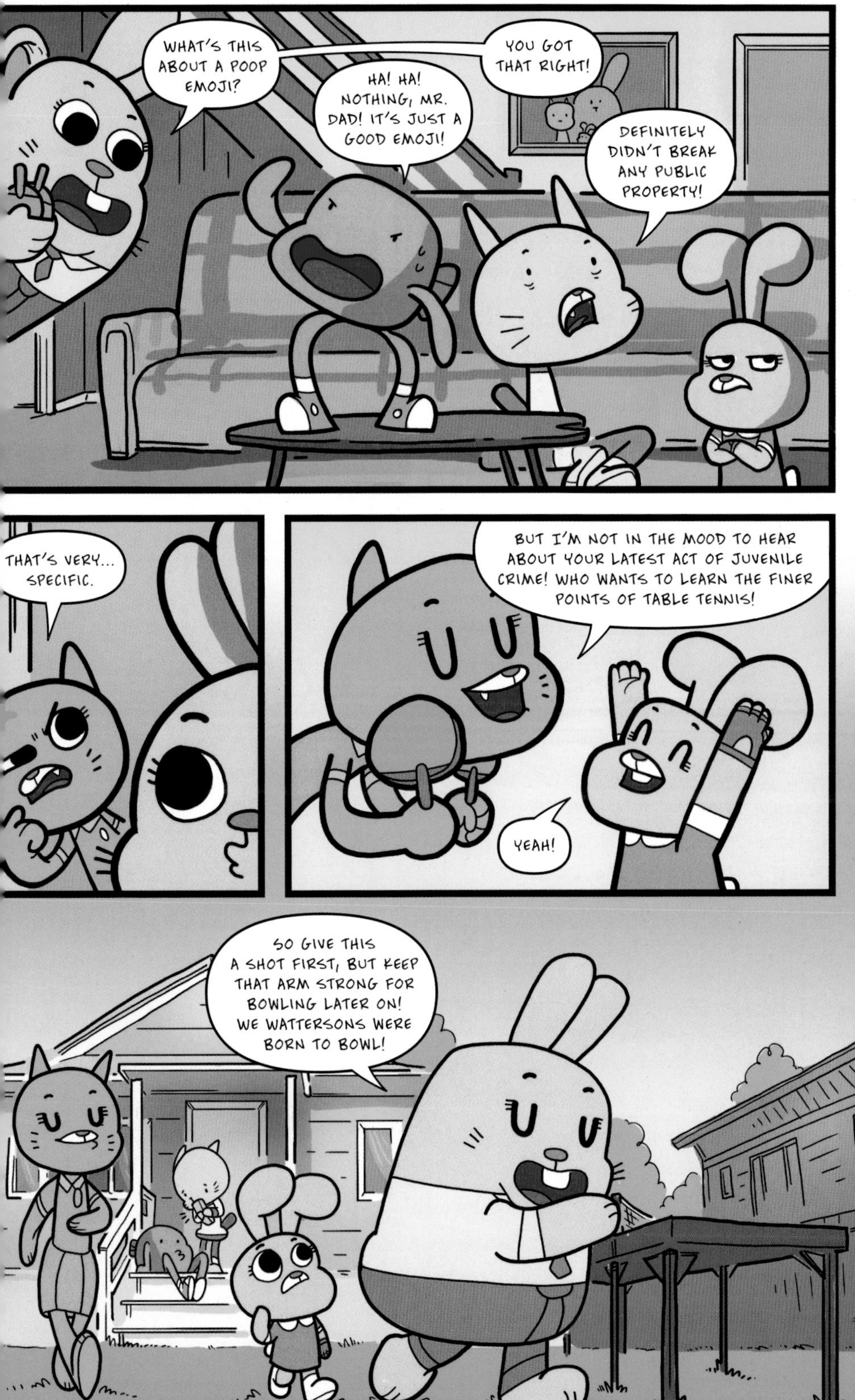
WHAT'S THIS ABOUT A POOP EMOJI?
YOU GOT THAT RIGHT!
HA! HA! NOTHING, MR. DAD! IT'S JUST A GOOD EMOJI!
DEFINITELY DIDN'T BREAK ANY PUBLIC PROPERTY!
THAT'S VERY... SPECIFIC.
BUT I'M NOT IN THE MOOD TO HEAR ABOUT YOUR LATEST ACT OF JUVENILE CRIME! WHO WANTS TO LEARN THE FINER POINTS OF TABLE TENNIS!
YEAH!
SO GIVE THIS A SHOT FIRST, BUT KEEP THAT ARM STRONG FOR BOWLING LATER ON! WE WATTERSONS WERE BORN TO BOWL!

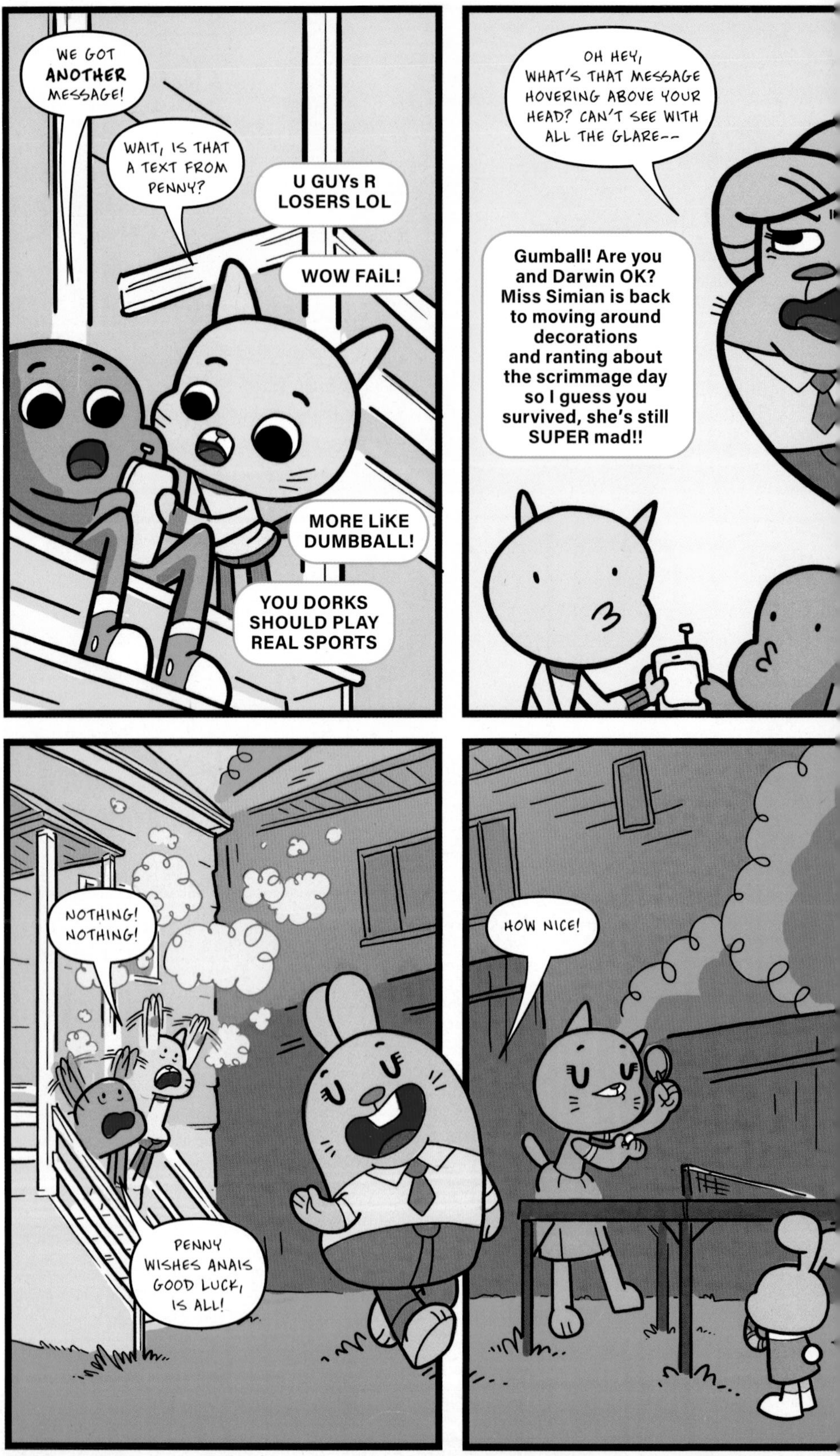
WE GOT ANOTHER MESSAGE!
WAIT, IS THAT A TEXT FROM PENNY?
U GUYs R LOSERS LOL
WOW FAiL!
MORE LiKE DUMBBALL!
YOU DORKS SHOULD PLAY REAL SPORTS
OH HEY, WHAT'S THAT MESSAGE HOVERING ABOVE YOUR HEAD? CAN'T SEE WITH ALL THE GLARE--
Gumball! Are you and Darwin OK? Miss Simian is back to moving around decorations and ranting about the scrimmage day so I guess you survived, she's still SUPER mad!!
NOTHING! NOTHING!
PENNY WISHES ANAIS GOOD LUCK, IS ALL!
HOW NICE!

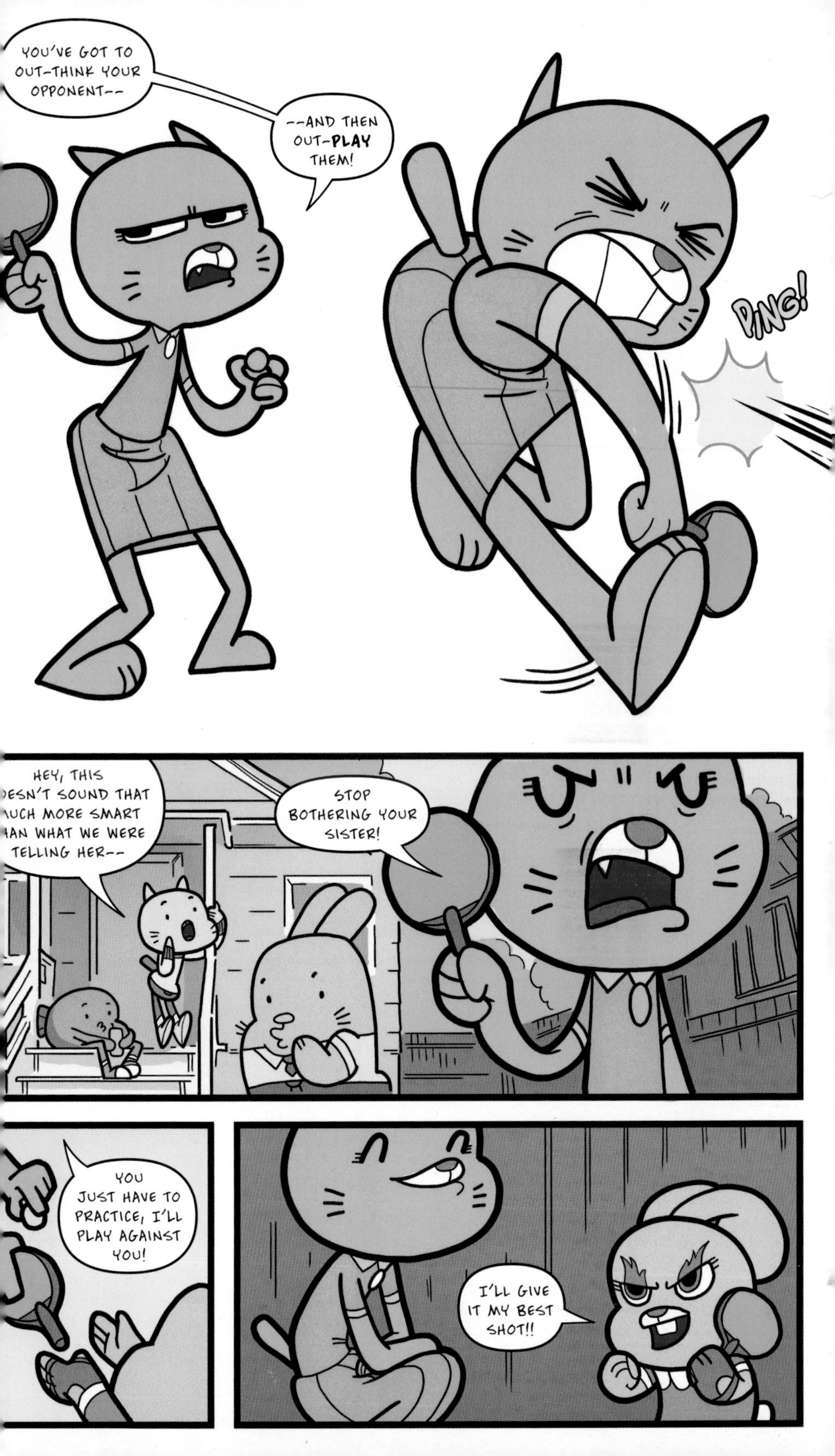
YOU'VE GOT TO OUT-THINK YOUR OPPONENT--
--AND THEN OUT-PLAY THEM!
PING!
HEY, THIS DESN'T SOUND THAT UCH MORE SMART HAN WHAT WE WERE TELLING HER--
STOP BOTHERING YOUR SISTER!
YOU JUST HAVE TO PRACTICE, I'LL PLAY AGAINST YOU!
I'LL GIVE IT MY BEST SHOT!!

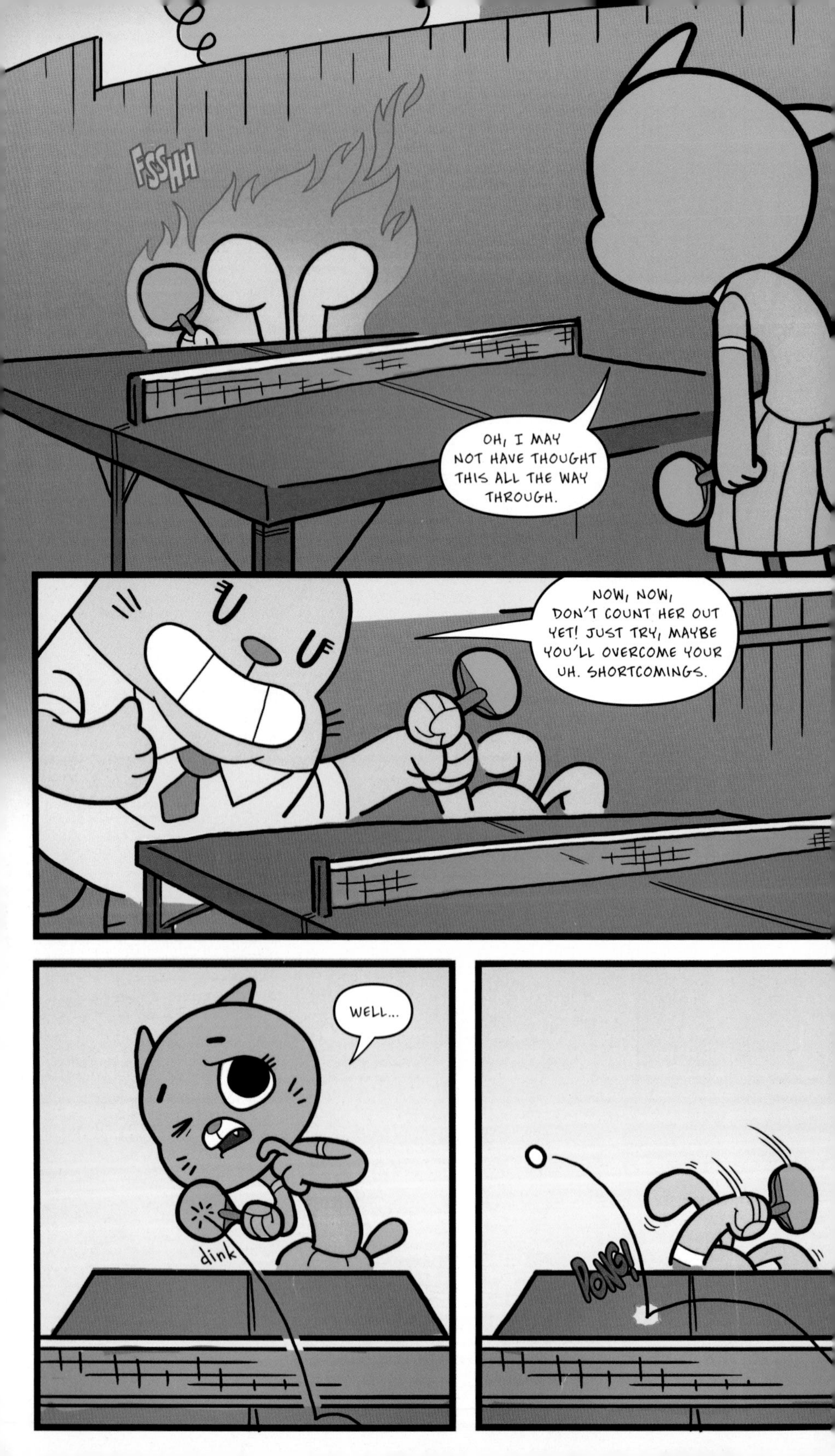
FSSHH
OH, I MAY NOT HAVE THOUGHT THIS ALL THE WAY THROUGH.
NOW, NOW, DON'T COUNT HER OUT YET! JUST TRY, MAYBE YOU'LL OVERCOME YOUR UH. SHORTCOMINGS.
WELL...
dink
PONG!

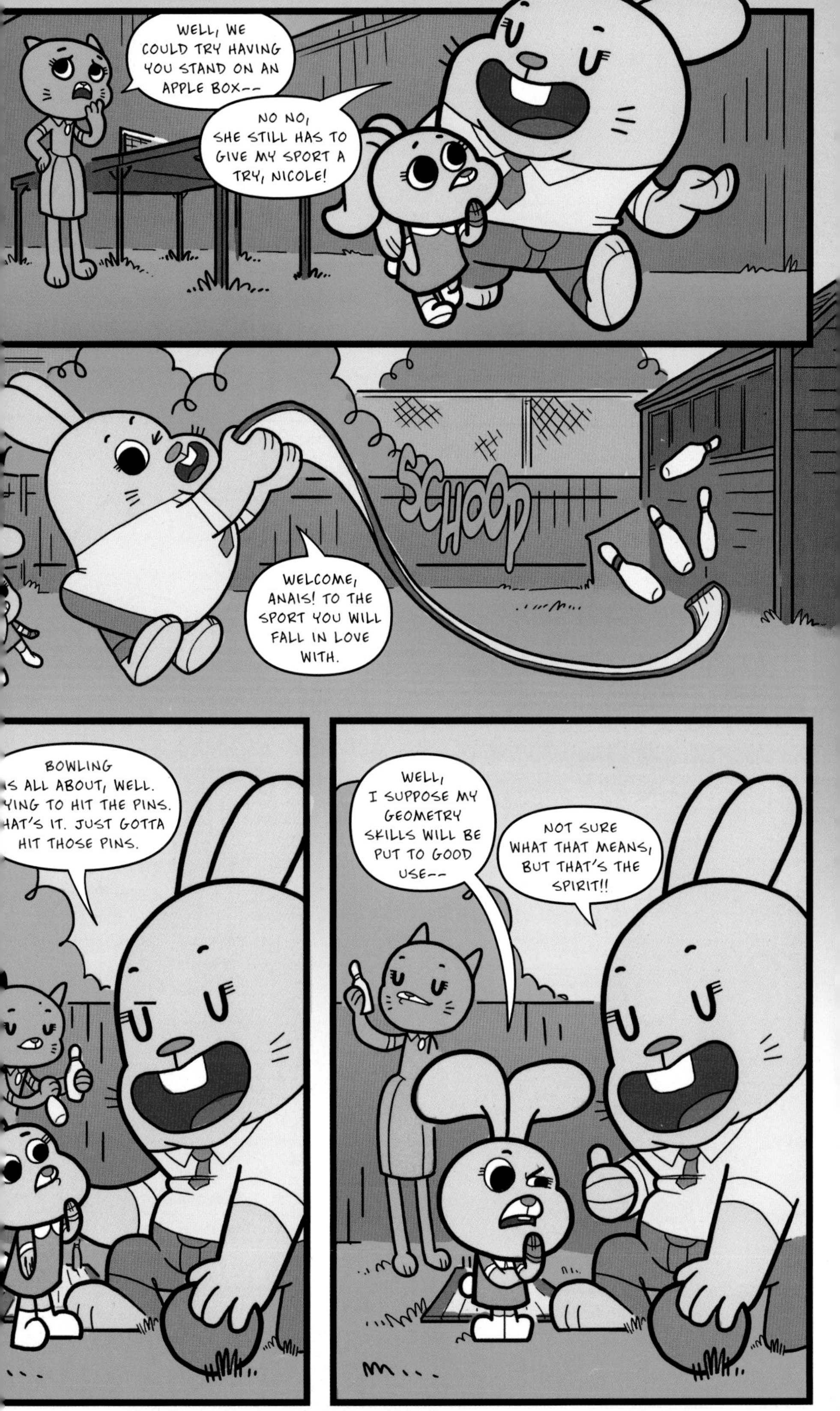
WELL, WE COULD TRY HAVING YOU STAND ON AN APPLE BOX--
NO NO, SHE STILL HAS TO GIVE MY SPORT A TRY, NICOLE!
SCHOOP
WELCOME, ANAIS! TO THE SPORT YOU WILL FALL IN LOVE WITH.
BOWLING S ALL ABOUT, WELL. YING TO HIT THE PINS. HAT'S IT. JUST GOTTA HIT THOSE PINS.
WELL, I SUPPOSE MY GEOMETRY SKILLS WILL BE PUT TO GOOD USE--
NOT SURE WHAT THAT MEANS, BUT THAT'S THE SPIRIT!!

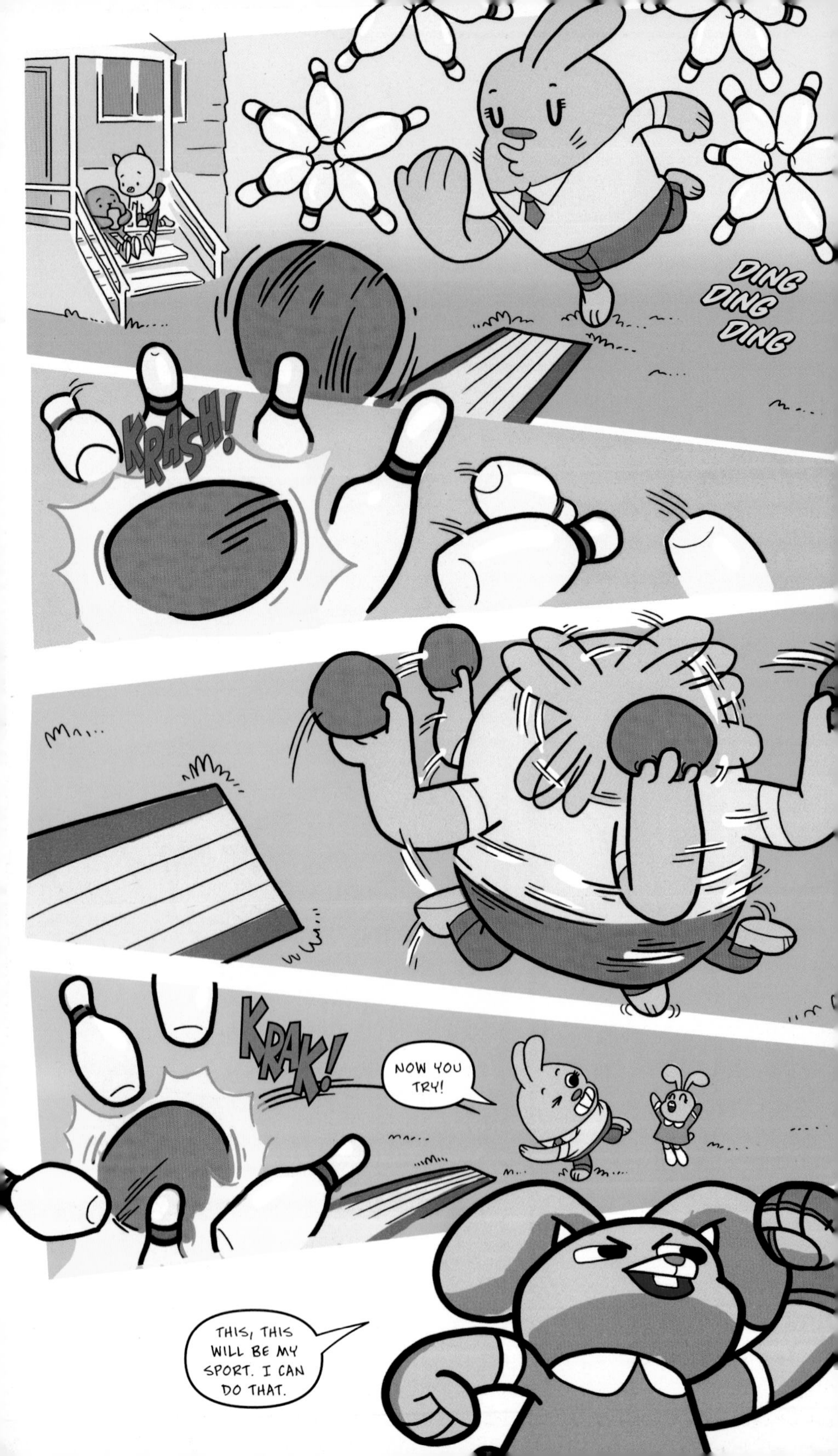
DING
DING
DING
KRASH!
KRAK!
NOW YOU TRY!
THIS, THIS WILL BE MY SPORT. I CAN DO THAT.

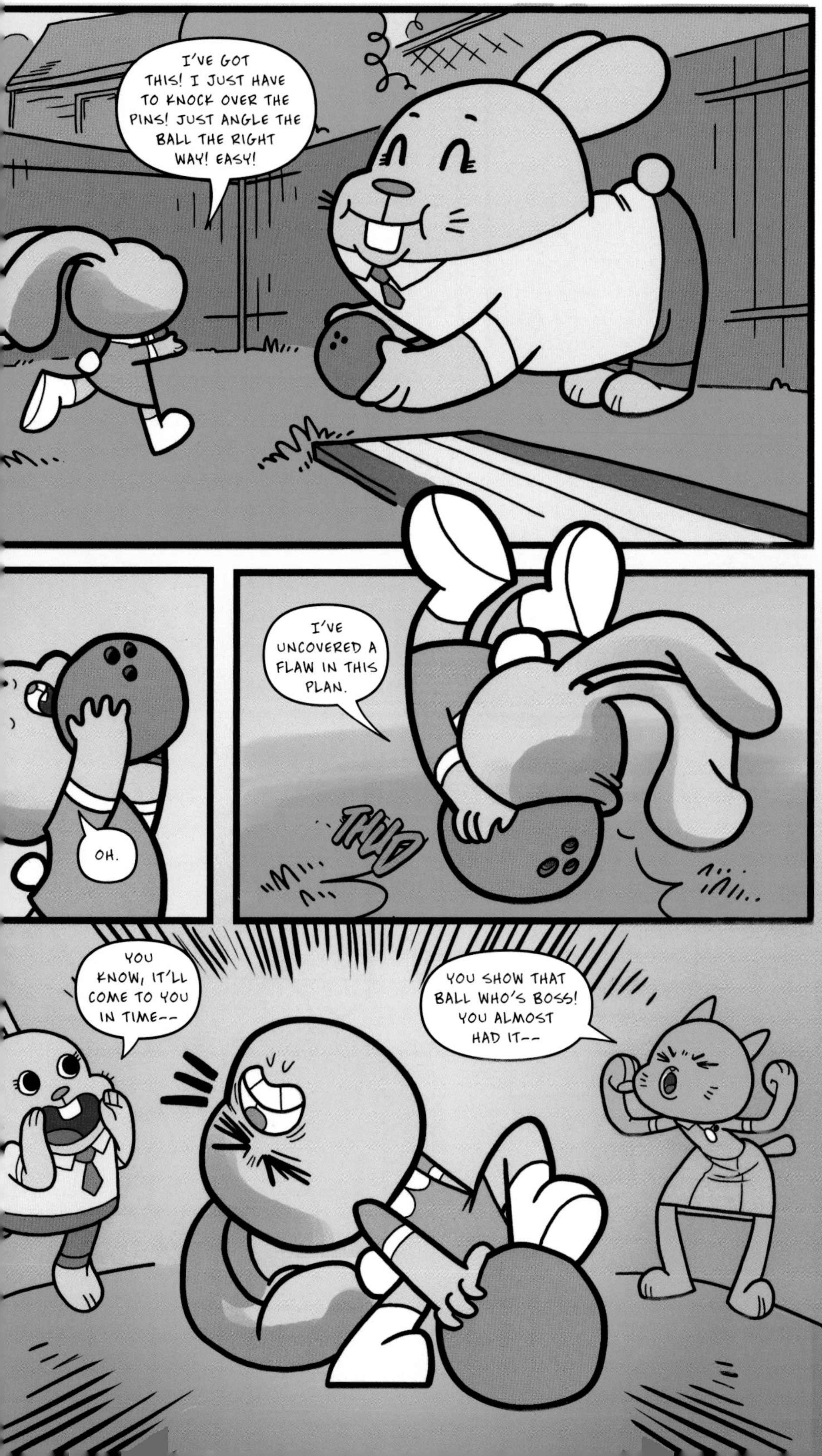
I'VE GOT THIS! I JUST HAVE TO KNOCK OVER THE PINS! JUST ANGLE THE BALL THE RIGHT WAY! EASY!
OH.
I'VE UNCOVERED A FLAW IN THIS PLAN.
THUD
YOU KNOW, IT'LL COME TO YOU IN TIME--
YOU SHOW THAT BALL WHO'S BOSS! YOU ALMOST HAD IT--

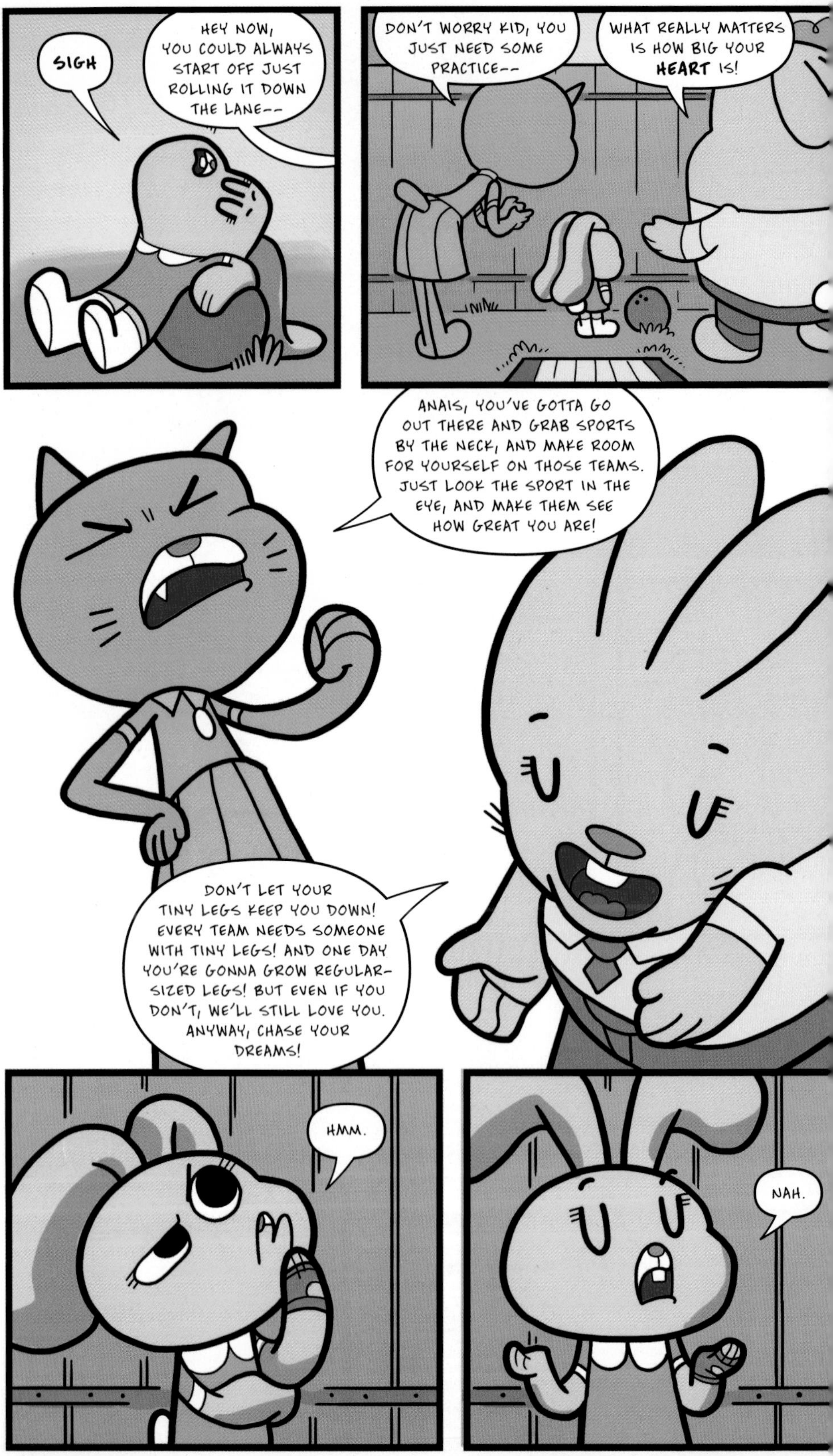
SIGH
HEY NOW, YOU COULD ALWAYS START OFF JUST ROLLING IT DOWN THE LANE--
DON'T WORRY KID, YOU JUST NEED SOME PRACTICE--
WHAT REALLY MATTERS IS HOW BIG YOUR HEART IS!
ANAIS, YOU'VE GOTTA GO OUT THERE AND GRAB SPORTS BY THE NECK, AND MAKE ROOM FOR YOURSELF ON THOSE TEAMS. JUST LOOK THE SPORT IN THE EYE, AND MAKE THEM SEE HOW GREAT YOU ARE!
DON'T LET YOUR TINY LEGS KEEP YOU DOWN! EVERY TEAM NEEDS SOMEONE WITH TINY LEGS! AND ONE DAY YOU'RE GONNA GROW REGULAR-SIZED LEGS! BUT EVEN IF YOU DON'T, WE'LL STILL LOVE YOU. ANYWAY, CHASE YOUR DREAMS!
HMM.
NAH.

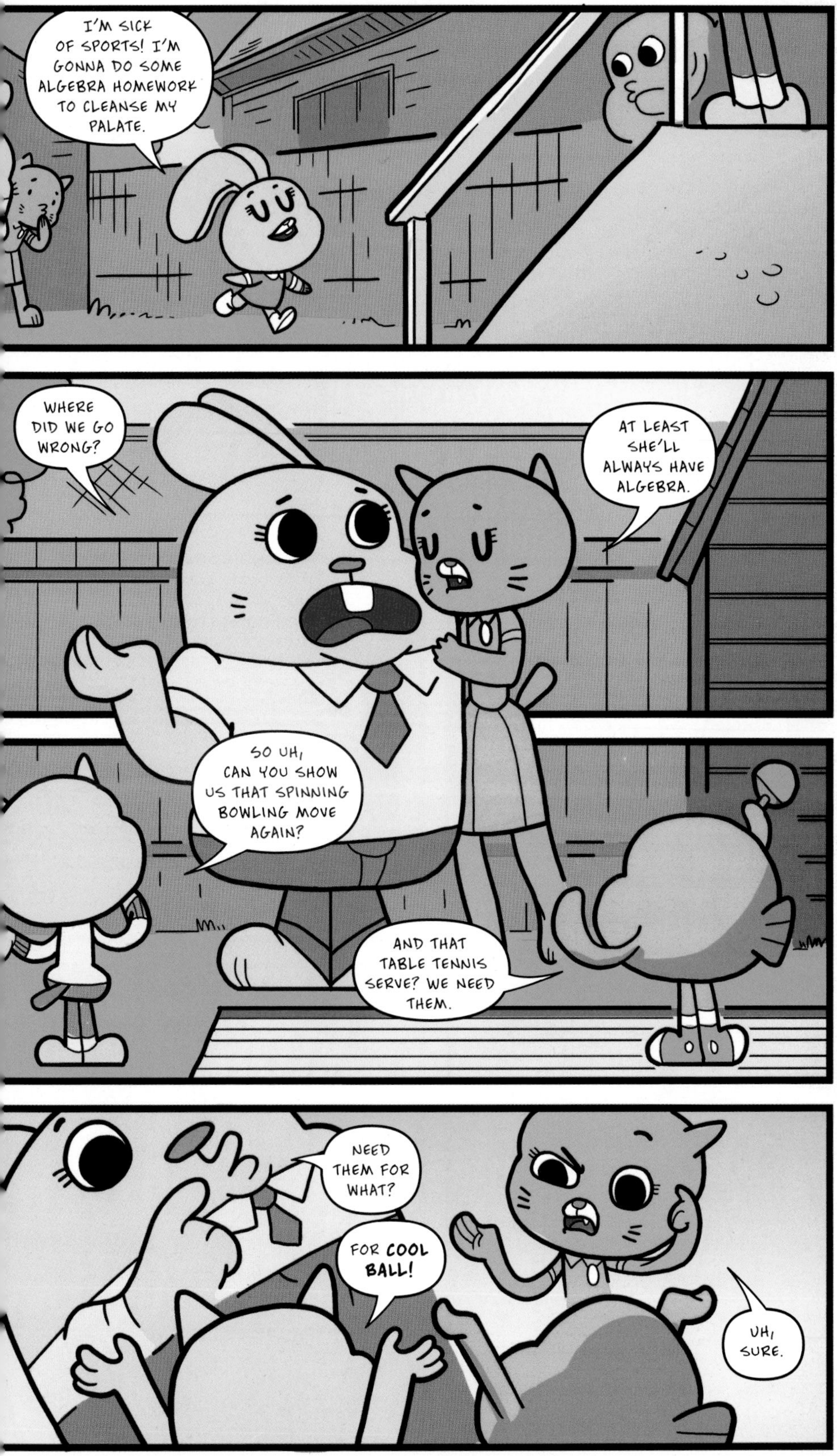
I'M SICK OF SPORTS! I'M GONNA DO SOME ALGEBRA HOMEWORK TO CLEANSE MY PALATE.
WHERE DID WE GO WRONG?
AT LEAST SHE'LL ALWAYS HAVE ALGEBRA.
SO UH, CAN YOU SHOW US THAT SPINNING BOWLING MOVE AGAIN?
AND THAT TABLE TENNIS SERVE? WE NEED THEM.
NEED THEM FOR WHAT?
FOR **COOL BALL!**
UH, SURE.

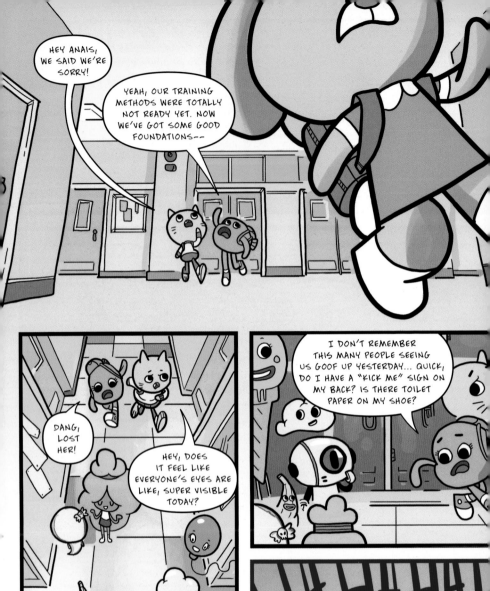

HEY ANAIS, WE SAID WE'RE SORRY!

YEAH, OUR TRAINING METHODS WERE TOTALLY NOT READY YET. NOW WE'VE GOT SOME GOOD FOUNDATIONS--

DANG, LOST HER!

HEY, DOES IT FEEL LIKE EVERYONE'S EYES ARE LIKE, SUPER VISIBLE TODAY?

I DON'T REMEMBER THIS MANY PEOPLE SEEING US GOOF UP YESTERDAY... QUICK, DO I HAVE A "KICK ME" SIGN ON MY BACK? IS THERE TOILET PAPER ON MY SHOE?

HAHAHAHAHAHAHAHAHAHAHAHAHA HA HA HA

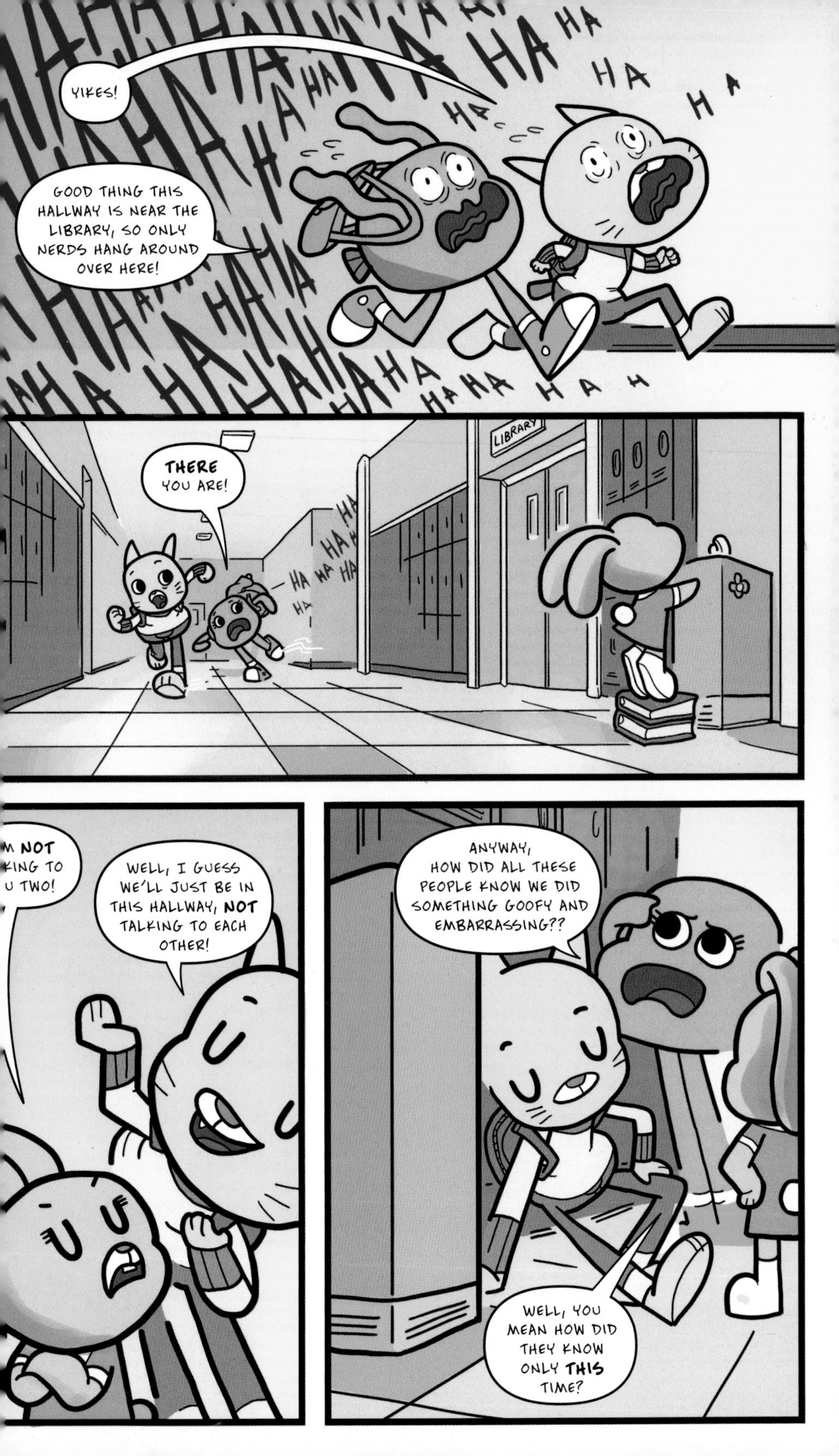
YIKES!
GOOD THING THIS HALLWAY IS NEAR THE LIBRARY, SO ONLY NERDS HANG AROUND OVER HERE!
HA HA HA HA
THERE YOU ARE!
LIBRARY
M NOT KING TO U TWO!
WELL, I GUESS WE'LL JUST BE IN THIS HALLWAY, NOT TALKING TO EACH OTHER!
ANYWAY, HOW DID ALL THESE PEOPLE KNOW WE DID SOMETHING GOOFY AND EMBARRASSING??
WELL, YOU MEAN HOW DID THEY KNOW ONLY THIS TIME?

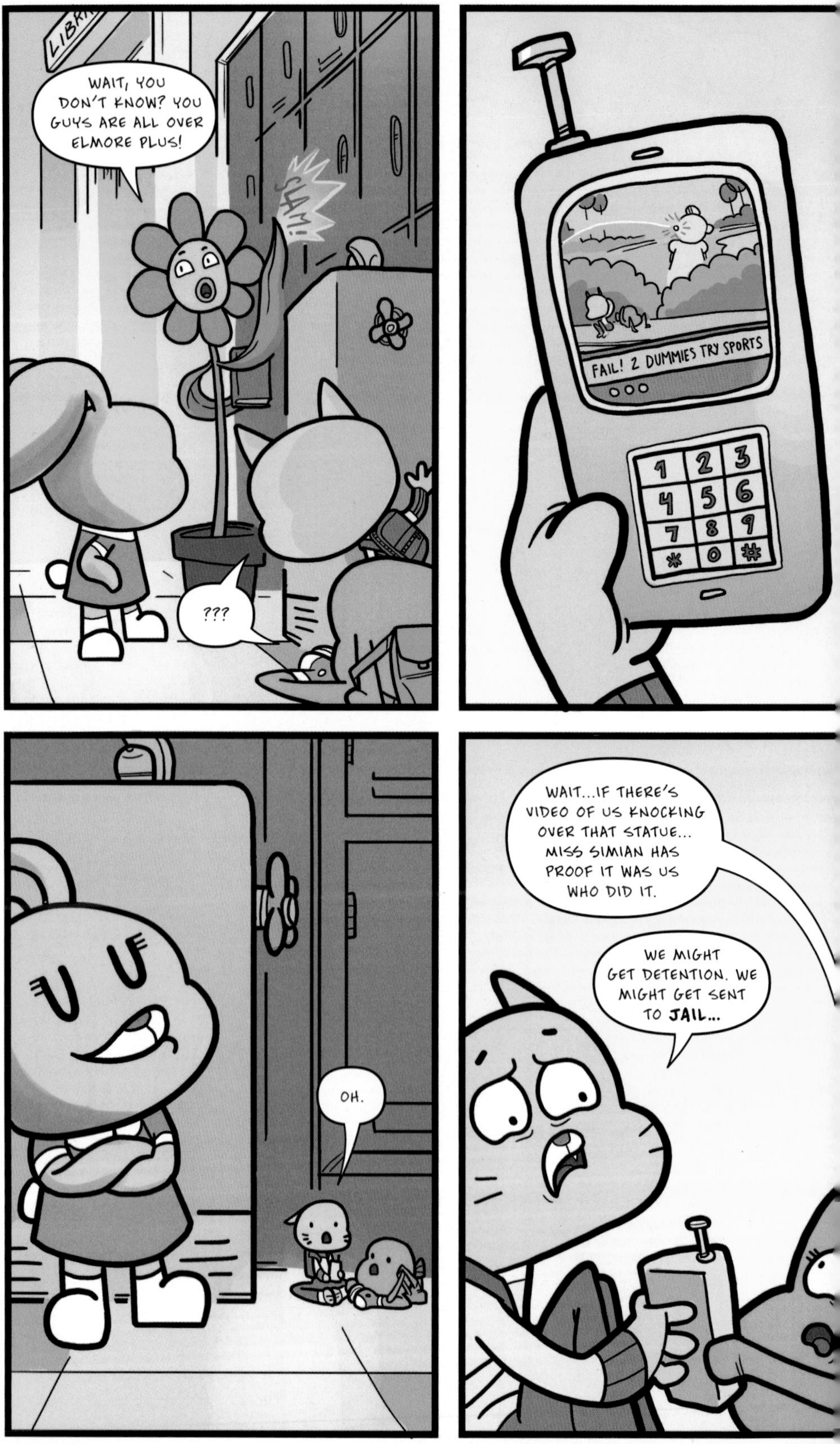
LIBR
WAIT, YOU DON'T KNOW? YOU GUYS ARE ALL OVER ELMORE PLUS!
SLAM!
???
FAIL! 2 DUMMIES TRY SPORTS
1 2 3 4 5 6 7 8 9 * 0 #
OH.
WAIT...IF THERE'S VIDEO OF US KNOCKING OVER THAT STATUE... MISS SIMIAN HAS PROOF IT WAS US WHO DID IT.
WE MIGHT GET DETENTION. WE MIGHT GET SENT TO **JAIL...**

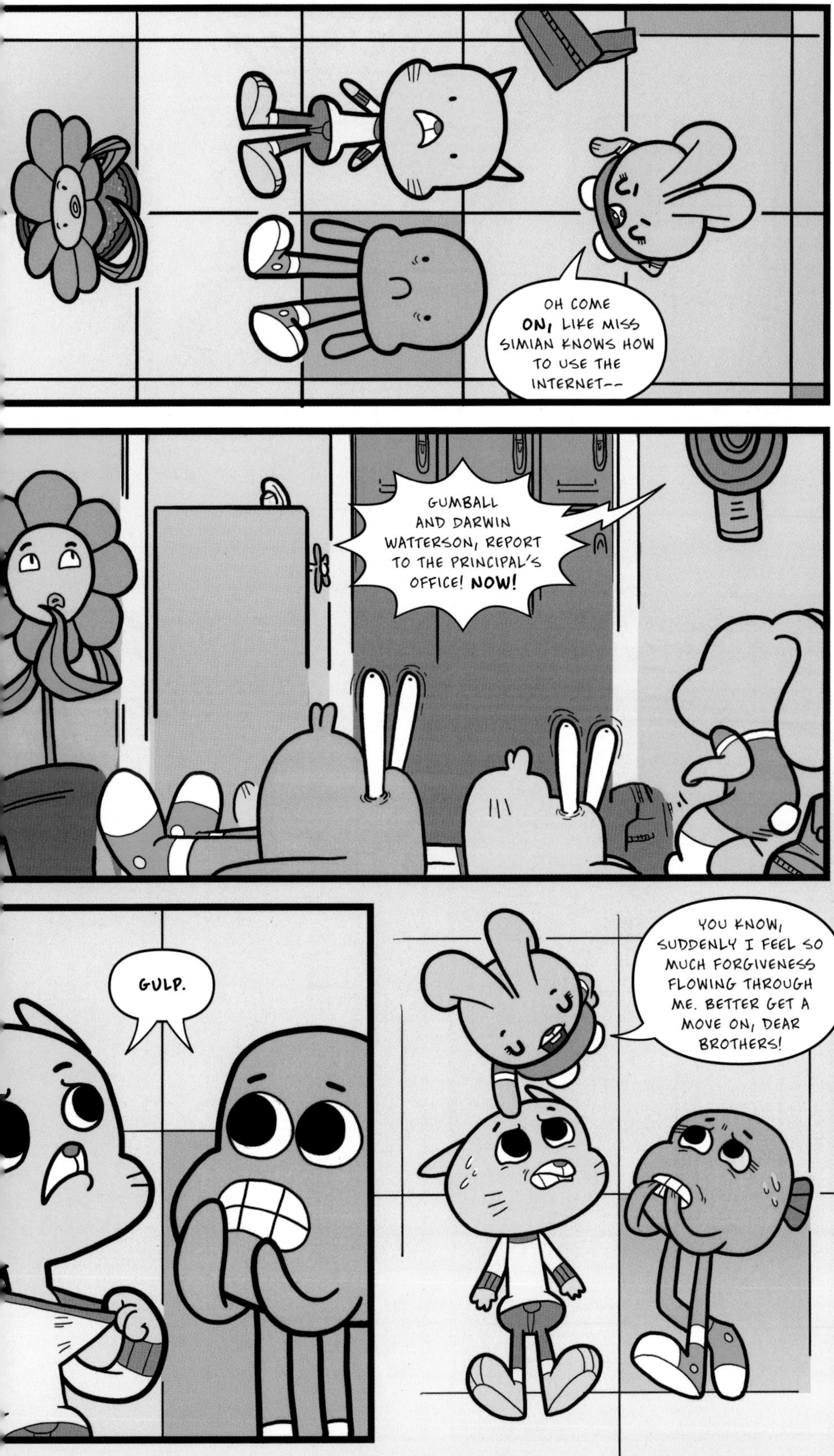

OH COME ON, LIKE MISS SIMIAN KNOWS HOW TO USE THE INTERNET--
GUMBALL AND DARWIN WATTERSON, REPORT TO THE PRINCIPAL'S OFFICE! NOW!
GULP.
YOU KNOW, SUDDENLY I FEEL SO MUCH FORGIVENESS FLOWING THROUGH ME. BETTER GET A MOVE ON, DEAR BROTHERS!

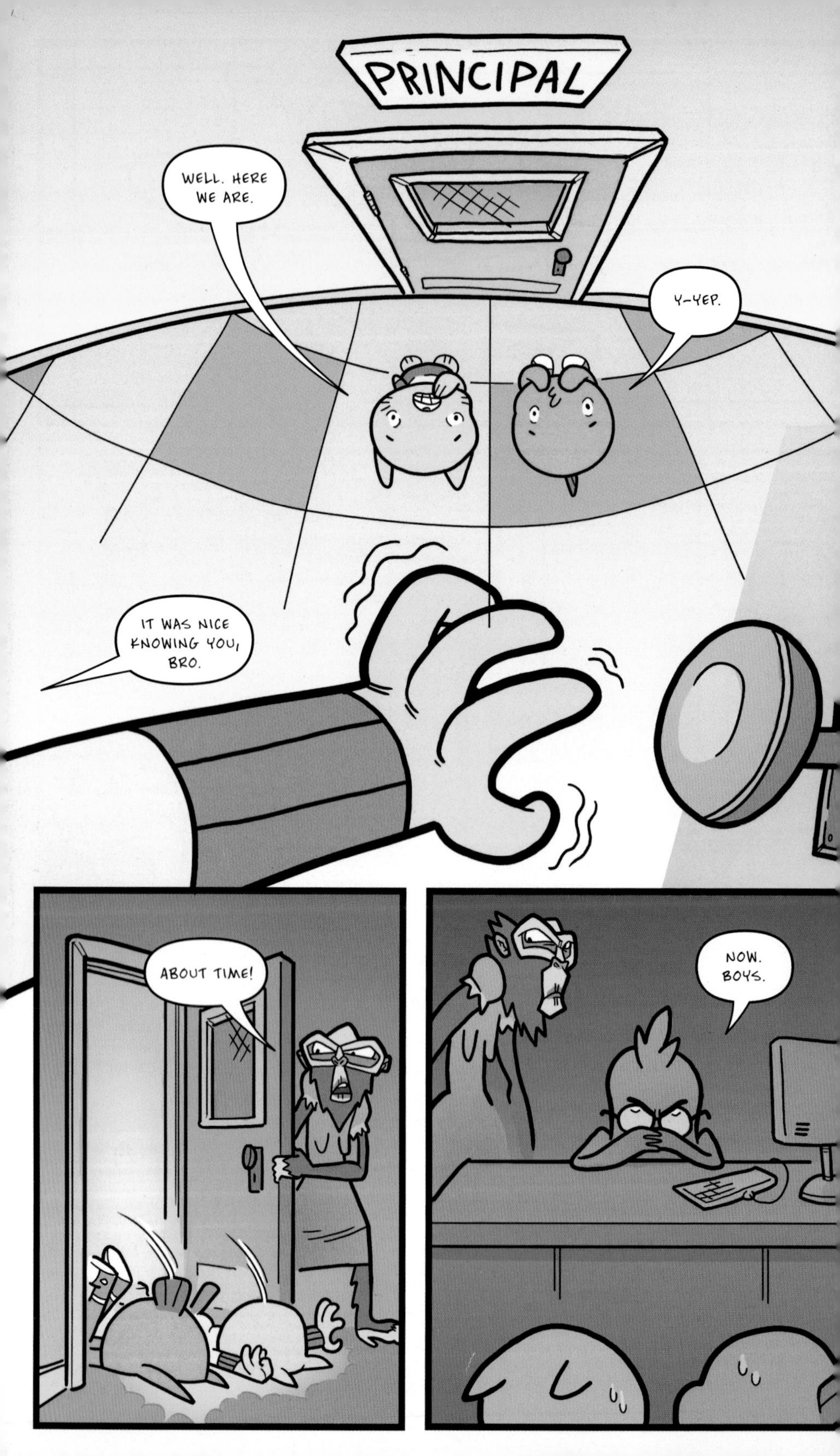
PRINCIPAL
WELL. HERE WE ARE.
Y-YEP.
IT WAS NICE KNOWING YOU, BRO.
ABOUT TIME!
NOW. BOYS.

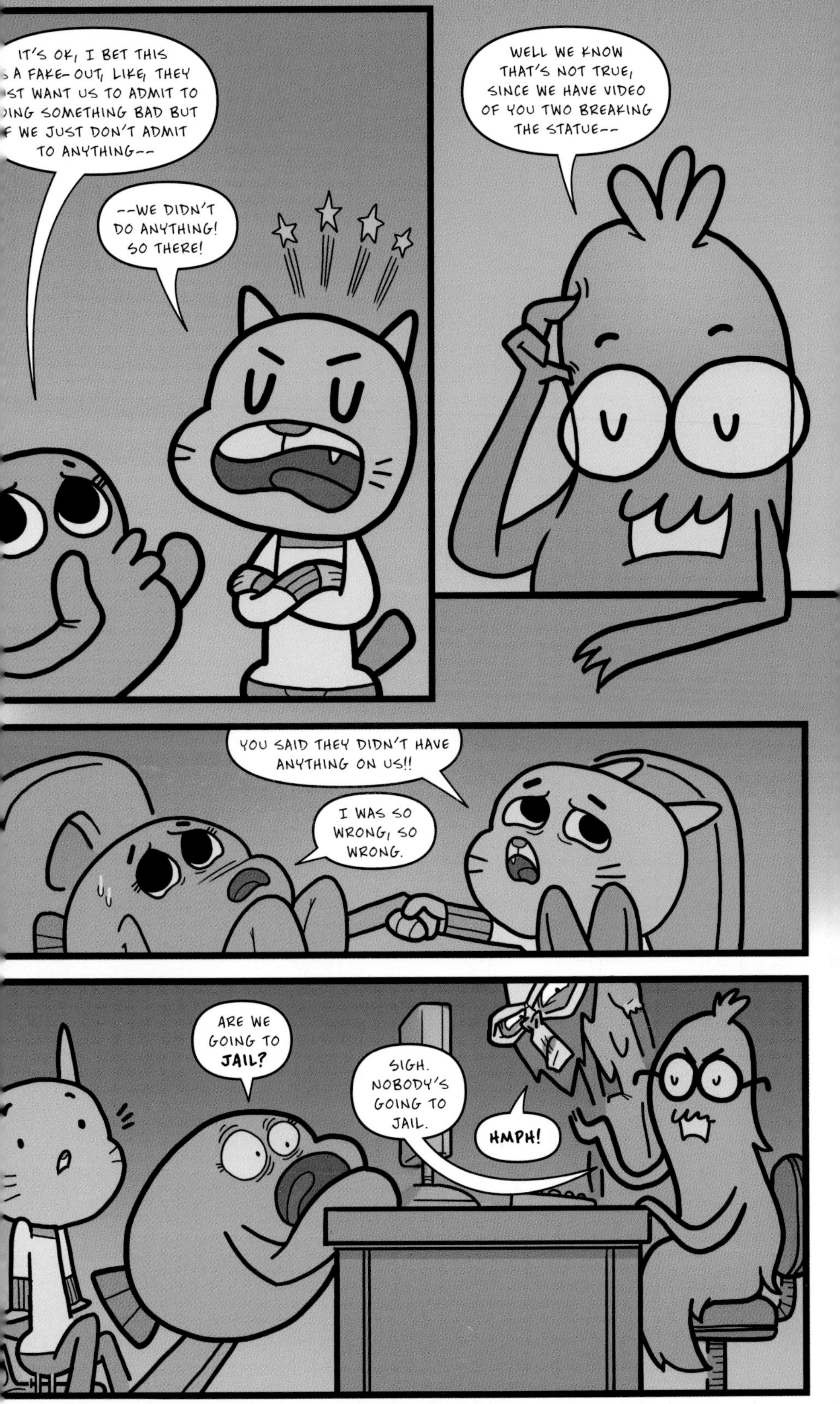
IT'S OK, I BET THIS
A FAKE-OUT, LIKE, THEY
WANT US TO ADMIT TO
SOMETHING BAD BUT
WE JUST DON'T ADMIT
TO ANYTHING--
--WE DIDN'T DO ANYTHING! SO THERE!
WELL WE KNOW THAT'S NOT TRUE, SINCE WE HAVE VIDEO OF YOU TWO BREAKING THE STATUE--
YOU SAID THEY DIDN'T HAVE ANYTHING ON US!!
I WAS SO WRONG, SO WRONG.
ARE WE GOING TO JAIL?
SIGH. NOBODY'S GOING TO JAIL.
HMPH!

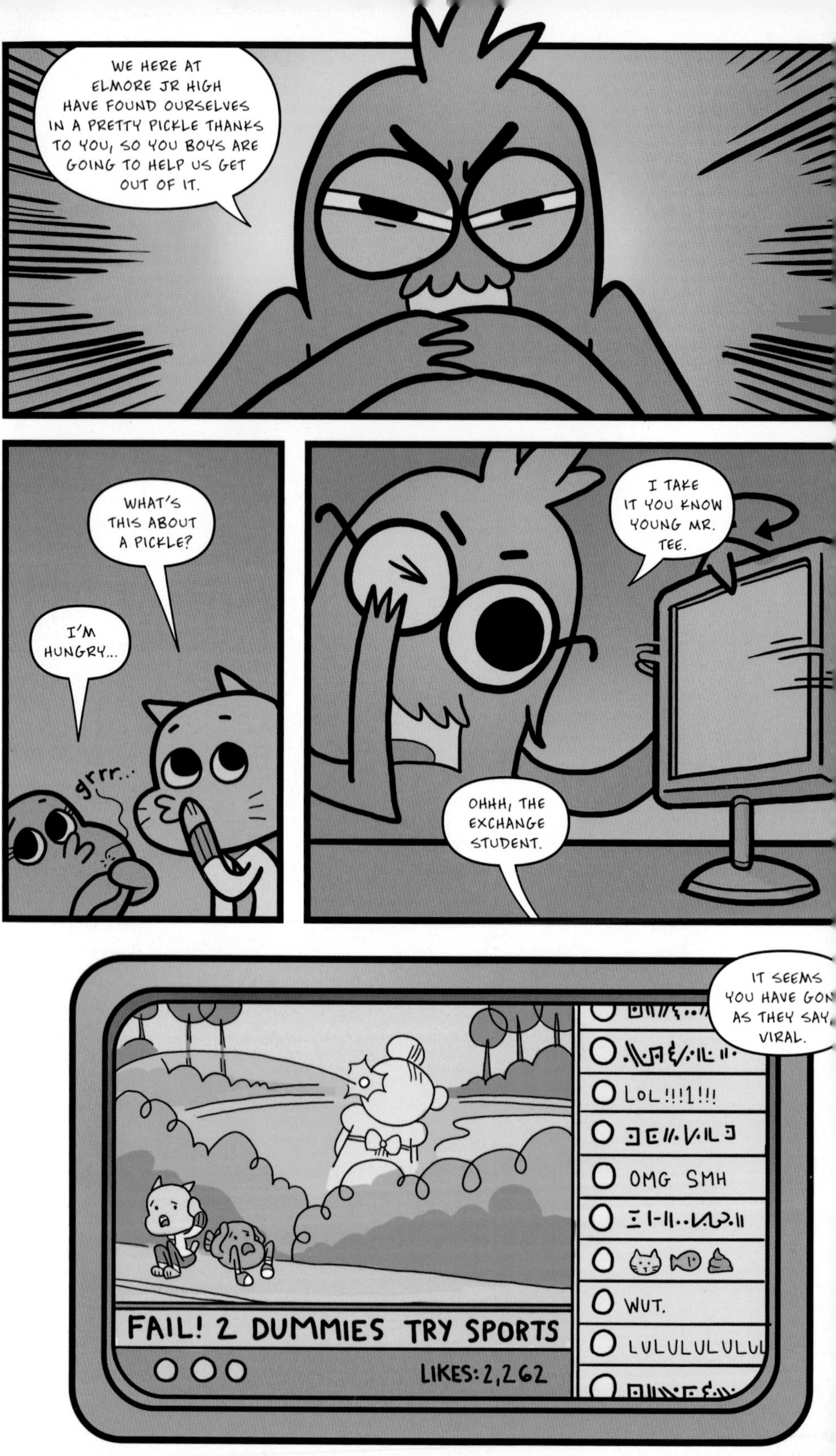
WE HERE AT ELMORE JR HIGH HAVE FOUND OURSELVES IN A PRETTY PICKLE THANKS TO YOU, SO YOU BOYS ARE GOING TO HELP US GET OUT OF IT.
WHAT'S THIS ABOUT A PICKLE?
I'M HUNGRY...
grrr...
I TAKE IT YOU KNOW YOUNG MR. TEE.
OHHH, THE EXCHANGE STUDENT.
IT SEEMS YOU HAVE GON AS THEY SAY, VIRAL.
LOL!!!1!!!
OMG SMH
WUT.
LULULULULUL
FAIL! 2 DUMMIES TRY SPORTS
LIKES: 2,262

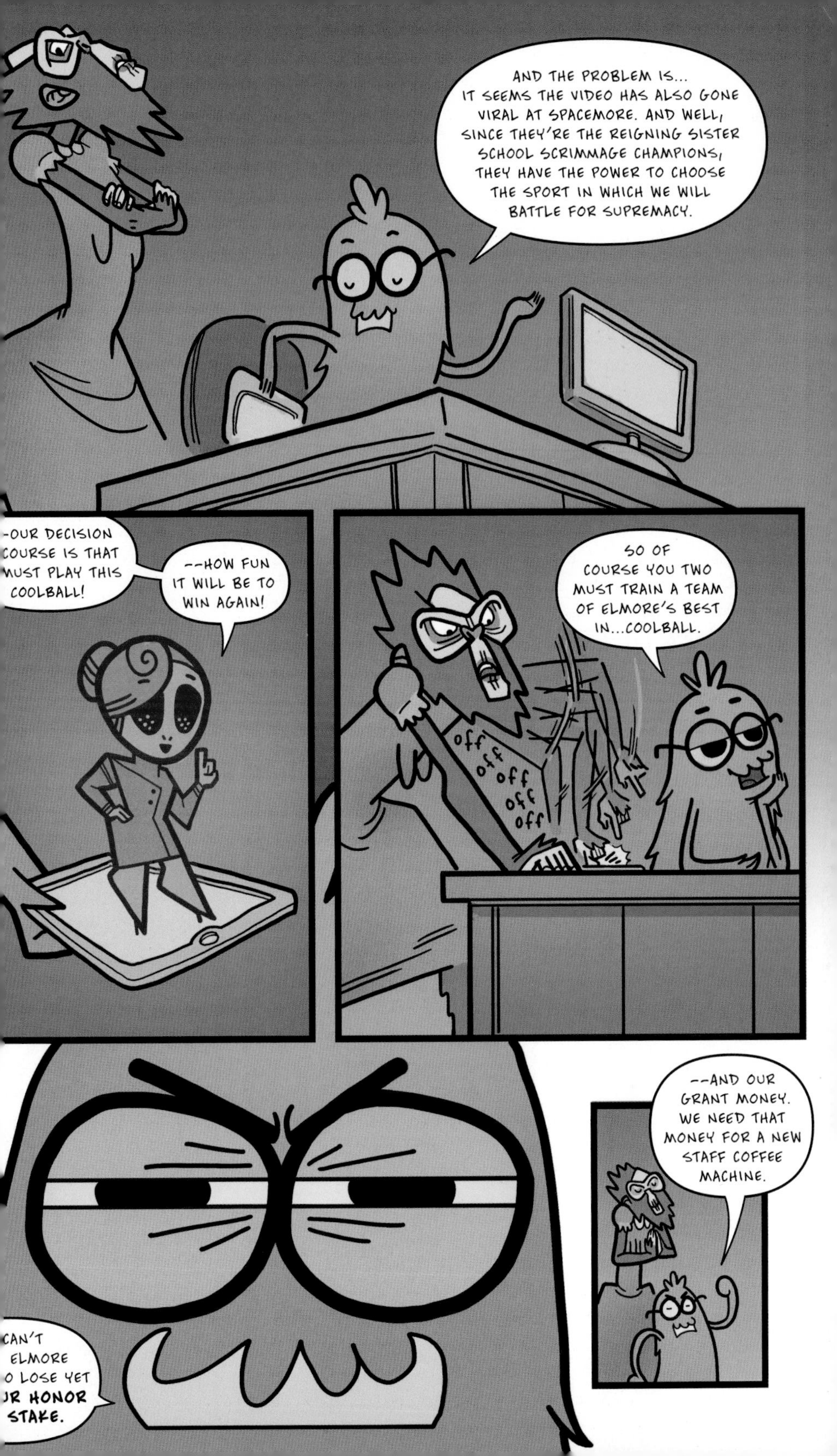
AND THE PROBLEM IS... IT SEEMS THE VIDEO HAS ALSO GONE VIRAL AT SPACEMORE. AND WELL, SINCE THEY'RE THE REIGNING SISTER SCHOOL SCRIMMAGE CHAMPIONS, THEY HAVE THE POWER TO CHOOSE THE SPORT IN WHICH WE WILL BATTLE FOR SUPREMACY.
-OUR DECISION COURSE IS THAT MUST PLAY THIS COOLBALL!
--HOW FUN IT WILL BE TO WIN AGAIN!
SO OF COURSE YOU TWO MUST TRAIN A TEAM OF ELMORE'S BEST IN...COOLBALL.
off off off off off off
CAN'T ELMORE O LOSE YET JR HONOR STAKE.
--AND OUR GRANT MONEY. WE NEED THAT MONEY FOR A NEW STAFF COFFEE MACHINE.

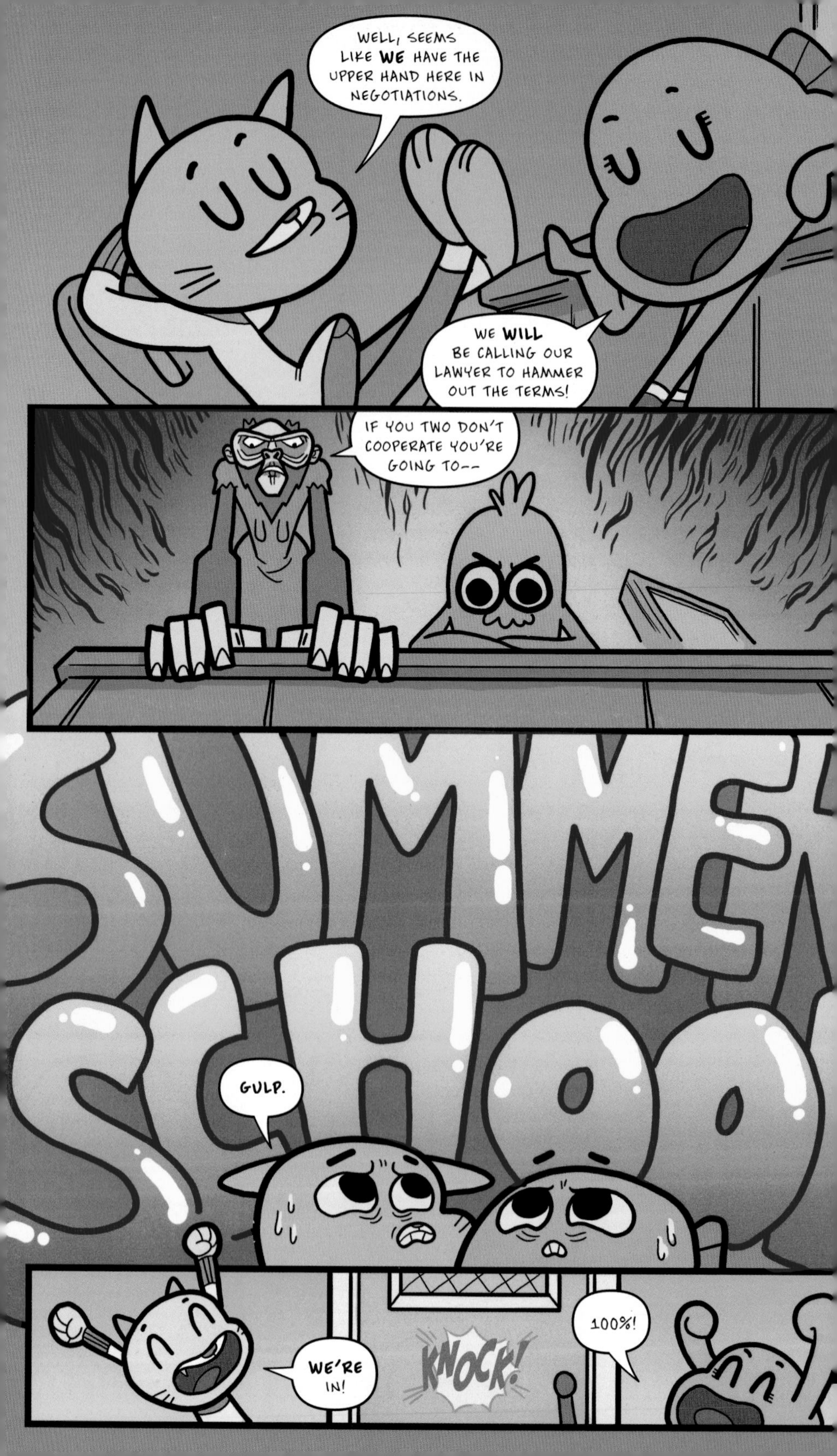
WELL, SEEMS LIKE **WE** HAVE THE UPPER HAND HERE IN NEGOTIATIONS.
WE **WILL** BE CALLING OUR LAWYER TO HAMMER OUT THE TERMS!
IF YOU TWO DON'T COOPERATE YOU'RE GOING TO--
SUMMER SCHOOL
GULP.
WE'RE IN!
KNOCK!
100%!

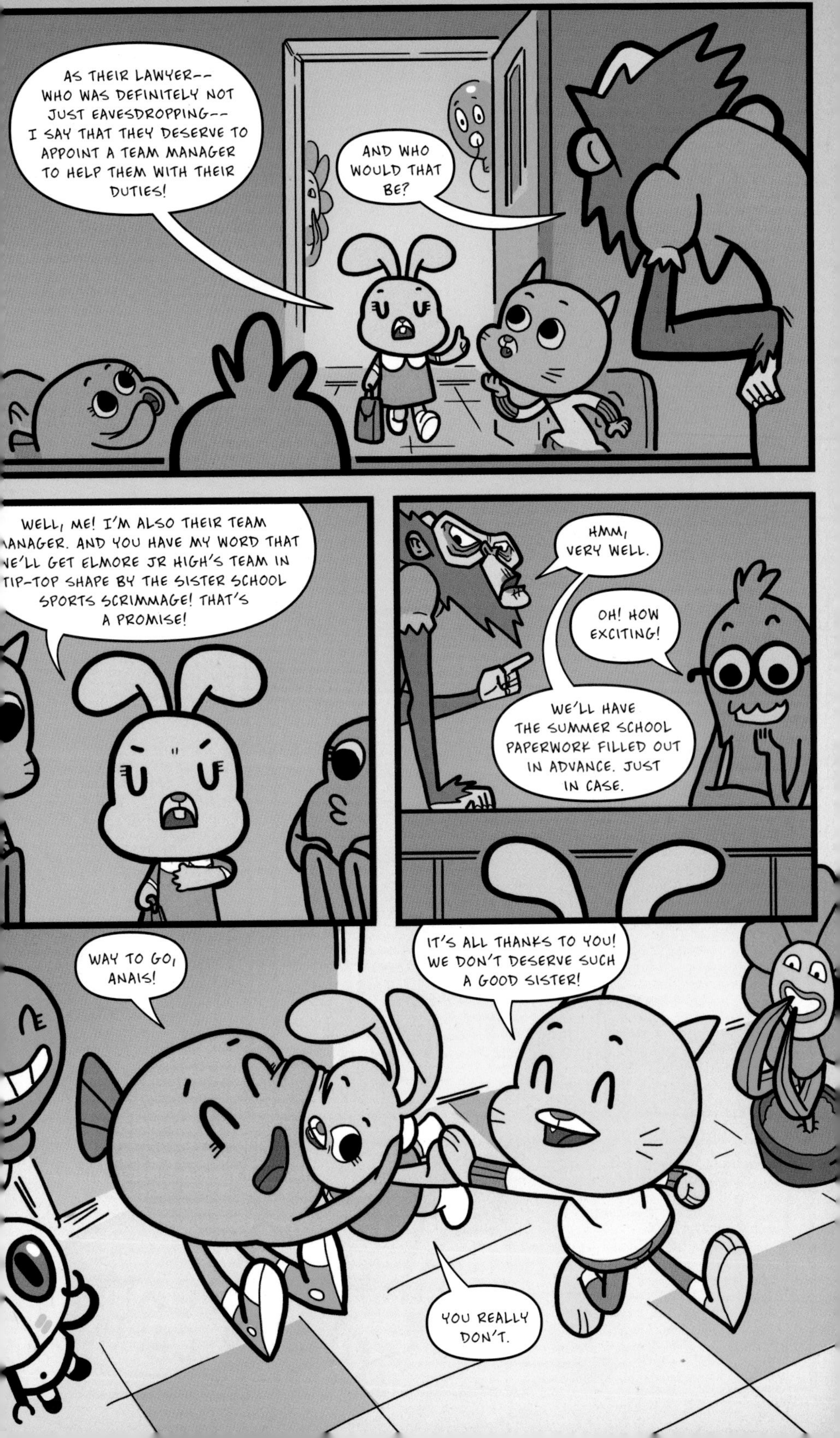
AS THEIR LAWYER-- WHO WAS DEFINITELY NOT JUST EAVESDROPPING-- I SAY THAT THEY DESERVE TO APPOINT A TEAM MANAGER TO HELP THEM WITH THEIR DUTIES!
AND WHO WOULD THAT BE?
WELL, ME! I'M ALSO THEIR TEAM MANAGER. AND YOU HAVE MY WORD THAT WE'LL GET ELMORE JR HIGH'S TEAM IN TIP-TOP SHAPE BY THE SISTER SCHOOL SPORTS SCRIMMAGE! THAT'S A PROMISE!
HMM, VERY WELL.
OH! HOW EXCITING!
WE'LL HAVE THE SUMMER SCHOOL PAPERWORK FILLED OUT IN ADVANCE. JUST IN CASE.
WAY TO GO, ANAIS!
IT'S ALL THANKS TO YOU! WE DON'T DESERVE SUCH A GOOD SISTER!
YOU REALLY DON'T.

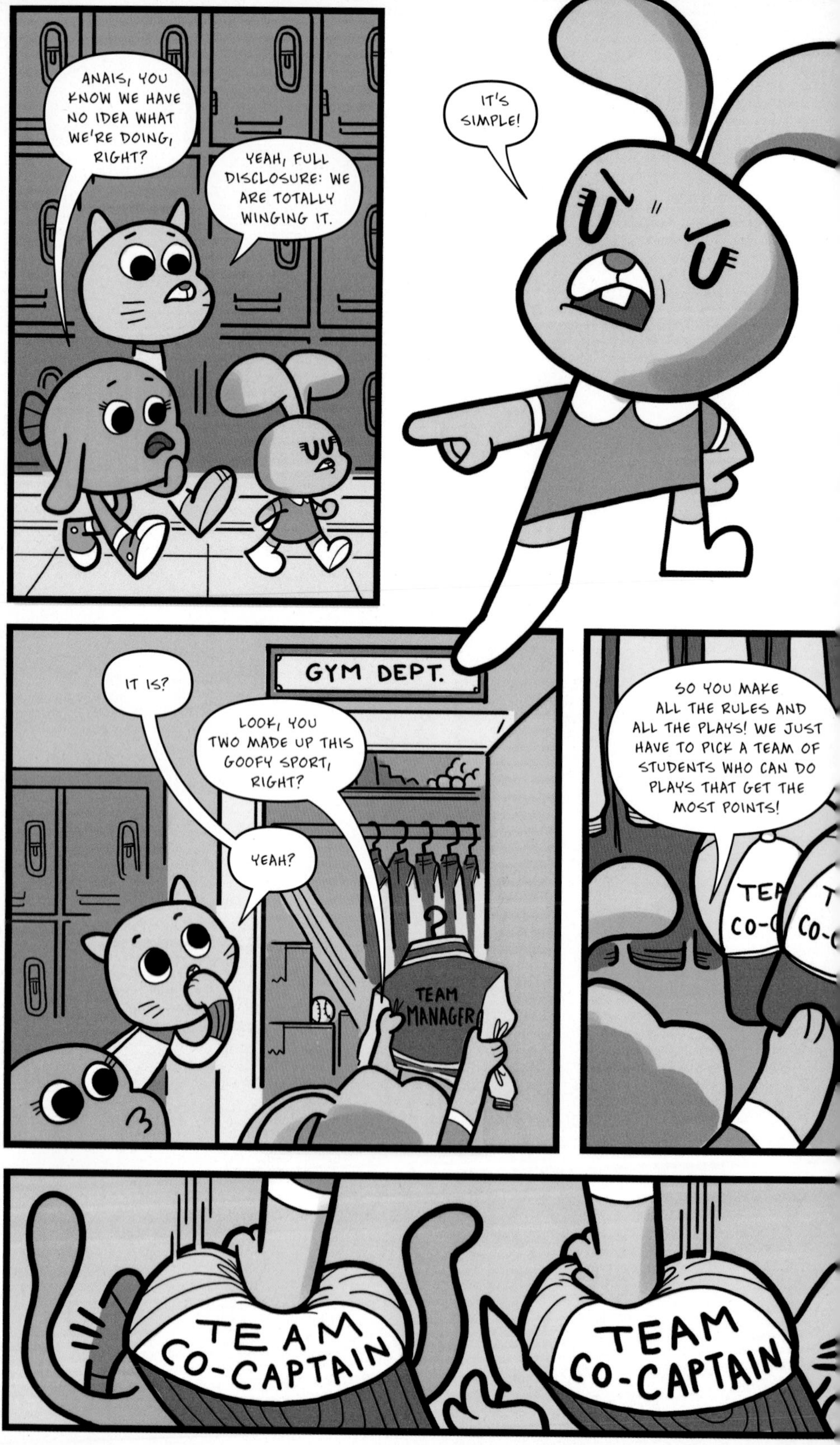
ANAIS, YOU KNOW WE HAVE NO IDEA WHAT WE'RE DOING, RIGHT?
YEAH, FULL DISCLOSURE: WE ARE TOTALLY WINGING IT.
IT'S SIMPLE!
GYM DEPT.
IT IS?
LOOK, YOU TWO MADE UP THIS GOOFY SPORT, RIGHT?
YEAH?
TEAM MANAGER
SO YOU MAKE ALL THE RULES AND ALL THE PLAYS! WE JUST HAVE TO PICK A TEAM OF STUDENTS WHO CAN DO PLAYS THAT GET THE MOST POINTS!
TEAM CO-CAPTAIN
TEAM CO-CAPTAIN

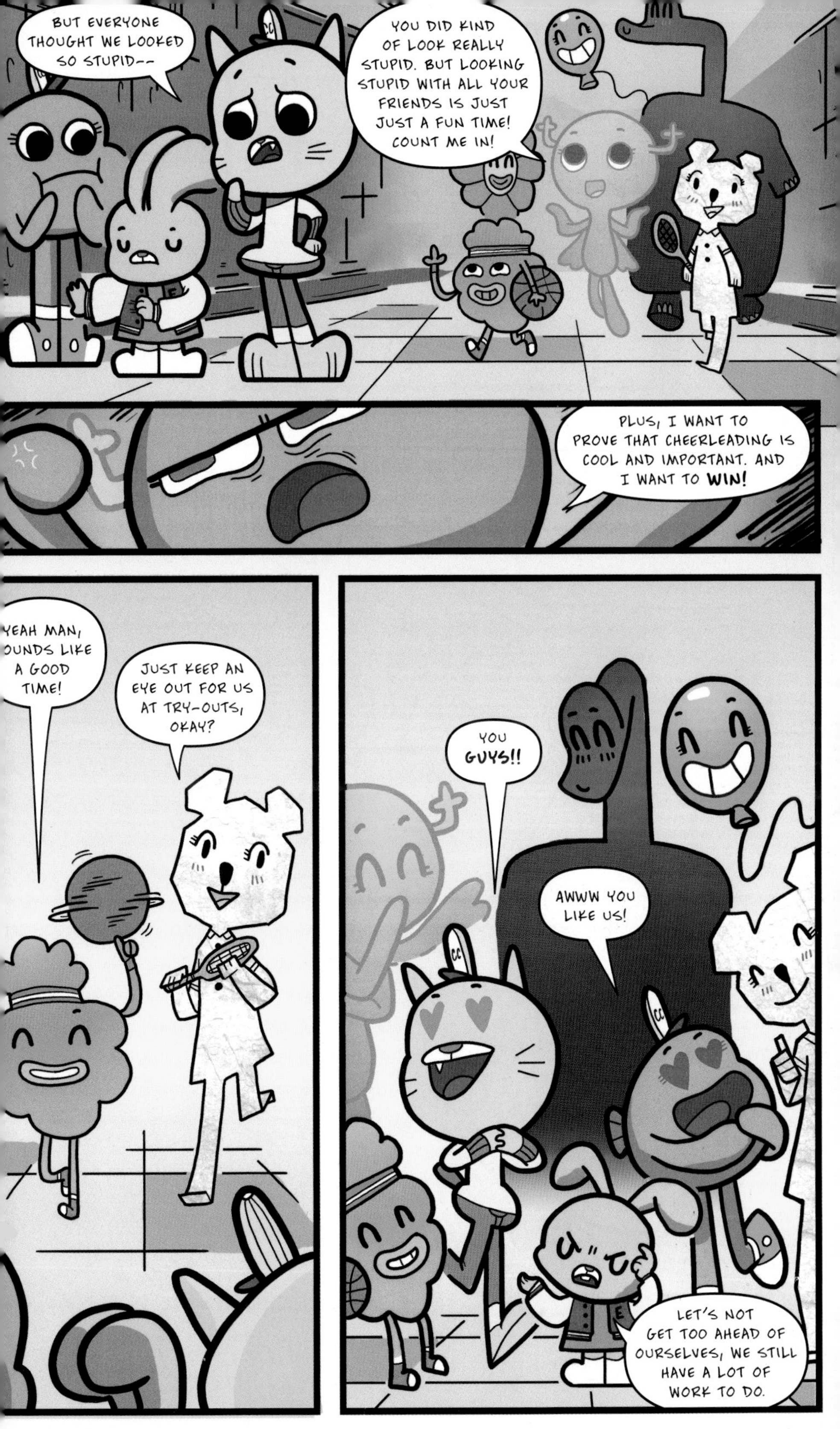

BUT EVERYONE THOUGHT WE LOOKED SO STUPID--
YOU DID KIND OF LOOK REALLY STUPID. BUT LOOKING STUPID WITH ALL YOUR FRIENDS IS JUST JUST A FUN TIME! COUNT ME IN!
PLUS, I WANT TO PROVE THAT CHEERLEADING IS COOL AND IMPORTANT. AND I WANT TO **WIN!**
YEAH MAN, OUNDS LIKE A GOOD TIME!
JUST KEEP AN EYE OUT FOR US AT TRY-OUTS, OKAY?
YOU **GUYS!!**
AWWW YOU LIKE US!
LET'S NOT GET TOO AHEAD OF OURSELVES, WE STILL HAVE A LOT OF WORK TO DO.

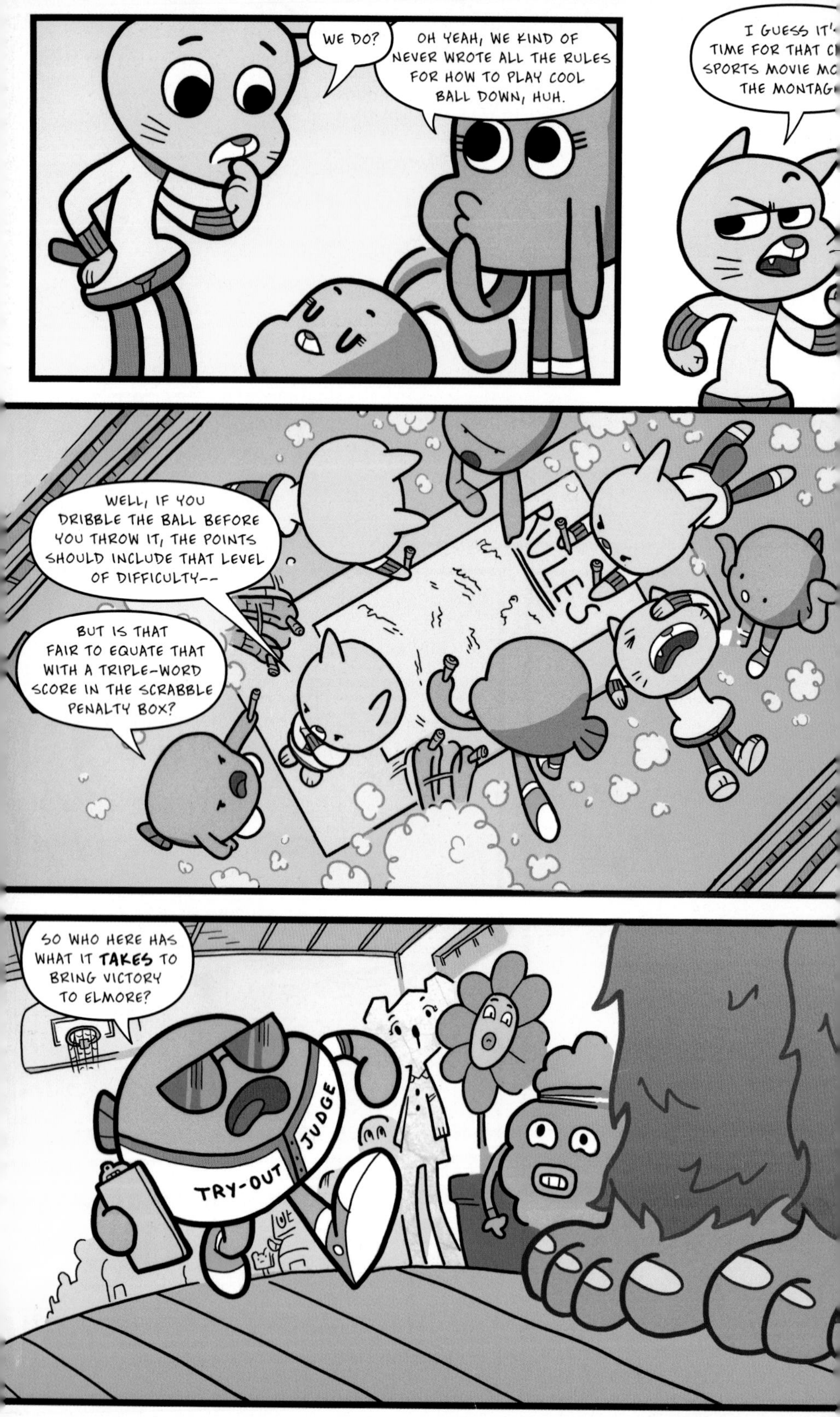
WE DO?
OH YEAH, WE KIND OF NEVER WROTE ALL THE RULES FOR HOW TO PLAY COOL BALL DOWN, HUH.
I GUESS IT'
TIME FOR THAT C
SPORTS MOVIE MO
THE MONTAG
RULES
WELL, IF YOU DRIBBLE THE BALL BEFORE YOU THROW IT, THE POINTS SHOULD INCLUDE THAT LEVEL OF DIFFICULTY--
BUT IS THAT FAIR TO EQUATE THAT WITH A TRIPLE-WORD SCORE IN THE SCRABBLE PENALTY BOX?
SO WHO HERE HAS WHAT IT TAKES TO BRING VICTORY TO ELMORE?
JUDGE
TRY-OUT

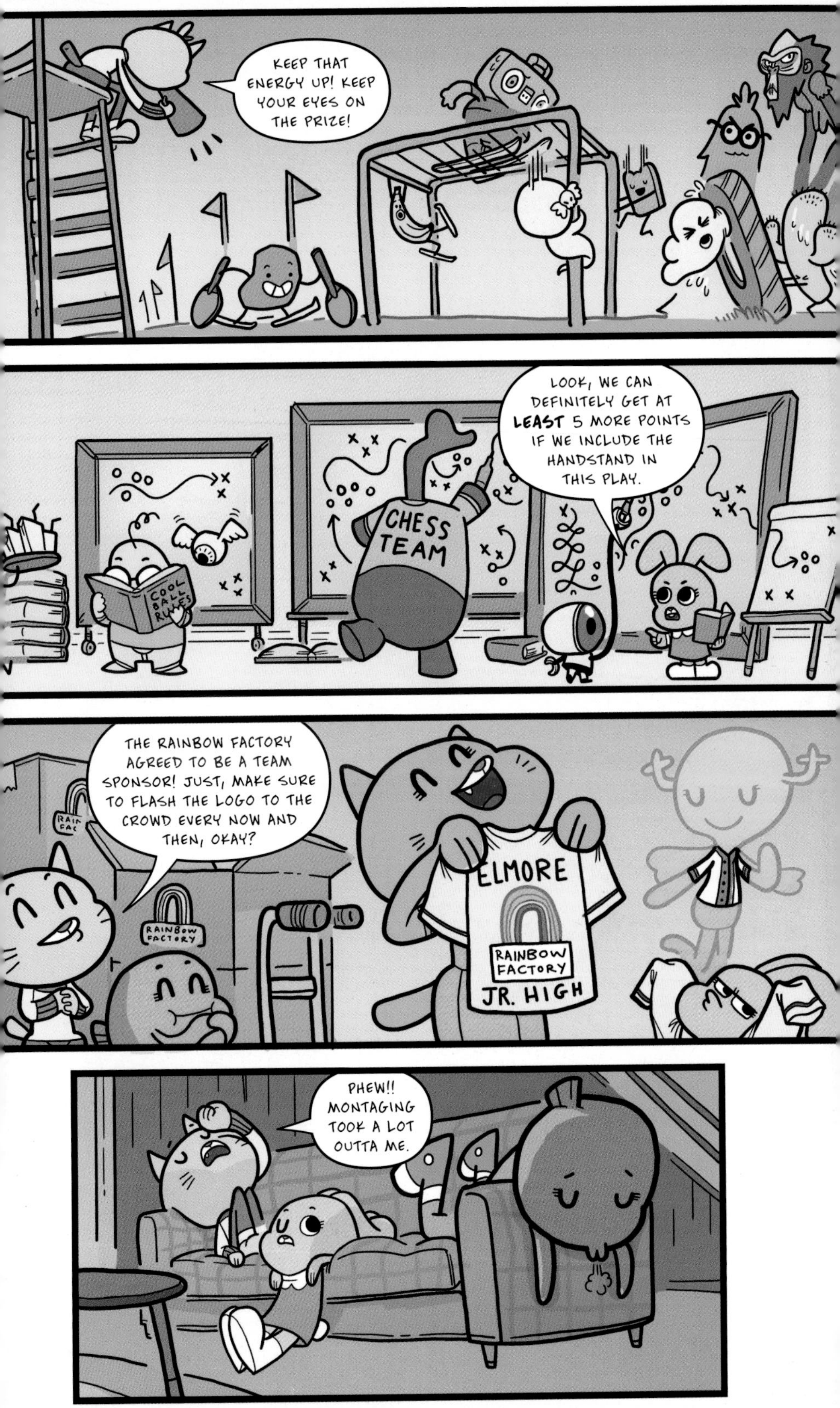
KEEP THAT ENERGY UP! KEEP YOUR EYES ON THE PRIZE!
LOOK, WE CAN DEFINITELY GET AT LEAST 5 MORE POINTS IF WE INCLUDE THE HANDSTAND IN THIS PLAY.
CHESS TEAM
COOL BALL RULES
THE RAINBOW FACTORY AGREED TO BE A TEAM SPONSOR! JUST, MAKE SURE TO FLASH THE LOGO TO THE CROWD EVERY NOW AND THEN, OKAY?
RAINBOW FACTORY
ELMORE
RAINBOW FACTORY
JR. HIGH
PHEW!! MONTAGING TOOK A LOT OUTTA ME.

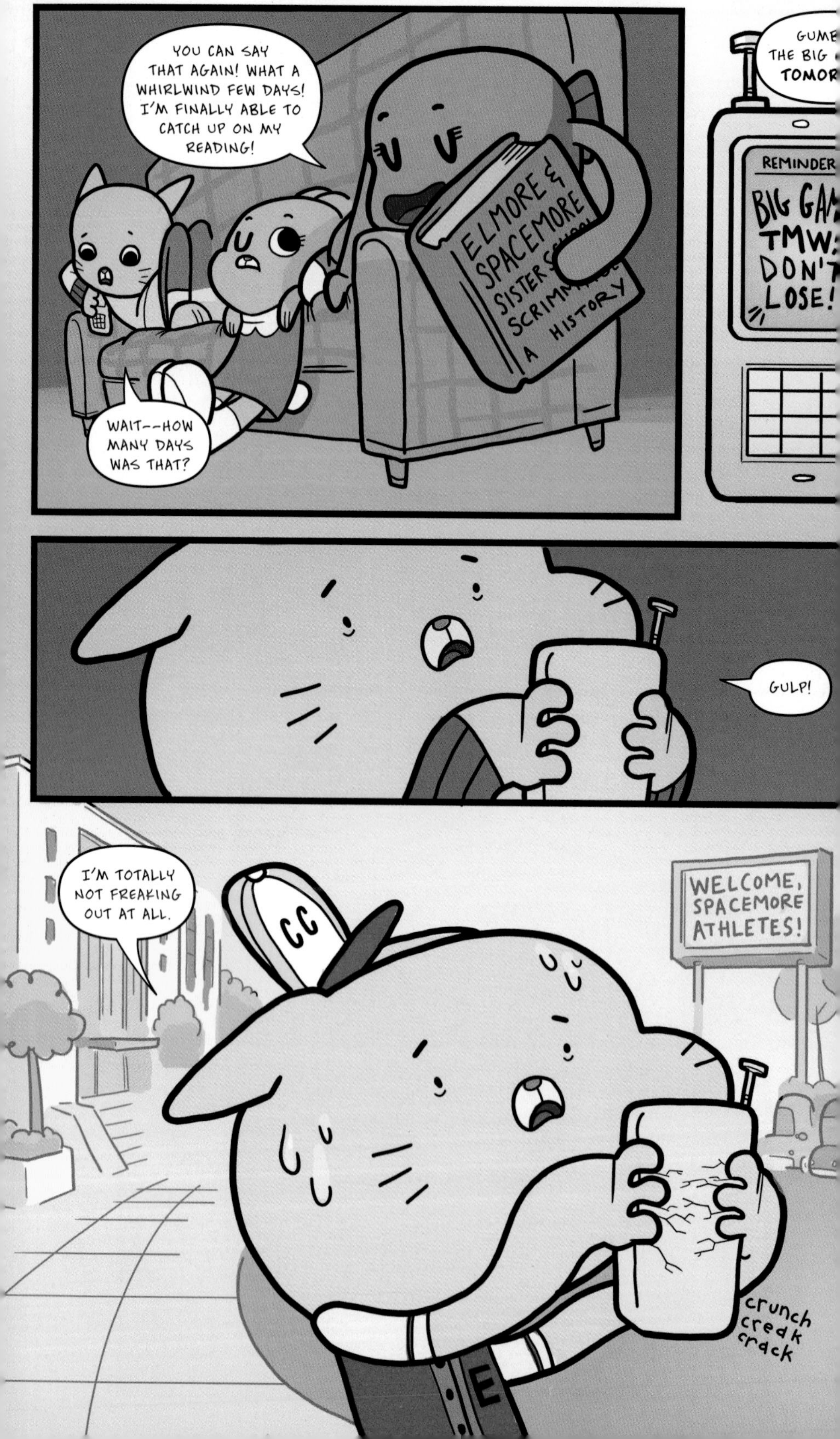
YOU CAN SAY THAT AGAIN! WHAT A WHIRLWIND FEW DAYS! I'M FINALLY ABLE TO CATCH UP ON MY READING!
ELMORE & SPACEMORE SISTER SCHOOL SCRIMMAGE A HISTORY
WAIT--HOW MANY DAYS WAS THAT?
REMINDER
GULP!
I'M TOTALLY NOT FREAKING OUT AT ALL.
CC
WELCOME, SPACEMORE ATHLETES!
crunch
creak
crack

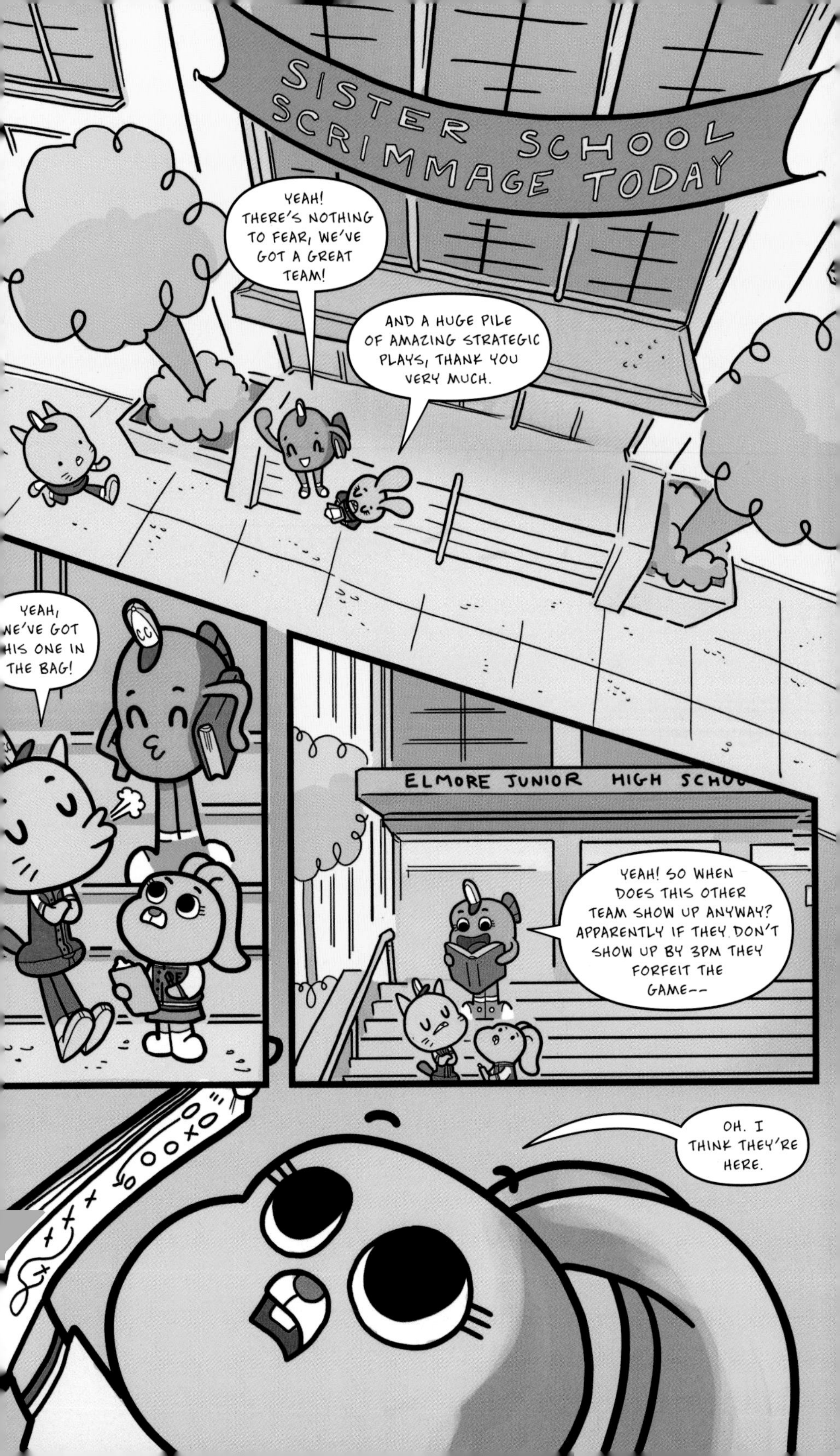
SISTER SCHOOL SCRIMMAGE TODAY
YEAH! THERE'S NOTHING TO FEAR, WE'VE GOT A GREAT TEAM!
AND A HUGE PILE OF AMAZING STRATEGIC PLAYS, THANK YOU VERY MUCH.
YEAH, WE'VE GOT THIS ONE IN THE BAG!
ELMORE JUNIOR HIGH SCHO
YEAH! SO WHEN DOES THIS OTHER TEAM SHOW UP ANYWAY? APPARENTLY IF THEY DON'T SHOW UP BY 3PM THEY FORFEIT THE GAME--
OH. I THINK THEY'RE HERE.

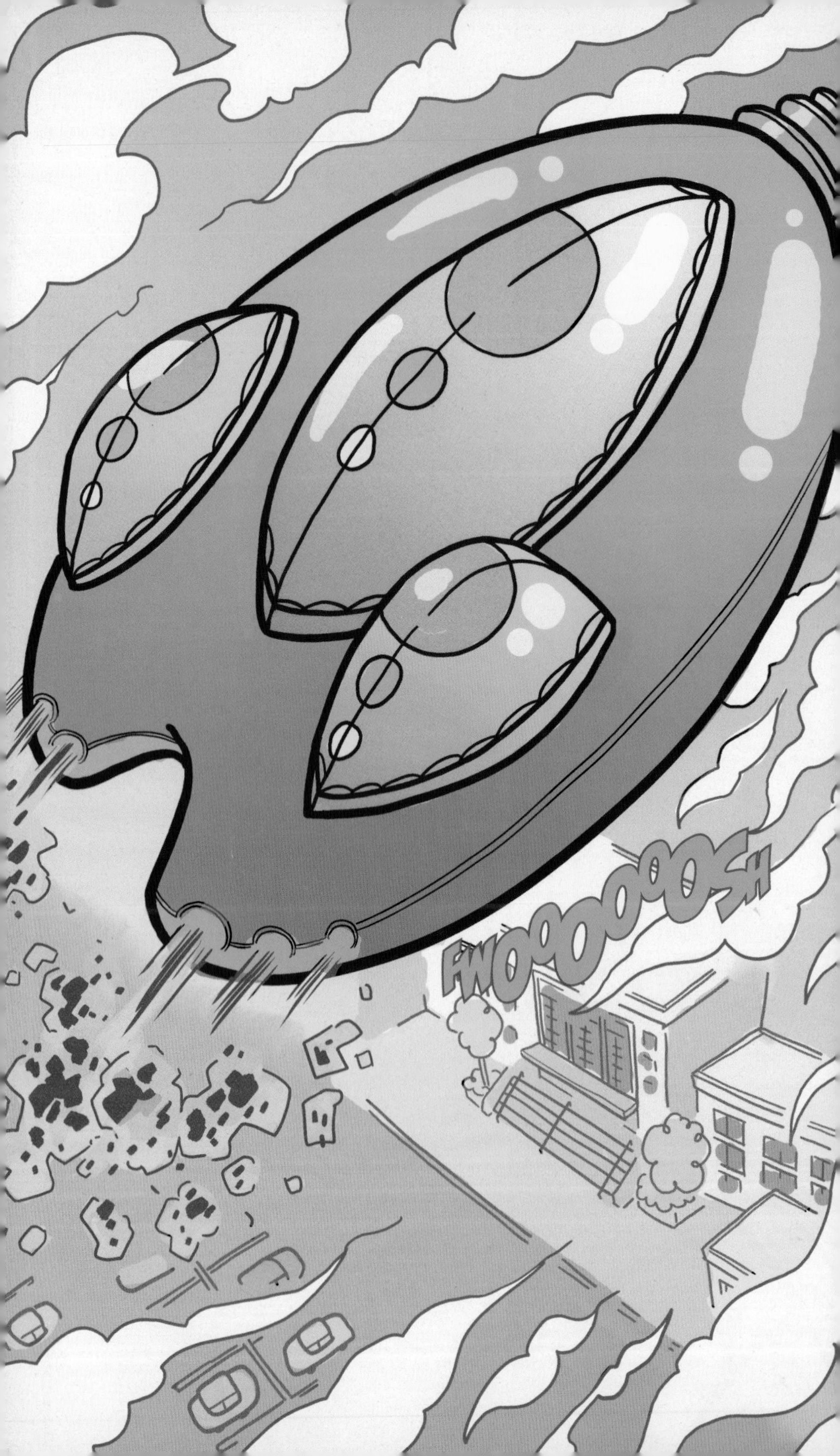
FWOOOOOOOSH

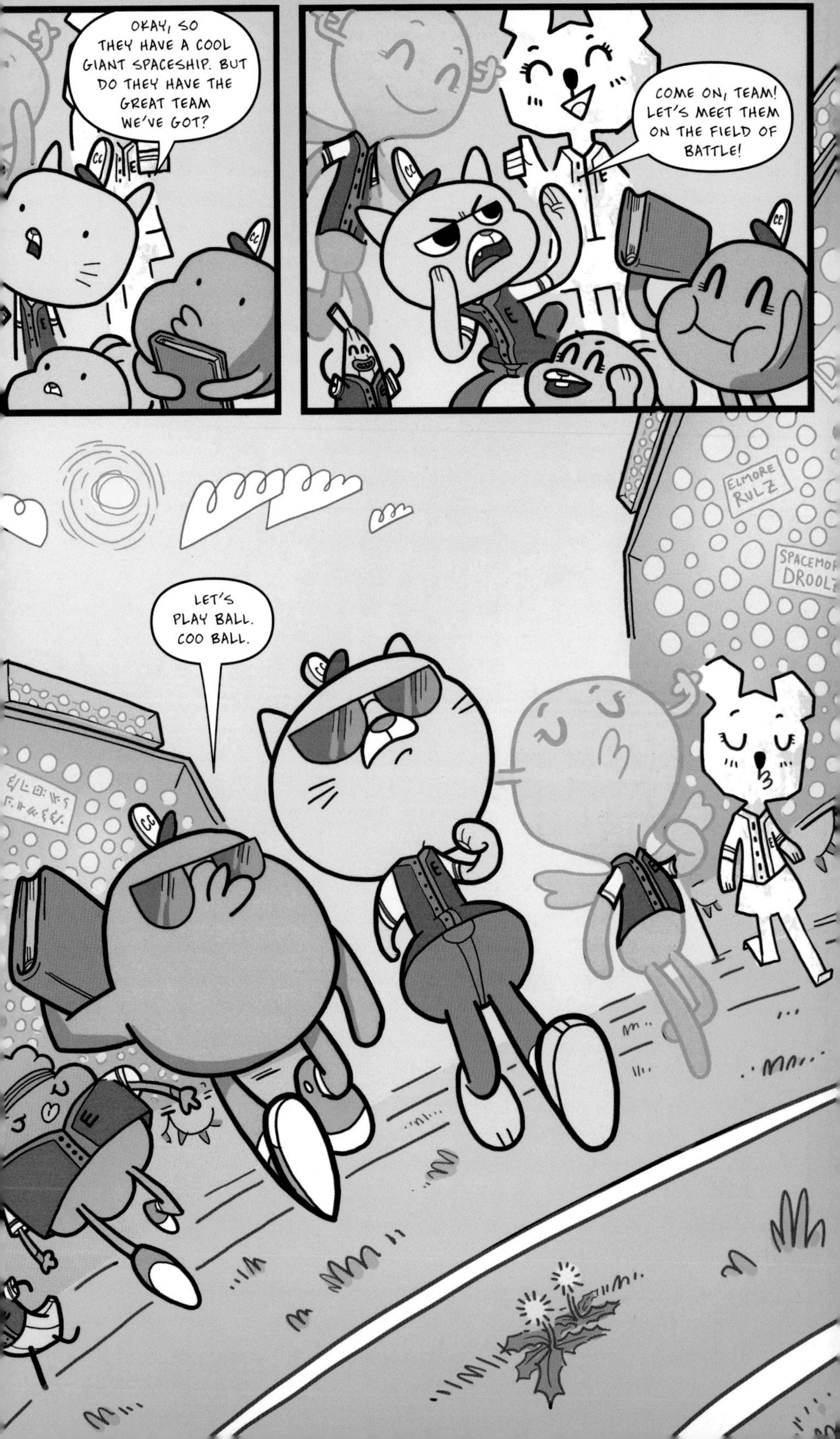
OKAY, SO THEY HAVE A COOL GIANT SPACESHIP. BUT DO THEY HAVE THE GREAT TEAM WE'VE GOT?
COME ON, TEAM! LET'S MEET THEM ON THE FIELD OF BATTLE!
ELMORE RULZ
LET'S PLAY BALL. COO BALL.

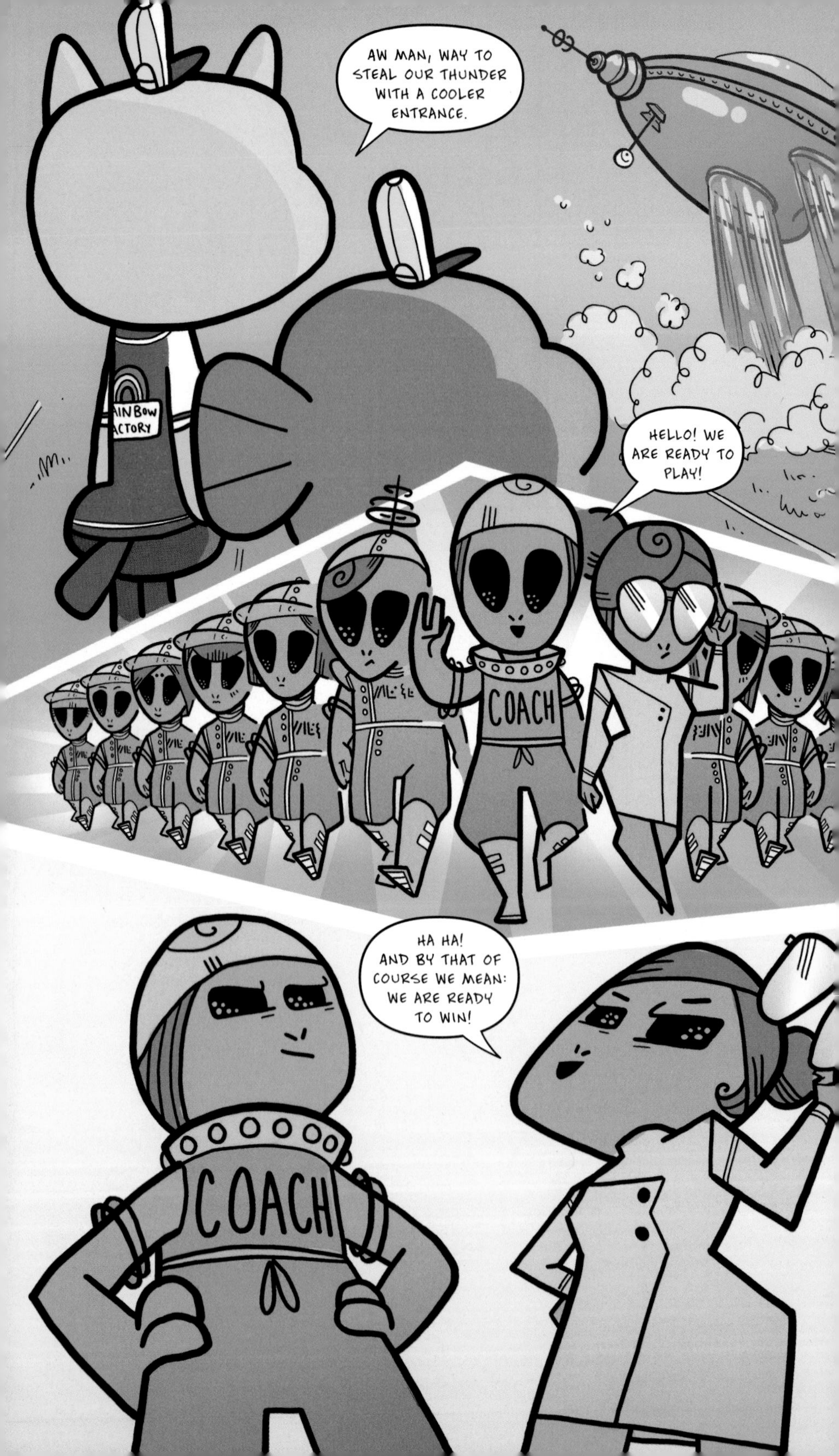
AW MAN, WAY TO STEAL OUR THUNDER WITH A COOLER ENTRANCE.
RAINBOW FACTORY
HELLO! WE ARE READY TO PLAY!
COACH
HA HA! AND BY THAT OF COURSE WE MEAN: WE ARE READY TO WIN!
COACH

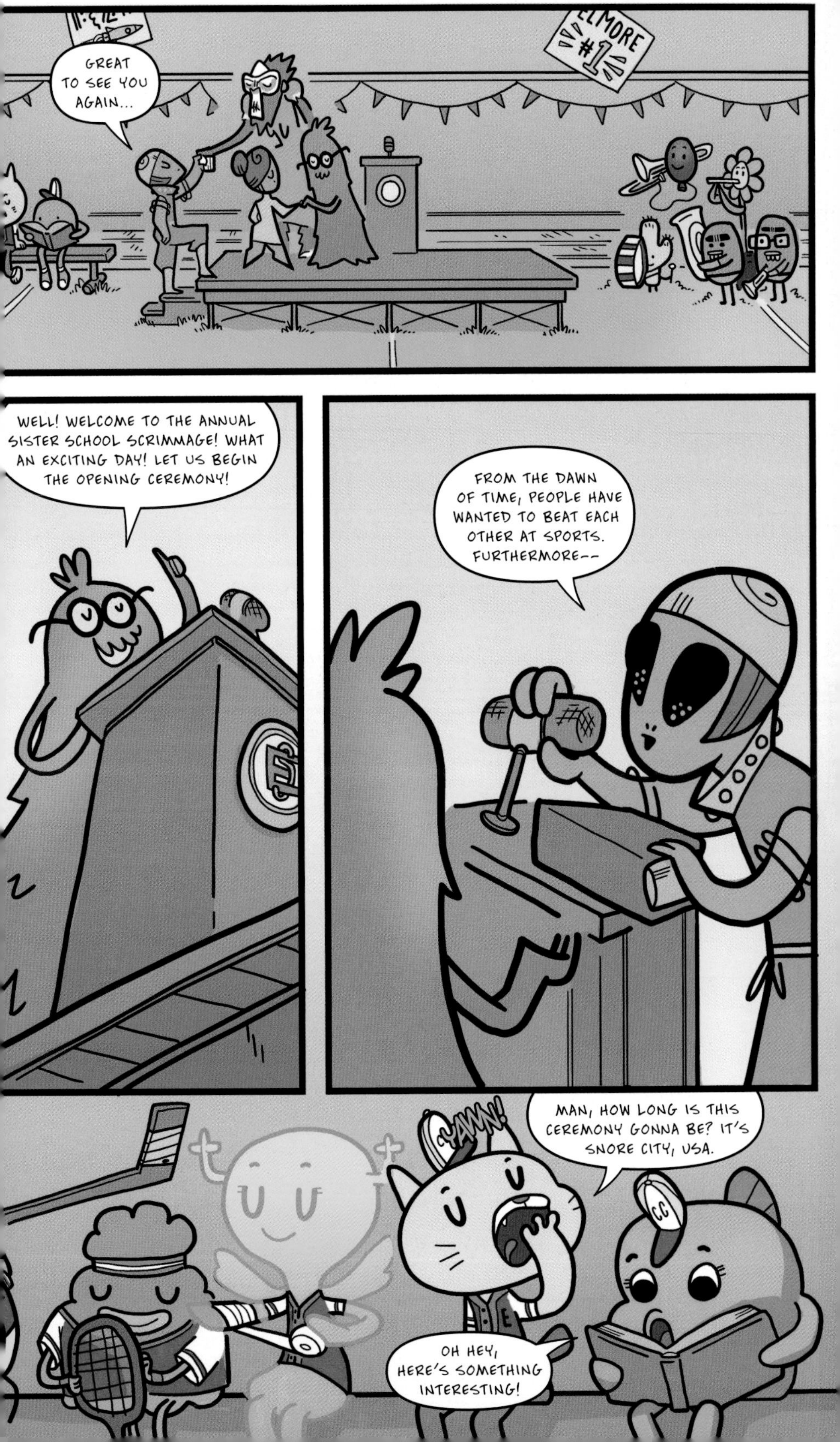
ELMORE #1
GREAT TO SEE YOU AGAIN...
WELL! WELCOME TO THE ANNUAL SISTER SCHOOL SCRIMMAGE! WHAT AN EXCITING DAY! LET US BEGIN THE OPENING CEREMONY!
FROM THE DAWN OF TIME, PEOPLE HAVE WANTED TO BEAT EACH OTHER AT SPORTS. FURTHERMORE--
YAWN!
MAN, HOW LONG IS THIS CEREMONY GONNA BE? IT'S SNORE CITY, USA.
OH HEY, HERE'S SOMETHING INTERESTING!

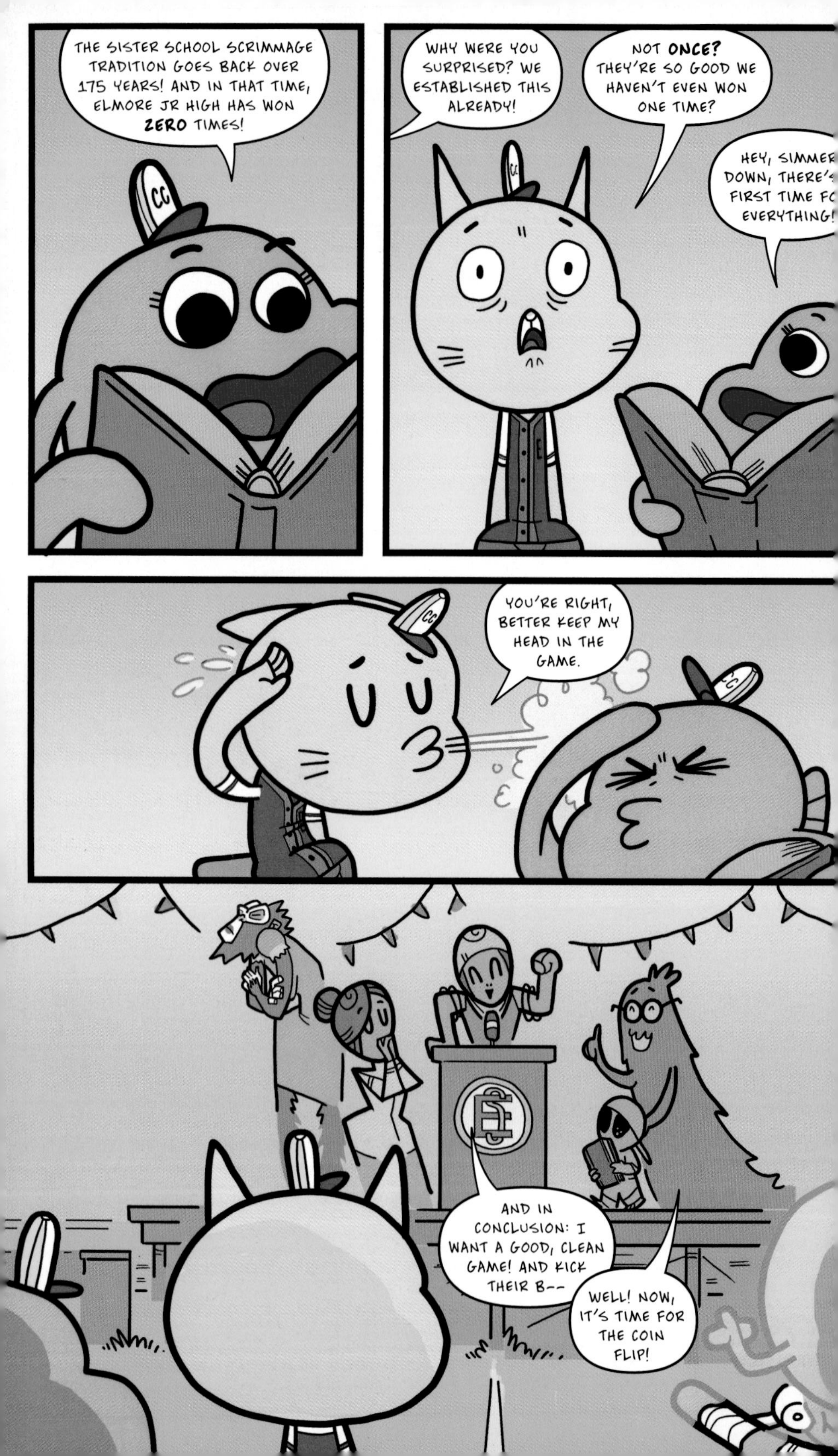
THE SISTER SCHOOL SCRIMMAGE TRADITION GOES BACK OVER 175 YEARS! AND IN THAT TIME, ELMORE JR HIGH HAS WON **ZERO** TIMES!
WHY WERE YOU SURPRISED? WE ESTABLISHED THIS ALREADY!
NOT **ONCE?** THEY'RE SO GOOD WE HAVEN'T EVEN WON ONE TIME?
HEY, SIMMER DOWN, THERE'S FIRST TIME FO EVERYTHING!
YOU'RE RIGHT, BETTER KEEP MY HEAD IN THE GAME.
AND IN CONCLUSION: I WANT A GOOD, CLEAN GAME! AND KICK THEIR B--
WELL! NOW, IT'S TIME FOR THE COIN FLIP!

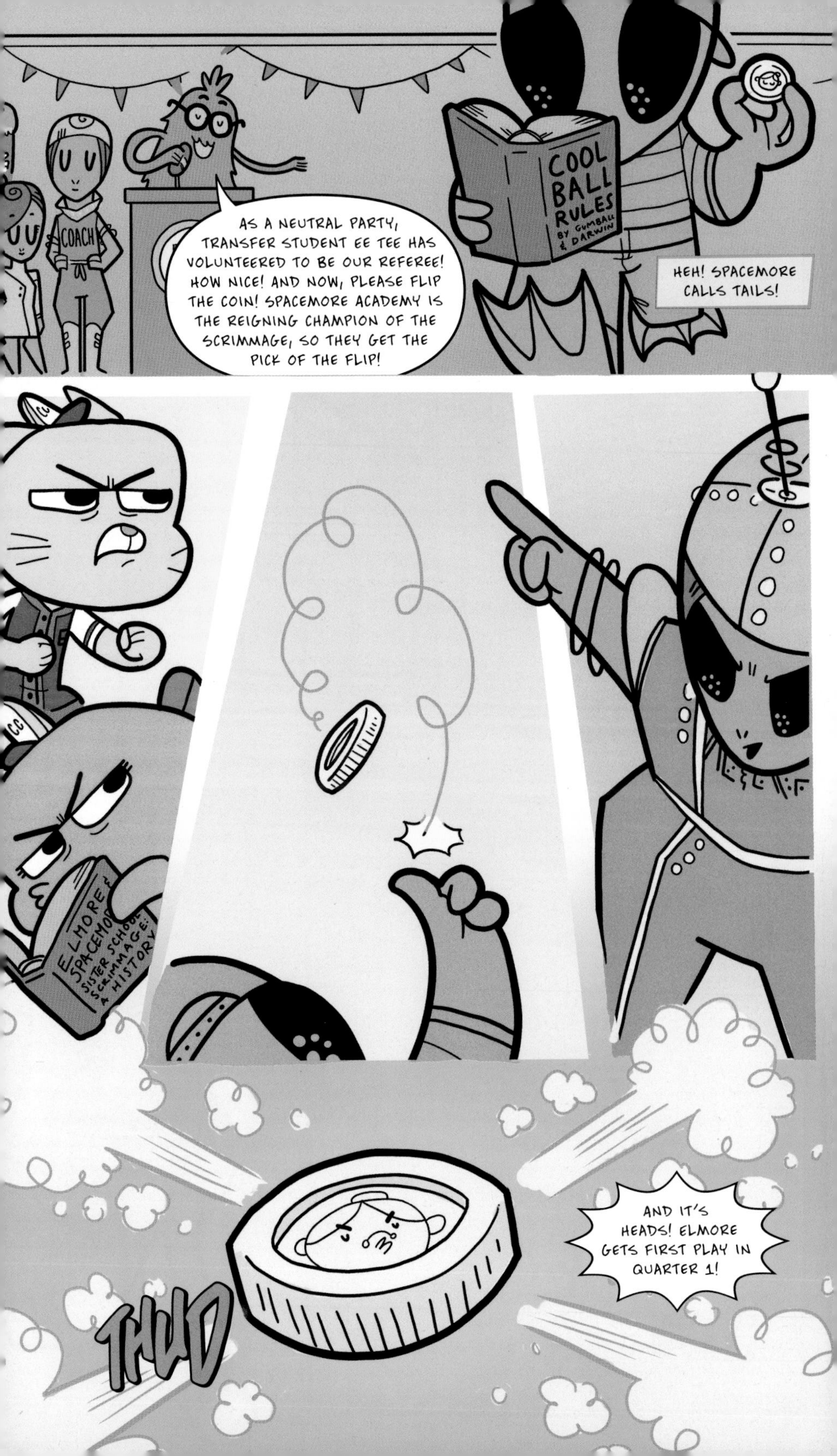
COACH
AS A NEUTRAL PARTY, TRANSFER STUDENT EE TEE HAS VOLUNTEERED TO BE OUR REFEREE! HOW NICE! AND NOW, PLEASE FLIP THE COIN! SPACEMORE ACADEMY IS THE REIGNING CHAMPION OF THE SCRIMMAGE, SO THEY GET THE PICK OF THE FLIP!
COOL BALL RULES BY GUMBALL & DARWIN
HEH! SPACEMORE CALLS TAILS!
ELMORE & SPACEMORE SISTER SCHOOL SCRIMMAGE: A HISTORY
AND IT'S HEADS! ELMORE GETS FIRST PLAY IN QUARTER 1!
THUD

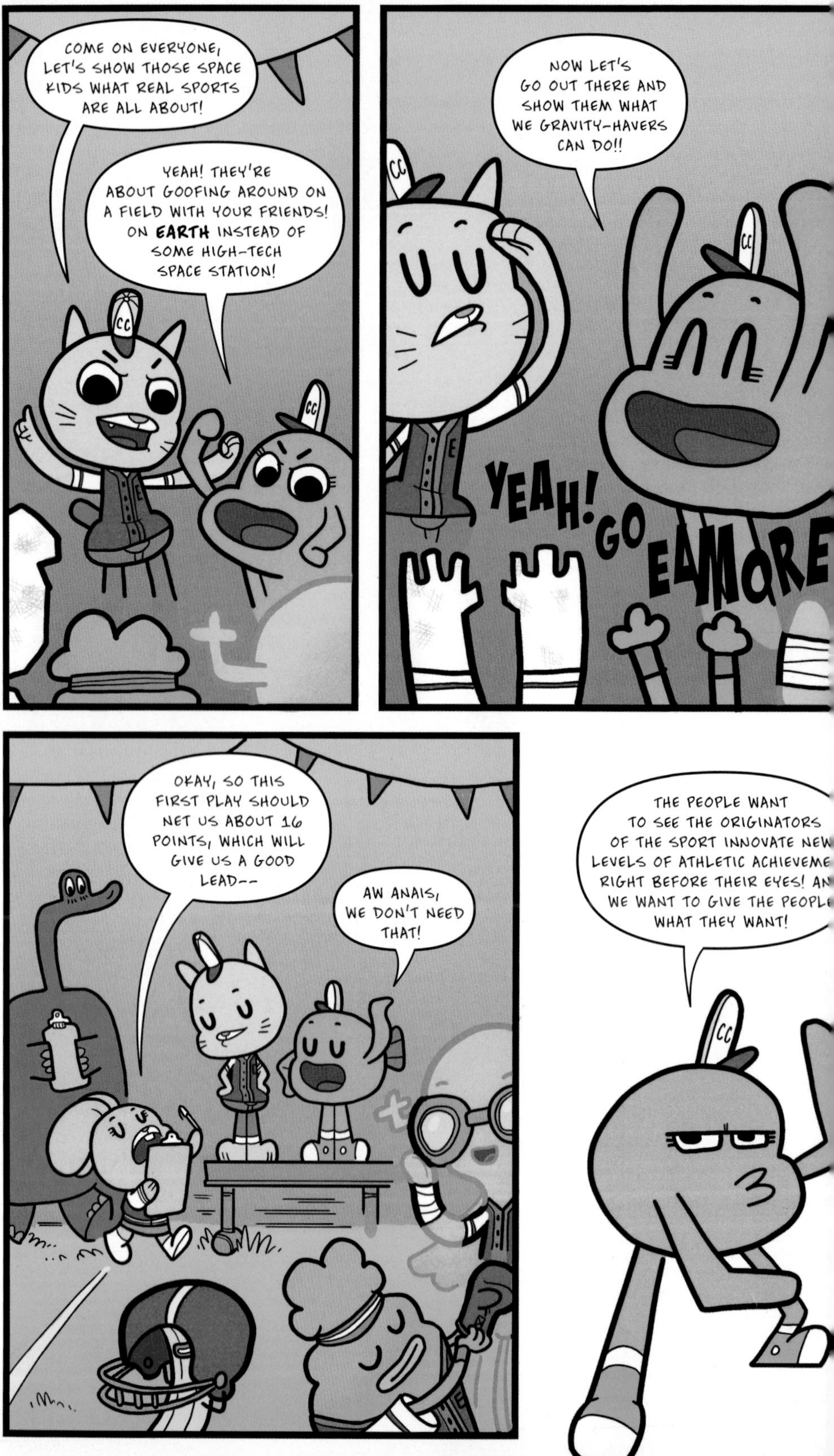
COME ON EVERYONE, LET'S SHOW THOSE SPACE KIDS WHAT REAL SPORTS ARE ALL ABOUT!
YEAH! THEY'RE ABOUT GOOFING AROUND ON A FIELD WITH YOUR FRIENDS! ON **EARTH** INSTEAD OF SOME HIGH-TECH SPACE STATION!
NOW LET'S GO OUT THERE AND SHOW THEM WHAT WE GRAVITY-HAVERS CAN DO!!
YEAH!
GO
ELMORE
OKAY, SO THIS FIRST PLAY SHOULD NET US ABOUT 16 POINTS, WHICH WILL GIVE US A GOOD LEAD--
AW ANAIS, WE DON'T NEED THAT!
THE PEOPLE WANT TO SEE THE ORIGINATORS OF THE SPORT INNOVATE NEW LEVELS OF ATHLETIC ACHIEVEME RIGHT BEFORE THEIR EYES! AN WE WANT TO GIVE THE PEOPL WHAT THEY WANT!

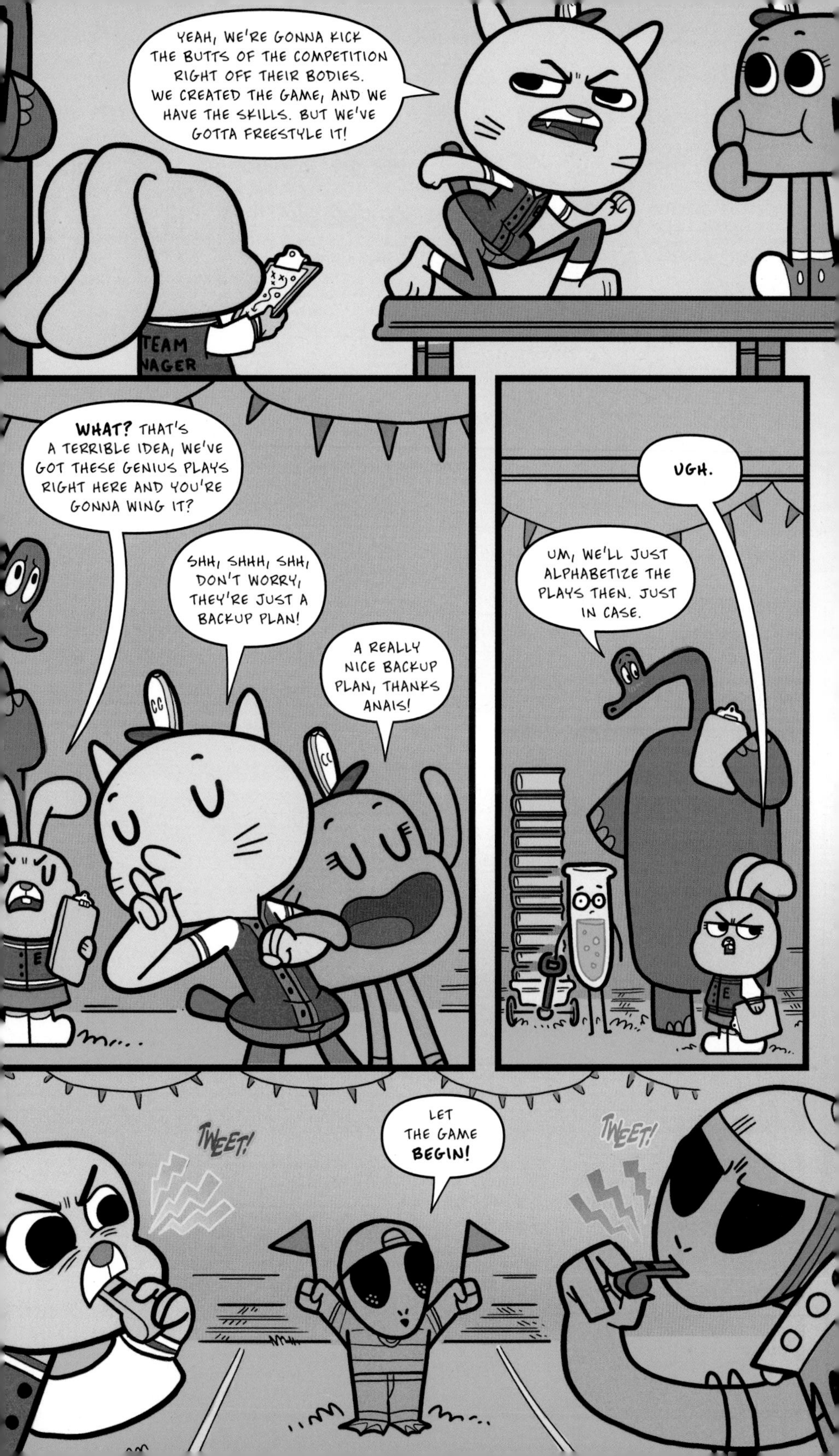
YEAH, WE'RE GONNA KICK THE BUTTS OF THE COMPETITION RIGHT OFF THEIR BODIES. WE CREATED THE GAME, AND WE HAVE THE SKILLS. BUT WE'VE GOTTA FREESTYLE IT!
TEAM
NAGER
WHAT? THAT'S A TERRIBLE IDEA, WE'VE GOT THESE GENIUS PLAYS RIGHT HERE AND YOU'RE GONNA WING IT?
SHH, SHHH, SHH, DON'T WORRY, THEY'RE JUST A BACKUP PLAN!
A REALLY NICE BACKUP PLAN, THANKS ANAIS!
UGH.
UM, WE'LL JUST ALPHABETIZE THE PLAYS THEN. JUST IN CASE.
TWEET!
LET THE GAME BEGIN!
TWEET!

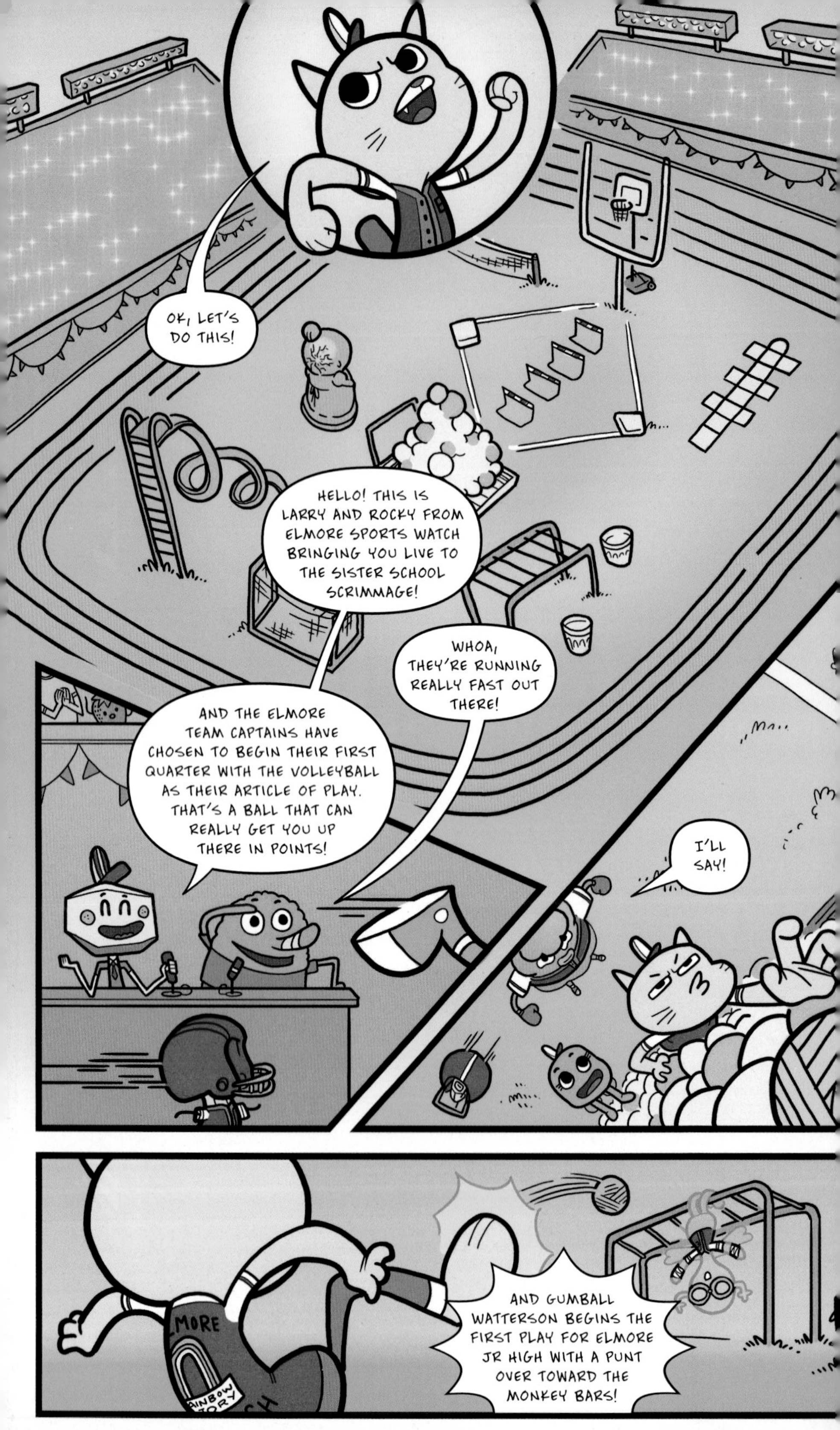
OK, LET'S DO THIS!
HELLO! THIS IS LARRY AND ROCKY FROM ELMORE SPORTS WATCH BRINGING YOU LIVE TO THE SISTER SCHOOL SCRIMMAGE!
AND THE ELMORE TEAM CAPTAINS HAVE CHOSEN TO BEGIN THEIR FIRST QUARTER WITH THE VOLLEYBALL AS THEIR ARTICLE OF PLAY. THAT'S A BALL THAT CAN REALLY GET YOU UP THERE IN POINTS!
WHOA, THEY'RE RUNNING REALLY FAST OUT THERE!
I'LL SAY!
AND GUMBALL WATTERSON BEGINS THE FIRST PLAY FOR ELMORE JR HIGH WITH A PUNT OVER TOWARD THE MONKEY BARS!

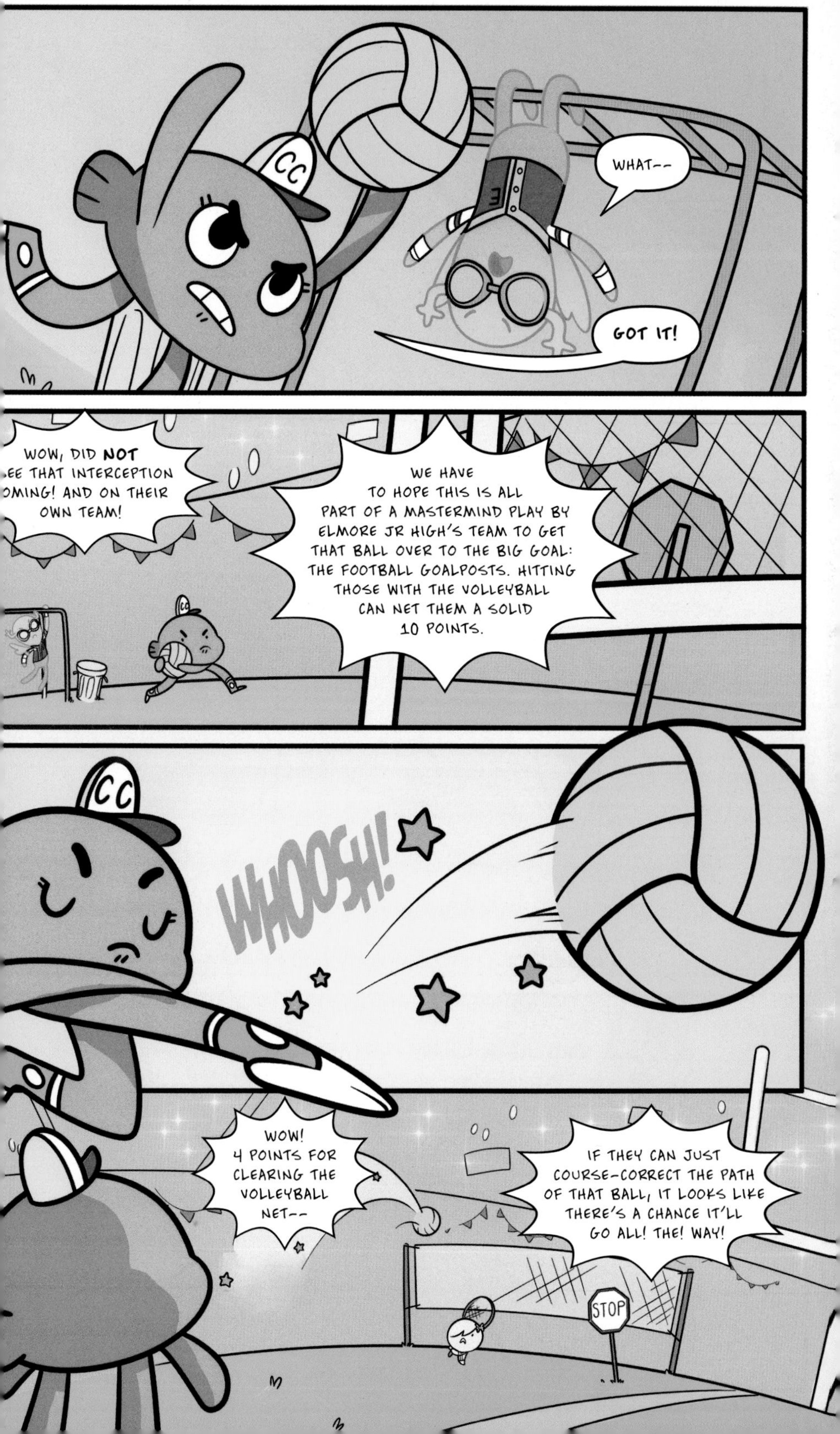
WHAT--
GOT IT!
WOW, DID **NOT** SEE THAT INTERCEPTION COMING! AND ON THEIR OWN TEAM!
WE HAVE TO HOPE THIS IS ALL PART OF A MASTERMIND PLAY BY ELMORE JR HIGH'S TEAM TO GET THAT BALL OVER TO THE BIG GOAL: THE FOOTBALL GOALPOSTS. HITTING THOSE WITH THE VOLLEYBALL CAN NET THEM A SOLID 10 POINTS.
CC
WHOOSH!
WOW! 4 POINTS FOR CLEARING THE VOLLEYBALL NET--
IF THEY CAN JUST COURSE-CORRECT THE PATH OF THAT BALL, IT LOOKS LIKE THERE'S A CHANCE IT'LL GO ALL! THE! WAY!
STOP

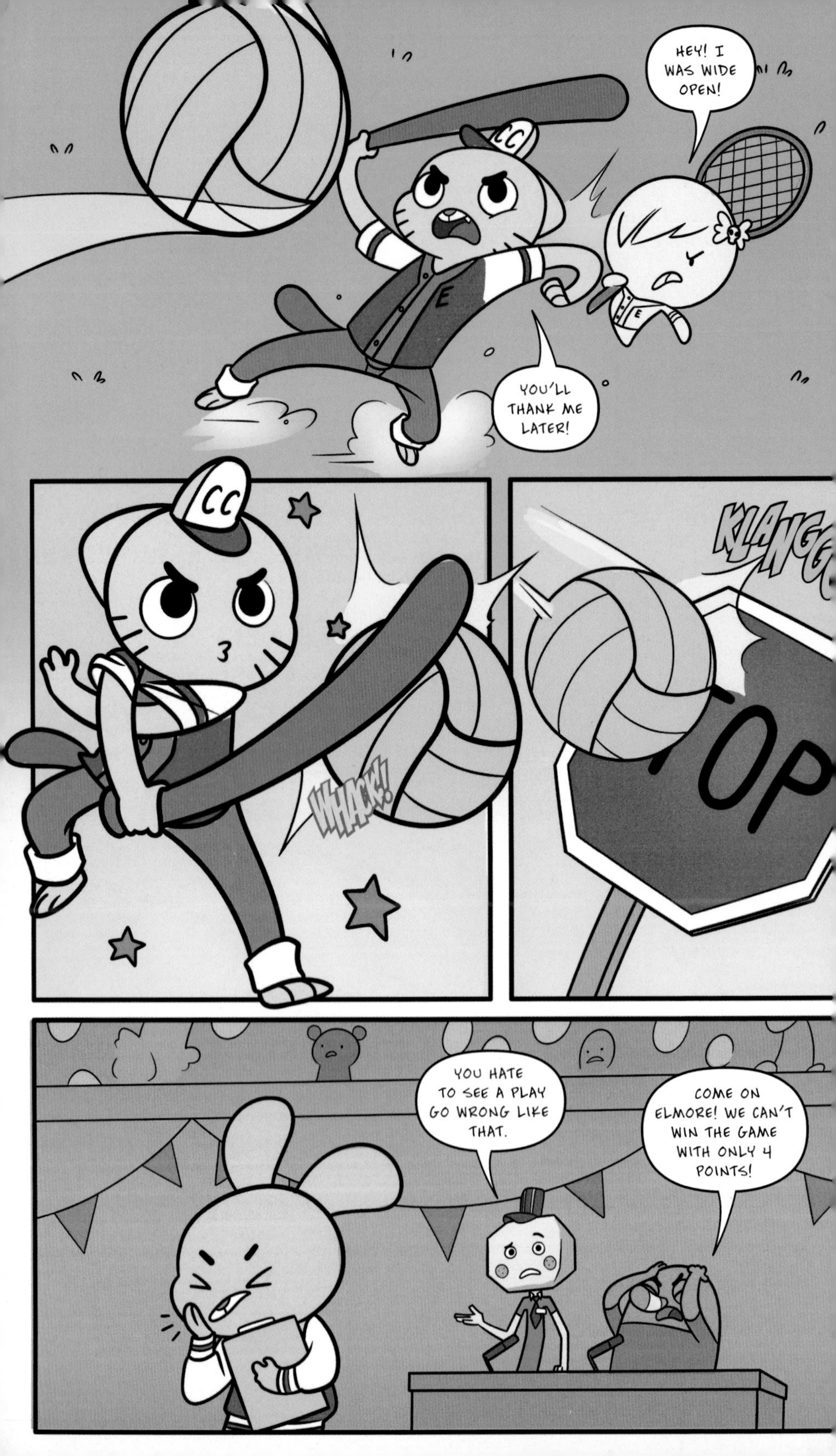
HEY! I WAS WIDE OPEN!
YOU'LL THANK ME LATER!
WHACK!
KLANGG
OP
YOU HATE TO SEE A PLAY GO WRONG LIKE THAT.
COME ON ELMORE! WE CAN'T WIN THE GAME WITH ONLY 4 POINTS!

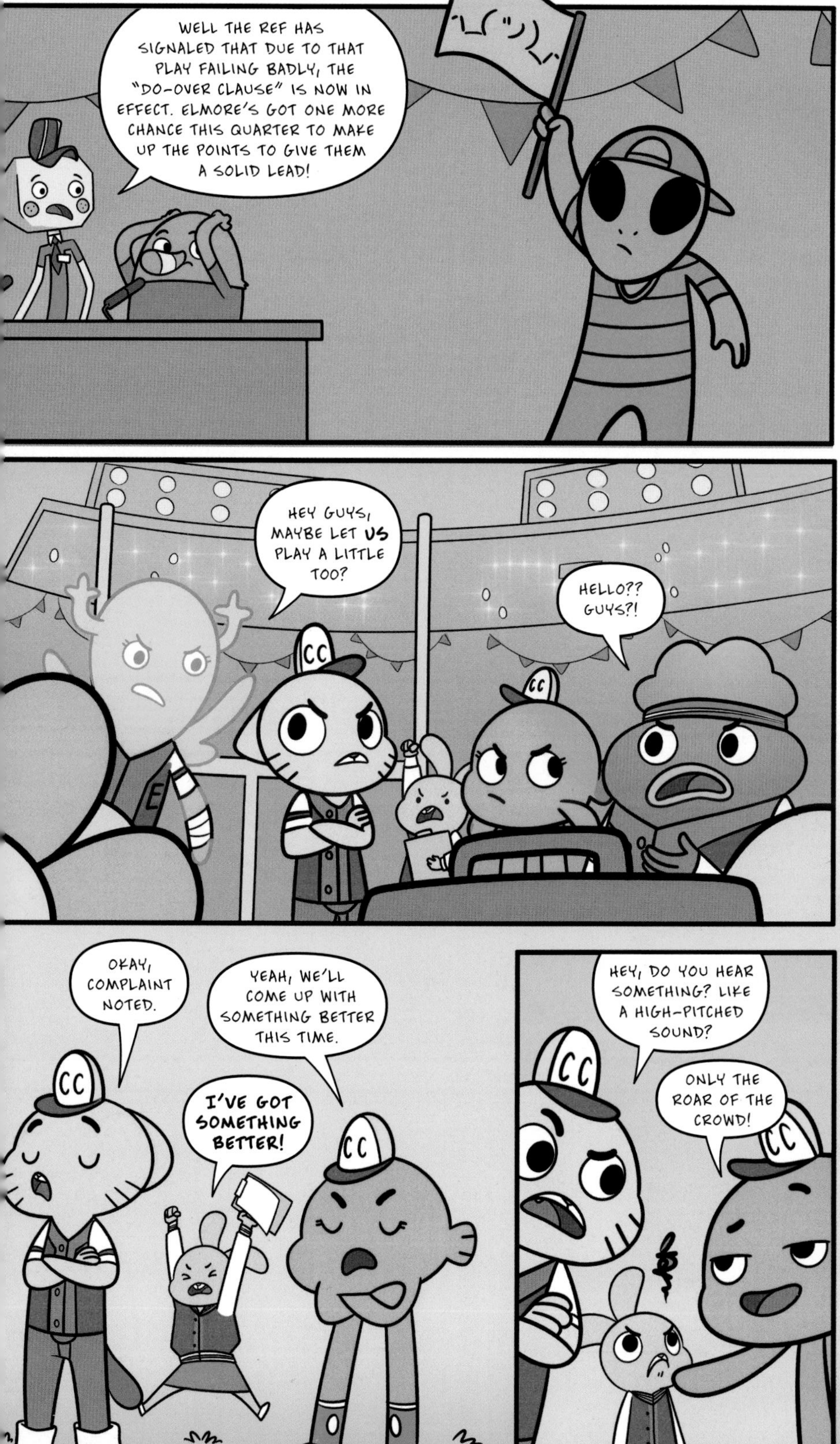
WELL THE REF HAS SIGNALED THAT DUE TO THAT PLAY FAILING BADLY, THE "DO-OVER CLAUSE" IS NOW IN EFFECT. ELMORE'S GOT ONE MORE CHANCE THIS QUARTER TO MAKE UP THE POINTS TO GIVE THEM A SOLID LEAD!
HEY GUYS, MAYBE LET **US** PLAY A LITTLE TOO?
HELLO?? GUYS?!
OKAY, COMPLAINT NOTED.
YEAH, WE'LL COME UP WITH SOMETHING BETTER THIS TIME.
I'VE GOT SOMETHING BETTER!
HEY, DO YOU HEAR SOMETHING? LIKE A HIGH-PITCHED SOUND?
ONLY THE ROAR OF THE CROWD!

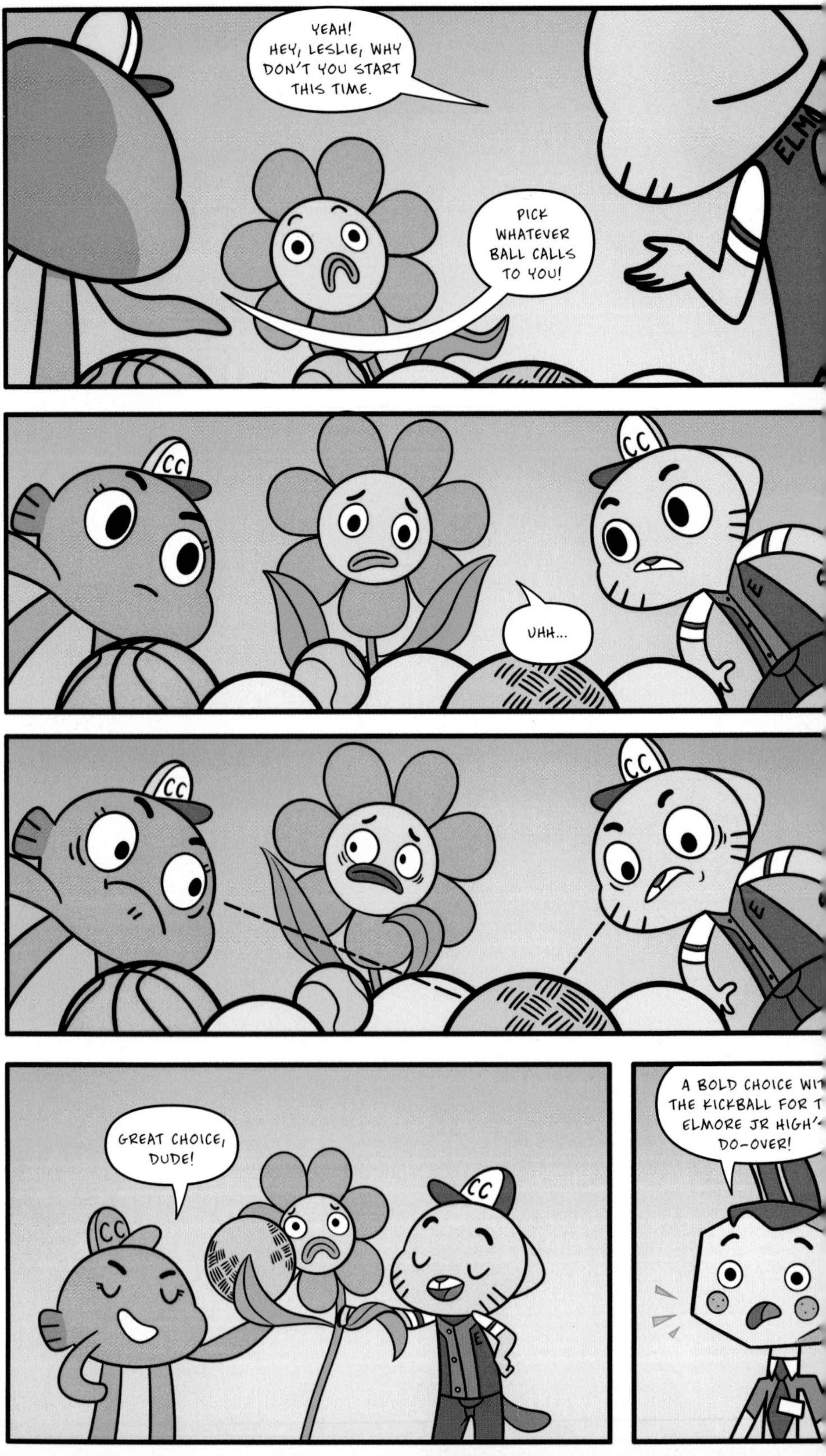
YEAH!
HEY, LESLIE, WHY DON'T YOU START THIS TIME.
PICK WHATEVER BALL CALLS TO YOU!
UHH...
GREAT CHOICE, DUDE!
A BOLD CHOICE WI
THE KICKBALL FOR T
ELMORE JR HIGH'
DO-OVER!

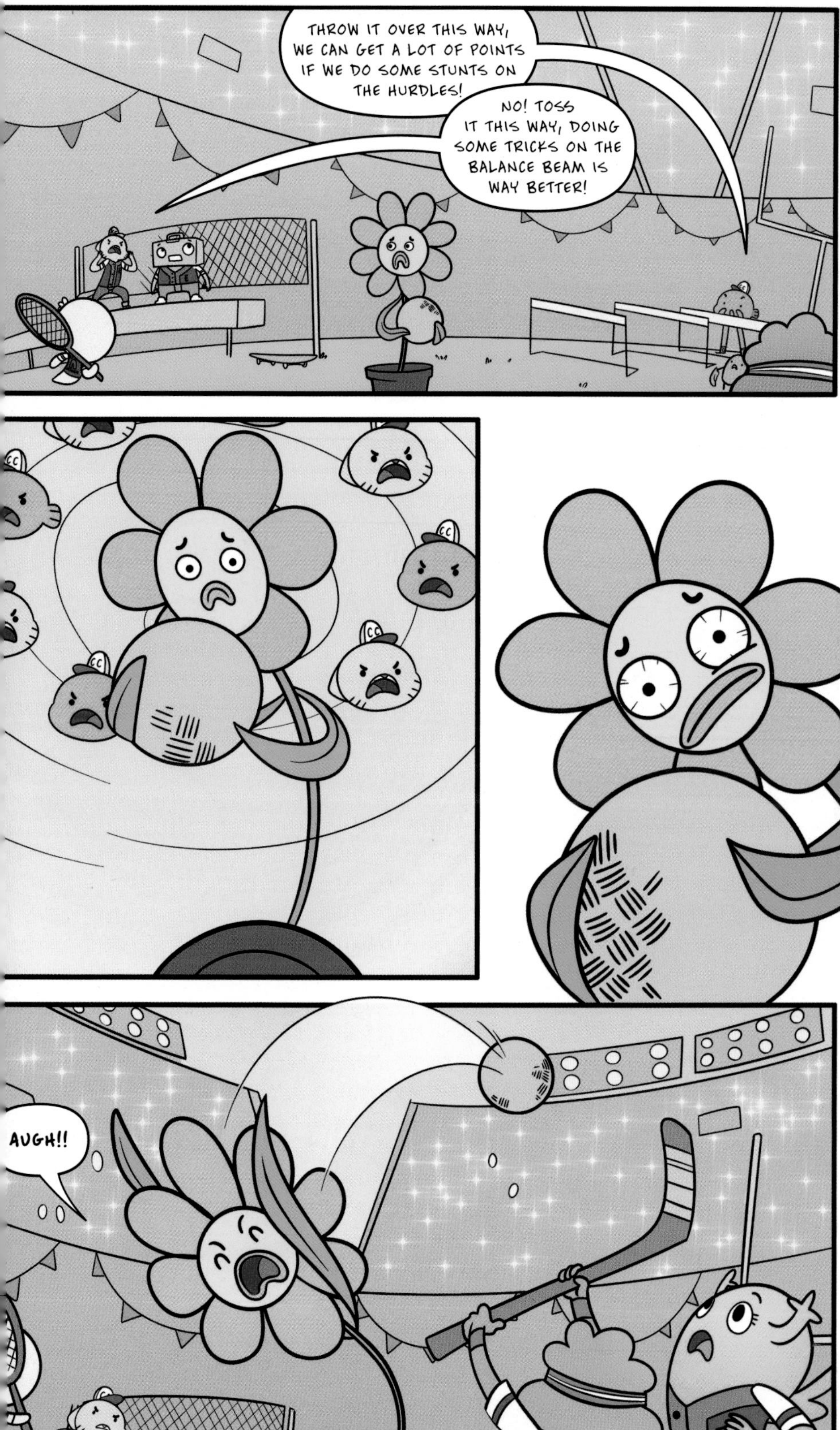
THROW IT OVER THIS WAY, WE CAN GET A LOT OF POINTS IF WE DO SOME STUNTS ON THE HURDLES!
NO! TOSS IT THIS WAY, DOING SOME TRICKS ON THE BALANCE BEAM IS WAY BETTER!
AUGH!!

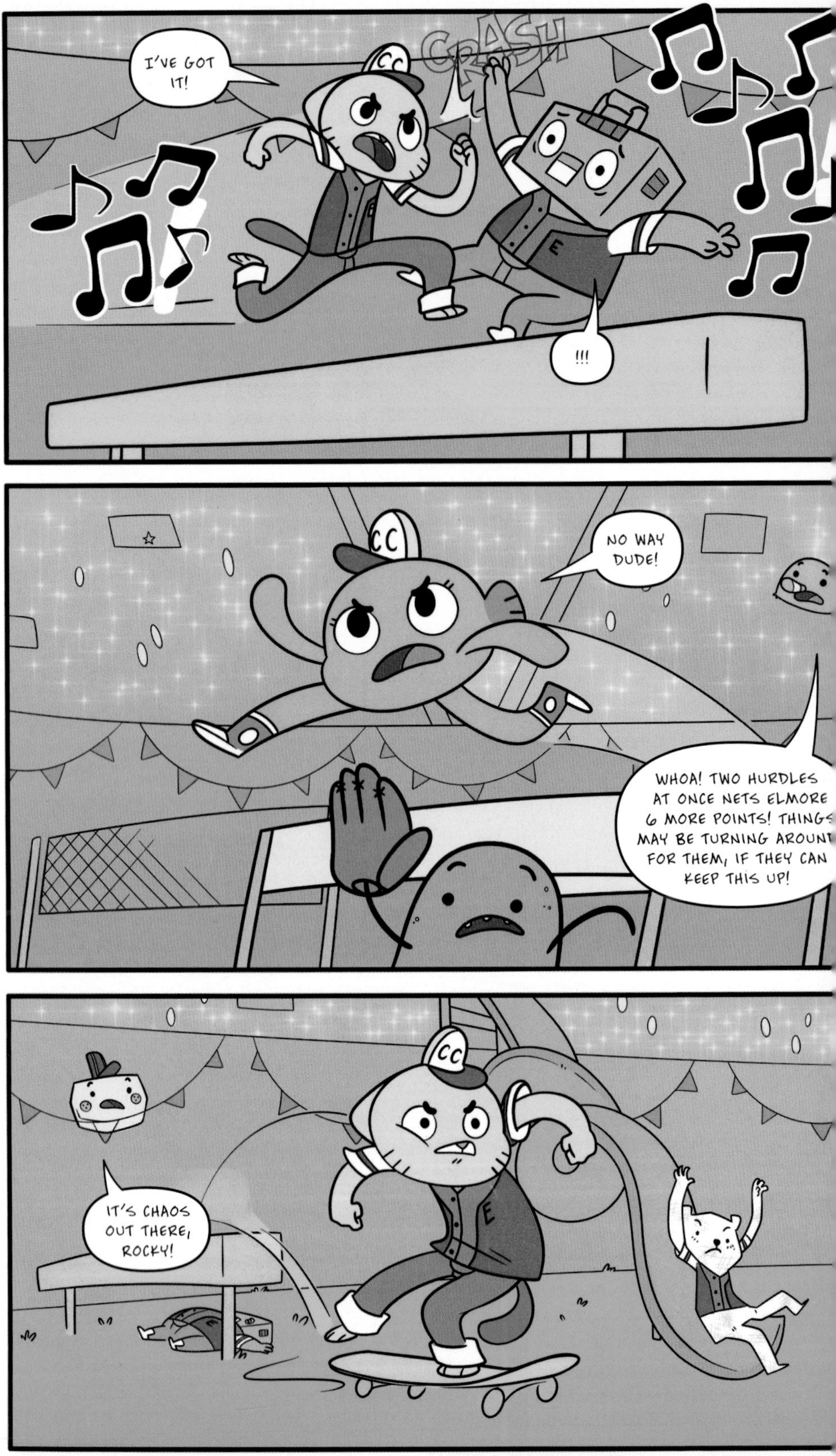
I'VE GOT IT!
CRASH
!!!
NO WAY DUDE!
WHOA! TWO HURDLES AT ONCE NETS ELMORE 6 MORE POINTS! THINGS MAY BE TURNING AROUND FOR THEM, IF THEY CAN KEEP THIS UP!
IT'S CHAOS OUT THERE, ROCKY!

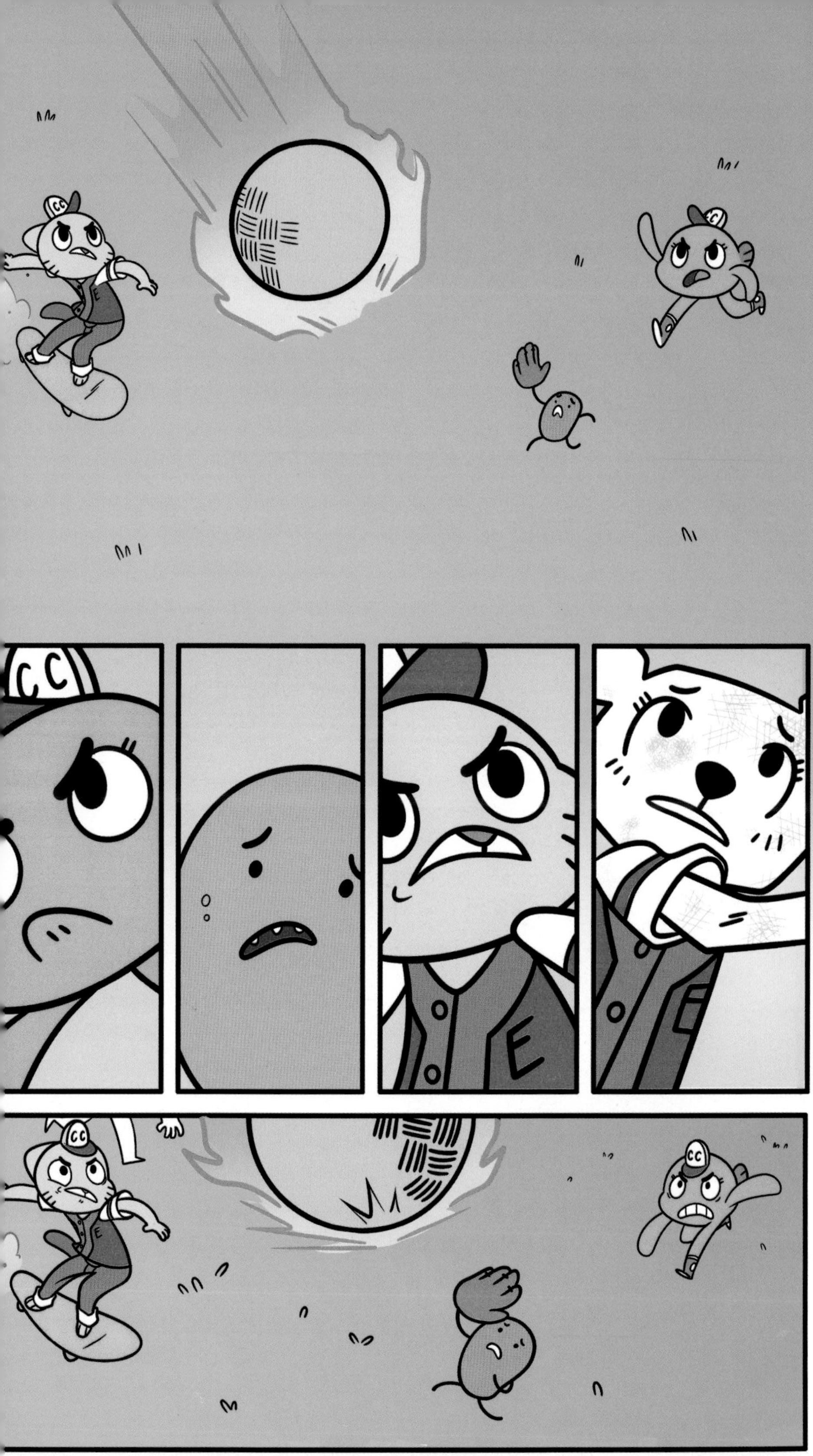

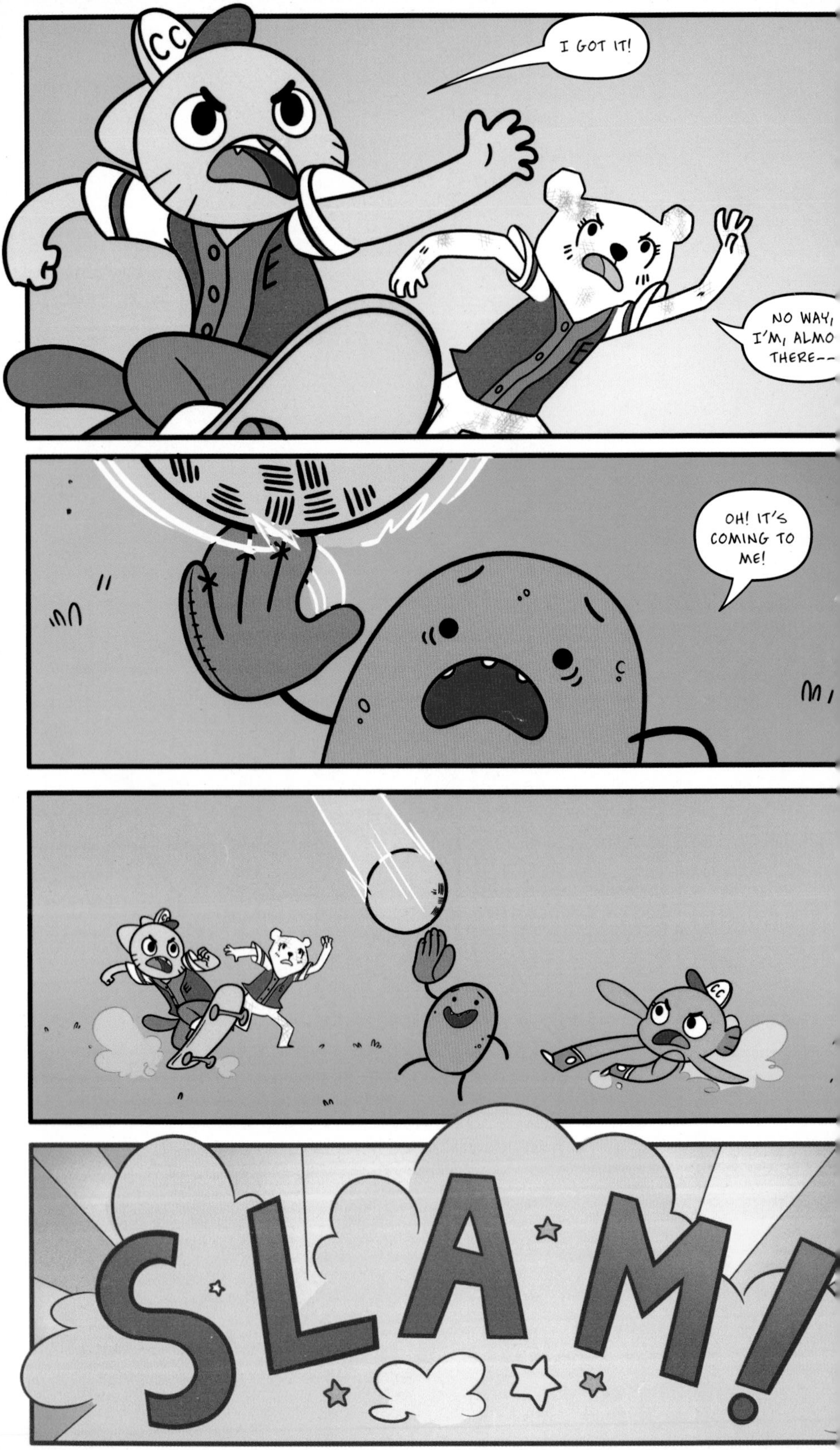
I GOT IT!
NO WAY, I'M, ALMO THERE--
OH! IT'S COMING TO ME!
SLAM!

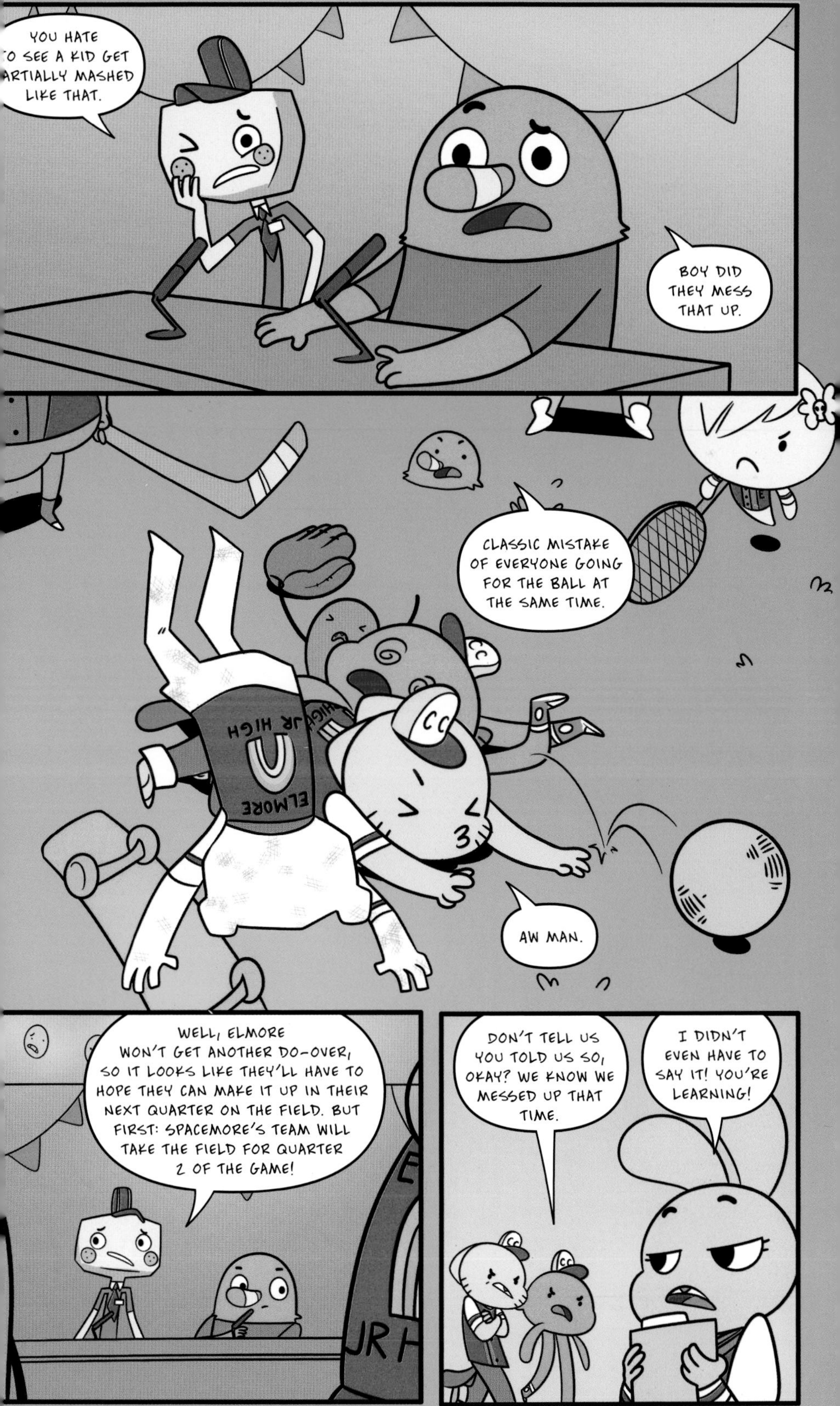
YOU HATE O SEE A KID GET ARTIALLY MASHED LIKE THAT.
BOY DID THEY MESS THAT UP.
CLASSIC MISTAKE OF EVERYONE GOING FOR THE BALL AT THE SAME TIME.
ELMORE JR HIGH
AW MAN.
WELL, ELMORE WON'T GET ANOTHER DO-OVER, SO IT LOOKS LIKE THEY'LL HAVE TO HOPE THEY CAN MAKE IT UP IN THEIR NEXT QUARTER ON THE FIELD. BUT FIRST: SPACEMORE'S TEAM WILL TAKE THE FIELD FOR QUARTER 2 OF THE GAME!
DON'T TELL US YOU TOLD US SO, OKAY? WE KNOW WE MESSED UP THAT TIME.
I DIDN'T EVEN HAVE TO SAY IT! YOU'RE LEARNING!

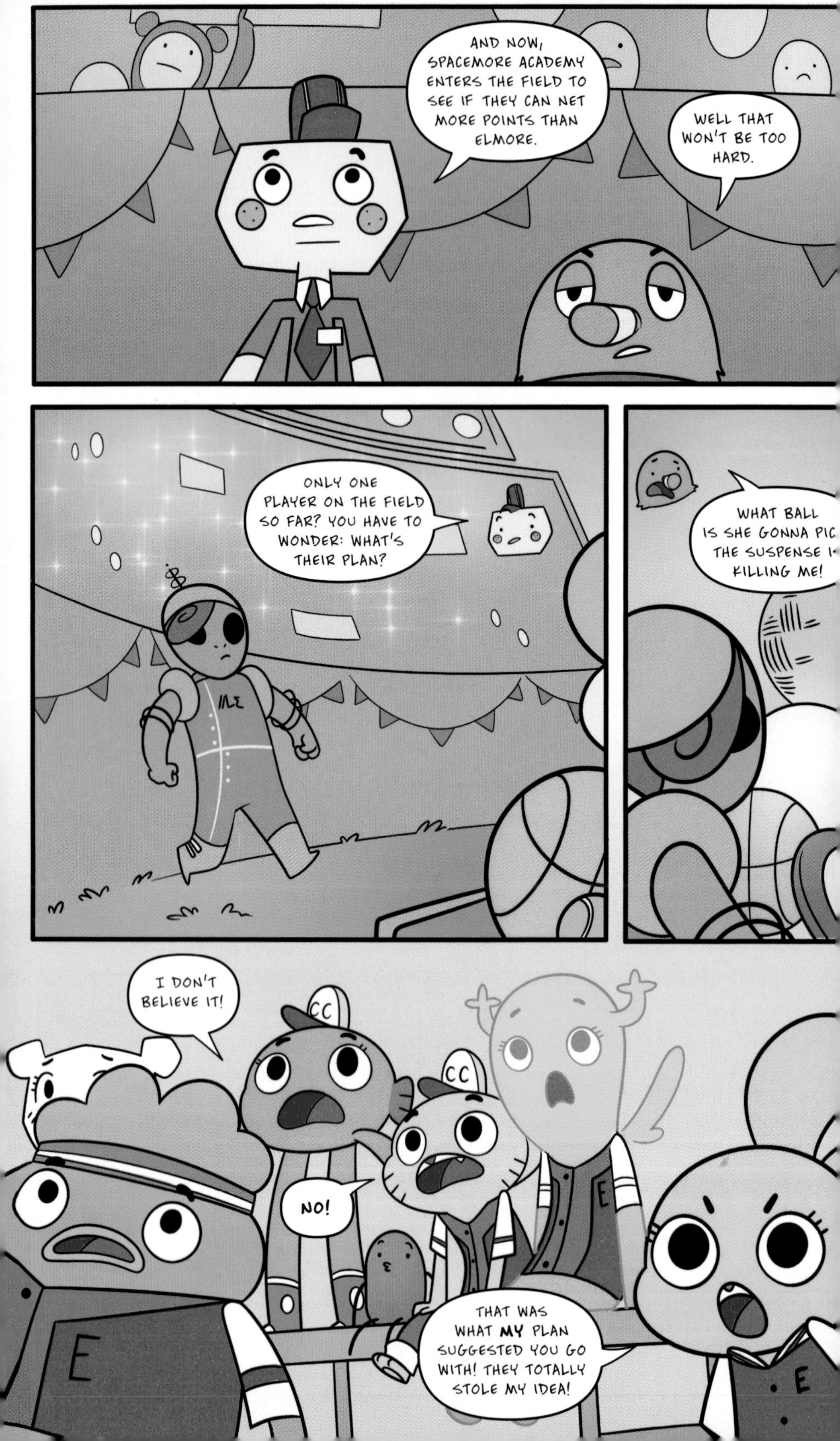
AND NOW, SPACEMORE ACADEMY ENTERS THE FIELD TO SEE IF THEY CAN NET MORE POINTS THAN ELMORE.
WELL THAT WON'T BE TOO HARD.
ONLY ONE PLAYER ON THE FIELD SO FAR? YOU HAVE TO WONDER: WHAT'S THEIR PLAN?
WHAT BALL IS SHE GONNA PIC THE SUSPENSE I KILLING ME!
I DON'T BELIEVE IT!
NO!
THAT WAS WHAT MY PLAN SUGGESTED YOU GO WITH! THEY TOTALLY STOLE MY IDEA!

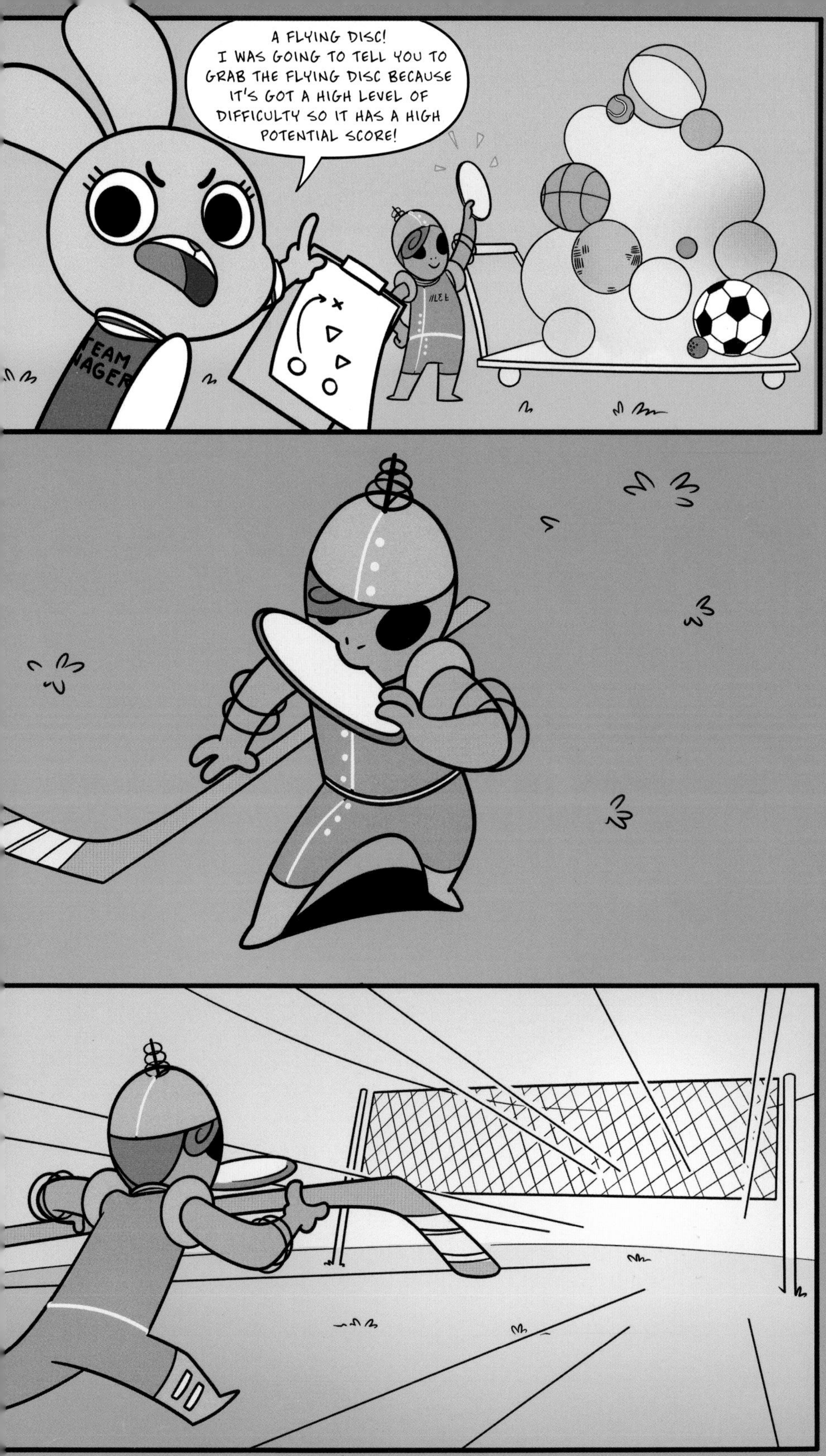
A FLYING DISC! I WAS GOING TO TELL YOU TO GRAB THE FLYING DISC BECAUSE IT'S GOT A HIGH LEVEL OF DIFFICULTY SO IT HAS A HIGH POTENTIAL SCORE!
TEAM
NAGER

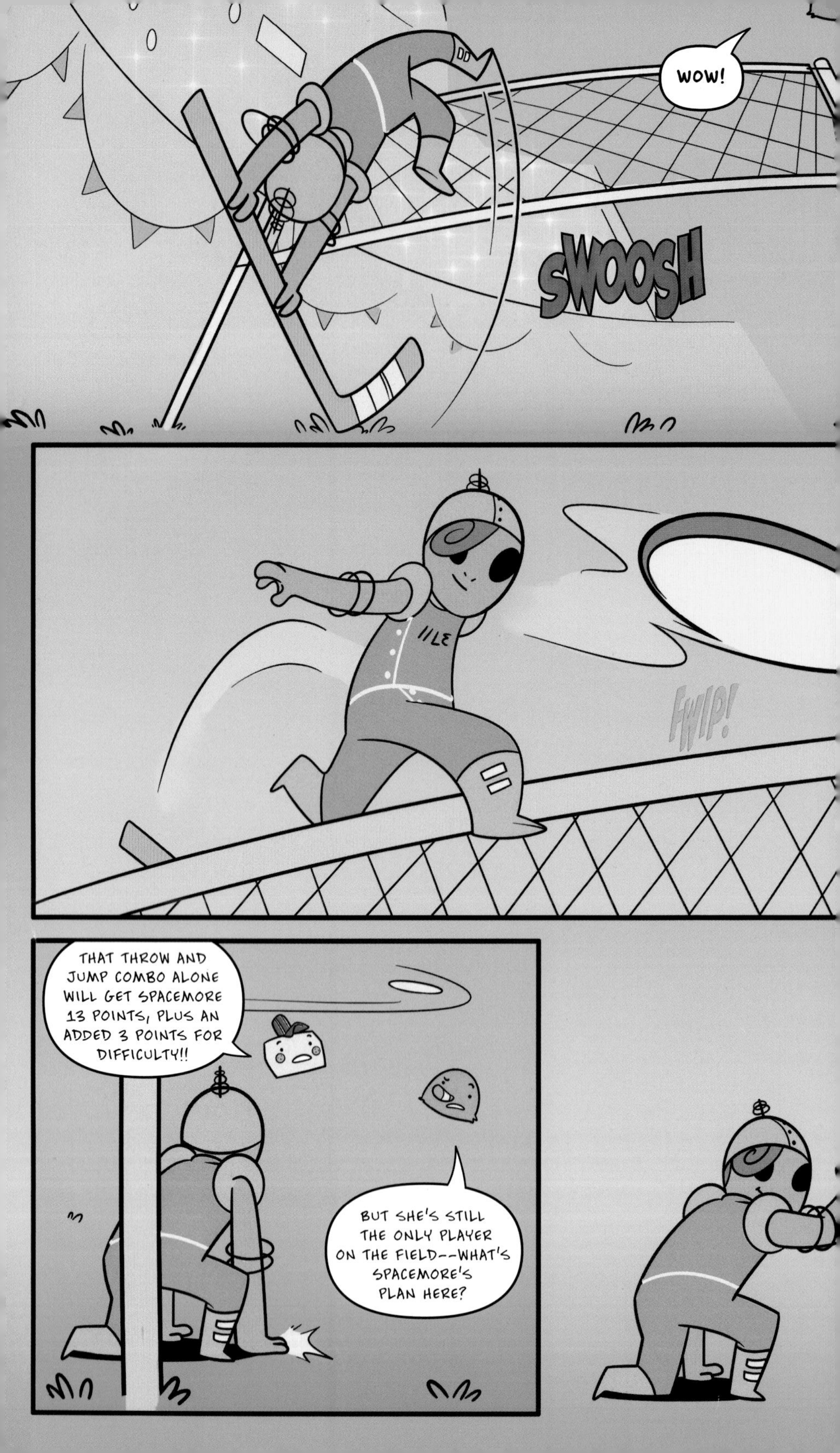
WOW!
SWOOSH
FWIP!
THAT THROW AND JUMP COMBO ALONE WILL GET SPACEMORE 13 POINTS, PLUS AN ADDED 3 POINTS FOR DIFFICULTY!!
BUT SHE'S STILL THE ONLY PLAYER ON THE FIELD--WHAT'S SPACEMORE'S PLAN HERE?

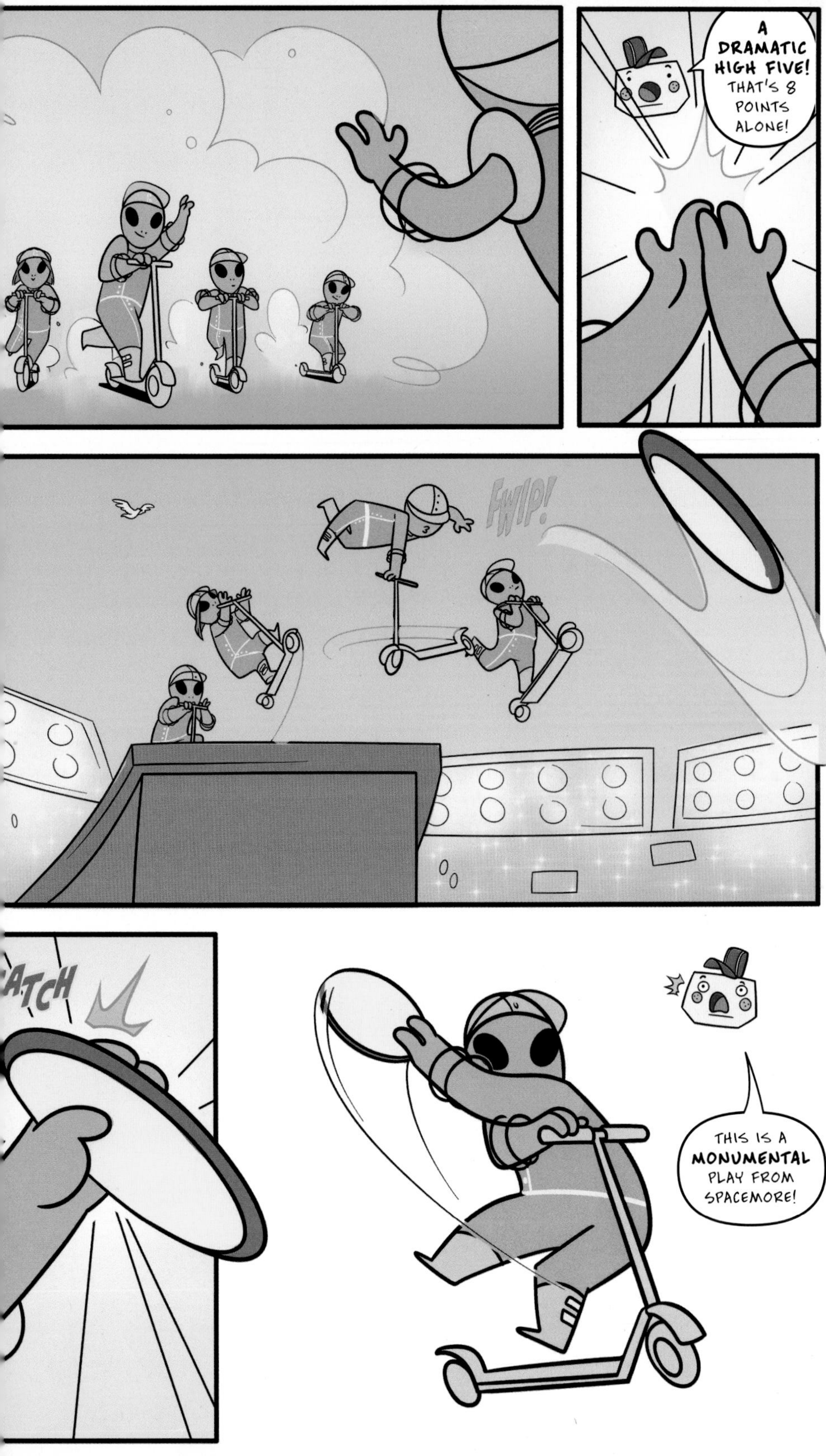
A DRAMATIC HIGH FIVE! THAT'S 8 POINTS ALONE!
FWIP!
CATCH
THIS IS A MONUMENTAL PLAY FROM SPACEMORE!

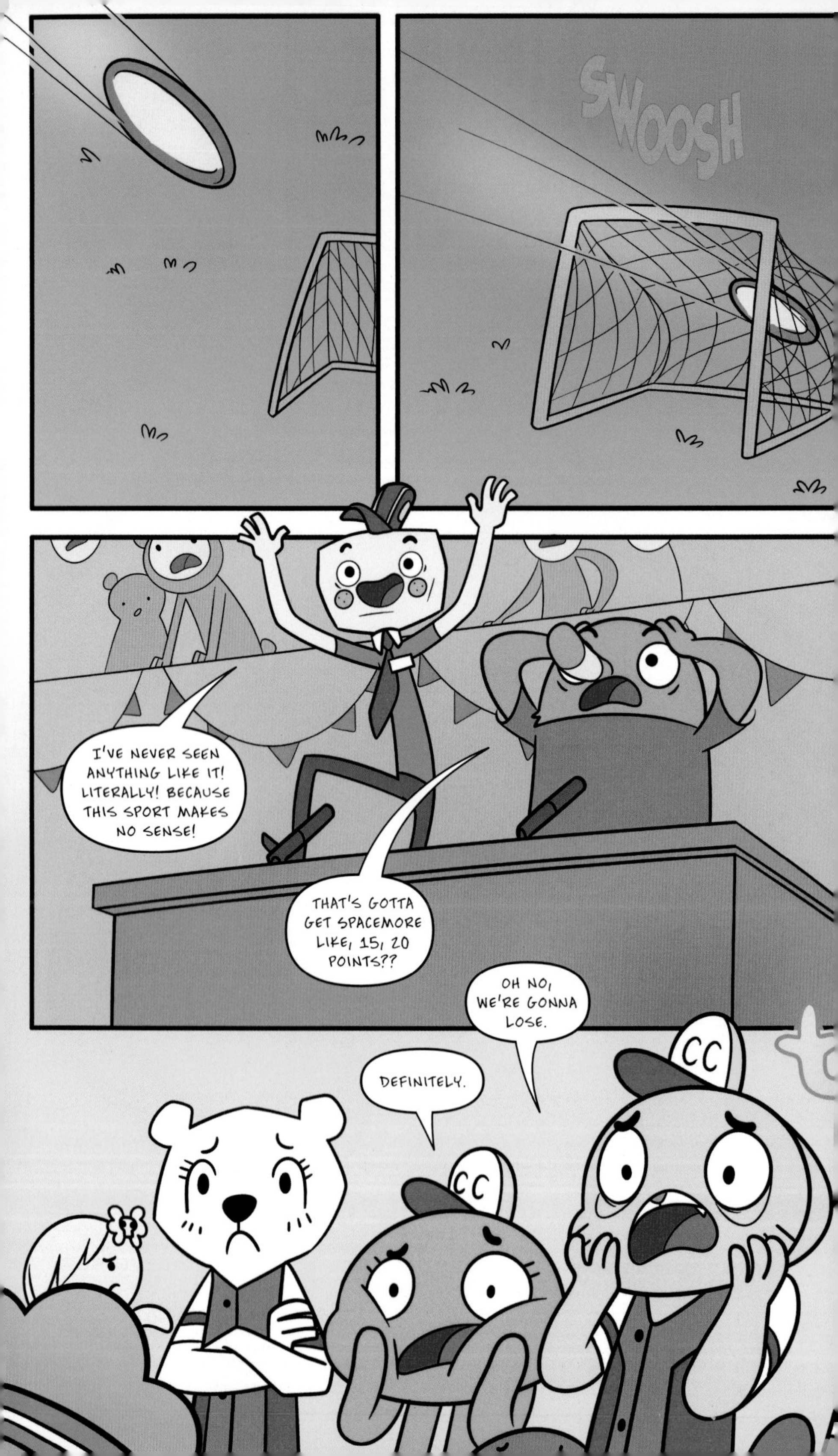
SWOOSH
I'VE NEVER SEEN ANYTHING LIKE IT! LITERALLY! BECAUSE THIS SPORT MAKES NO SENSE!
THAT'S GOTTA GET SPACEMORE LIKE, 15, 20 POINTS??
OH NO, WE'RE GONNA LOSE.
DEFINITELY.
CC
CC

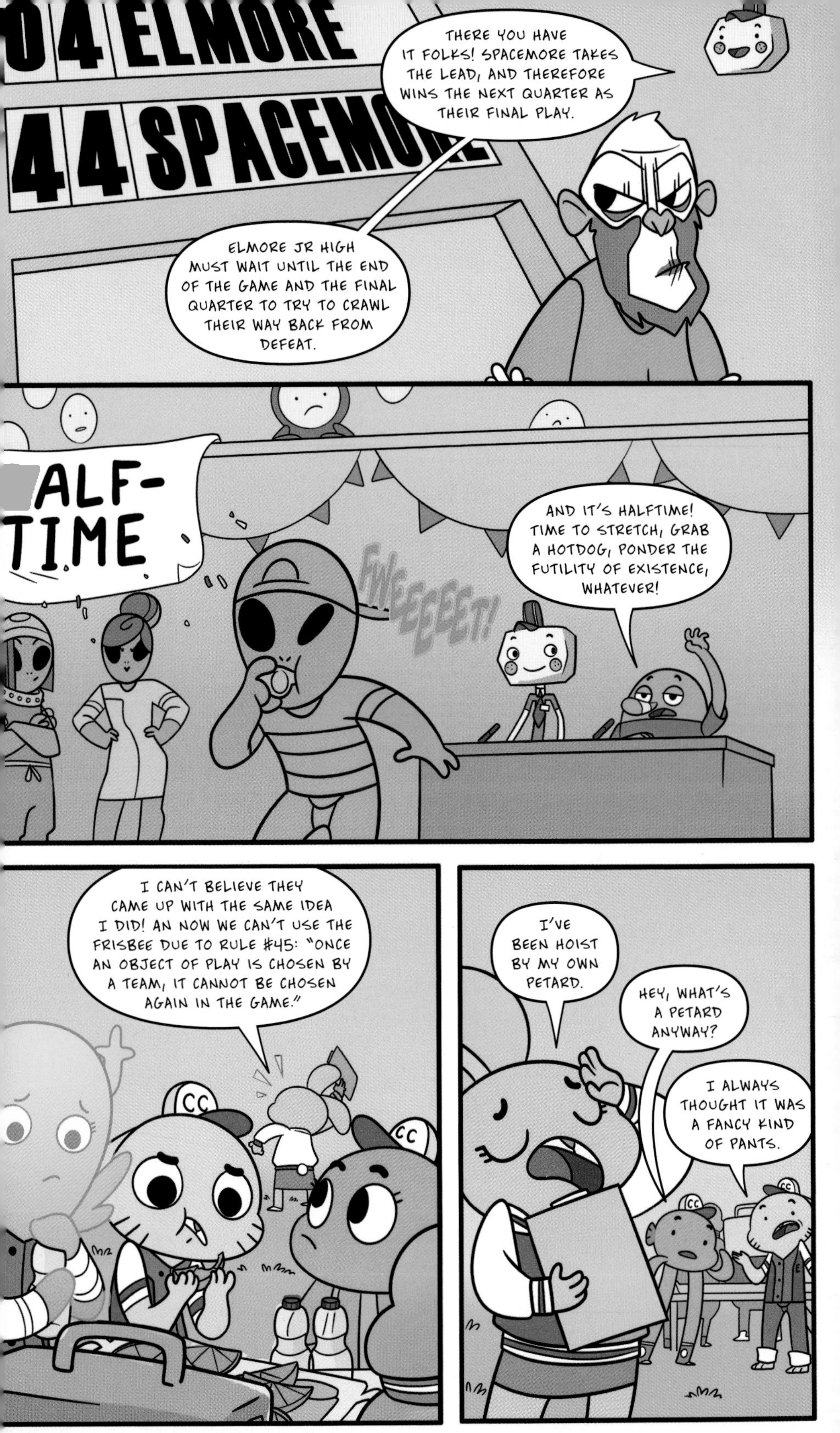
04 ELMORE
44 SPACEMORE
THERE YOU HAVE IT FOLKS! SPACEMORE TAKES THE LEAD, AND THEREFORE WINS THE NEXT QUARTER AS THEIR FINAL PLAY.
ELMORE JR HIGH MUST WAIT UNTIL THE END OF THE GAME AND THE FINAL QUARTER TO TRY TO CRAWL THEIR WAY BACK FROM DEFEAT.
ALF-TIME
FWEEEEET!
AND IT'S HALFTIME! TIME TO STRETCH, GRAB A HOTDOG, PONDER THE FUTILITY OF EXISTENCE, WHATEVER!
I CAN'T BELIEVE THEY CAME UP WITH THE SAME IDEA I DID! AN NOW WE CAN'T USE THE FRISBEE DUE TO RULE #45: "ONCE AN OBJECT OF PLAY IS CHOSEN BY A TEAM, IT CANNOT BE CHOSEN AGAIN IN THE GAME."
I'VE BEEN HOIST BY MY OWN PETARD.
HEY, WHAT'S A PETARD ANYWAY?
I ALWAYS THOUGHT IT WAS A FANCY KIND OF PANTS.

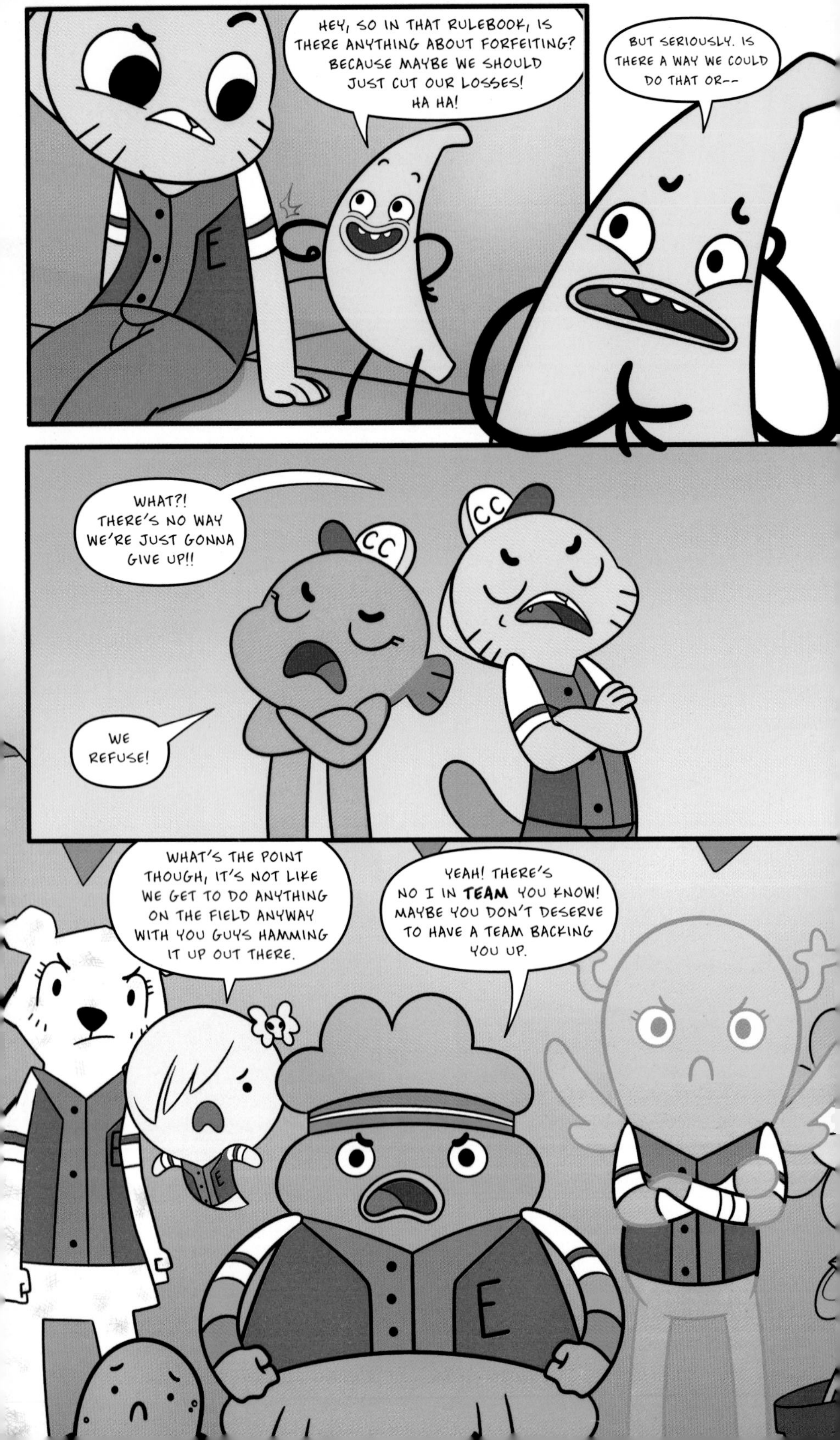
HEY, SO IN THAT RULEBOOK, IS THERE ANYTHING ABOUT FORFEITING? BECAUSE MAYBE WE SHOULD JUST CUT OUR LOSSES! HA HA!
BUT SERIOUSLY. IS THERE A WAY WE COULD DO THAT OR--
WHAT?! THERE'S NO WAY WE'RE JUST GONNA GIVE UP!!
WE REFUSE!
WHAT'S THE POINT THOUGH, IT'S NOT LIKE WE GET TO DO ANYTHING ON THE FIELD ANYWAY WITH YOU GUYS HAMMING IT UP OUT THERE.
YEAH! THERE'S NO I IN **TEAM** YOU KNOW! MAYBE YOU DON'T DESERVE TO HAVE A TEAM BACKING YOU UP.

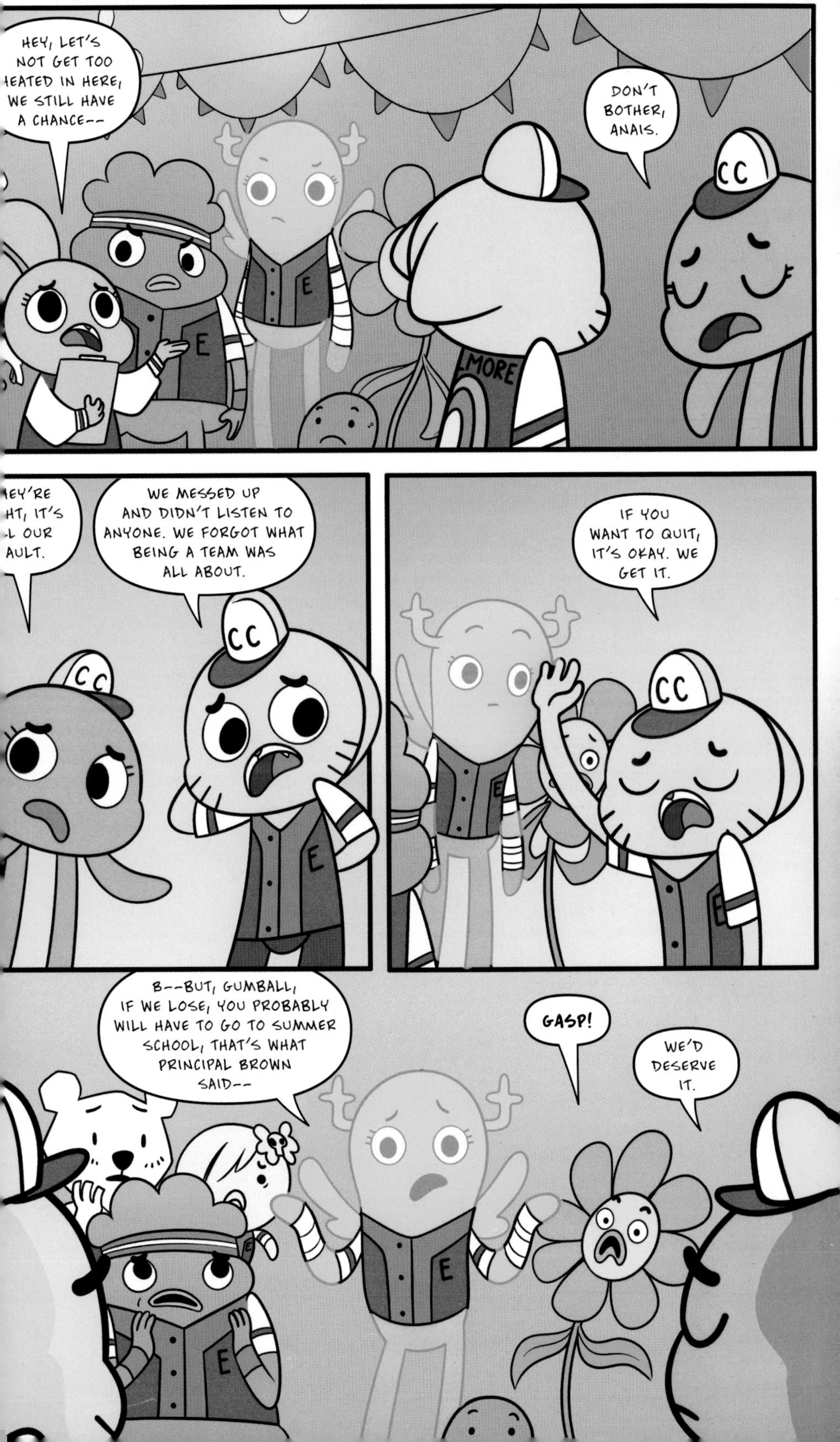
HEY, LET'S NOT GET TOO EATED IN HERE, WE STILL HAVE A CHANCE--
DON'T BOTHER, ANAIS.
EY'RE HT, IT'S L OUR AULT.
WE MESSED UP AND DIDN'T LISTEN TO ANYONE. WE FORGOT WHAT BEING A TEAM WAS ALL ABOUT.
IF YOU WANT TO QUIT, IT'S OKAY. WE GET IT.
B--BUT, GUMBALL, IF WE LOSE, YOU PROBABLY WILL HAVE TO GO TO SUMMER SCHOOL, THAT'S WHAT PRINCIPAL BROWN SAID--
GASP!
WE'D DESERVE IT.

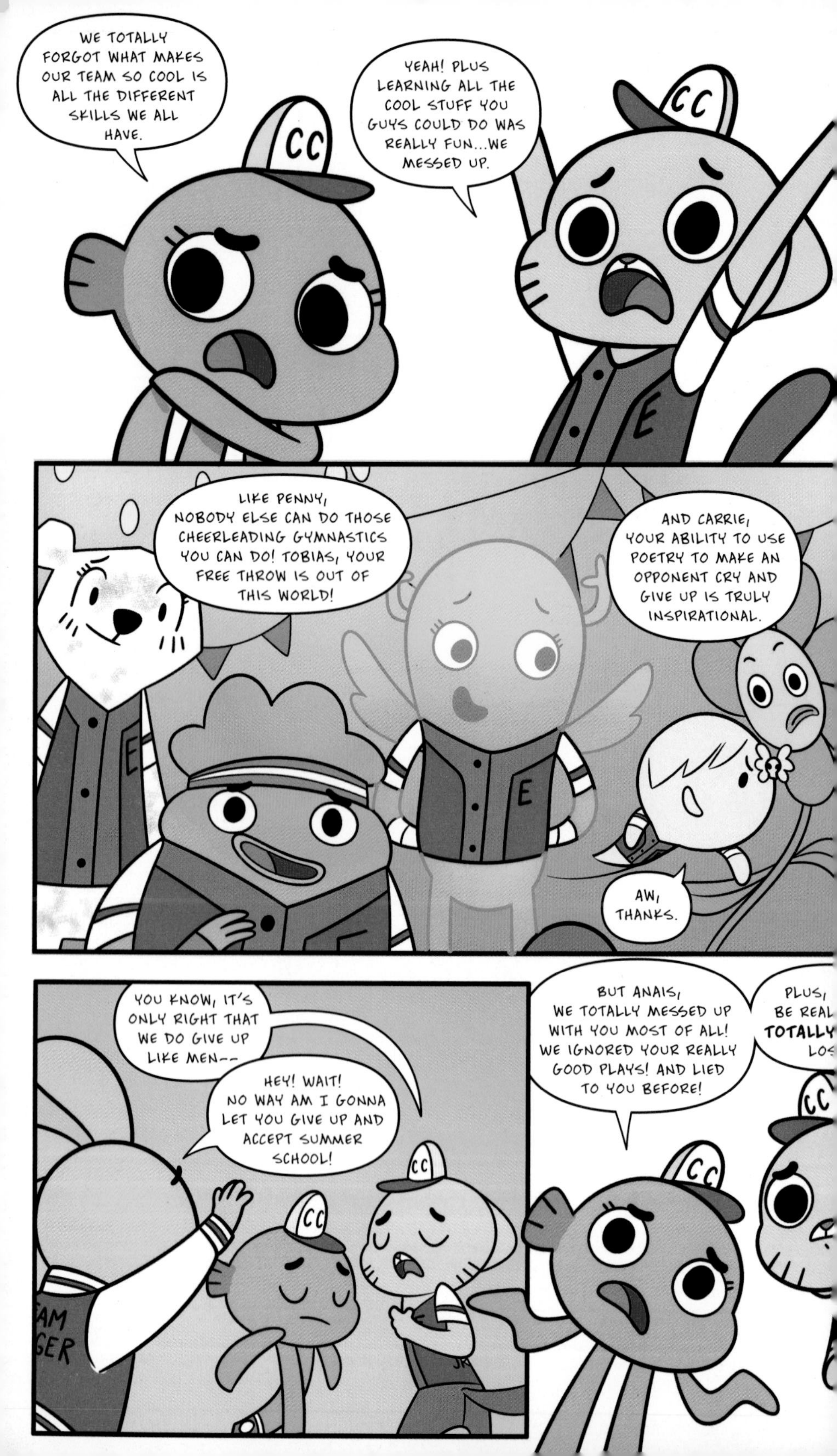
WE TOTALLY FORGOT WHAT MAKES OUR TEAM SO COOL IS ALL THE DIFFERENT SKILLS WE ALL HAVE.
YEAH! PLUS LEARNING ALL THE COOL STUFF YOU GUYS COULD DO WAS REALLY FUN...WE MESSED UP.
LIKE PENNY, NOBODY ELSE CAN DO THOSE CHEERLEADING GYMNASTICS YOU CAN DO! TOBIAS, YOUR FREE THROW IS OUT OF THIS WORLD!
AND CARRIE, YOUR ABILITY TO USE POETRY TO MAKE AN OPPONENT CRY AND GIVE UP IS TRULY INSPIRATIONAL.
AW, THANKS.
YOU KNOW, IT'S ONLY RIGHT THAT WE DO GIVE UP LIKE MEN--
HEY! WAIT! NO WAY AM I GONNA LET YOU GIVE UP AND ACCEPT SUMMER SCHOOL!
BUT ANAIS, WE TOTALLY MESSED UP WITH YOU MOST OF ALL! WE IGNORED YOUR REALLY GOOD PLAYS! AND LIED TO YOU BEFORE!

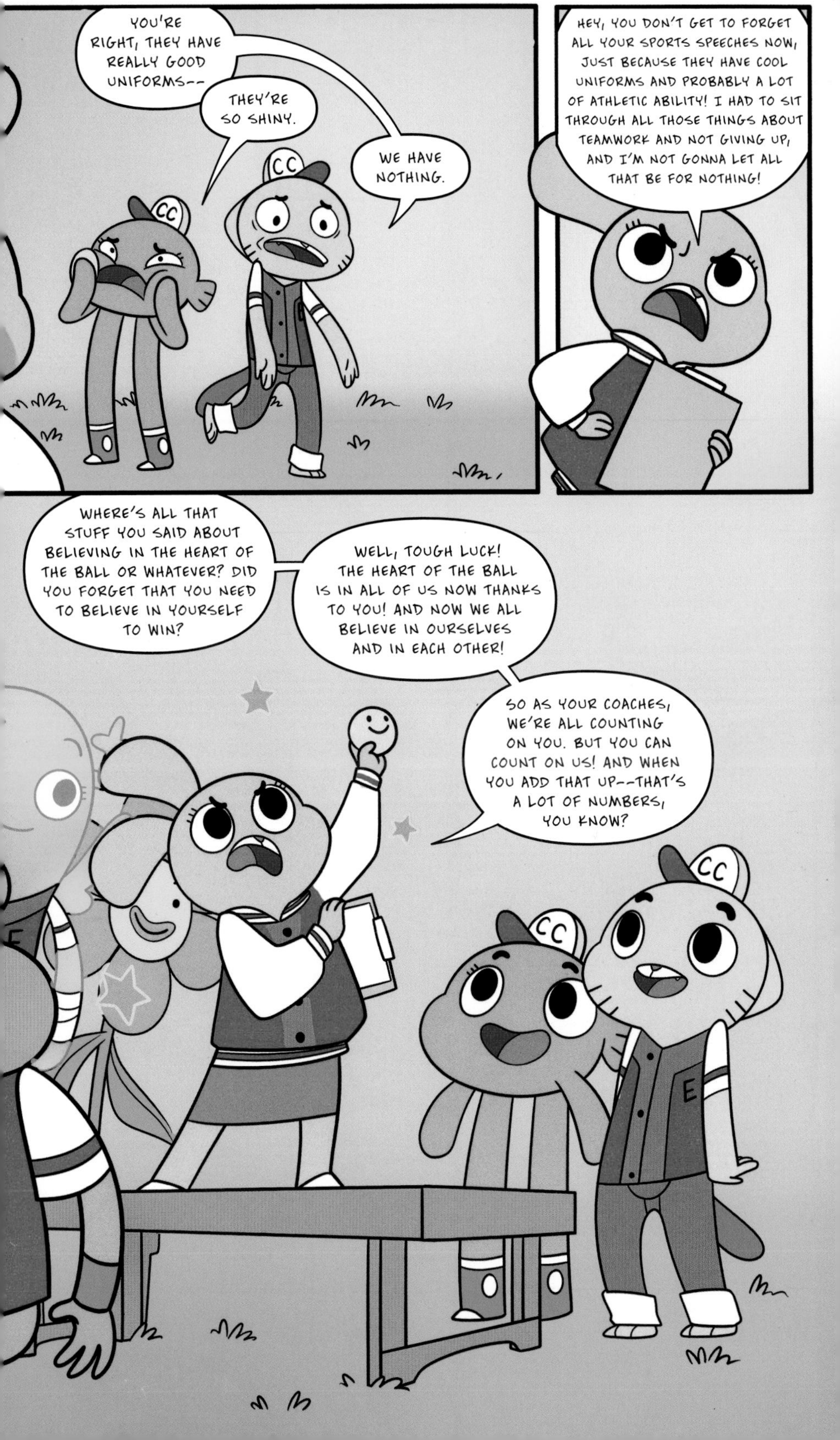
YOU'RE RIGHT, THEY HAVE REALLY GOOD UNIFORMS--
THEY'RE SO SHINY.
WE HAVE NOTHING.
HEY, YOU DON'T GET TO FORGET ALL YOUR SPORTS SPEECHES NOW, JUST BECAUSE THEY HAVE COOL UNIFORMS AND PROBABLY A LOT OF ATHLETIC ABILITY! I HAD TO SIT THROUGH ALL THOSE THINGS ABOUT TEAMWORK AND NOT GIVING UP, AND I'M NOT GONNA LET ALL THAT BE FOR NOTHING!
WHERE'S ALL THAT STUFF YOU SAID ABOUT BELIEVING IN THE HEART OF THE BALL OR WHATEVER? DID YOU FORGET THAT YOU NEED TO BELIEVE IN YOURSELF TO WIN?
WELL, TOUGH LUCK! THE HEART OF THE BALL IS IN ALL OF US NOW THANKS TO YOU! AND NOW WE ALL BELIEVE IN OURSELVES AND IN EACH OTHER!
SO AS YOUR COACHES, WE'RE ALL COUNTING ON YOU. BUT YOU CAN COUNT ON US! AND WHEN YOU ADD THAT UP--THAT'S A LOT OF NUMBERS, YOU KNOW?
CC
CC
CC
CC
E

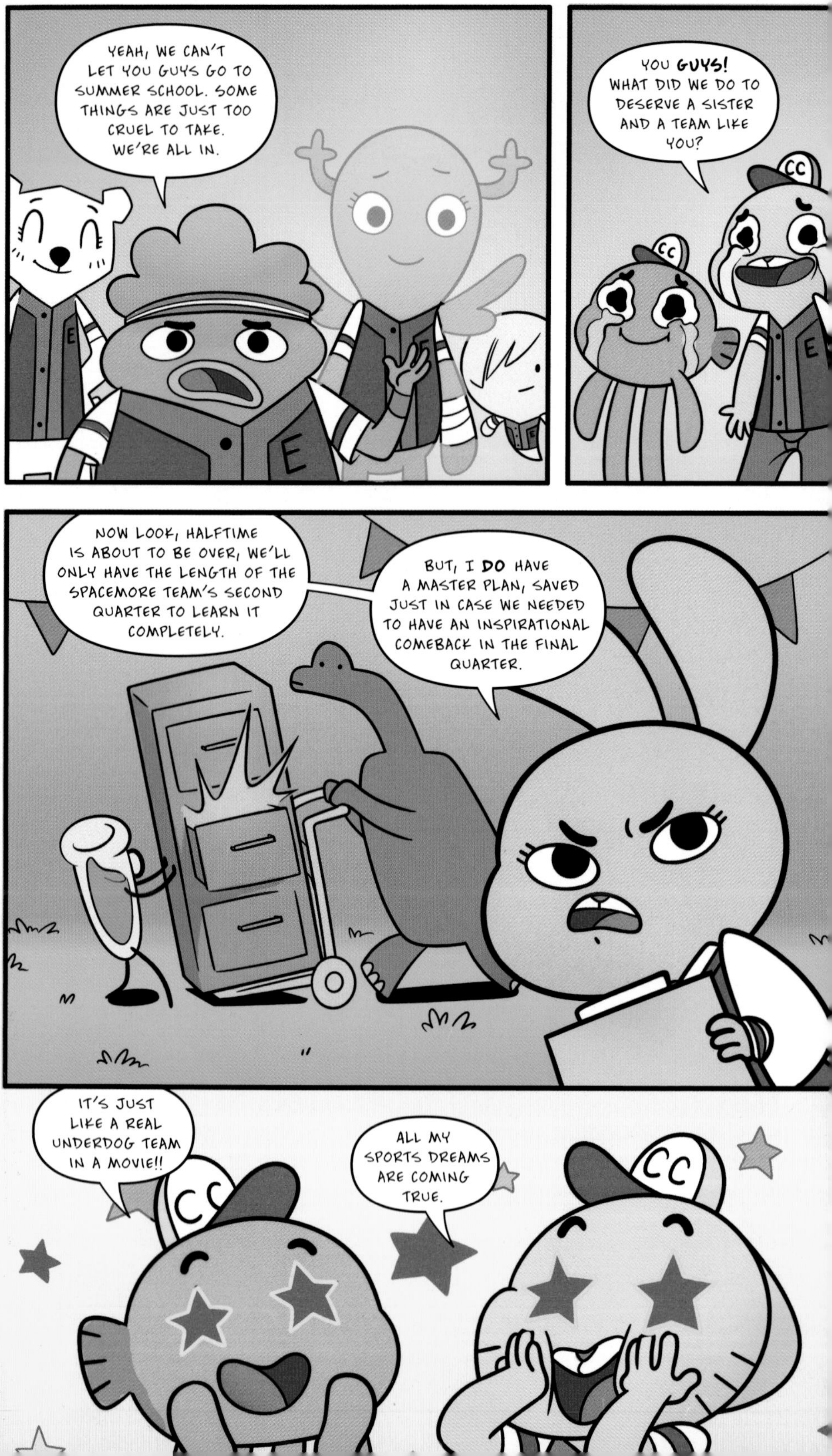
YEAH, WE CAN'T LET YOU GUYS GO TO SUMMER SCHOOL. SOME THINGS ARE JUST TOO CRUEL TO TAKE. WE'RE ALL IN.
YOU **GUYS!** WHAT DID WE DO TO DESERVE A SISTER AND A TEAM LIKE YOU?
NOW LOOK, HALFTIME IS ABOUT TO BE OVER, WE'LL ONLY HAVE THE LENGTH OF THE SPACEMORE TEAM'S SECOND QUARTER TO LEARN IT COMPLETELY.
BUT, I **DO** HAVE A MASTER PLAN, SAVED JUST IN CASE WE NEEDED TO HAVE AN INSPIRATIONAL COMEBACK IN THE FINAL QUARTER.
IT'S JUST LIKE A REAL UNDERDOG TEAM IN A MOVIE!!
ALL MY SPORTS DREAMS ARE COMING TRUE.

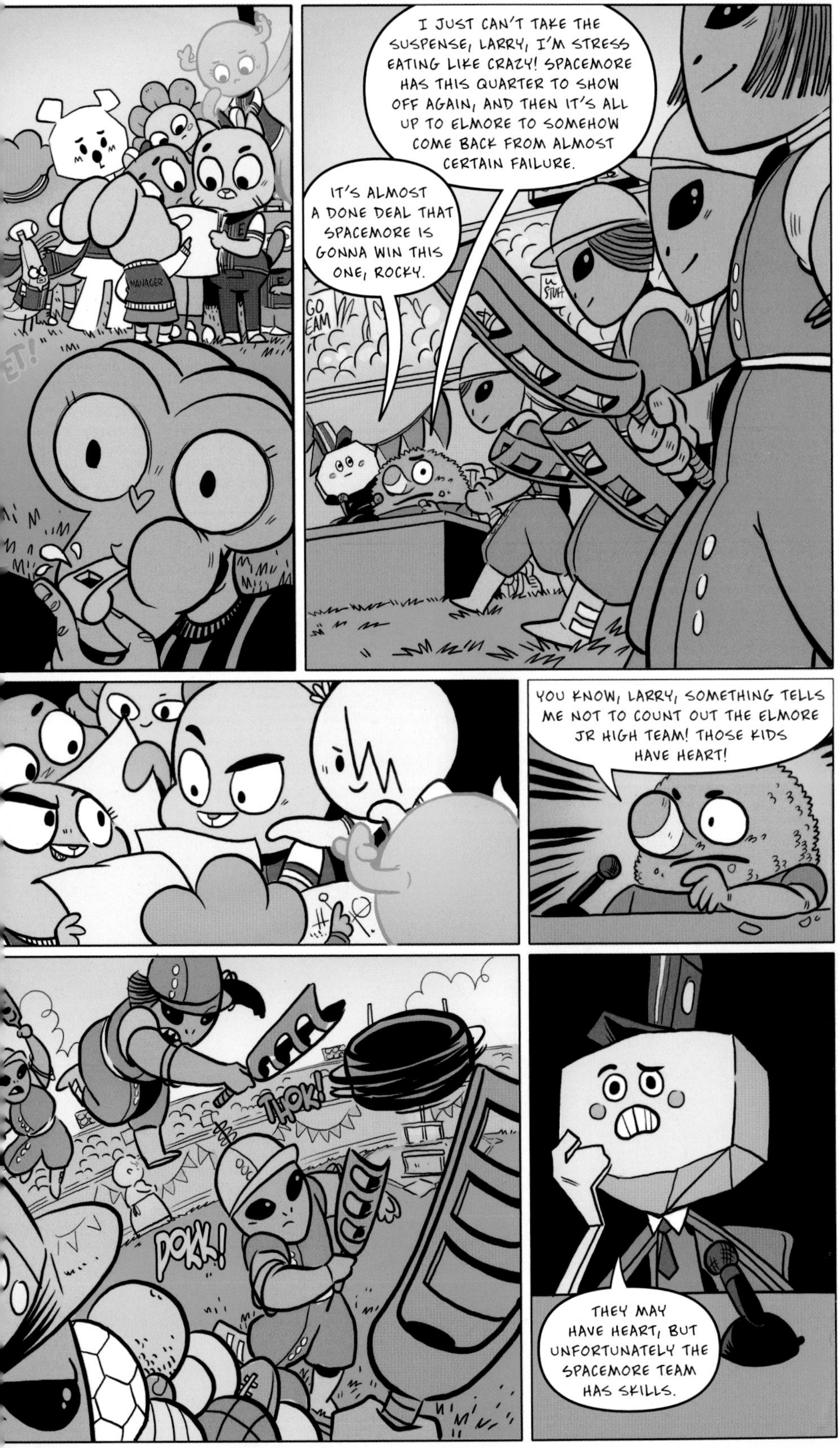
ET!
I JUST CAN'T TAKE THE SUSPENSE, LARRY, I'M STRESS EATING LIKE CRAZY! SPACEMORE HAS THIS QUARTER TO SHOW OFF AGAIN, AND THEN IT'S ALL UP TO ELMORE TO SOMEHOW COME BACK FROM ALMOST CERTAIN FAILURE.
IT'S ALMOST A DONE DEAL THAT SPACEMORE IS GONNA WIN THIS ONE, ROCKY.
YOU KNOW, LARRY, SOMETHING TELLS ME NOT TO COUNT OUT THE ELMORE JR HIGH TEAM! THOSE KIDS HAVE HEART!
THOK!
DOKK!
THEY MAY HAVE HEART, BUT UNFORTUNATELY THE SPACEMORE TEAM HAS SKILLS.

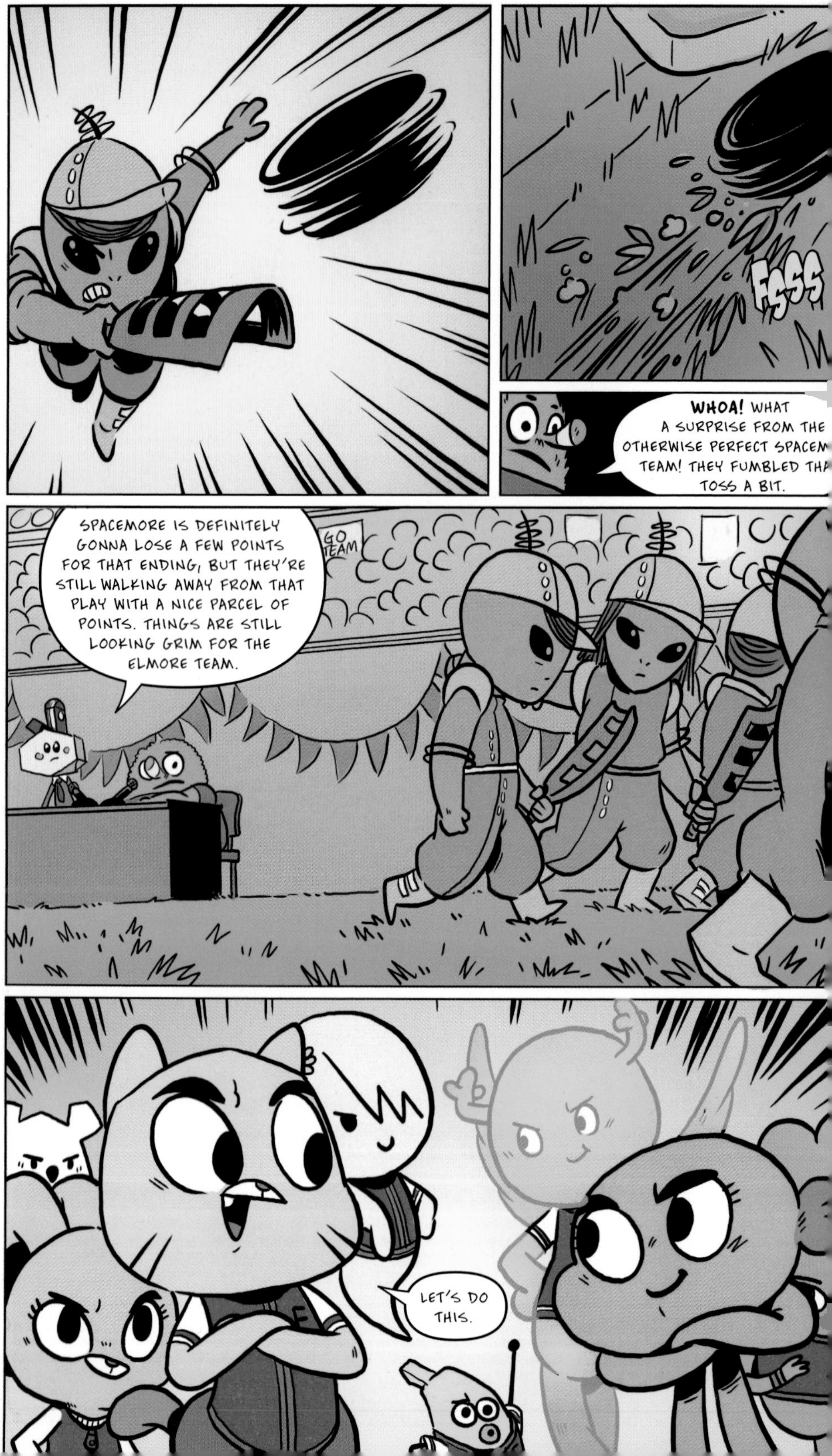
FSSS
WHOA! WHAT A SURPRISE FROM THE OTHERWISE PERFECT SPACEM TEAM! THEY FUMBLED THA TOSS A BIT.
SPACEMORE IS DEFINITELY GONNA LOSE A FEW POINTS FOR THAT ENDING, BUT THEY'RE STILL WALKING AWAY FROM THAT PLAY WITH A NICE PARCEL OF POINTS. THINGS ARE STILL LOOKING GRIM FOR THE ELMORE TEAM.
GO TEAM
LET'S DO THIS.

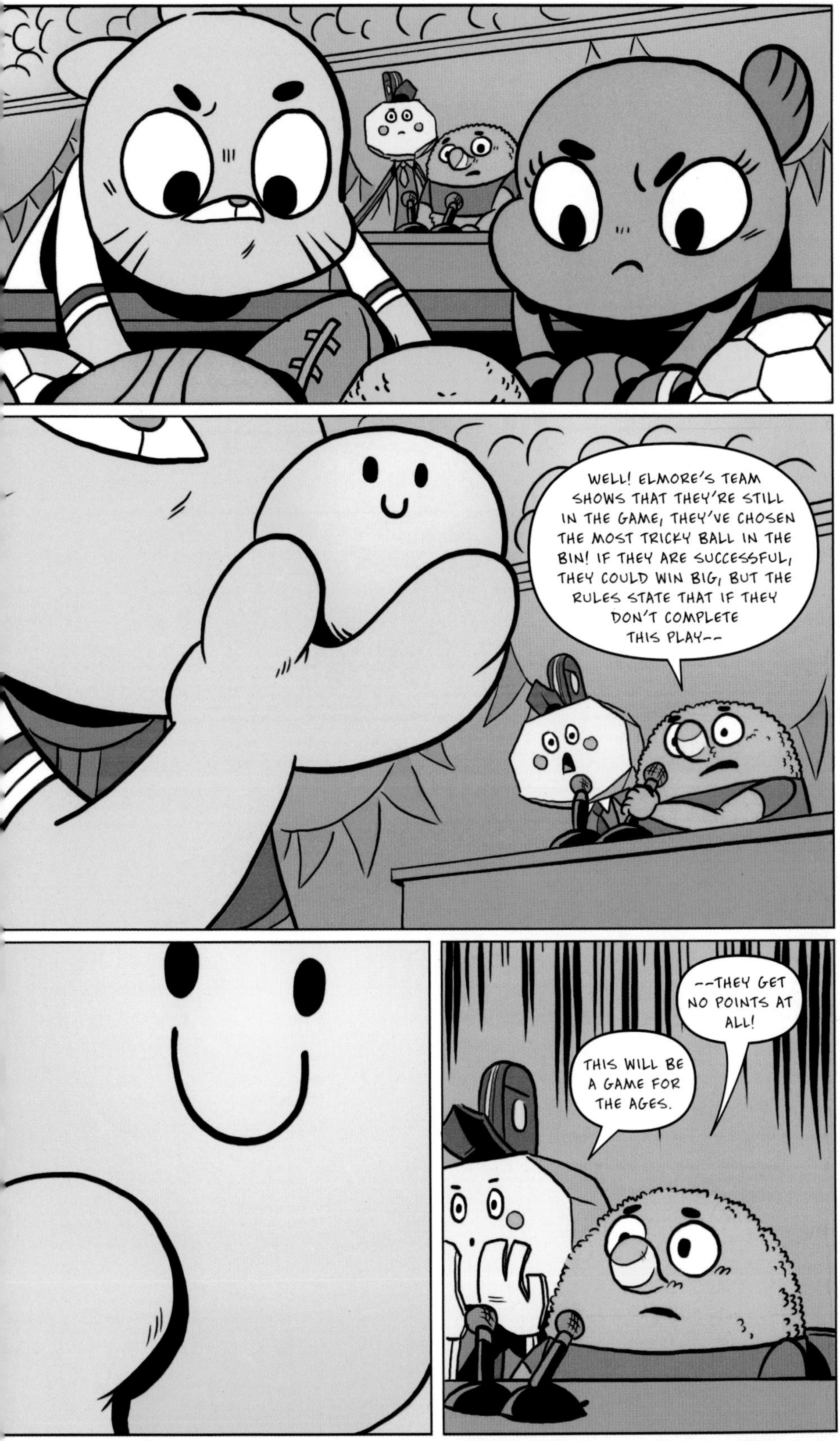
WELL! ELMORE'S TEAM SHOWS THAT THEY'RE STILL IN THE GAME, THEY'VE CHOSEN THE MOST TRICKY BALL IN THE BIN! IF THEY ARE SUCCESSFUL, THEY COULD WIN BIG, BUT THE RULES STATE THAT IF THEY DON'T COMPLETE THIS PLAY--
--THEY GET NO POINTS AT ALL!
THIS WILL BE A GAME FOR THE AGES.

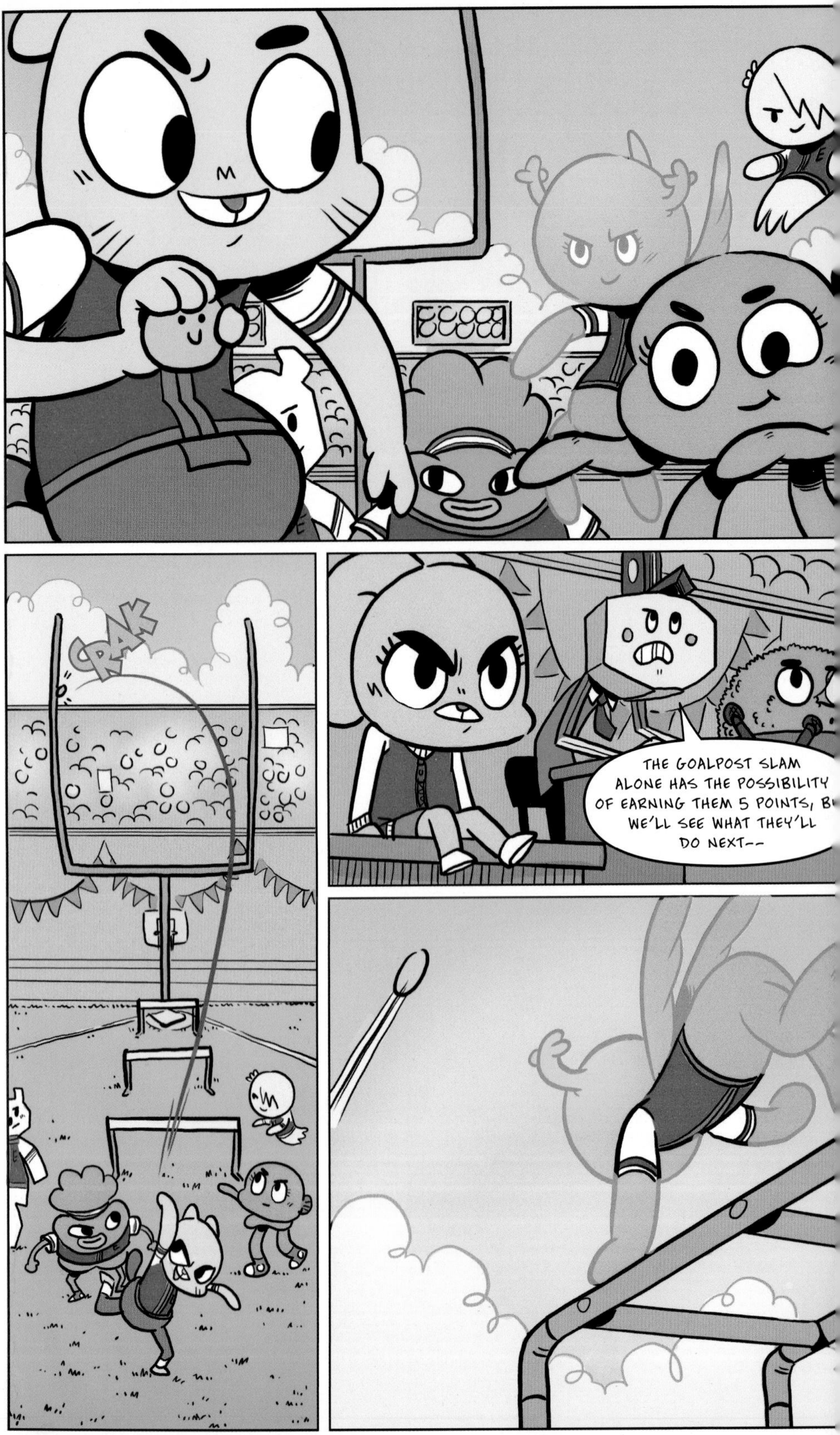
CRAK
THE GOALPOST SLAM ALONE HAS THE POSSIBILITY OF EARNING THEM 5 POINTS, B
WE'LL SEE WHAT THEY'LL DO NEXT--

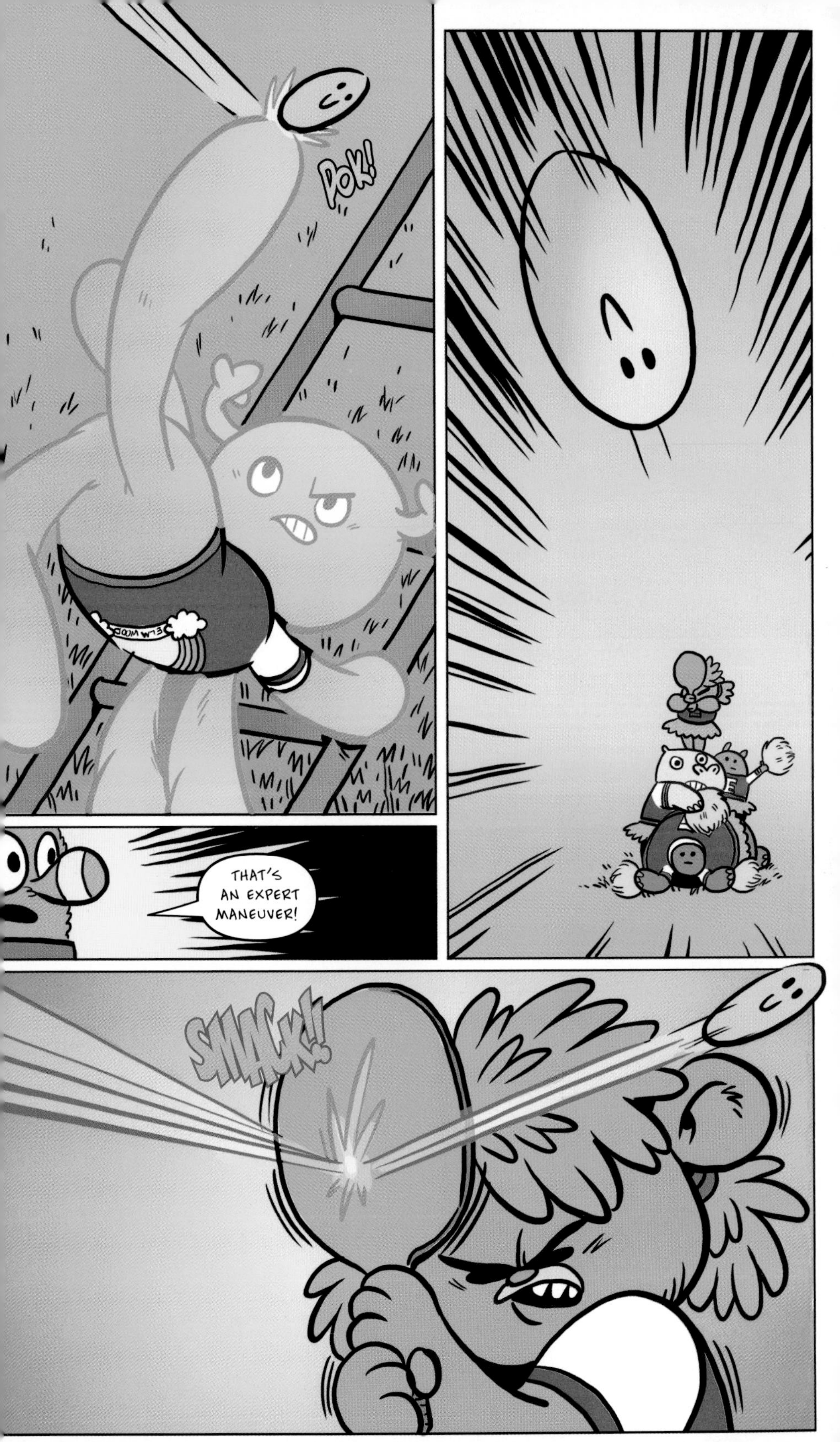
POK!
THAT'S AN EXPERT MANEUVER!
SMACK!!

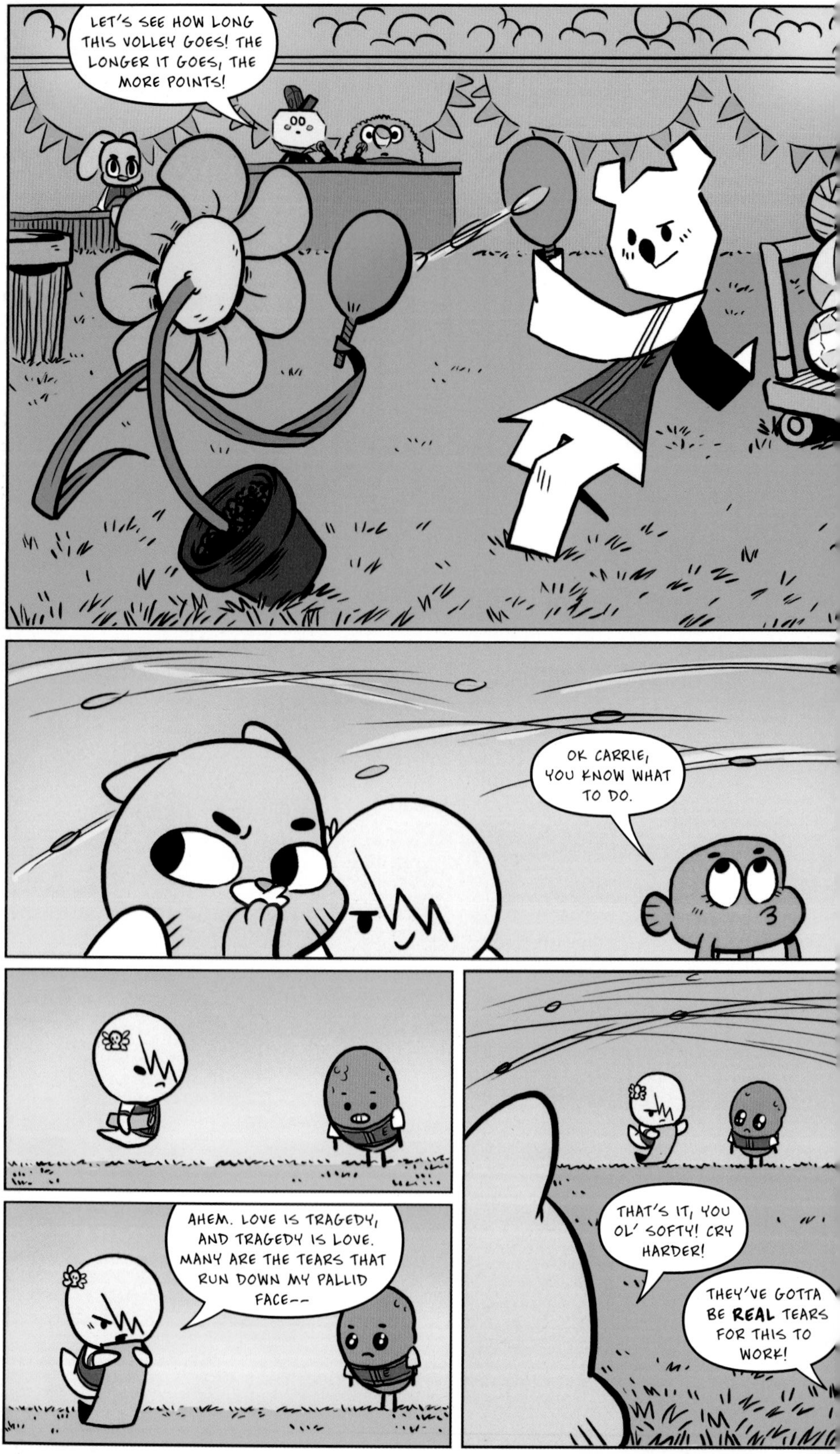
LET'S SEE HOW LONG THIS VOLLEY GOES! THE LONGER IT GOES, THE MORE POINTS!
OK CARRIE, YOU KNOW WHAT TO DO.
AHEM. LOVE IS TRAGEDY, AND TRAGEDY IS LOVE. MANY ARE THE TEARS THAT RUN DOWN MY PALLID FACE--
THAT'S IT, YOU OL' SOFTY! CRY HARDER!
THEY'VE GOTTA BE **REAL** TEARS FOR THIS TO WORK!

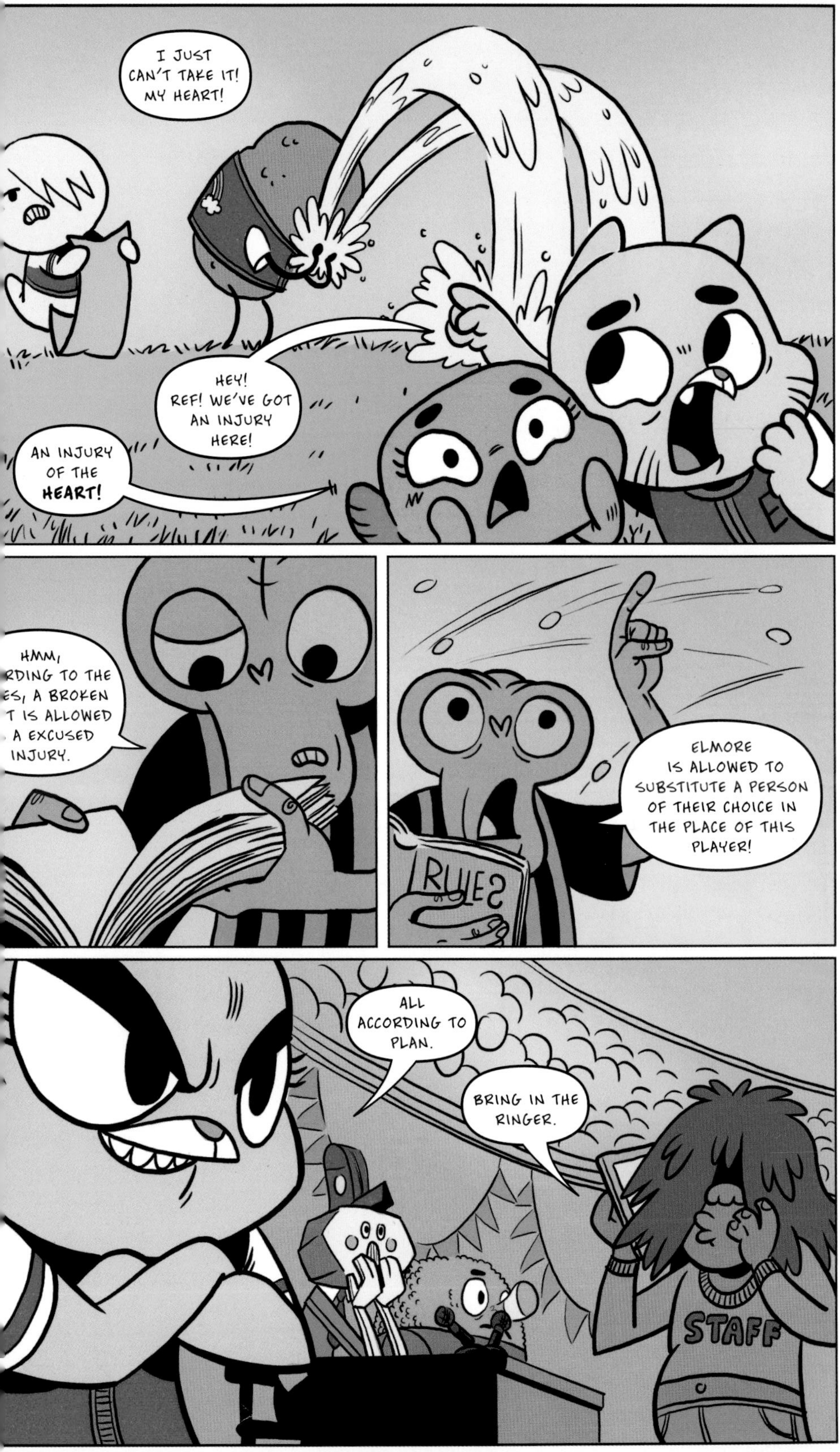
I JUST CAN'T TAKE IT! MY HEART!
HEY! REF! WE'VE GOT AN INJURY HERE!
AN INJURY OF THE **HEART!**
HMM, RDING TO THE ES, A BROKEN T IS ALLOWED A EXCUSED INJURY.
ELMORE IS ALLOWED TO SUBSTITUTE A PERSON OF THEIR CHOICE IN THE PLACE OF THIS PLAYER!
RULES
ALL ACCORDING TO PLAN.
BRING IN THE RINGER.
STAFF

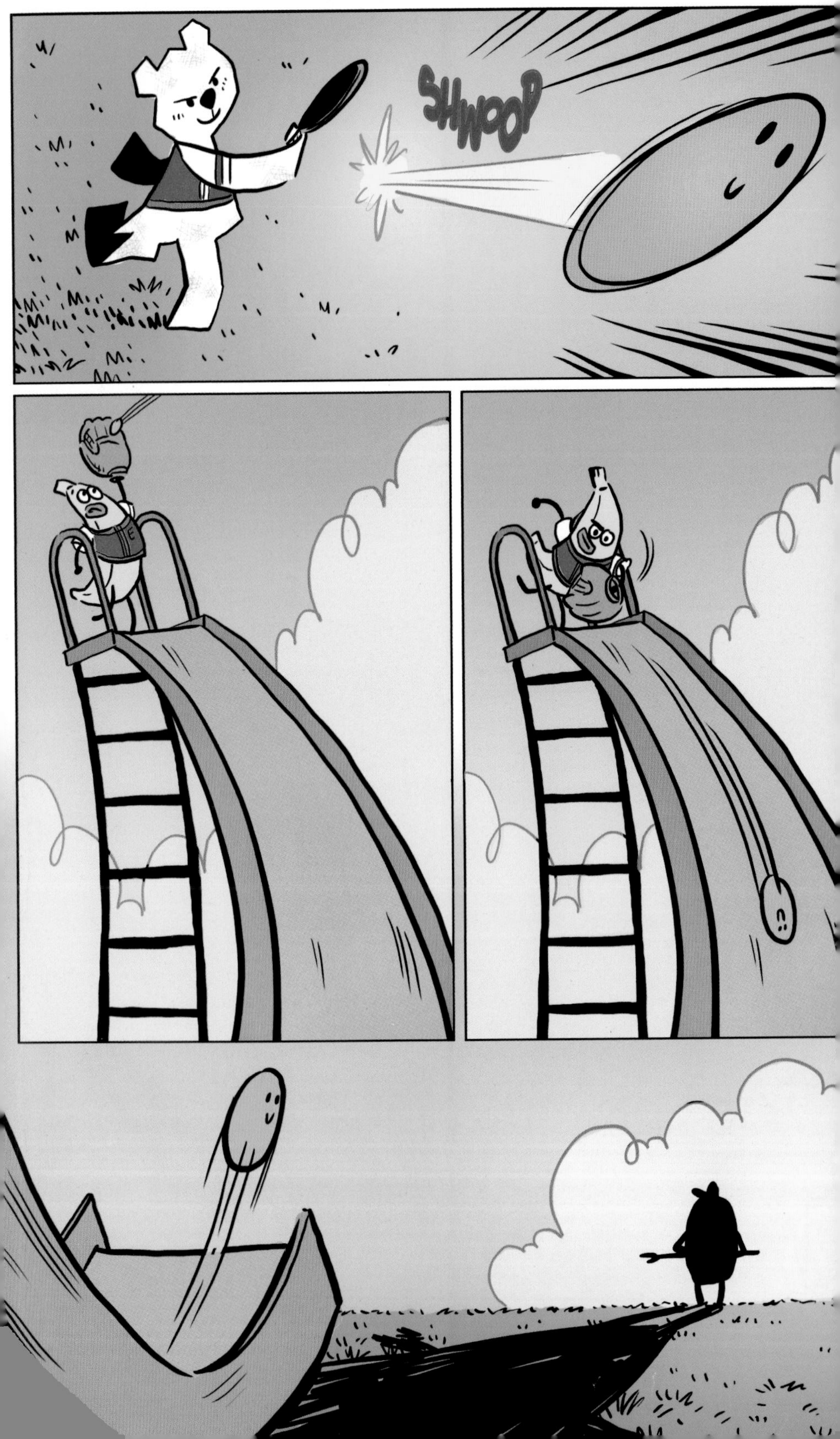
SHWOOP

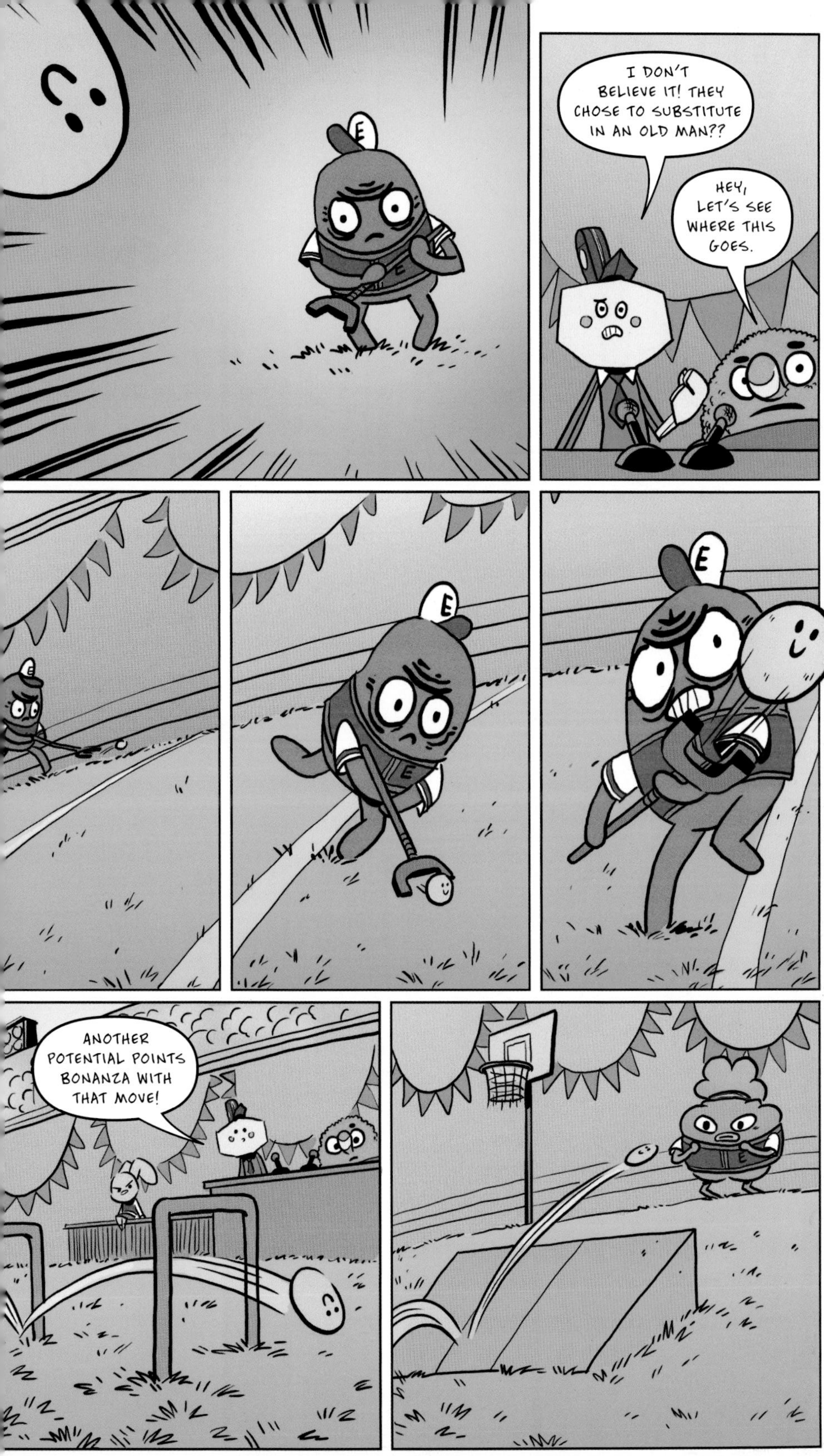
I DON'T BELIEVE IT! THEY CHOSE TO SUBSTITUTE IN AN OLD MAN??
HEY, LET'S SEE WHERE THIS GOES.
ANOTHER POTENTIAL POINTS BONANZA WITH THAT MOVE!

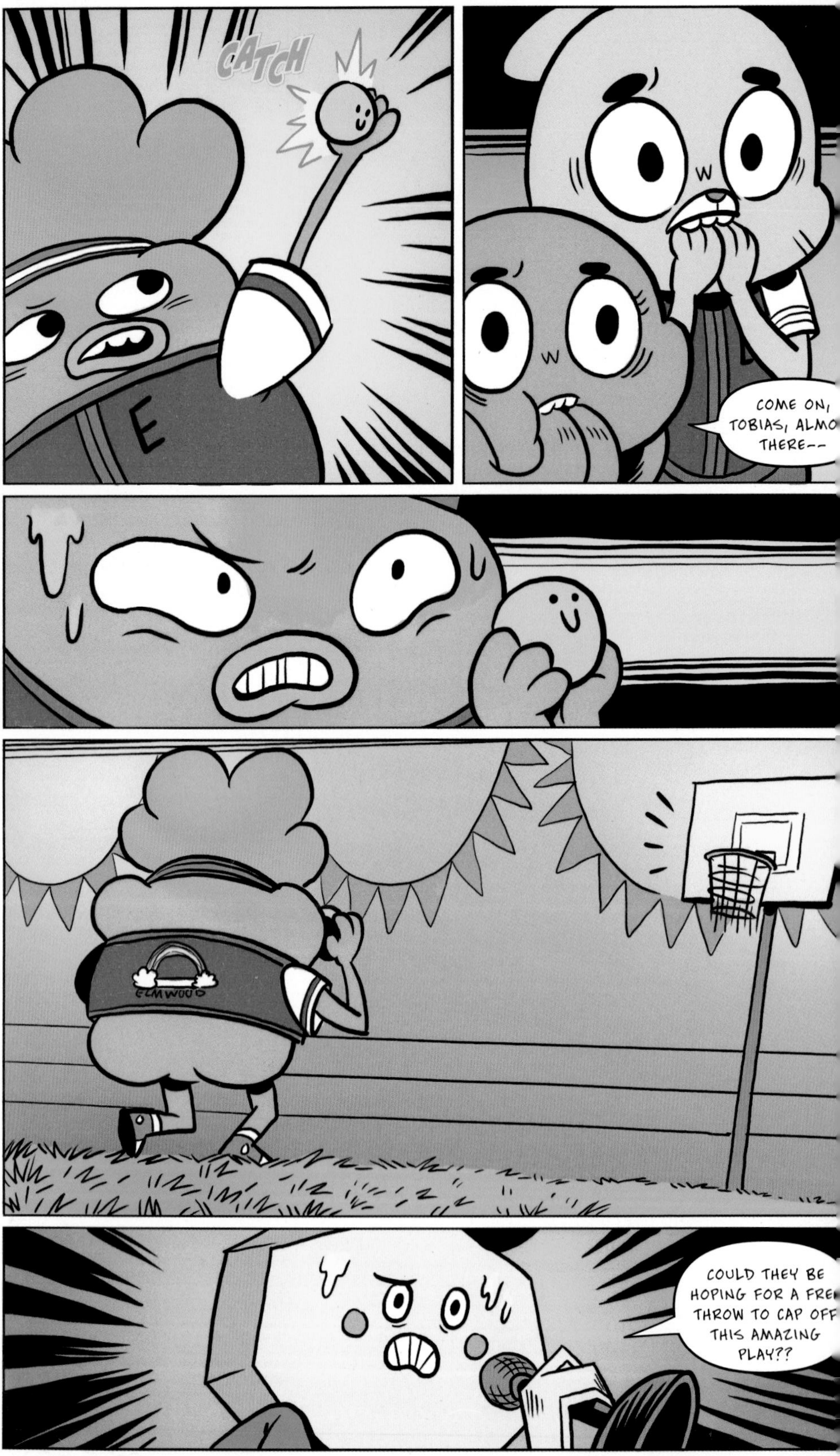
CATCH
COME ON, TOBIAS, ALMO THERE--
ELMWOOD
COULD THEY BE HOPING FOR A FRE THROW TO CAP OFF THIS AMAZING PLAY??

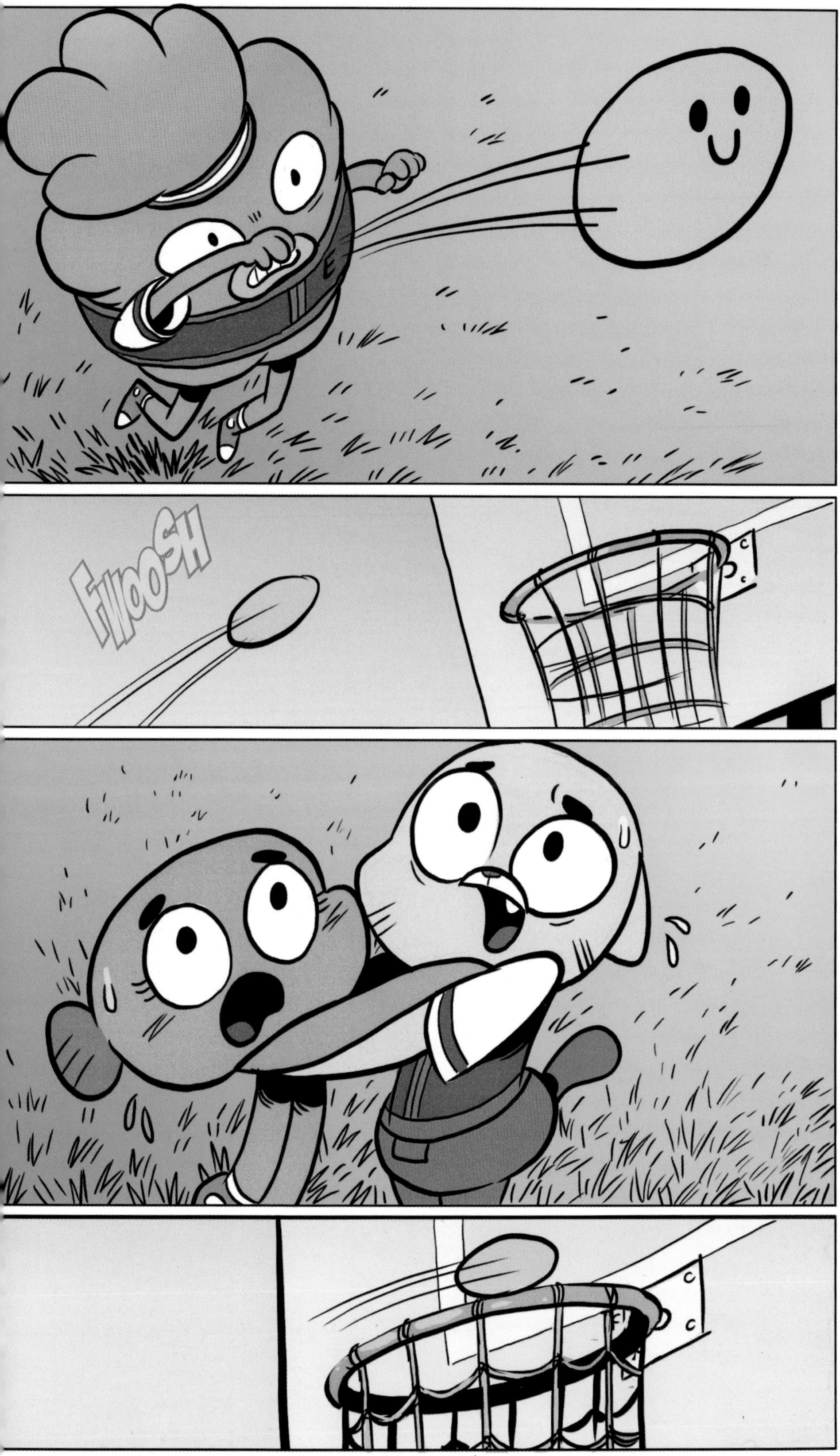
FWOOSH

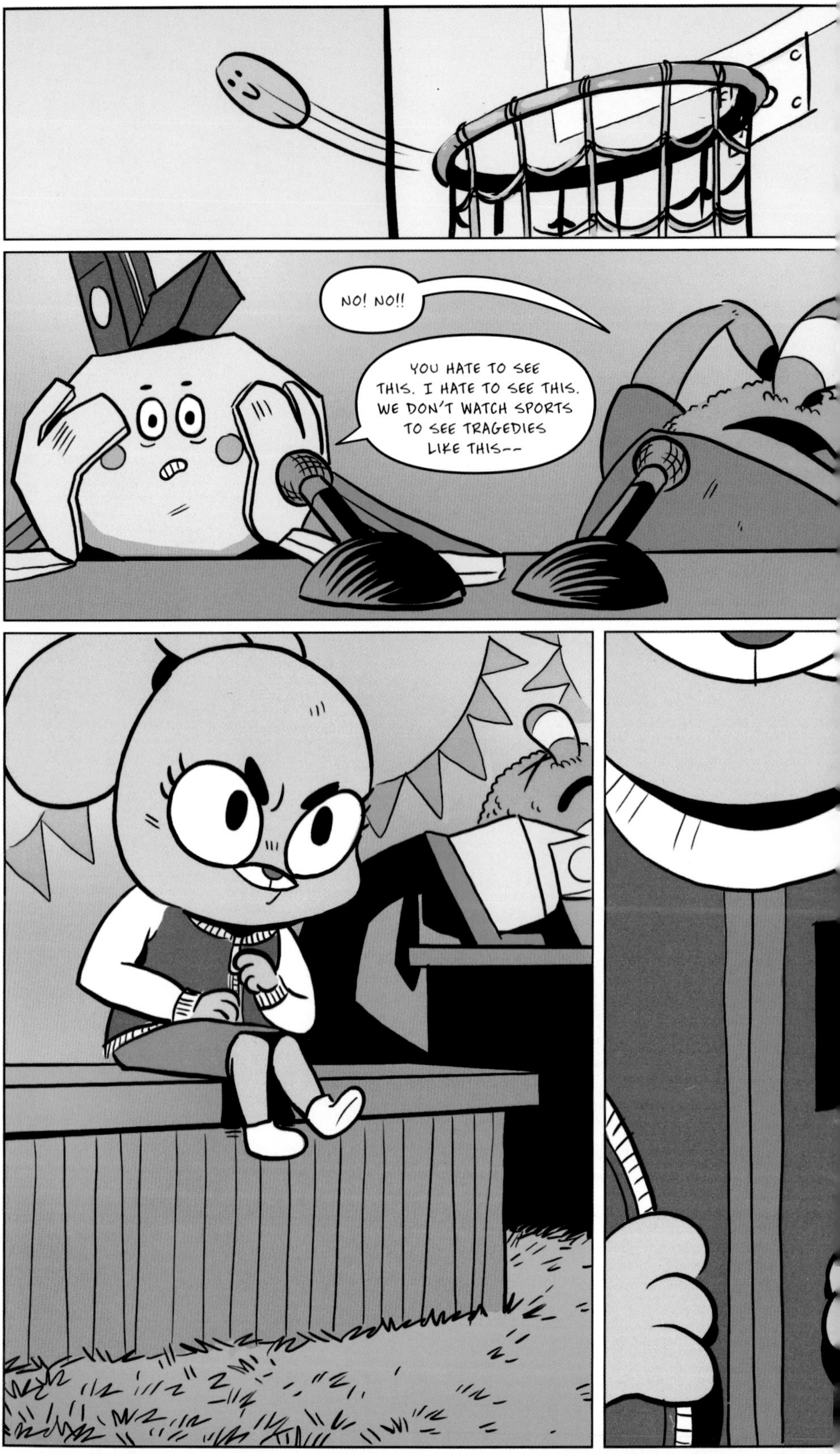
NO! NO!!
YOU HATE TO SEE THIS. I HATE TO SEE THIS. WE DON'T WATCH SPORTS TO SEE TRAGEDIES LIKE THIS--

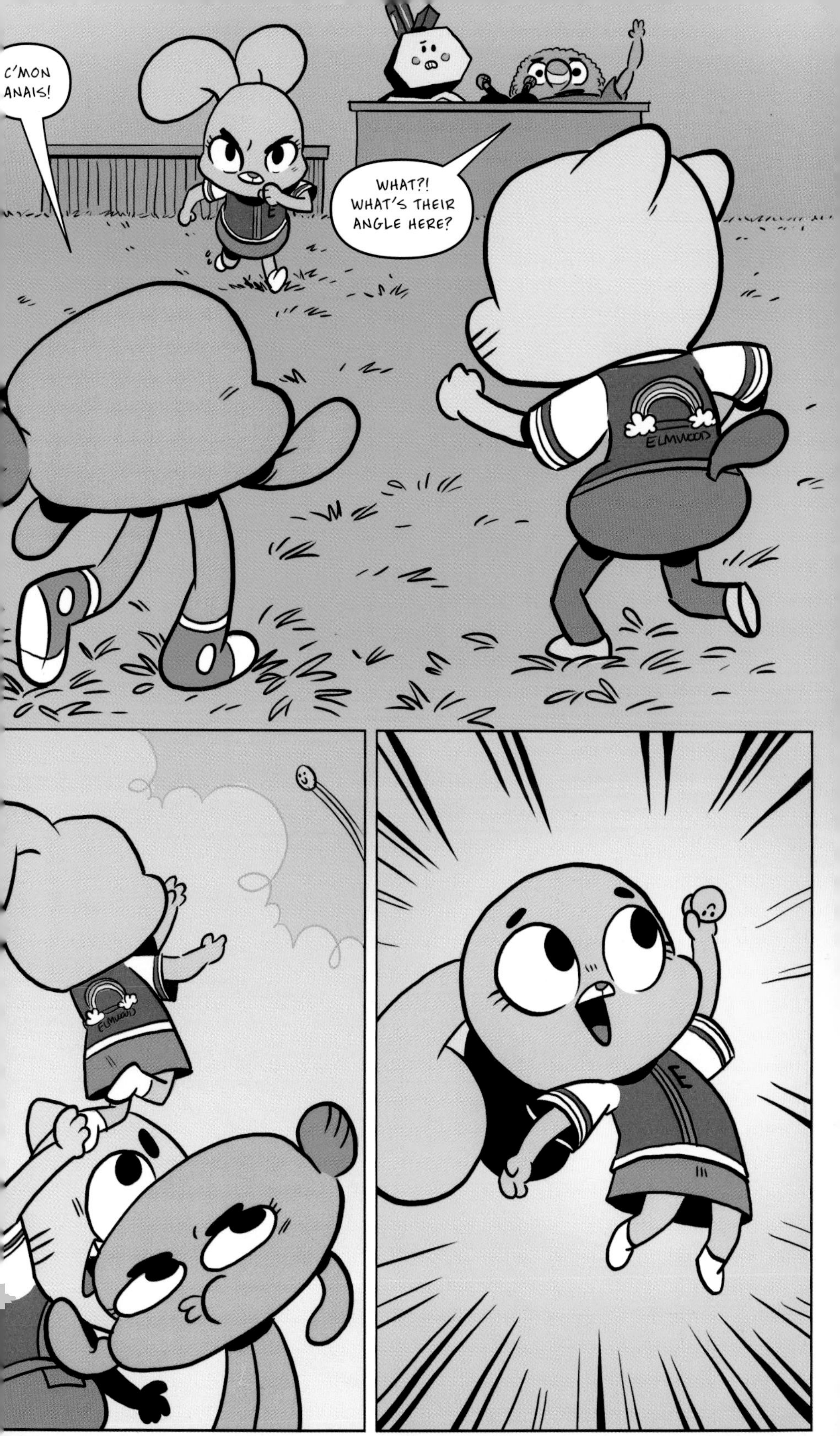
C'MON ANAIS!
WHAT?! WHAT'S THEIR ANGLE HERE?
ELMWOOD
ELMWOOD

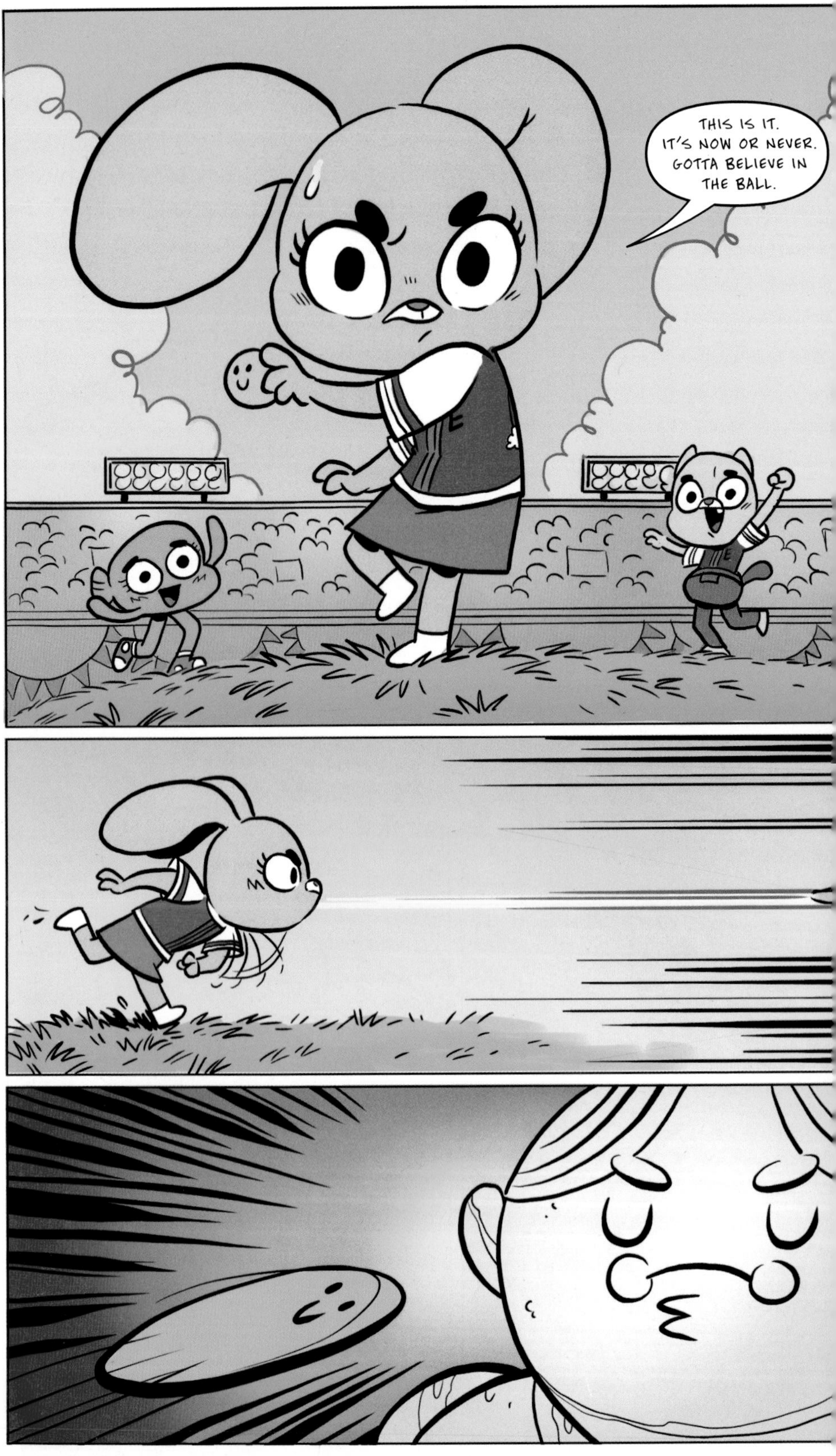
THIS IS IT. IT'S NOW OR NEVER. GOTTA BELIEVE IN THE BALL.

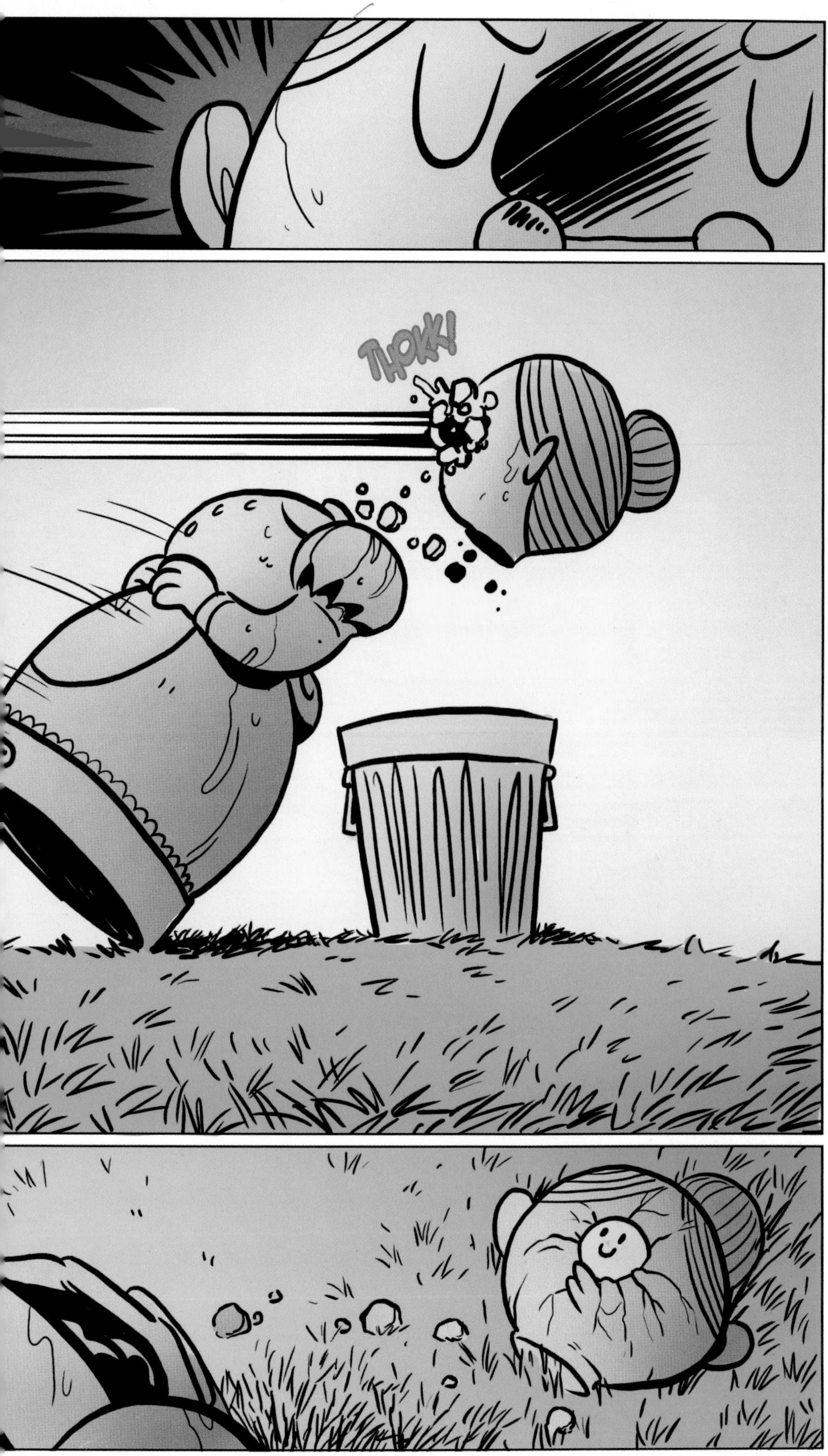
THOKK!

THAT'S....100 POINTS. JUST THE PART WITH THE STATUE IS 100 POINTS.

CLAP CLAP

WOOOOOOOO

WITH THAT SCORE, THERE'S NO DOUBT THAT ONCE THE POINTS ARE ALL TABULATED ELMORE WILL WIN THE GAME!

WHAT A DAY! WHAT A GAME! ELM WINS THE SISTER SC SCRIMMAGE FOR THE TIME IN HISTORY

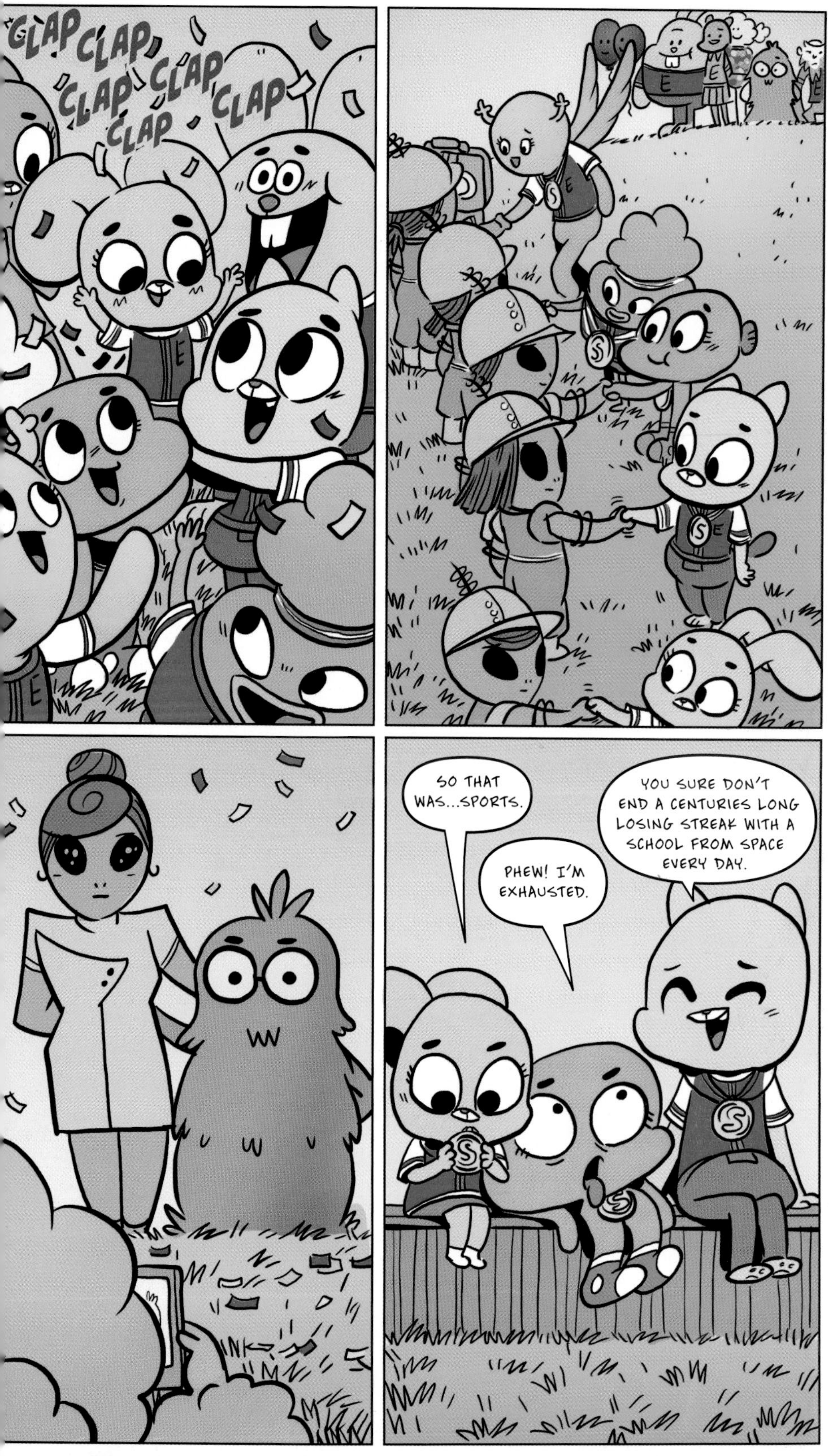
CLAP CLAP CLAP CLAP CLAP CLAP
SO THAT WAS...SPORTS.
PHEW! I'M EXHAUSTED.
YOU SURE DON'T END A CENTURIES LONG LOSING STREAK WITH A SCHOOL FROM SPACE EVERY DAY.

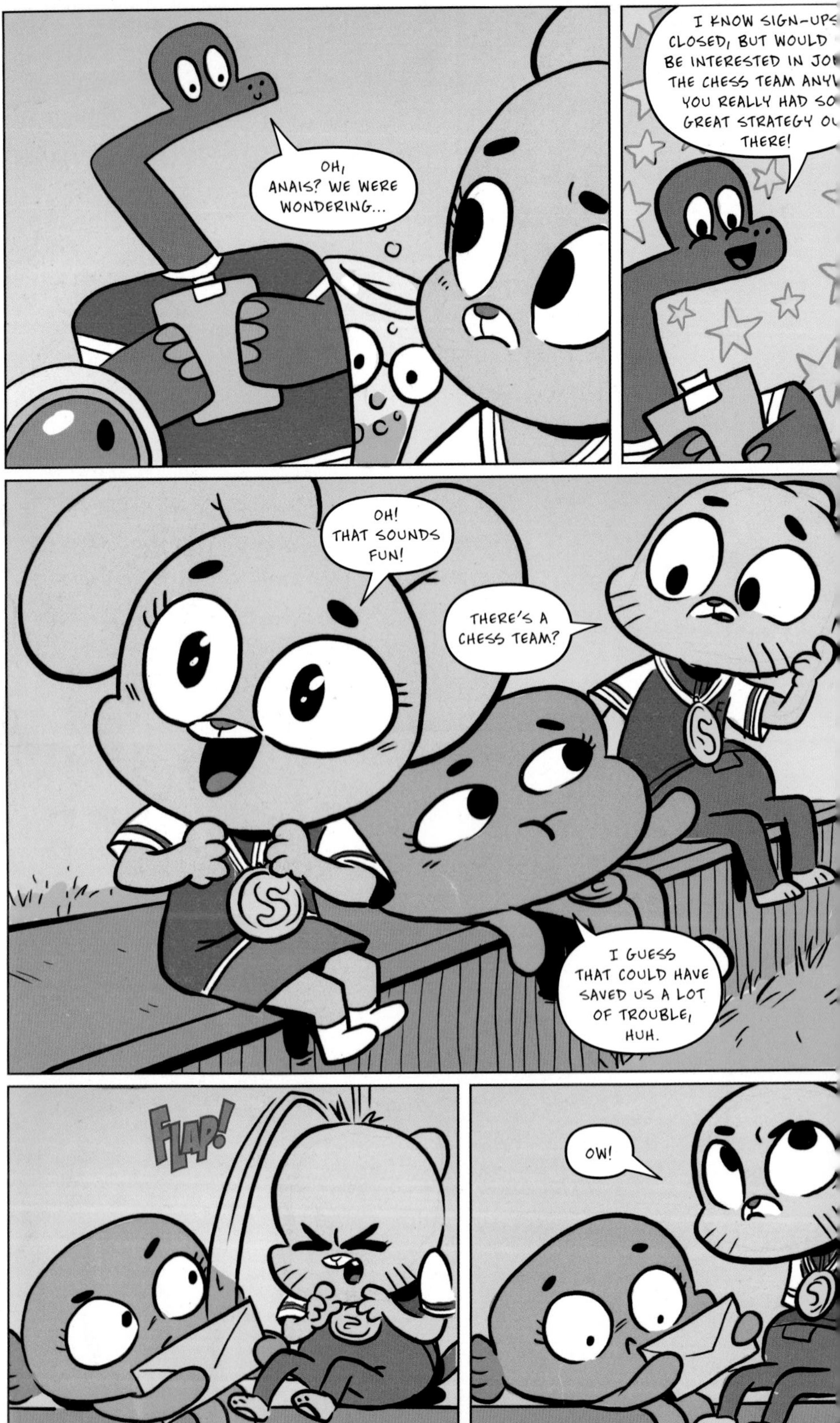
OH, ANAIS? WE WERE WONDERING...
I KNOW SIGN-UPS CLOSED, BUT WOULD BE INTERESTED IN JO THE CHESS TEAM ANY YOU REALLY HAD SO GREAT STRATEGY O THERE!
OH! THAT SOUNDS FUN!
THERE'S A CHESS TEAM?
I GUESS THAT COULD HAVE SAVED US A LOT OF TROUBLE, HUH.
FLAP!
OW!

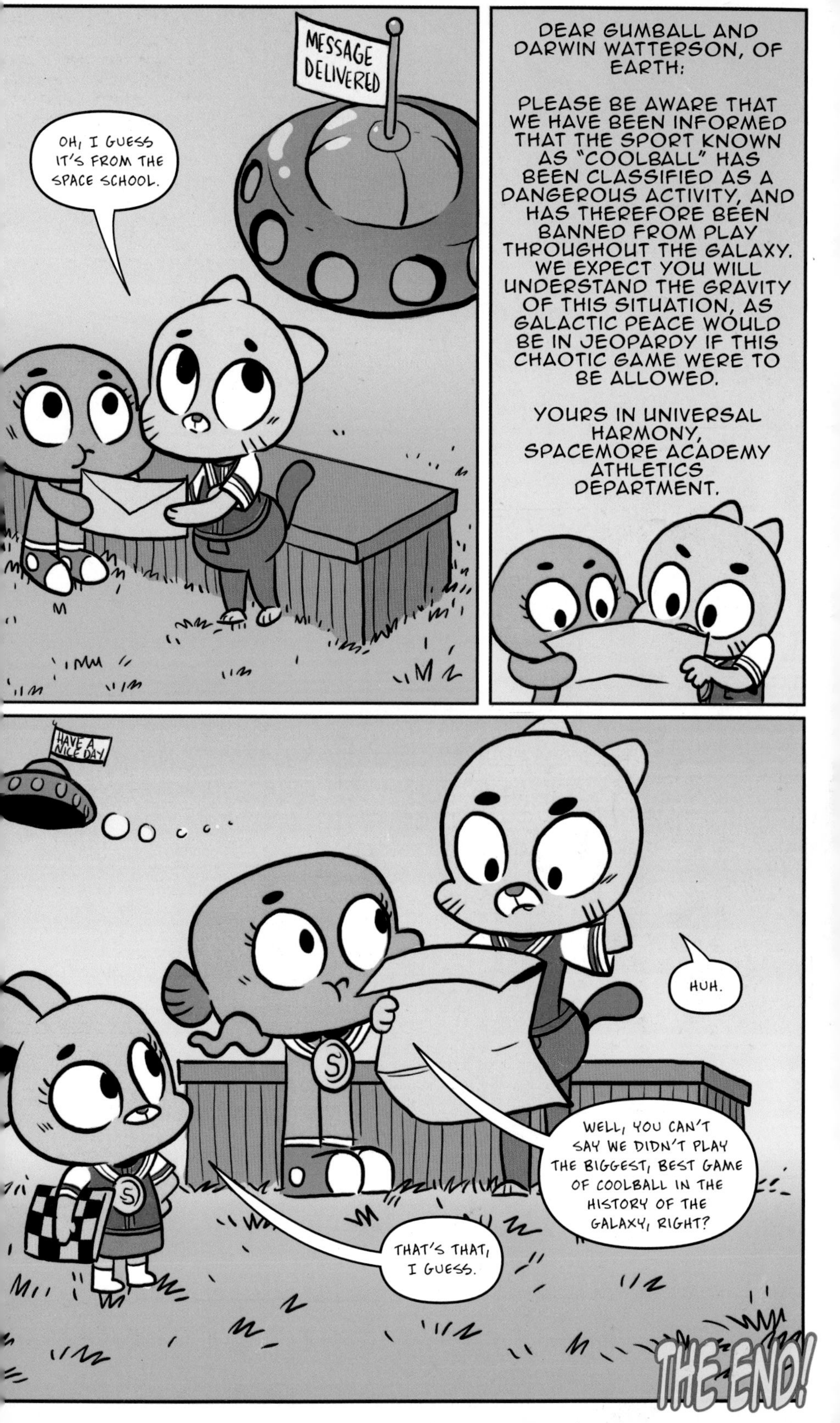
MESSAGE DELIVERED
OH, I GUESS IT'S FROM THE SPACE SCHOOL.
DEAR GUMBALL AND DARWIN WATTERSON, OF EARTH:
PLEASE BE AWARE THAT WE HAVE BEEN INFORMED THAT THE SPORT KNOWN AS "COOLBALL" HAS BEEN CLASSIFIED AS A DANGEROUS ACTIVITY, AND HAS THEREFORE BEEN BANNED FROM PLAY THROUGHOUT THE GALAXY. WE EXPECT YOU WILL UNDERSTAND THE GRAVITY OF THIS SITUATION, AS GALACTIC PEACE WOULD BE IN JEOPARDY IF THIS CHAOTIC GAME WERE TO BE ALLOWED.
YOURS IN UNIVERSAL HARMONY, SPACEMORE ACADEMY ATHLETICS DEPARTMENT.
HAVE A NICE DAY!
HUH.
WELL, YOU CAN'T SAY WE DIDN'T PLAY THE BIGGEST, BEST GAME OF COOLBALL IN THE HISTORY OF THE GALAXY, RIGHT?
THAT'S THAT, I GUESS.
THE END!

DISCOVER
EXPLOSIVE NEW WORLDS

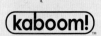